Between Nab being carried aloft and the hounds scuttling between men's legs below, the great hall was a squirming mass of unwieldy limbs. Then to cap the pandemonium, the door burst open and a hoary breath of winter washed over the company.

And blew in William Douglas, Laird of Badenoch, with it.

He stomped his booted feet on the threshold, shaking free great chunks of white. Even though he'd drawn the end of his plaid over his head, his dark hair was dusted with snow. His brows were drawn together in a frown over his fine straight nose.

Something tingled to life in Katherine's chest at the sight of him, but she tamped it down. Hope hurt too much. She'd thought herself safe from him for Christmas since a howling storm had roared since midday, but he'd evidently ridden through the blizzard to come after her.

Devil take the man's stubbornness.

More from Mia Marlowe

Touch of a Thief

Touch of a Rogue

Touch of a Scoundrel

Plaid to the Bone (eBook novella)

Plaid Tidings

Once Upon A Plaid

MIA MARLOWE

ZEBRA BOOKS
KENSINGTON PUBLISHING CORP.
http://www.kensingtonbooks.com

ZEBRA BOOKS are published by

Kensington Publishing Corp.
119 West 40th Street
New York, NY 10018

All Kensington titles, imprints, and distributed lines are available at special quantity discounts for bulk purchases for sales promotion, premiums, fund-raising, educational, or institutional use.

Special book excerpts or customized printings can also be created to fit specific needs. For details, write or phone the office of the Kensington Special Sales Manager: Attn. Special Sales Department. Kensington Publishing Corp., 119 West 40th Street, New York, NY 10018. Phone: 1-800-221-2647.

Zebra Books and the Z logo Reg. U.S. Pat. & TM Off.

First Printing: October 2014
ISBN-13: 978-1-4201-3534-3
ISBN-10: 1-4201-3534-1

First Electronic Edition: October 2014
eISBN-13: 978-1-4201-3535-0
eISBN-10: 1-4201-3535-X

10 9 8 7 6 5 4 3 2 1

Printed in the United States of America

The boar's head in hand bear I
Bedeck'd with bays and rosemary.

—From "The Boar's Head Carol"

"However many pretty leaves and sweet-smelling spices
ye put on the sorry thing, 'tis still just the head of a
deid pig, aye?"

—An observation from Nab,
fool to the Earl of Glengarry

Chapter One

"Christmastide is no time for such a Friday-face, Kat."
Katherine quickly turned up the corners of her
mouth. The frozen smile she forced into place felt
almost natural. Heaven knew, she'd had enough practice, but her sister-in-law, Margaret, had caught her in
an unguarded moment and that would never do. She
flashed her teeth, praying no one in her father's hall
would know the difference between this mask she
donned and a genuine expression of pleasure.

"I'm just a wee bit tired." She forced down a gulp of
her small beer and moved her food around her trencher
without eating it. If Katherine had a single bite of songbird pie, she feared she'd retch. She picked out a sliver

of meat and held it beneath the table for Angus. Her little terrier nibbled daintily, then licked the drippings from her fingers.

Angus cringed each time the deerhounds by the fire cracked the bones flung to them by the earl's men-at-arms or fell to snapping and snarling among themselves over some choice tidbit. He didn't dare stray far from Katherine's side.

"After the work we did this day, I'm surprised ye're not all in as well, Margie," Katherine said.

The women had plenty to show for their labors. The great hall sparkled in the light of dozens of dear beeswax candles. The large end of the Yule log was crammed into the massive fireplace, roaring away cheerfully. Since it was long and thick enough to burn for the required twelve days of Christmas, most of the log stuck out into the hall between the trestle tables. Earlier in the day, before snow had begun falling in earnest, Katherine and Margaret had gathered armloads of greenery and festooned the hall with fragrant wreaths and garlands. The kissing bough, fashioned of ivy, fir, and mistletoe, had taken hours to construct and hang just so.

Not that I'll have occasion to use it. An aching lump of loneliness swelled in Katherine's chest.

"Right glad I am that ye decided to come celebrate Christmas with us." Margaret finished the last of her pie with a satisfied sigh. "Thanks to ye, good-sister, I did more supervising than working. But if ye must know, women near their time don't get tired, we get hungry." She eyed Katherine's trencher. "If ye're not going to eat that . . ."

Kat shoved her food in front of her sister-in-law. After all, Margie was eating for two. Possibly three, given the way the fine fabric of her leine bulged.

Katherine forced herself to smile a bit wider so no one would suspect she died a little each time she looked at Margaret's round belly. She raised her beer again.

It was comforting to hide behind the flagon. No one could know this Christmastide held not a drop of joy for her. Not even William, who ought to have known, who by rights ought to feel the same, had any idea what was festering inside her.

Or if he did, he didn't care.

Katherine was dragged from her dark musings when Ranulf MacNaught, the most bellicose of her father's pledge-men and her first cousin, snatched the bagpipes from the boy who'd been attempting to play them in fits and starts all evening. MacNaught started a wheezing squeal of his own. Even though he was Lord Glengarry's nephew, Ranulf was given far more attention than Katherine thought he deserved. A certain faction of her father's retainers fawned on Ranulf with hound-like servility. Now Lord Glengarry's men-at-arms upended their drinking horns and banged them in time with the droning melody on the dark, scarred wood of the long tables. The pounding rhythm echoed in Katherine's chest.

Her nose twitched. The smells of too much rich food, damp wool, unwashed dogs, and unkempt men couldn't be completely obscured by evergreens and spice balls. The bright hall seemed suddenly very close, as if the stone walls were inching toward her.

"Odds bodkins, 'tis Christmas, Lady Katherine," murmured a soft voice behind her. "Why are ye sad?"

When she turned toward the sound, she found Nab, her father's fool, fingering the drooping ends of his ridiculous cap. His carrot-red hair shot out from under the cap in snarls and stringy braids. His multihued

motley costume was stained with bits of the feast. Since
Nab was usually the fastidious sort, except for his hair,
which resisted all efforts to subdue it, Katherine guessed
that food had been tossed at him, as if he were one of
the deerhounds.

Apart from his odd appearance, she'd never understood why Lord Glengarry chose Nab to serve as his
resident entertainer. Most court fools were sly and
cruel in their comedy.

Nab was shy and quiet and hadn't a mean bone in his
slight body. But he had a habit of saying the most unusual things at the wrong time, which her father found
hilarious. Nab's gaze darted about, looking anywhere
but at her. In truth, he rarely looked anyone directly in
the eye. Even so, she knew his attention was fixed upon
her, waiting for a response.

"Ye're mistaken, Nab. I'm not sad. I'm tired."

"Nay, tired is when ye yawn. Sad is when ye pretend to
smile." He frowned down at the turned-up tips of his
own shoes. "I'm thinkin' ye are the one who's mistaken.
When I'm confused, I go to sleep and it all becomes
clear in my dreams. Ye should find yer bed then. That
way, ye willna still be sad tomorrow."

Margaret chuckled. "The fool's right in an odd sort
of way. Find your bed, lass. Ye've worked yourself into
a frazzle since ye came home to help me. Things will
only get more boisterous here in the hall this night."

As if to prove her right, Ranulf laid aside the pipes
and bellowed, "If we're to get this Yuletide under way,
we must crown a Laird of Misrule."

Katherine's father rose from his place on the dais,
leaned his heavy knuckles on the table, and skewered
MacNaught with a gimlet eye. His grey brows lowered in
a frown, though everyone chuckled, sensing that their

laird didn't mean it. Each Yuletide, this sham deposing of their true leader was but the signal that the revels were to begin in earnest.

"Are ye saying ye dinna like the way I do things around here, MacNaught?" Lord Glengarry boomed.

"Nay, milord. Rest assured, we'd follow ye blithely to Hades, singing as we go all the rest of the year." MacNaught scraped a quick bow. "But Christmastide needs a master of revels, a proper Abbot of Unreason, and my Lord Glengarry is the soul of reason and benevolent rule. What we need now is a decadent despot, a feeble-minded tyrant." He scanned the room till his gaze fell on Nab. "What we need is a fool! Get him, lads."

"No." Katherine leaped to her feet, but she was too late. Some of the nearby men snatched up Nab, who hated to be touched at the best of times, and bounced him hand to hand over their heads across the hall. He made pitiful bleating noises, sounding like the mournful Glengarry sheep when shearing season was upon them.

"Put him down this instant," Katherine demanded, but no one seemed to hear her, least of all her father, who was roaring with laughter along with the rest of them.

She stumbled after Nab, accidentally stepping on wee Angus in the process. The terrier yipped, alerting the deerhounds to his presence in the hall. The two largest bitches scrambled to their feet and lunged after him, as if he were a hare in the thicket. Angus skittered beneath the long trestle table with the deerhounds on his stubby tail, upending benches and knocking over diners who didn't scatter out of their way quickly enough.

Between Nab being carried aloft and the hounds

scuttling between men's legs below, the great hall was a squirming mass of unwieldy limbs. Then to cap the pandemonium, the door burst open and a hoary breath of winter washed over the company.

And blew in William Douglas, Laird of Badenoch, with it.

He stomped his booted feet on the threshold, shaking free great chunks of white. Even though he'd drawn the end of his plaid over his head, his dark hair was dusted with snow. His brows were drawn together in a frown over his fine straight nose.

Something tingled to life in Katherine's chest at the sight of him, but she tamped it down. Hope hurt too much. She'd thought herself safe from him for Christmas since a howling storm had roared since midday, but he'd evidently ridden through the blizzard to come after her.

Devil take the man's stubbornness.

Angus, however, seemed relieved to see him. He made a beeline for William and, with a flying leap, launched himself into the man's arms. The deerhounds surrounded them, snapping and growling.

"Ho there, wee beastie!" William grabbed the wriggling terrier and held him aloft to keep him from the deerhounds' jaws while he set down his oilskin bag.

That bag boded ill. It seemed to be full, which meant he planned on staying at Glengarry Castle for a while.

When the terrier stilled, William tucked the little dog into his plaid. Angus snuggled into as small a ball as he could, safe in the folds of the tartan. He didn't stir a hair when Will thundered at the deerhounds, "Back then, ye worm-eaten bitches!"

The hounds tucked in their tails and scuttled away, casting backward glances at William. Angus peeped out from between William's shirt and the swath of plaid draped over his shoulder, watching the bigger dogs slink back to the fire.

But Will had evidently already dismissed Lord Glengarry's pack from his mind. As if he sensed her eyes on him, William lifted his dark head and turned to meet Katherine's gaze. She was still halfway across the great hall, and yet, he seemed to know exactly where she was.

He always did.

How does he do that?

And if he could do that, why could he not also sense how very much she wished him gone?

But at least he didn't fight his way across the crowded space to her. Nab was still being tossed from one group of men to another, wailing as he sailed through the air. William strode toward the mob.

When Nab landed on a group of hands near him, William grabbed the fool and pulled him down to stand on his own two feet. "The fool's not a sack of barley to be flung about. What's this great stramash about then?"

Ranulf MacNaught's lip curled, but he did no more than clench and unclench his fists at his sides.

Will was a braw fellow, standing half a head above most of the men in the hall. His shoulders were as broad as a stone dresser's and his reputation for feats of arms bordered on legendary. Katherine didn't blame Ranulf for being intimidated. Better men than he had cringed under the Black Douglas glare.

"We're crowning our Abbot of Unreason," Ranulf said. "Not that it's any concern of yours."

"Well, then if Nab's to be your king for the next twelve days, ye ought to give him a bit more respect." William turned to the fool. "As the Abbot of Unreason, d'ye ken ye can give any order and your subjects must obey?"

"In truth?" Nab's gaze flitted around like a midge, refusing to light on any one person for longer than a blink.

"Aye, in truth." William could be as hard as flint when he chose, but now the kindness in his tone made Katherine's chest ache. It would be so much easier to do what she must if he were a terrible bully. "What say ye, Laird Nab?"

"I say . . . I say . . ." Nab held his hands out at arms' length. "Everybody step back."

MacNaught grumbled, but he and the rest of his cohorts did as they were bid.

"Ye can order them to stand on their heads if it pleases ye," Will suggested.

Nab's red brows drew together. "It might leave a terrible boot print if Ranulf were to try to stand on his own head."

William laughed at Nab's misunderstanding. "It might at that. Though as hard as Ranulf MacNaught's head is, I've doubts on that score. But it doesna change the fact that ye've been chosen as laird till Twelfth Night. Ye can make your own rules."

"Odds bodkins, I'm not a laird." Nab sneaked a glance at Katherine's father. Lord Glengarry shot his fool a toothy grin and gave him a nod of encouragement. Nab blushed to the tips of his oversized ears. "Leastwise, I dinna feel like a laird."

"Perhaps we can remedy that." Will knelt to rummage in his oilskin bag. He pulled out a long object wrapped in soft doeskin and handed it to Nab.

With care, the fool unwrapped the parcel to reveal a small scepter. It was no longer than a child's bow, but the gilt-edged silver was engraved with mystical symbols, whose meanings were far older than living memory. The polished stone atop its length gleamed as if it were lit with fire from within.

He would have to bring that benighted thing, Katherine thought, as she folded her arms over her chest.

Nab handed it back to William.

"Nay, 'tis not for me." The fool sidled a few steps away. "'Tis too fine."

"Nothing's too fine for the Laird of Misrule," William said with a smile that nearly broke Katherine's heart. She'd fallen in love with that smile.

Loving the man had come later.

"Besides, this is a true scepter of power, mind ye," Will went on. "'Tis old beyond reckoning and has been handed down in the Douglas family since the beginning, from father to son."

"Is that so?" Ranulf MacNaught found his voice and a bit of his courage, but Kat noticed he hadn't drawn any closer to William. "The scepter seems small for something ye'd have us believe is so great."

"Just because something is small doesna mean it willna do the job," Will said. "Is that not what ye're counting on your women to believe, MacNaught?"

The hall rang with laughter at that. Ranulf's face turned an unhealthy shade of purple, but William ignored his growing rage, turning back to Nab.

"Legend has it that the scepter came to the Douglas clan from the Fair Folk, and as ye know, many of the fey peoples are smaller than we. But it is a mistake to underestimate them." William laid a hand on Nab's shoulder and held out the scepter to him again. "Sometimes the small, the seemingly weak, are really the strongest of all."

Nab reached out and haltingly took the scepter this

time. Then he clutched it tight to his chest. "I'll take good care of it till Twelfth Night, Lord Badenoch."

"Call me William. Ye're the laird now. And I know ye'll have a care for the scepter, else I'd not have lent it to ye. Come, lads. Raise a glass to Laird Nab. Well may he reign, though it be not long!"

After the men drank to the Laird of Misrule's health, Nab waved the scepter while he instructed his new subjects in the fine art of balancing on one foot while hopping in a circle. The half-drunken crowd followed suit to great hilarity.

William gave Katherine's father a quick bow in nominal acknowledgment of his host, and then left the foolery behind to head across the room to her.

She wanted to pick up her skirts and flee, but she couldn't stir a step. It was as if she were trapped in her recurring night phantom, the one where an ogre pounds down a mountainside toward her but she can't move. Just as in her dream, her feet seemed rooted to the flagstone floor.

Will stopped before her, reached into his plaid, and pulled out Angus, offering the little dog to her as if he were a loaf of bread. Of course, this particular loaf squirmed and whined, his stubby legs churning the air as though he might swim through it to her if only William would turn him loose.

"This is yours, I believe."

Katherine took the terrier from him. Angus melted into her, nuzzling her neck and pressing nosy doggie kisses against her skin. "Thank ye, Will."

"I have somewhat else with me that's yours as well."

She knew better than to ask him what that might be. His dark eyes were speaking for him. Will could be silver-tongued when he wished to be, and she couldn't bear to hear his protestations of love. Anything he said would ring false. She could endure much, but she drew the line at untruths.

"I suppose ye'll be wanting to refresh yourself after your journey." Normally, Margaret served as chatelaine since she was married to Katherine's brother. It was her place to cater to the needs of guests, but since Margie was in the final days of her confinement, Katherine had taken over those duties when she arrived at Glengarry Castle two days ago. "I'll show ye to your chamber."

"So long as it's also your chamber," William said, shifting his oilskin pack on his shoulder. "Or has it slipped your mind that ye're my wife?"

O, yonder she's comin', over yon lea.
With many a fine tale unto thee,
An' she's gotten a baby on her knee
And another one comin' home.

—From "The Gaberlunzie Man"

"Dinna this song make ye wonder where she got those
bairns? Sounds as if she picked 'em up along the
hedgerows, does it not? O' course, I hear tell that's where
quite a few of 'em get their start."

—An observation from Nab,
fool to the Earl of Glengarry

Chapter Two

"Nay, what's between you and me is topmost on my mind," Kat said. "Though I rather think ye've not given it much thought of late. In fact, I'm surprised ye noticed I was gone."

William kept his expression carefully neutral. She was right. It had been a day and a half before he realized she'd absented herself from Badenoch Castle. "I'm here, aren't I?"

"Aye. Just in time for the goose and trimmings."
One of her russet brows cocked up.

William wished he could smooth down that brow,
but she'd probably bat his hand away. She'd pushed
him away for weeks. "D'ye really want to have this
argument in your father's hall before God and everybody?"

Katherine's lips tightened into a thin line. She lib-
erated a candle from one of the sconces and led the
way out of the great hall. She didn't say a word as she
preceded him up the twisting spiral staircase that ex-
clusively served the family portion of the castle. But
her hips twitched with each step, warming Will more
than the fire in the great hall ever would.

*Yet if she turned around, my darling wife's frown would
freeze me quicker than the north wind.*

William had to half stoop as he ascended behind
her. Even then he nearly smacked his forehead on the
lintel each time they passed through a corner of a
room and reentered the private stairs.

The family chambers were stacked one upon another on succeeding levels of the tower, all joined to
the same twisting staircase. They passed through Lord
Glengarry's spartan room first. After Katherine's
mother had died, the earl had removed all hint of feminine frippery from his chamber, content with only the
most basic of necessities—a comfortable bed, a chest
for his clothing, and a larger one for his weapons. His
only extravagance was the private garderobe, where he
could bathe in a copper hip bath on occasion and use
the latrine built into the castle wall.

The next chamber up belonged to Donald, Lord
Glengarry's heir and Kat's only brother. He obviously
shared it with his wife, Margaret, because the walls were

covered with tapestries and the space was crammed with furniture in the heavy new Tudor style. The pads on the kneeling bench of the prie-dieu in the corner were deeply indented, proof of Lady Margaret's piety.

William was sure Donald spent little time on his knees.

Finally at the top of the tower, as befitted a daughter of the house, Katherine's chamber was situated in the most secure place in the keep. It was the room she'd occupied all her life until she became his bride four years ago.

She set the candle down before her silvered glass mirror, where its light could be magnified and cast back into the space. Then she crossed over to the hearth and poked the banked fire into a flickering dance.

Katherine stooped and set down wee Angus, his short legs scrambling even before his feet met the fragrant rushes on the stone floor. The terrier made a running jump and planted himself firmly in the center of the string bed.

"That bed will be a tight enough fit with just you and me, Kat," Will said as he set down his oilskin sack. "I dinna think there's room for the wee beastie as well."

He was marginally ashamed of the fact that he envied the terrier. His wife lavished a goodly amount of affection on that little flea trap. William would be pleased with even a small portion of it.

"You presume a great deal if ye think ye'll be allowed to join me in that bed."

"Ye're my wife, Katherine. Ye promised before God to obey me. If I want to sleep with ye, I damned well will."

It was worse than a sore tooth that he had to force the issue. Before he'd married, William had been invited into plenty of feminine beds, though he hadn't accepted any of the offers. He'd been betrothed to Katherine when they were both children and to tup another woman hadn't seemed respectful, either to her or to the agreement their fathers had made. He was spoken for and he was determined to honor his marriage bed. Even though his young body had burned with curiosity about what passed between a man and a woman, William made sure he and his bride had learned together.

And the lessons they'd given each other were sweet indeed. She was warm and responsive, and beneath her gown, his wife was curved and soft. Will had thanked God and set out to explore his new kingdom with thoroughness. Katherine returned the favor.

At least, at first.

The invitations to other ladies' beds hadn't stopped after he'd given his vow to Katherine. He still turned away from those welcoming smiles but it was getting harder. After all, the one woman who ought to be most welcoming of all seemed to want nothing to do with him.

"If ye mean to bring God into this," his wife was saying, "let me remind ye that the Scriptures teach us that if the wife's body belongs to her husband, the husband's body likewise belongs to his wife." Kat's green eyes sparked dangerously. "So if I choose to see that your body sleeps elsewhere, husband, 'tis my God-given right."

Suffering Lord. He never should have let Father Simon tutor her. She'd become far too good a theologian for him to cross verbal swords with. He decided to take a different tack.

"I dinna know what ye have to be angry about." He fisted his hands at his waist.

"Then let me refresh your memory." Her neat

brows drew closer together over her pert nose. "Does Lady Ellen ring a bell?"

"Lady Ellen?"

"Aye, the nubile young thing ye've seen fit to add to our household."

Nubile? William would have called the girl hopelessly skinny. He liked a woman with a bit of meat on her bones, all soft and curved. Like his Katherine. "Lady Ellen's but a child."

"She's fifteen. Younger than she are mothers made."

"That's what her family fears. She's to be betrothed to my cousin John, ye see. My uncle asked would we foster her until the wedding next May. Her family lives in the Lowlands and John will be worth less than nothing to his father if he's running off to court her instead of tending to his father's holding."

"I see." Her shoulders relaxed a bit, as if she were a coracle with the wind spilling from her sails.

"Besides, her family wanted us to vouchsafe her purity since they feared the girl was apt to run away with John unless she was closely watched."

"Oh." Katherine worried her lower lip.

"Dinna fret. I've set Duncan to sheep-dogging her." Will was certain the girl was safe in Duncan's care. Their grizzled, one-eyed retainer didn't suffer fools gladly. Especially not young ones. "He'll not let anything befall the lass. No matter how much she might wish it."

"Why did ye not tell me these things?"

"Ye haven't exactly been wanting to talk with me of late." In fact, since Michaelmas she'd insisted on separate bedchambers, as if they were damned English nobility whose reputation for chilly marriages was well known even in the Highlands. "Do ye really think so ill of me that ye supposed I'd bring a mistress under the same roof as my wife?"

Her shoulders stiffened again. "So are ye telling me ye keep a light-o-love elsewhere?"

"God's Teeth, what do ye take me for, Kat?" he growled. "One woman in my life is trouble enough. What would I do with two? Ye've no right to be angry." He stomped over to the only chair in the room and plopped down in it to tug off his boots. "I'm not the one who went haring off in the dead of winter without so much as a word. Did ye not think I'd be worried about ye?"

The left boot slipped off with ease, but try as he might, William couldn't seem to get the correct angle on the right one. Katherine sighed and came over to help him. At least she didn't neglect all her wifely duties.

"My brother's wife is about to give him another child," she said as she straddled his outstretched leg and gave the boot a yank. It wouldn't budge. "Did ye not suppose she'd appreciate a kinswoman with her for her lying-in?"

"Aye." But would it have hurt her to tell him her plans? "That's why I came straight here once I realized ye weren't out visiting sick crofters or delivering food baskets to every gaberlunzie begging by the side of the road again."

Any beggar with a sad story to tell found an easy meal or a coin forthcoming from his Katherine. William thought her devotion to giving obsessive, especially since it meant she often neglected her other duties as his chatelaine to attend the poor.

"Seems ye think every scruffy mendicant who turns up at our gate is a chance for you to host an angel unaware."

And of more importance than your husband, he thought with bitterness.

He put his stockinged foot on her backside and gave it a push to help remove the other boot. It finally eased over his heel and Kat stumbled forward. She'd have fallen headlong if he hadn't caught her by the waist and pulled her back onto his lap.

"Ye make my charity sound silly," Katherine said accusingly. She struggled to rise, but he held her fast.

"No, 'tis not silly." If married life had taught him anything, it was that sometimes it was wise to hold back his true thoughts. "But there are those who take advantage of your good heart."

She hung her head. "Ye only believe my heart's good because ye dinna ken *why* I give alms."

She stopped straining against his arms and was still for a moment. William drew in a deep lungful of her scent, a sweet breath of spices and evergreens, and then let all the tension in his body flow out along with his exhalation. It was restful to hold her like this, as if they had stepped outside of time while the rest of the world went on without them for a bit.

He lived for such moments—quiet, tender times when he could simply hold the woman he loved. Pity they were so few and far between.

"Sometimes," she said in a small voice, "I imagine if only I could do enough for others, if only my deeds were balanced against my sins and found to outweigh them, then maybe my dearest wish would be granted."

He didn't have the courage to ask what that wish might be. He already knew. Hearing her voice it would break something inside him.

Her head came to rest on his shoulder. "So ye see, Will, if I do acts of kindness only because I hope to gain, my heart isna all that good."

"I'll be the judge of that." William slid a finger under

her chin and tipped her face up to him. Her eyes were enormous with the light of the fire sparking in them. But the unspoken burden behind them was even bigger.

He bent and covered her mouth with his, wishing he could take her sorrow on himself. But if he couldn't bear to hear her speak it, how could he lift it from her?

So instead he poured his love for her into his kiss.

She opened to him, answering his tongue with hers, and the world went wet and soft and welcoming.

This much is right between us.

In their fifteen hundred days or so of wedded life, Will had kissed this woman countless times and, contrary to his friends' predictions, it was always new to him. How could it not be when he was never sure what was rolling around in Kat's head while their mouths made love?

Perhaps it was all right not to know. Perhaps they were better together if only their bodies did the talking. He brushed her breast through her soft gown. She made a small noise, a soft coo like a nesting dove, into his mouth. That sound never failed to go straight to his groin, though it had been some months since he'd heard it.

William stood, with her still in his arms, and carried her to the bed. Angus scrambled up to hide under one of the pillows. Will decided he'd deal with that little furball later, after he laid his wife out and covered her sweet body with his.

But when he lay down atop her, she pressed both palms on his chest. "No, Will, I canna."

"Och, love, dinna be cruel." He planted a string of baby kisses along her jaw and neck. She seemed to melt under them. "Not to a man who rode through a blizzard to come to your bed."

When he suckled her earlobe, she shivered and he figured he was halfway to heaven. But when he made to kiss her mouth again, she turned her face aside.

"'Tis not that I dinna want ye. I do. More than ye know." Her voice broke. "My courses are upon me."

Her words were a punch to his gut. William rolled off her and lay flat on his back beside her, staring up at the underside of the tower thatching.

Devil seize it.

She'd lost another one. By his reckoning, she'd been more than three months gone with child, but he couldn't be sure since she'd not shared her hopes with him this time. Still, he could count. She ought to have known he was waiting for her to tell him, to reveal her secret so they could rejoice together.

Now all he could share with his wife was the bitter end of yet another failure. Another loss.

'Tis not your fault.

The words died on his tongue. He'd said them before. Many times. She never seemed to hear them. He'd give half his holding if someone would tell him what to do, what to say, to ease his Katherine's pain.

He started to reach for her, to draw her into his arms, but she rolled onto her side facing away from him. She didn't say anything, but in the dimness, her shoulders shook.

She wept without a sound.

Even in her grief, she shut him out.

Wee Angus crept out from under the pillow and nestled against the small of her back. She didn't push him away.

God's Teeth, I canna even best a dog.

Will sat up and swung his legs over the side of the bed.

"Where are you going?" she said softly.

"To get roaring drunk, my love. I may even pick a fight with that clotpole Ranulf MacNaught." He stomped to the doorway and promptly banged his forehead on the low lintel. William swore softly under his breath. "I canna think of a better way to celebrate Christmas, can you?"

Ding Dong! Merrily on high
in heav'n the bells are ringing:
Ding dong! Verily the sky is riv'n with Angels singing.
Gloria, Hosanna in excelsis!

—Set to a sixteenth-century tune

"Is it wrong, ye think, that I want to dance over so somber a thing as our Lord's birth? I dinna think ye could blame me when even the angels are cutting up such a great stramash."

—An observation from Nab,
fool to the Earl of Glengarry

Chapter Three

The chapel bells woke William, boring into his brain a little deeper with each rolling chime. He rolled over in the bed, searching with one hand for Katherine. When he didn't find her, he forced his eyes open.

She'd been gone for some time. There wasn't the least bit of warmth left on her pillow. Angus, however, wiggled his way out from under the coverlet and licked Will's face.

"Looks like we've both been abandoned," William said to the dog. "Trust our Kat to rise for Christ's Mass.

She's pious enough; no doubt her prayers will count for all of us."

Good thing. Will hadn't had much to say to the Almighty for a while.

He threw back the bedclothes and, ignoring the ripple of gooseflesh across his bare skin, stalked across the chamber to the pitcher and ewer on the stand in the corner. The water had a thin crust of ice on it, but Will broke through and splashed his face in any case. The bracing cold swept the last of the cobwebs from his brain.

Last night, he'd tromped back down to the great hall and consumed far too much ale. Later, after the rest of the party was snoring under the tables, his father-in-law had brought out the good whisky, and between the two of them, they'd polished off the rest of the bottle.

He didn't remember too much of what the laird and he had talked about. He seemed to recall that Lord Glengarry grumbled about the fact that Ranulf MacNaught was garnering more followers among the clan. The laird's son, Donald, couldn't be bothered to absent himself from court long enough to learn the names of his own men. Since Katherine's father had suffered an apoplectic fit last winter, he'd lost flesh. No doubt he fretted about whether Donald was ready to lead the clan in case he should pass. Ranulf's increased popularity was giving the laird reason to drink.

Not that Will's father-in-law needed a reason.

William didn't give much weight to Lord Glengarry's complaints. His conversations with Katherine's father were always sojourns on a roundabout trail that circled Lord Glengarry himself. William had troubles of his own. However, by the time the candles guttered in the late watches of the night, Will was beginning to feel more in charity with the whole world.

But that may have just been the whisky.

"I dinna know what's amiss betwixt ye and my wee Katikins, and I'm not wantin' to know. I'll not say I understand my daughter at the best of times. Women are chancy creatures," the old man had said, "but this one thing I ken about my Kat. She loves ye, lad. More than anything. On that ye could lay your hope of heaven."

Will tugged his shirt over his head quickly in the cold chamber. Then he wrapped the belted plaid about his body. It would've been much easier if he'd had Katherine's help pleating the length of cloth. But by the time he draped the excess fabric over one shoulder and secured it with a pewter pin, William was more or less decently covered and much warmer.

His heart, however, still felt the chill of the empty room.

"She loves me, Angus," he told the dog because he wanted to hear the words again.

He looked once more at the rumpled bedclothes. His memories of last night were a bit fuzzy, but it seemed to him that after he'd stumbled back up to her chamber, Kat had risen and helped him undress. The fact that his shirt and plaid had been neatly folded instead of tossed on the floor was proof positive Katherine had had a hand in it.

Then once they'd snuggled back under the covers for warmth, she hadn't pushed him away when he'd spooned his body around hers. His last coherent memory of the previous night was burying his nose in her abundant hair and breathing her in.

If he hadn't been so far gone with drink, perhaps he wouldn't have sunk so quickly into slumber. Maybe he'd have roused to her and she to him, whether the custom of women was upon her or not, whether it was a sin for them to join then or not, and she'd have forgotten all about being so unhappy.

The chapel bell tolled again and he pulled back the heavy curtain to peer out the arrow notch that served as a window. The storm had blown itself out in the night, leaving a fresh layer of sparkling white on the world. Below in the bailey, Katherine and Lady Margaret were trudging from the chapel to the keep through the crisp snow.

If he hurried, he'd be able to join his wife as she broke her fast on Christmas morning.

"That'll be a good start," he told Angus. "A fresh start."

The little dog whined and burrowed back under the covers.

William snorted. "I guess ye dinna much like my chances."

Truth to tell, he didn't either.

Her three young nephews ran past Katherine and their mother, shrieking like boggles and lobbing icy handfuls at each other. Margaret stumbled as she dodged one of the snowballs that went astray. She would have gone down if Katherine hadn't grabbed her and kept her upright at the last moment.

"Dermid, ye wee heathen, look what ye nearly did to your mother. Lachlan and Monroe, dinna encourage him," Katherine said crossly to her nephews. "Settle yourselves, all of ye."

"Dinna scold, Auntie Kat. 'Tis Christmas morn, after all, and that'll put any lad in high spirits," Margaret said with far more charity than Kat was able to muster.

"A bearing woman should be coddled, not caught in the crossfire of a snowball fight."

"No harm done." Margie bent down to speak to her offspring, who had the good grace to look chagrined. Fidgeting and shuffling their feet, they lined up before their mother and aunt like a small flight of stairs, oldest to youngest. Even though Katherine had reprimanded them, Margie narrowly resisted the urge to kneel and gather them into her arms to kiss their snub-nosed, plump-cheeked faces. "Hurry off to the kitchen now and tell Cook I said ye could have fresh bannocks and jam with extra clotted cream."

The boys whooped and shot toward the keep as if they'd been slung from a sling.

"Here, give me your arm, Margie," Katherine said as she watched the boys with a small ache in her chest. "We canna have ye going tail over teakettle in the snow."

"The drifts are deep enough t'would be a soft landing if I did." Margaret chuckled. "What a handful those wee imps have become. And just wait till Lucas and wee Tam leave the nursery and join them. This castle will be overrun with small boys."

"Five sons in eight years," Katherine said. All of Margaret's lads were thriving. In a time when illness and death struck the laird's child as often as his cottar's, it was a minor miracle to have so many living offspring. "Ye and my brother have been truly blessed. Donald must be so pleased."

As they walked in step with each other, a shadow passed over Margaret's face. "I expect he will be once the boys are older. They aren't of much interest to him now, ye ken."

"Oh?" Katherine wondered if all men felt that way about their children. If so, that explained why William had never expressed any grief over their losses. It didn't excuse him, though. The wind swirled up a snow-sprite of white around them and Katherine steadied her sister-in-law while they trudged across the bailey.

"To Donald, they're bairns yet, unable to hold either a conversation or a dirk like a man. Though last time he was home, your brother did spend a bit more time with Dermid." Margaret's face lit with pride. "He's all of seven now and trying mightily to please his father by learning to speak French."

"French?"

"Aye. Donald says if our sons hope to go to court, they must learn French. 'Tis the language of diplomacy, he says."

Donald was twelve years Katherine's senior, so she had never really spent much time with her brother as she was growing up. If he ignored his sons so, she was beginning to think not knowing her brother well wasn't much of a loss.

"And is that what *you* want?" Kat asked. "For your boys to be courtiers and diplomats?"

Margaret shrugged. "It doesna matter a flibbet what I want. Their father will decide for them when the time comes. Of course, Dermid is his heir, so he'll be trained in running the estate and military strategy, but Donald will have plans for the others too. It'll be the Church for one of them, I warrant. And I'm so afraid he'll send at least one to sea."

"If ye dinna want your sons to go to sea, ye should tell Donald how ye feel."

"And have ye told your husband how *you* feel?"

"About what?"

"About whatever it is that brought you here without him," Margie said. "Of course, I'm grateful for your company as my time nears, but I've a feeling seeing your newest nephew or niece safely into the world isna all that brought ye home."

Katherine pressed her lips together for a moment. If Margaret knew what she was planning, she suspected her sister-in-law wouldn't encourage her. "We aren't talking about me now."

"Pity. We should, so you can settle this thing, whatever it is. At least ye have your husband close by." Margaret smiled sadly. "When would I have occasion to talk to Donald? Your brother is hardly ever home. Your father oversees the running of the estate, but Donald spends his time at court. 'Looking to Glengarry's future,' he says."

James V was seventeen now, in 1529, and finally out from under the thumbs of the men who'd ruled in his name. It made sense to cultivate the favor of the young king for the good of the earldom, but the birth of a child should count for something.

"Surely he'll be here for your lying-in."

Margaret laughed, but there was little mirth in the sound. "Leave court at Christmas? I highly doubt it. Besides, Donald has no patience for a sickroom. He'll come when the child is to be christened and I've been churched. Not before."

Silence fell between them, interrupted only by the crunch of snow underfoot.

"To be honest, when your man swept into the keep last night," Margaret said softly, "I hoped it was my Donald."

Kat squeezed Margie's arm tighter. "I wish it had been."

"Never say that, Katherine. Ye dinna know how lucky ye are to have a man who'll leave everything and follow after ye simply because he wants you."

"He wants something, but I'm not sure 'tis me."

"Give the man credit for being here. After this one's born, Donald will come home long enough to get me with another bairn, which willna take much doing, I'm afeared. Last time, he barely had time to hang his plaid on the peg before I was breeding again." Margaret sighed. "Then once he's done his duty by me, he'll be gone."

Margaret conceived and carried babes so easily. Katherine seldom felt more useless and less womanly than when she was in her sister-in-law's presence. It wasn't Margie's fault. She never said anything to demean Kat directly. Her swollen belly was indictment enough.

"At least you can give my brother children."

Margaret must have heard the wistfulness in her tone for she stopped walking. "Oh, Katherine, I'm sorry. I didna think. I didna mean to complain. Truly, I did not. It'll happen again for you. Have faith."

It had happened. Many times. But Katherine's body couldn't seem to keep a child growing inside it. Of course, Margaret only knew about the stillborn boy Katherine had delivered about a year after she and William wed. For months afterward, that small ghost had hovered around Kat. Now he had a handful of unborn siblings.

"Have faith," Katherine repeated. "So ye think that's what it takes?"

In the pause between the Gloria and the Credo that morning, Katherine had come to a decision. She knew what she must do. It was best for William, and the only way she could truly demonstrate her love for him. Now she needed the courage to do it. The remembered words of a Psalm hardened her resolve.

"'Like arrows in the hand of a warrior, so are the

sons of one's youth,'" Katherine quoted, trying to keep bitterness from bleeding into her tone. "'Blessed is the man whose quiver is full of them.' That's how it goes, isn't it?"

"Donald's quiver is full enough." Margaret patted her belly. "I'm praying this one's a girl."

William burst into the bright sunlight, wishing mightily for typical overcast Scottish weather. The heavens seemed determined to remind him that he'd imbibed far too much whisky last night. He ignored the stab of pain behind his eyes and plowed toward Katherine and her sister-in-law.

"Happy Christmas, good-sister," he said courteously to Margaret. It would pay him to keep in her good graces. Katherine was devoted to Margie and a man never knew when he'd need a feminine ally.

"Happy Christmas to you too, good-brother." She smiled impishly at him and then tossed a wink to Kat. Will suspected Margaret knew more about the state of his marriage than he did. "If ye want me later, Katherine, I'll be in my chamber with my feet up."

"Good," his wife said. "Ye need your rest."

"Rest? Not likely with this one doing somersaults and squirming about." She laid a protective hand on her belly. "The best I can hope is to keep my ankles from swelling."

When Katherine would have followed her into the keep, William caught her elbow. "Walk with me, wife."

"In the snow?"

"There was a time when we'd brave drifts deeper than this to have a moment alone." He brought her hands to his lips and blew his warm breath on them.

Her fingers were icy. She ought to have worn gloves. "Of course, we could always go to our chamber."

"In the middle of the morning?"

"Not so long ago that wouldn't have mattered either." He tucked one of her hands into the crook of his elbow and started walking, measuring the length of his stride so she could stay even with him easily. He led her up the steps to the parapet that topped the curtain wall. The view was fine from there. The edge of the loch was rimed with ice. Further out, the deep open water sparkled like jet.

Will ran his thumb over the back of her hand. "I mind a time when folk said we were so uncommon close, it was impossible to slip a piece of parchment between us. We couldna keep our hands off each other."

The way her cheeks pinkened had little to do with the chilly weather. Making his wife blush counted as a win. He cupped her cheek, reveling in the satiny softness of her skin. "I miss those times, love."

She closed her eyes and leaned into his touch. "I do, too, Will. So much."

He lowered his mouth to hers, intending to give her a soft, gentle kiss. But it had been so long since he'd had the comfort of her sweet body, the kiss turned dark and demanding between one breath and the next. Before he knew it, he had her pinned against the stone parapet, pressing his hardness against her. Need flared between them, white hot and relentless.

Sweet Lord! She arched into him and he feared he might spend on the spot.

If anyone had told him a man could be so bewitched by his own wife, he'd never have believed it.

"Oh, Kat, my bonnie Kat." He started kissing down her neck. God help him, he was ready to lift her skirt and tup her right there within sight of the bailey. It would be quick. Lord, just a thrust or two would send him right over the edge. Then he'd lure her back up to their chamber, where he'd strip off her Christmas finery and—

Katherine wedged her arms between them and broke off their kiss.

"Stop it, Will. Anyone might see."

"No one's looking. Most of your father's men are still asleep and the servants are busy with preparations for the Christmas feast."

Katherine used to be the adventurous sort. He remembered the breathless coupling they managed in the shadow of the portcullis one night as watchmen prowled the curtain wall above. She'd had to cover her mouth to keep from crying out as she came that time.

Now she covered her face simply to keep from crying.

"What happened to us, Kat?"

Do ye love me no longer? The words hovered on his tongue, but he wouldn't let himself voice them. A man shouldn't need like that.

She sighed and dropped her hands. Tears trembled on her lashes, but she didn't let them fall.

"I remember how it was, Will," she said slowly, "but I think the proper question now is how *it should* be for us in the future."

"What do you mean?"

She squared her shoulders, but didn't meet his eyes. "After Epiphany, I mean to send a letter to Rome, asking for our marriage to be annulled. I've thought long and hard about it, ye see, and . . ."

Will knew she was still talking because her lips moved, but he couldn't understand the words coming from her mouth. Once in a while he caught a few snippets—something about asking the bishop to hand deliver the request and wondering if a generous donation to the local abbey might speed the proceedings—but the rest of her words made no sense to his brain.

"Ye have no grounds for an annulment," he finally said to stop her.

"I'll find one."

William didn't see how. They weren't closely related. Sometimes annulments were granted when a couple discovered they were cousins within a few degrees. But that couldn't be the case with them since no one in the Douglas clan had ever taken a Glengarry bride before.

The age of consent was another possible reason to rule a marriage invalid. They'd been betrothed as children, but they were both of age at their wedding. Sometimes birth records were spotty, and could be falsified, but no one who'd attended their ceremony would have mistaken Katherine and Will for children under the ages of twelve and fourteen.

"Ye canna claim we've never consummated," William said. "No one would believe it."

"People will believe anything if ye repeat it often enough."

"Not in this case," he said softly. "We had the one."

"Stephan. His name is Stephan. Why can ye not—" Her voice cracked, but she pressed on. "Even now, ye canna say his name."

Will turned away and leaned on the parapet. Something in his chest went suddenly as cold and icebound as the loch. They hadn't been allowed to name the child officially since he never drew breath, but Kat insisted on calling him after her father.

The boy had been buried without ceremony in a bit of unconsecrated ground near the woods around Badenoch. They weren't even supposed to mark the grave, but William knew to a finger width exactly where the child lay. Father Simon told them the baby's soul was in limbo, but he assured them it would be released to heaven if only they prayed hard enough.

Will hadn't said a word to the Almighty since. Any deity who wouldn't take his stillborn son straight to heaven wasn't one with whom he cared to converse.

"Some things dinna bear speaking of," he said. She'd only work herself into more of an upset. "Besides, talking willna change a thing."

"Good. I'm glad ye see it too."

He suspected the subject had been changed while he was unaware of it. "See what?"

"Our marriage will never be what it once was." Katherine's chin trembled, but her eyes were dry now. "So I release you."

"I dinna wish to be released. We can go back to the way we were, as if none of this ever happened." He reached for her again, but she stepped back, out of the circle of his arms. The stricken look on her face told him he'd said exactly the wrong thing.

"But it did happen. Stephan happened. We canna go back. 'Twill never be the same. Trust me, Will, 'tis better this way. Ye'll be free to take a bride who can give ye the son and heir ye deserve and ye can pass that . . ." She paused, drawing her lips into a tight line. ". . . that scepter ye're so proud of on to the next generation of Douglas males. In time, ye'll thank me." Then she fled from him, down the steps and across the bailey.

Feeling as dead as his son, William watched her

go. Only his hitching puffs of breath in the frosty air convinced him that his heart was still beating.

"Lady Katherine is right," a small voice said once she was gone. "'Twill never be the same, William. Nothing ever is."

His head jerked at the sound, and he saw a gargoylelike face peeping at him from between the stone crenellations a little way down the wall.

It was Nab. The small fellow had been scrunched down in a hollow embrasure a few feet away from them, invisible to anyone on the narrow walkway. Now he was leaning inward toward the bailey, the floppy ends of his hat dangling. He still looked the fool, but he was clutching the scepter Will had given him tight to his chest.

"But why would ye want it to be?" Nab asked.

William didn't understand the fool at the best of times, and now he had little patience for his cryptic question. "Be what?" he asked gruffly.

"The same," Nab said. "Yer marriage willna be the same. That's not so bad when ye think about it."

"Aye, it is." Having Katherine want to leave him was the worst that could happen. Will leaned on the stone crenellations and stared down at the frigid loch.

"But since Lady Katherine is so sad and doesna seem to like ye much, the same isna all that good, is it?"

In a strange way, Nab was making sense.

"It canna be the same," the fool repeated. "So that leaves only two choices. It can be better."

The words struck Will with the force of a crossbow bolt.

"Or worse," Nab continued. "Odds bodkins, it could always be worse. It usually is."

Better. He could make things better. As laird of his

own estate, William was a problem solver by nature. He resolved disputes between his crofters all the time. Just because he was a party to this dispute, it didn't mean he couldn't hammer out a solution that would please both him and Katherine. He ground his fist into his other palm. He could fix this. He could—

"I know!" Nab's mouth curved into an awkward grin and he waggled the scepter over his head. "Since I'm Laird of Misrule, I could order Lady Katherine to be happy and love ye. She has to obey me. It's a Christmastide tradition."

"Power has gone to your head, my friend." Will started to pat Nab on the shoulder, but when the smaller fellow shied from his touch, he stopped short. "I'm obliged to ye, Laird Nab, but no man can give a woman that order and expect to see it obeyed. Besides, your rule only extends till Twelfth Night and I intend for Kat and me to last far longer than that."

Will paced along the parapet, the wind stinging his eyes. "I can start afresh, do things differently this time." He smacked his thigh with an open palm. "I could woo her."

Nab raised a quizzical brow.

"I didna have to the first time. We were promised to each other so young, ye see. I never had to court Katherine." He was both excited and daunted by the prospect. "I'll win her heart."

"I'll help."

"Thank ye, Nab, but I—"

"Lasses like poems, or so I've heard. I know lots of poems. Do ye want to hear a poem, William?"

"Not now, Nab, I'm thinking." His mind churned furiously. There was so much to do, so many things he ought to have done before. He headed for the steps leading down to the bailey. "I have to go. Wish me luck."

"Luck," Nab repeated, waving the scepter, the stone atop it sparkling in the sunlight. "What d'ye need luck for?"

"I'm off to make my wife want to wed me all over again," he called over his shoulder.

Nab sighed. "Ye'll need more than luck. Ye'll need a poem, William. Maybe two."

I saw a fair maiden, sitten and sing.
She lulléd a little child, a sweeté lording.

—Fifteenth-century carol

"Dinna ye think the child might sleep better if there was
less singin' and more tiptoein'?"

—An observation from Nab,
fool to the Earl of Glengarry

Chapter Four

Somehow, Katherine kept her composure as she hurried through the great hall. She even managed to listen when Jamison, her father's seneschal, stopped her to complain about the ravages to the castle's larder.

"I urge ye to moderation, my lady. I've tried to tell Lady Margaret, but she willna heed me. If we continue feasting like this till Twelfth Night, mark my words, stomachs will be knocking on backbones around here before winter is gone," he predicted dourly.

"Glengarry canna stint at Christmastide," she said. "Not before the laird's guests."

"We might ask a few of them to leave," Jamison grumbled.

There was only one Katherine would wish to see gone.

No, that wasn't true. She never felt truly alive unless she breathed the same air as William Douglas. She just wished taking the breath didn't hurt so much.

"If needs be, my father will take the men hunting and ye'll have a boar and a stag and heaven knows what else to hang and dress in the larder before ye know it. In fact, it would do them all good to clear out of the hall for a time." She and the Glengarry servants might be able to sweep out the soiled rushes and freshen the place if it sat empty for a while. It would do her good to have a job to do. Something mindless, so she wouldn't have to think anymore. Or feel. "Now let me pass."

She pushed by Jamison, still holding back the tears that pricked the backs of her eyes, and made her way up the winding staircase to Margaret's chamber. When she stepped into the room, her sister-in-law was humming a lullaby to wee Tam. The bairn slept in her arms. His rosebud mouth made little sucking motions, but otherwise he didn't stir.

Katherine couldn't keep the ache in her heart from leaking out of her eyes any longer. Seeing her distress, Margie signaled to the waiting maid.

"Here, Dorcas," Margaret said as she transferred the babe to her servant's arms, "do ye take the lad. He'll sleep sweet now, I'll be bound." After Dorcas carried the child away, Margie hurried to Katherine's side. "Dorcas says his wet nurse wants to wean him because he's teething and has started biting her something fierce. I daresay those new little teeth are sharp as a dirk's edge, but . . . ye aren't here for me to regale ye with tales of my nursery. What news? Tell me."

The floodgates opened. Tears streamed down Katherine's cheeks, and mopping them up with a handkerchief didn't stem the tide much. Still, she managed to choke out her plan to have her marriage annulled and William's objections to it.

"He's right. Ye have no grounds," her sister-in-law said with annoying practicality. "Ye're getting yourself in a fret over nothing."

Kat glared at her.

"I didna mean that," Margie said. "Of course, if ye're this upset, 'tis not nothing. But if ye mean to go ahead with the annulment, ye must know ye have no cause the Church will recognize."

"What if I was pre-contracted?"

"Before ye were betrothed to William?"

"Aye. Rabbie MacDonell. He and I pledged ourselves to each other when we were six or seven. We were young, I'll admit, but I'm sure he'll remember it." She dried her eyes and stuffed the soggy handkerchief up her sleeve. "We used the most excellent oaths we could think of and swore in the haymow one day to plight our troths."

"Since ye were all of six and in a stable, are ye sure ye and Rabbie didna plight your *troughs*?" Margie said with a chuckle.

"Dinna laugh at me." Kat sank into one of the heavy Tudor chairs. "I'm serious as a case of the pox."

"Then ye'll have to come up with something better than a pre-contract with a lad in a stable," Margie said. "Katherine, I love ye. Ye know I do, but ye're a goose for even thinking of leaving a man like William."

Kat stood. "If ye'll not help me, I'll go in peace."

"Nay, steady on. Of course, I'll help if I can." Margaret waved one hand in a small circle. Katherine recognized it as the same gesture she used with her boys when she wished to cut to the heart of the matter. Usually this was before she was forced to check their sporrans for toads and other unchancy things that found their way into a small lad's treasure trove. "Tell me more about this contract with Rabbie. Were your parents aware of it?"

"No, but a pre-contract need not have been formalized to be held valid."

"That's true. Though ye'll need a verra good advocate to convince Rome to give the claim any weight." Margie paced the length of her chamber, arching her back and surreptitiously grinding a fist into the small of it. She never complained, but Katherine saw signs that the last few days of her sister-in-law's confinement were becoming increasingly uncomfortable.

"But here's the problem," Margaret said. "The pre-contract is unenforceable. Rabbie has already wed the daughter of Owen MacNulty, aye?"

"Aye, but if I'm granted an annulment, I dinna mean to hold Rabbie to his troth." Katherine straightened her spine. "I plan to take the veil. I'd not want to disturb his peace."

"From what I hear, the daughter of Owen MacNulty gives Rabbie no peace. Him nor anyone else within earshot." Margaret pulled up the stool she'd been using to elevate her feet and plopped it down before Katherine. Then she sat on it and grasped both of Kat's hands. "Why are ye doing this? Will loves ye something fierce. Anyone with eyes can see it, and while I'm about it, he's fair easy on the eyes himself. Why in creation would ye want to be severed from a man like that?"

Kat's face crumpled. "Because I love him."

"Weel, that's no sort of sense." Margie snorted. "Have ye gone softheaded?"

"Nay, I've never been more clear. As Laird of Badenoch, Will is a man of property and power. He needs an heir." She shook her head sadly. "I canna give him one."

"Ye've only been wed a few years. Give it time." A wistful smile lifted Margaret's lips. "Enjoy the making of a child. When all ye can hear in the night is one or another of your bairns crying, ye'll be wishing for the days when the only reason ye lost sleep was trying to give your man his heir."

Katherine wouldn't be deterred. It was important that someone understood her reasons. Lord knew, William certainly didn't. Her sister-in-law was her best hope. "Margie, ye ken we buried our little boy, but ye dinna ken about the others."

"Others?" Margaret gripped Kat's hands tighter.

"I've lost four more since then." She hadn't even told Will about all of them. At first when she suspected she was bearing, she'd practically sing out that her courses were late and she and William would be deliriously happy together. But after two disappointments in close succession, it was easier to try to pretend it hadn't happened again. By keeping a pregnancy to herself, she was the only one who suffered the loss when it ended badly. "I didna bear them long. Not even long enough for them to quicken."

She'd only felt that joyful invasion, that beloved Other fluttering in her belly, when she carried Stephan. "It seems I canna bear a child."

Thank God, Margaret didn't mouth any comforting platitudes. She didn't try to deny the truth. She just put her arms around Katherine and let her weep.

When she finally had no more tears, she discovered Margaret's cheeks were wet too.

"Margie, I'm sorry. Ye shouldna be crying. 'Tis not good for the bairn."

"I canna help it. Dinna fret about the babe. 'Tis in no danger from my tears. The child will give me more of them once it comes. Of that ye may be certain. They all do sooner or later." Margaret dried her eyes. "Besides, no one weeps alone if I am with them."

Katherine couldn't help wondering if things might be different, if she might have the courage to go on in her marriage, if just once, William had wept with her.

She gave herself a brisk inward shake. That was a selfish thought. "An heir is important to William, even if he denies it. Did ye mark that scepter Will gave Nab to use while he's Laird of Misrule?"

"Aye, 'tis a thing of beauty and of no small value. I wonder that he trusts it to the fool."

"He gave it up because he knows as long as he's wed to me, he'll have no son to hand it on to." Katherine curled her fingers into fists. "Time out of mind, that scepter has passed through an unbroken line of Douglas fathers and sons. I canna bear to let the lineage die with William."

"What does Will say about it?"

"What can he say? Each time he learns I lost another, he simply wants to try again." Katherine stood and walked to the window. The sun had disappeared behind a cloudbank. The world of sparkling white was suddenly marked with cold, grey shadows advancing on the snowdrifts in the bailey. "Oh, Margie, I canna hope any longer. It hurts too much."

Margaret came and put an arm around Kat's shoulders. "If there was no sorrow, we'd never know joy. Ye must hope, Katherine. Even if it hurts to hope. Life has a way of evening things out. The sorrow ye feel now will make a future joy shine all the brighter."

Katherine laid her head on her good-sister's shoulder. "How did ye become so wise?"

"'Tis all the extra sweetmeats I've been eating, no doubt. Come. Let's see if my wee heathens have left any bannocks and clotted cream for the rest of us." Margie shuffled to the head of the stairs leading down to the great hall. "Failing that, I've a strong craving for one of those gooseberry tarts."

Katherine didn't see William for the rest of the day, which struck her as odd since there were only so many places in Glengarry where a man might betake himself. He wasn't in the great hall with the other revelers who'd been tossing knucklebones and wagering loudly. He wasn't pacing the ramparts of the castle walls. Even without looking, she was certain William wasn't in the chapel.

He had little use for the Church, even on high holidays.

Finally, as the sun started its western slide to the horizon, she visited the stable on the pretext of checking on a mare that was in foal. What she really wanted to see was whether her husband's mount was still there. Wee Angus dogged her steps, snuffling at her heels and leaping through the snow to keep up with her.

Once they cleared the stable doorway, the terrier darted after a rat and disappeared, only his stubby tail was visible above the loose straw. Katherine wandered down the line of stalls alone.

Relief washed over her when Greyfellow, William's dappled gelding, whickered to her over one of the gates. She was more than a little ashamed of being glad her husband was still in the castle. It would be better for both of them if he were gone.

"There's a fine boy." She reached over to stroke the horse's soft nose. Then she dug into her pocket for the apple core she'd brought for him and offered it to the gelding on a flattened palm. Greyfellow's lips brushed her skin as he took the gift. "I'm glad to see ye, but he really ought to go home."

"Who ought to go home?" William came up behind her, carrying the gelding's saddle.

It seemed rude to tell him he should leave to his face. After all, it was Christmastide and he was still her husband.

"My cousin Ranulf MacNaught," she said quickly. "He's been terrifying Nab something fierce."

"Still?" William opened the stall and settled the saddle on the gelding's back. "I thought he led the charge to see the fool crowned Laird of Misrule."

"Aye, it was his idea. But I suspect it was only so he could taunt Nab more easily. I think Ranulf has repented of putting him into a place of power, however ridiculous it might be."

Will bent to cinch Greyfellow's girth. The sight of his broad back sent a feminine thrill down her spine, but she tamped down the feeling. No good could come of mooning over her husband since she was determined he wouldn't be hers much longer.

"Nab set the lot of them to sweeping the solar this morning after breakfast to save the maids from having to do it. Somehow in the process, a great bucket of wash water was accidentally dumped on Ranulf. I know it wasna hot, but he complained so loudly, ye'd have thought he was a scalded cat."

Will chuckled. "Nab may not be a warrior, but he has his own ways of evening the score. Wish I'd seen it."

Katherine resisted the urge to ask where William had been. He might think his whereabouts mattered to her and that would never do.

He fitted the halter over his mount's head, then slid in the bit.

"Are ye leaving?" she asked, wishing her voice hadn't chosen that moment to break.

"Would ye care if I did?"

Of course, she'd care. She'd go to her grave loving this man, but if he wasn't around for her to see, to hear, to simply breathe the same air, perhaps the ache in her chest would ease. "Ye do have things at home that require your attention."

"So do ye, but I dinna see ye packing to head back to Badenoch."

"Margaret needs me."

"So do I." His dark eyes burned into hers. Then his intent expression was replaced by a grin. "And right now, I need ye to ride pillion. We canna go far on Greyfellow this day with all the snow, so he needs more of a load to get the same exercise."

Without waiting for her response, he put both hands on her waist and lifted her to sit on the padding behind his saddle. Then he climbed up into the saddle ahead of her, swinging his booted right foot over Greyfellow's head. The gelding whickered at the indignity of such an unorthodox mounting.

"But what about Angus?"

"The wee fleabag will be fine here chasing mice till we return."

As if the matter were decided, Will dug his heels into the gelding's sides and they were off at a trot. Katherine was forced to wrap her arms around William's waist, lest she slide off the horse's rump. They picked up speed as they shot through the portcullis and over the drawbridge.

Will chirruped to the gelding, urging him to climb the hill that rushed up from the loch. Greyfellow's great haunches bunched and flexed beneath Katherine with every lunge. Once they reached the tree line, they turned right to shadow the edge of the loch. The gelding sank into the powdery snow past his fetlocks, but Will urged him to more speed. Sprays of white fluttered around them with each pounding step.

Katherine tightened her grip around William's waist and pressed her cheek to his warm back. His heart hammered under her ear, thunderous and strong.

He'd do anything for her. She knew that. The only trouble was there was nothing he could do about her barrenness. She sighed and held him tighter. He was the love of her life, but it wasn't enough. It was selfish of her to cling to him. It was time she made a fresh break. . . .

But he was so strong and alive and wonderful. How many more times would she be able to hold him like this?

Just when she was beginning to wish they could keep riding forever, moving as one, nothing to stop them, nothing to separate them, William reined in the horse. It danced in circles, still wanting to run.

"Settle then, ye wicked beast," he growled to the gelding. Greyfellow stopped fidgeting and stood still.

"I'll give ye your head when we turn back to the castle and ye can gallop your silly hooves off then."

Will threw one leg over the horse's head and slid to the ground. He helped Katherine down, his hands lingering on her waist. After he hobbled the gelding, he took Kat's hand and led her to the rocky promontory overlooking the loch.

A biting wind lifted the bottom of Katherine's cloak. She shivered but didn't complain. The view was too lovely to spoil by quibbling over chattering teeth. The loch stretched below them, long but fairly narrow in either direction, its choppy surface cradled between ragged peaks. In the distance, the grey sky and water seemed to join as the clouds lowered.

"More snow this night, I'll be bound," William said. When he turned his head so she could see his profile, Katherine caught a glimpse of the son she should have given him. He'd have been strong and sturdy, with laughing eyes and a firm chin, a smaller version of his father. A dull ache throbbed in her chest, and she forced herself to look away to the rough water of the loch.

She had to find new thoughts. The ones rolling around in her head now were likely to make her heart stop beating.

"I wonder how the waterhorse will manage if the loch freezes solid," she said.

"Waterhorse?"

"Aye, did ye never hear tell of the waterhorse of Loch Ness?"

Will chuckled. "O' course I have. Since St. Columba saw the monster ages ago, there have been stories. I just never expected ye to believe in it."

"I grew up here, remember. The loch's full of secrets." She shrugged and pulled her cloak tighter.

When the dark water of the loch rippled and swirled on a still day for no reason, it was hard not to imagine something large and otherworldly moving silently beneath the surface. "Nab saw it once, ye ken."

"Did he?"

"Aye, so they say. It happened when he was but a young lad. Afterward, his mother found him standing like a pillar of salt by the edge of the loch, staring down into the dark water. He could scarcely move. She led him home, but he didna speak for a week. Then he finally said 'Weel, that was a hell of a sight.'"

William moved closer, positioning his body to shield her from the wind. "That doesna sound like Nab."

"No, it doesna. His father beat him for swearing, though I've no doubt he learned the word at his father's knee, but his mother claims Nab never would have sworn unless he'd seen the waterhorse."

"I guess that would do it."

"Some folk say that's what turned Nab so queer, but my father says he was born thus."

"I expect your father's right. We are as God made us."

She looked at him sharply then. He was staring into the distance with a hard set to his jaw.

"So ye're saying I am as God made me."

He smiled at her then, but it seemed hollow, like the one she forced herself to wear sometimes. A cat's smile. A smile that held unspeakable secrets. "I should remember to thank Him because He made ye specially for me to love."

"No, that's not what ye were thinking. Ye were thinking if ye canna lay the blame on your wife, 'tis God's fault we have no child."

"'Tis no one's fault."

"Good. Ye shouldna blame the Almighty," she said primly. "I fear for your soul if ye do."

"He hasna struck me down yet, and trust me, I've had plenty of blasphemous thoughts."

"Will, dinna say that. 'Tis my fault and we both know it."

"Kat, for once in your life, will ye please stop? I didna bring ye here to talk. In truth, I'm weary to death of words. There've been too many between us already, and more will only make things worse." He moved to stand behind her, put his arms around her, and pulled her close to his chest. "I just want to be alone with the girl I love."

"Oh, Will." She ought to pull away from him. If she didn't, it would only make things harder on both of them, but she couldn't seem to help herself. She sank back into his embrace, soaking up his warmth and the strength of his body.

"That's more like it." He kissed her neck just the way she liked for him to. A little pleasure-sprite danced over her skin. "Besides, I've a present for ye."

"A present?" She really ought not to accept it. Not when in her mind, she was still composing a letter to His Holiness, Clement VII, asking for an annulment. "I've not been good enough to deserve a gift."

"Probably not, haring off as ye did and making me and Greyfellow tramp through a blizzard after ye, but I'm prepared to overlook that." He nuzzled her neck again, the stubble of his beard tickling her in a very good way indeed. "Besides, 'tis Christmas, and we all deserve a bit of leeway at this time of year. In any case, I want ye to have it. Ye've need of it."

He trudged back through the snow to Greyfellow and pulled something out of his saddlebag. "'Tis a wee pretty I picked up for ye in Edinburgh last time I was there. They say all the ladies at court have one for winter."

William handed her a rectangle of rabbit fur.

A puzzled frown knitting her brows, Katherine ran her palm over the softness. "I thank ye, Will, for the . . . er . . . what is it?"

"They call it a muff. There are openings on either side and ye stick your hands into it. Here. Let me show ye."

Standing behind her, he guided her hands into the dense fur and stayed there, his arms around her, his chin resting on the crown of her head.

"Och, 'tis so soft."

"And if ye give it a moment, your hands will warm the space and your fingers will be toasty even without gloves."

"'Tis lovely, Will. And verra fine. But I have nothing for ye."

He turned her in his arms and drew her close. Then he leaned down to touch his forehead to hers. "Let's away to your chamber and I'm sure if we try hard enough we'll discover something ye might give me."

Without thinking about it, she slipped her muff-covered hands over his head, resting the fur against the back of his neck. His scent enveloped her—all leather and warm horse and undeniably male. His dark eyes searched her face, asking for—no, demanding—a response. Katherine tipped her chin up a wee bit.

He brushed her lips with his, a soft, glancing caress. This man had a way of kissing her that made each time feel as if it were the first. As if no one had ever kissed before and he and Katherine were making it up as they went. This time it was as if he were trying to divine her secrets by teasing them from her mouth.

Then, deep and demanding and true, William covered her lips in a hungry bruising. He claimed her, and even though the kiss was rougher than usual, Kat roused to him.

Desire flared to life and she felt herself go soft and liquid in her inward parts. Everything in her responded to his dark summons. Katherine was falling a bit on the inside, tumbling into that place where nothing and everything made perfect sense, and when she did, she knew William would be there to catch her.

She'd do anything for this man.

It would be so easy to rush back to the keep and lie with him. So easy to give him release and take some for herself. So easy to worship him with her body. She'd often thought she needed to esteem either William less or God more, lest she be guilty of idolatry. It was so easy to adore her husband.

But could she do the hardest thing and show she truly loved him?

Love would free him to find another woman who could give him a dozen sons.

With effort, she pulled away. "No, Will, I canna."

"If ye're still—"

"Nay, 'tis not that. My courses are ended." She edged away from him. "And so is our marriage. The sooner ye accept that, the better 'twill be for us both."

Hurt flicked over his features, but it was so quickly replaced by anger, Katherine couldn't be sure she hadn't imagined it. She'd seen Will's wrath aimed at the marauding Campbells who stole cattle whenever they could and at crofters who were too lazy to work the land he'd assigned them, but it had never been turned in her direction before. She stepped back another pace under the blistering heat of his scowl.

"As ye will, milady," he said, his voice taut with fury. Then, without another word, he picked her up and deposited her on Greyfellow's back as if she were a sack of meal. But this time, she wasn't on the pillion. He'd placed her squarely on the saddle.

He unhobbled the gelding. Katherine barely had time to throw a leg over to slip both feet into the stirrups before William gave the horse a whack on the backside. Greyfellow took off at a mile-eating canter back to the warmth and light and oats waiting for him in the castle stable.

As Katherine streaked under the portcullis, she realized in her effort to hang on to Greyfellow's reins, she'd lost her new muff, her Christmas gift from William, somewhere along the path.

It was just as well. She didn't deserve it.

Sire, the night is darker now
and the wind blows stronger.
Fails my heart, I know not how I can go no longer.

—From "Good King Wenceslas"

"If a body's that weary, why does he not lie down and sleep? And they call me a fool!"

—An observation from Nab,
fool to the Earl of Glengarry

Chapter Five

William trudged through the snow trying to stay in the trampled path left by Greyfellow's hooves. At one point, he found Katherine's muff tossed carelessly aside into a snow-covered gorse bush.

She'd thrown away his gift just as she was throwing away their marriage. Damned if he'd let her do it. He pricked his fingers on the sharp thorns several times, but finally managed to extricate the muff from the shrubbery. He stuffed it into the folds of his plaid and pressed on.

He was chilled to the bone by the time he made it back to Glengarry Castle. Night fell early in the Highlands in December. He stomped his frozen feet to coax some feeling into them while the watchmen challenged him. After several impertinent questions, which he felt were entirely unnecessary—he was wed to the daughter of the house, after all—William was finally allowed back in.

"Ought to have let *her* walk home," he grumbled as he headed for the great hall. At the time, his only thought had been to get Katherine out of his sight before he said or did something he'd later regret.

Now he wondered why he had bothered since she didn't seem to regret anything. She wounded him afresh with each rejection and didn't care a flying fig.

He wouldn't have named her heartless before.

When he entered the great hall, supper was still in progress, despite the fact that Lord Glengarry's place on the dais was empty. Will wasn't surprised. The laird was getting older, and since he'd had that apoplectic fit last winter, he tired more easily.

The whole castle had been in an uproar of panic when their laird was stricken. For weeks, one side of the old man's face sagged and his speech was slurred. William and Katherine had been summoned to Glengarry and even Donald abandoned court to rush to his father's bedside.

The earl was made of stern stuff. He had rallied and regained his speech. But now the constant merry-making of Christmastide probably wearied him more than usual. Will figured his father-in-law had likely taken a bowl of parritch in his chamber.

The fire blazing in the gigantic hearth called to him.

"God be praised," William murmured under his breath as he worked his way through the throng to stand before the flames. The smell of steaming wool warned him he was a bit too close. It felt so good to let his muscles thaw and unbunch before the fire, he decided it was worth the risk of singeing his plaid.

He didn't even look around to see if Katherine was there until the blood came screaming back into his fingers and toes once more.

As it happened, she wasn't in the hall, but he was determined not to go in search of her.

For the first time, the idea that she might be right crept into his brain. Perhaps no true marriage had been made between them if she was willing to set it aside so easily.

But just because his head entertained this thought, it didn't mean his heart agreed. His chest ached as if someone had opened his ribs and hollowed him out.

William plopped down at one of the tables and snagged a bannock from the basket filled with them. Then a serving girl brought him a trencher laden with a generous slice of humble pie.

"Fitting." He wondered if his wife had ordered it especially for him.

But the crusty pastry was light and flaky. When he cut it open, the rich mixture of deer heart, liver, and brains smelled savory enough to make his mouth water. There was even a healthy portion of spicy frumenty on the side.

"Thank ye," he said to the serving girl before he tucked in. "Ye're Dorcas, are ye not?"

"Aye, milord." The girl dropped a curtsey. With eyes as pale as rainwater, she was still comely in a freckle-nosed, round-cheeked sort of way. "I'm ever so honored ye remember me."

He narrowed his gaze at her, trying to recall exactly where he'd run across her in the keep. It seemed that Katherine had been gushing about the girl's skills once and wondering if they might coax her away from Glengarry Castle. "Ye dinna usually serve in the hall."

"Nay, I tend Lady Margaret and her children mostly."

That explained it. When Katherine was bearing the first time, she had wanted to send for Dorcas to come serve in their nursery. William convinced her to wait till the child was born before bringing on a nursemaid. Then in the end, there was no need. He shoved away the memory of that small coffin.

Reliving the past never changed it.

"But they wanted extra hands in the hall this night, and to be honest, I'm that grateful to be spending Christmas with those who can cut their own meat for a change," Dorcas nattered on. "Shall I pull an ale for ye or would ye prefer a wee dram?"

Before William could answer, Ranulf MacNaught climbed atop a table and shouted for quiet.

"As ye all know, we've crowned our Laird of Misrule. As befits Christmastide royalty, he's been given a scepter by Lord Badenoch." Ranulf cast a grudging nod in Will's direction. "But far be it from a MacNaught to be outdone by a Douglas, so me and the lads have fashioned a throne for our Abbot of Unreason. Bring it in!"

Four of MacNaught's boon companions plodded into the great room from the solar, chanting a bastardized hymn in praise of Laird Nab as they came. The men held a chair fashioned from stag antlers and draped with purple velvet hoisted high above their heads. Laughing and stumbling, the mock procession wobbled toward the dais. They positioned the new throne with overblown ceremony next to the real Laird of Glengarry's heavy chair.

Kat's father would have laughed if anyone had

called his seat a throne. It was simply a sturdy place from which he meted out justice and issued orders.

"Come out, come out, wherever you are, Laird Nab, and take your rightful place," Ranulf singsonged.

Nab peeped from one of the shallow alcoves that notched the hall. The fool seemed uncomfortable in large crowds at the best of times. Now, from clear across the room, William saw that there was a sheen of sweat on his brow.

After a chorus of encouragement from the assembled revelers, Nab shuffled up to stand next to MacNaught and squinted at the antler-throne. "It doesna look verra comfortable, Ranulf, what with the points and all."

"A position of power isna intended to be comfortable, your wee lordship. But the velvet will cushion your backside well enough if that's what troubles ye. Go on. Take your throne, Nab."

"Laird Nab," the fool corrected. "I'm Laird Nab. Ye all said so."

"So be it. Laird Nab. Aye, an' it please ye, your lordship," Ranulf said with a sarcastic bow, "move your arse."

He gave Nab a shove and the fool stumbled up the rush-strewn steps leading to the dais. When his left foot reached the top step, a snare pulled taut around his ankle. Suddenly Nab was jerked to the ground, dragged along the steps by a rope that had been hidden beneath the rushes, and finally yanked into the air. Suspended by a loop of hemp, he bounced helplessly, dangling from a hook bolted to the ceiling. Nab tried to free his foot, but kept getting tangled up in his kilt, which was flapping around his armpits.

He might have been able to free himself, if he hadn't clung so tenaciously to the scepter. Instead, he swung upside down as the rope recoiled, first dropping him about six feet, then jerking him back up. Since his clothing draped downward, he was bare-assed to the world and from its nest of carrot-red hair, the fool's sex waggled free. Through it all, Nab could only make incomprehensible bleating sounds of disbelief at his mistreatment.

"The bastards," Will growled under his breath. He pushed away from the table and stood. Rage had been simmering in him all the way back to Glengarry Castle. He couldn't aim it at Katherine, though she was the cause. It had threatened to overflow and surge out in all directions, but now he had a suitable target upon which to unleash it.

"Weel, would ye look at that? The fool's been hiding his light under a bushel," MacNaught said with a barking laugh. "The wee shite is hung like a stallion. Guess he'll not have trouble finding a Lady of Misrule after this."

William plowed toward Ranulf. "And what do ye think your chances of finding a lady will be once ye have no teeth, MacNaught?"

He delivered a solid clout to Ranulf's jaw and the man staggered backward. But only a pace or two. Blood trickled from the corner of his lips. MacNaught ran his tongue around his mouth and spat out one of his eyeteeth. Then he wiped away the smear of red from his chin whiskers with the back of his hand.

"Been wantin' to have a go at ye, Douglas." His face split in a bloody smile. "Expect this is going to be fun."

MacNaught launched himself at William, fists flying. The brawl boiled up and across the dais in a flurry of jabs and wild swings. The rest of the revelers formed a moving circle around the fighters, the better to see this new entertainment. From the corner of his eye, Will caught one enterprising fellow laying odds and collecting bets on the outcome from atop one of the trestle tables.

Will landed a blow to MacNaught's temple that sent him teetering, but then he reared back against one of the tables and kicked William in the center of his chest with both booted feet.

All the air rushed from Will's lungs. He sucked wind, trying to fend off the darkness that gathered at the edges of his vision.

William's world spiraled down to the next punch, the next blow to his ribs, the next stinging jab to the jaw. He fought doggedly on, not thinking about strategy or form, but only focusing on connecting his fists with MacNaught's unyielding flesh.

Then suddenly Ranulf was giving ground, stumbling back toward the foot of the staircase that led to the family portion of the keep. Will followed up his advantage with a hail of punishing strikes.

Above the din of catcalls and raucous encouragement, Will could hear Nab, still bleating out his distress.

"For the love of God, somebody cut down the fool," he grunted as he put the power of his whole body behind his punch to MacNaught's belly. Ranulf doubled over as most of the onlookers realized there was another spectacle they'd forgotten about and milled back toward the dais, where poor Nab still hung upside down by one foot.

Ranulf was holding the short straw in the fight, so he took advantage of the crowd's inattention to call out to his companions, "Get him, lads."

Winded and sore, Will suddenly found himself faced with four fresh pairs of fists. And they didn't seem inclined to take turns. He circled, trying to face his attackers, but he couldn't prepare for a blow because he never knew which of them would dart within his reach to jab at him. Again and again, MacNaught's cronies struck him in the back at the base of his ribs. He managed to pop a couple of them in the face a time or two, but the fight had become markedly one-sided.

Finally, one of MacNaught's men picked up a chair and brought it crashing down over William's head. He crumpled to the flagstones. His vision tunneled, and the last coherent thought skittering through his brain was, "Thank God. Nab's finally stopped making that infernal noise."

Make we joy now in this fest
In quo Christus natus est.

—From "Make We Joy Now"

"I like the music. Ye can dance to it. But for the life of me, I dinna ken why we sing in a language no one but God and them who pass for educated understand."

—An observation from Nab,
fool to the Earl of Glengarry

Chapter Six

Nab tore the loaf in two and took a bite. The barley bread was still warm, but he took no pleasure in it. Even so, he forced himself to wolf it down. He didn't want to wake later and be tempted to wander back down into the main part of the keep in search of food. Then he stopped himself from demolishing the whole loaf in one sitting. He might be truly hungry tomorrow. He wrapped the rest of the bread in his handkerchief and set it aside. He never wanted to go back to the great hall, even though he was pretty sure his appetite would return sometime.

But then again, maybe not.

His stomach roiled uncertainly. Nab was used to being thought the fool and made the butt of countless jokes, but never before this night had he felt so helpless, so small, so . . . exposed.

He didn't express himself well. He knew that. But what the rest of them didn't understand was that he thought as well or better than any of them.

Just a wee bit differently.

The Earl of Glengarry ought to see it, but he never did.

Maybe out of all of them, only William could see him clearly. Maybe he knew there was something more to Nab than motley and a fool's cap. He must since he'd entrusted him with such a precious thing as the scepter. And William had stood up to Ranulf MacNaught for him.

But William was the only one.

Nab settled on the old rug and laid down the scepter so that the silver rod rested by his thigh. The smooth metal was restful and helped quiet the fidgets inside him.

He cracked open his book. No one in the castle, not even his friend William, would believe Nab could read. He'd started by studying the Latin inscriptions carved into the walls of the chapel, and before long, he'd puzzled out the code of the written word on his own.

The priest thought he was just parroting what he'd heard instead of reading. It made Nab smile. Sometimes it was good to be underestimated. If folks expected less of him, it gave him fewer chances to fail.

Lord Glengarry had a small library in his solar. The shelf held nearly half a dozen bound volumes, an unspeakable trove of riches meant to impress visitors to the keep. Nab was sure the earl himself couldn't read. He'd certainly never seen his master with a book in his hand unless he was showing it to someone else. Lord

Glengarry wasn't likely to miss one of them. Nab just had to be stealthy about borrowing in case the maids who dusted the books could count.

He reminded himself to feel grateful that he was able to stay at Glengarry Castle, even if he did have to play the fool. His parents had been glad to be shed of him. They had no idea what to do with the likes of him. There'd even been superstitious talk in the village about Nab being a changeling, some queer offspring from the hollow hills. Everyone in his family was relieved when Lord Glengarry took him on as his fool. Nab was slight enough of frame that manual labor would have been a hardship, and this way, at least he never knew hunger or lacked a roof over his head.

There was another good thing about living in a place like Glengarry. The keep had been added to piecemeal over the years, a new dovecote here, a barbican there. As the centuries rolled by, certain things were forgotten. Like the derelict passageway that led into the old tower room where he took sanctuary.

One particularly rainy day last January when the sky was falling like shards of grey glass, Nab had slipped away from his place by the earl's side and set off to explore the lower regions of the castle. In a deserted portion of the souterrain, he'd discovered a bricked-over passage. After pulling out enough of the crumbling mortar and bricks to slither through, he'd followed a set of uneven stairs to the top of a secret tower. It was flush up against the newer square tower that held the family quarters, and served to buttress that structure, but it was much shorter and smaller.

The room at the top of the tower wasn't big enough to fit a bed. Nab could scarcely lie down without his head touching one wall and his feet another. He guessed it had once served as a lookout of sorts, but judging from the thick layer of dust, he figured it had been abandoned for far longer than living memory.

"Odds bodkins, a secret place," he'd said to himself. "And it's all mine."

Whenever the taunting laughter that earned him his daily bread became too much to bear, Nab slipped away to his own little hidey-hole. After discovering the place, he'd spent several weeks furnishing it with threadbare, cast-off rugs and a small chest whose latch was broken. No one missed them.

Nab was a hopeless magpie. Bits of twine, fishing hooks, and oddly shaped rocks that reminded him of the scaly back of the waterhorse he'd once seen all found their way into his secret cache.

How to stay warm was a problem. The small fireplace in the tower room had collapsed in on itself and, in any case, to light a fire might alert others to the chamber's existence. Nab made do with wrapping a thick blanket around his shoulders.

Despite the eternal chill leeching from the stone walls, the tower room's good points outweighed the bad. Its window overlooked the loch and wasn't visible from any point on land.

Usually Nab read there by the light of a tallow candle through the dark watches of the night, but now he couldn't seem to make his eyes focus on the leather-bound volume of *Le Morte d'Arthur*. After hanging upside down in the great hall, his face still burned and he felt all hot and jittery inside.

He stood and limped to the window. It was a wonder his leg hadn't been yanked out of the socket. His hip joint pained him something fierce.

But Nab had a good imagination and picturing

Ranulf MacNaught dangling over the loch from the tower window with a rope looped around *his* ankle cheered him tremendously. It was a long drop to the water.

The earl's men had taunted him unmercifully about the helpless little sounds he'd made while he hung upside down in the great hall. Nab wondered what sort of noises Ranulf would make if someone sawed on the rope with his boot knife ever so slowly. . . .

"Nab!" A hissing whisper echoed up the spiral steps.

Someone had found him. He scuttled away from the window and plopped back down on the rugs, hugging the blanket around him. Had they heard his wicked thoughts about Ranulf? He hadn't thought them very loudly.

"Are ye there?" the voice came again.

"Nay, I'm here," he called back. "Ye're there."

"Quiet, ninny. D'ye want the rest of them to find ye?"

He recognized the voice now. It belonged to Dorcas. She was either the serving girl or the upstairs maid. Nab had trouble keeping track of her since she could never be counted upon to turn up where he expected. He liked things and people to be tidy and in their place. Dorcas should stay where she belonged.

He thought the same about Lady Katherine.

Which was why he had to help William find a way to take his lady wife home. Those two belonged together, whether they realized it or not.

But he couldn't think about that now. A soft swish of kid soles told him Dorcas was coming up the stairs. His stairs. The secret ones.

Nab grasped the scepter Will had given him and twisted his hands around the cold metal, wishing Dorcas would turn around and go back down. William had told him the rod was a thing of power, but Nab felt none coming from it. If the scepter had a bit of glamour about it, Nab would use it to wish himself to blend into the cold stone of the tower, invisible as a spirit, so Dorcas wouldn't see him and would go away. But since he could still see his own hands, he figured the scepter didn't work that way.

Dorcas peered over the lip of the floor as she cleared the last of the stone steps. "What are ye doing here, Nab?"

She'd never believe he was reading. He tucked the book under a flap of his kilt.

"I'm . . . I . . . ye canna be here."

"And yet, here I am, so I most certainly can." She tipped her round face to the side and raised a brow at him. "But ye probably shouldna be here either. The stairs are in such disrepair, I shouldna wonder if the whole tower isna about to tumble into the loch."

"Nay, 'tis safe enough." He'd made sure of that, pacing the length of the small chamber and examining the walls for crumbling mortar. "Leaks a bit when the weather turns soft, though."

She peered at the overhead thatch. A watermark stained the stones to the right of the window. "Someone needs to scrub that or it'll go black with mold. I'll bring a pail and brush when I come next time, shall I?"

"Next time. Ye mean to come again?"

"Aye, and why not? D'ye think ye're the only one who'd like a place to disappear to from time to time?"

Yes, he had. That was exactly what he'd thought. He was the only one who needed to get away, who needed to distance himself from all the noise and chatter. All the poking and prodding and people pressed up against each other . . . Sometimes living in such close quarters with so many others made him feel like a swarm of midges were loose inside him.

Dorcas turned her pale eyes on the contents of the small room, her gaze darting from the chest to the sorry-looking rugs and meager stash of candles. Seeing it as she did, he realized the place was hopelessly shabby, but surprisingly enough, she grinned at him.

"We canna bring more furniture up the stairs. The opening in the bricks below is too small and even a pair of chairs would overwhelm this wee space. But I found an old wolf pelt in the lumber room last week. It would warm the floor better than those rugs, I'll warrant."

"Ye want to change things?"

"Only for the better, Nab."

"When things change, 'tis usually not better. Things usually get worse." Hadn't he warned William of that?

"Not necessarily. Dinna ye have a hope of something better?" Her cheeks pinkened as her gaze darted away from him. "Findin' a lass and gettin' married someday, perhaps?"

There was a strange twinge in his chest at that. He'd never considered getting married, but he supposed it was different for a girl. Working in service, Dorcas had little chance of making a decent match. Nab felt sorry for her. He decided to try to cheer her up about it.

"I wouldna worry that ye're not a wife, or be in a hurry to marry, were I ye."

"Did I say I was in a hurry to wed?"

"Nay, but—"

"Then I'll thank ye not to put words in my mouth."

Who knew girls were so touchy? Nab hunched his shoulders, making himself as small as possible. "I just mean that since ye have no property or dowry, any husband ye might find is likely to be some old boar with no teeth and one foot in the grave, so marriage isna something ye should covet. Especially since—"

"Let me be the judge of that," she interrupted and then went on to denigrate his parentage for several generations.

Her words tumbled on top of his. He sometimes imagined that words hovered in the air like little soap bubbles, unheard until they burst in someone else's ear. Now he wondered if his wee floating wordlets felt as overwhelmed as he did by the way she ran roughshod over them.

"And have a care with yer predictions, Master Nab," she said archly. "In my family, women have the Sight. And I know I shall marry for love."

"Ye'll not wed at all unless Lord Glengarry approves it and he doesna trouble himself overmuch with what his servants want." Nab was on solid ground now. If there was anything he was an expert on, it was his laird's benevolent neglect. "Besides, he thinks girls are only good for making alliances and babies, even his own daughter. Ye know—"

"What I know is that a younger son whose family didna know what to do with him is only good for serving as a fool." She looked down her freckled, slightly too long nose at him.

That stung, but he couldn't let her see it. He was nothing to his parents except a burden from which they were relieved to be free. That knowledge was a small keening ache that never quite stilled. It didn't help that someone else apparently knew how he felt about it either.

"At least if I decide to wed, I willna have to crawl into bed with some gouty old—" He stopped when her little chin began to quiver. "Forget about what I said, Dorcas. I didna mean it. Ye'll not have to marry an old ogre if ye dinna want to. Besides, ye'd have to find an ogre ye wish to marry first and that might take a long—"

"Not so long as ye might think," she interrupted while rolling her eyes at him. Even though of the pair of them he was sure he was the only one who could read, she made him feel like a dunderheid. "Girls grow up quicker than boys, ye ken."

He snorted.

"My mother bore my brother Malcolm when she was fourteen. Ye've a passel of brothers and sisters at home. Which of yer older brothers is a husband?"

She had him there. At twenty-eight, his oldest brother, Stewart, wasn't even promised yet. Her smug smile reminded him of a cat with a mouse's tail hanging from one corner.

"So dinna dispute my word when I tell ye I shall marry for love, Nab," she said decisively. "And he willna be an old ogre either."

He decided to let her keep her delusions for now. Life had a way of knocking the dreams out of a body without the need for him to take a part in the beating.

Of course, allowing her to think she could join him in his tower room might actually encourage those unreasonable dreams.

"If two of us are using the tower—" he began.

"Stop fretting."

"I'm not fretting." He was wondering why the middle of his strings of words kept interrupting the beginning of hers. It had happened five times now. It made him wonder. His words usually weren't that careless.

She tucked her skirts around herself and settled beside him, letting the shawl-like portion of her arisaid slip from her shoulders.

He stopped wondering about words completely.
Odds bodkins, a girl in my tower.

It had seemed so unlikely a happenstance that he'd
never considered it. He'd never considered how good
one might smell either. Dorcas had a whiff of something sweet wafting about her, clinging to the folds of
her arisaid.

The real surprise was that Nab didn't mind that she
sat so close to him. He cut a glance at her and then pretended complete absorption with his hands in his lap.

"The worst that will happen is that we'll be found
out here and the stairs will be resealed," she said.

That would definitely be worse. Where could he
read if the tower was closed to him?

"I brought ye something. I'm thinkin' ye didna have
much supper," she said, pulling a small bundle wrapped
in cloth from her pocket. "'Tis a bit of Clootie Dumpling. Are ye fond of sweeties?"

He was. And Clootie Dumpling was his favorite—a
rich, dense pudding flavored with currants and raisins.
He took it from her with thanks and made short work
of it.

"I like to see a man enjoy his food," Dorcas said.
"But yer hand's all sticky now. Here. Let me."

She took him by the wrist, and amazingly enough,
he didn't mind too much that she was touching him.
But he was shocked to his curled toes when she licked
off his fingers, one by one. It made him feel a whole
different kind of hot and jittery inside.

He pulled his hand away.

Dorcas tucked her knees up and leaned her arms
across them. "So what do ye do when ye're here by yerself, Nab?"

Did he dare tell her? She might laugh and he didn't
think he could bear more laughter this night. Still, she

had brought him a Clootie Dumpling, so he decided to risk it. After all, when someone has licked a body's fingers, a body ought to be able to trust them.

"I read."

Dorcas snorted. "Ye never do."

At least she didn't laugh.

"'Tis true. I'll show ye." Nab pulled the book out from under his plaid and handed it to her. The maid's eyes grew round as she opened the pages and looked at the ornate script.

"What does it say?"

"'Tis the story of Arthur and his knights." But *Le Morte d'Arthur* by Sir Thomas Mallory was far more than that to Nab. It was a whole world where the good fought to protect the weak and might didn't always equal right.

It was a world he dearly wanted to visit, and if he ever reached it, he'd never willingly return.

There was enough action and adventure in the tome to please him and enough courtly love nonsense to have Dorcas sighing in short order. Girls liked that sort of thing, he'd heard. Maybe he could read it to her if she ever—

"Read it to me." Somehow, even the middle of his thoughts managed to interrupt the beginning of her words. She handed the book back to him.

He turned to the story about the Lady of the Lake. Sometimes when he gazed out on the loch, he wished the Lady would rise up for him, sword in hand, her eyes blazing with destiny. He glanced down at Dorcas. She was peering intently at the ornate script, but from this angle her eyes were downcast, their pale blue irises obscured by the fringe of blond lashes. She looked as demur and fragile as any lady needing rescue he'd ever imagined.

Nab began to read.

"What's this?" she interrupted yet again, sounding anything but demur or fragile. "It may as well be a mass."

"I suppose it does seem like that to ye. 'Tis in Latin."

Dorcas crossed her arms. "Makes no more sense to me than a mass either. I think ye're making all this up."

"Nay, I'm reading. Truly." Nab removed his fool's cap and scratched his head. "Suppose I read a bit to myself and then tell ye what it says in words ye will understand."

Nab thought he'd never seen anything finer than the way sunlight danced on the water of the loch as the sun came up. It never failed to make his chest swell with the joy of simply being alive. Nothing could be better.

But that was before he saw Dorcas really smile.

She lifted a corner of his blanket, draped it over herself, and laid her head on his shoulder. "Tell me the story, Nab."

Something new stirred in his chest. He felt bigger. Stronger. As if he were all the Knights of the Round Table rolled into one.

"One day," Nab began, "King Arthur decided to seek an adventure, so he . . ."

Make we merry in hall and bower
And this glorious lady we honor
That to us hath borne our Savior
Homo sine femine
To increase our joy and bliss,
Christus natus est nobis.

—From "Make We Merry"

"This is a song about the deep magic of how women make things new . . . er, I mean make new things. That sort of power should cause men to have a bit of a rethink about how they treat them."

—An observation from Nab,
fool to the Earl of Glengarry

Chapter Seven

"We'll need another leech under that eye if we dinna want it to swell shut for days," a calm feminine voice said from somewhere above.

"If we must. I can barely abide the nasty things," said another with a sigh. "Have ye any fresh ones?"

"Aye, I think so. Let me check in the . . ."

The voices faded and William sank back into the black pool of forgetfulness, hovering in the deep. It was peaceful and dark and undemanding. There was no pain. Well, not much. The eye the voices had mentioned did ache a wee bit and his back throbbed.

Cool feminine hands fussed with his clothing. It dragged him closer to the surface of consciousness and, therefore, closer to more pain. The skin around his eye was drawn so tight, it felt as if it might crack open. Fire licked at his ribs. He sank back and skimmed beneath full awareness, struggling to stay in that warm, shadowy oblivion.

"I'd almost forgotten about that scar." One of the voices dipped down to him. A fingertip, as light as a feather, traced the hard ridge that snaked over his ribs on the right side.

"That fair surprises me since your father gave it to him."

A memory bubbled up in Will's brain, but he still made no effort to rejoin the world of light and increasing pain. Even though he and Kat had been pledged to each other for most of their lives, when William came of age, Lord Glengarry had demanded that he demonstrate his worthiness of Katherine's hand. Kat's father had challenged him to single combat, and though it was not a serious sword fight, both of them were bloodied before Lord Glengarry called a halt and declared himself satisfied.

"We canna lift him into the bath ourselves."

"We'll call for a couple of pages to help us once we get him undressed. And ye ought not to be lifting anything heavier than wee Tam in any case."

There was another rustle of fabric, followed by a low hum of approval.

"Oh, Katherine. He's so well made in all his parts. Tell me ye dinna mean to leave a man as fine as this."

Will's eyes shot open at that. Or rather one of them

did. He was unable to pry his eyelid open more than a thin gap on the right side. Still, it was enough for him to tell that he was lying naked on a clean sheet with his wife and his sister-in-law peering down at him.

He tried to sit up. "Where am—"

Margaret stopped him with a palm to his chest. It was so covered with fresh bruising, the barest touch made him wince, and he eased back down.

"Ye're in the earl's chamber, his being the only one with a bath, ye ken," she said in the no-nonsense tone he'd heard her use with her troop of boys when it was time for them to wash. She draped a square of cloth over his genitals. "There. If it'll ease your modesty to be covered while we doctor your hurts, so be it." Her grey eyes sparked impishly. "But truth to tell, good-brother, ye have nothing to be ashamed of."

Katherine cleared her throat loudly. "I think I can manage now, Margie. If William can get into the bath on his own power, that is."

"That I can." He started to rise again, but Margaret stopped him with another hand to the chest.

"I'll be taking my leeches back first, if ye please." She gently poked at the slugs attached above and beneath his swollen eye. The bloated things obediently released their hold on William's flesh. Margaret leaned down to examine his face more closely. "Ye'll still bruise, but ye'll have use of the eye tomorrow. Ye may not be pretty for a while, William Douglas, but ye'll mend. Ranulf MacNaught, on the other hand, will be straining his stew through that new gap in his teeth forever."

Then she turned to Katherine. "Make him drink some willow bark tea after the bath and apply this to any open wound before he dresses again." Margaret handed Kat a jar of pungent, oily cream, gathered up her leeches, and left with the waddle common to women in the late stages of breeding.

"Ye've made an enemy of Ranulf, ye ken," Katherine said softly.

"He was never my friend, for all that he's your kinsman."

"Dinna remind me. I've other cousins I wish were here in Glengarry instead, but with Donald gone so much, my father has come to depend on Ranulf."

That could be a problem. When the earl had his apoplexy last year, it had seemed the keep teemed with more MacNaught supporters than usual. If Lord Glengarry had died, would Ranulf have challenged Katherine's brother for the clan chieftainship?

"Well, ye said ye could get yourself into the bath so . . ." She waved a hand toward the waiting tub.

His father had always warned him against promising that which he could not perform, so he forced himself to sit upright. Every muscle in his body screamed as he strained to get himself out of the bed. Katherine came alongside him and put his arm around her shoulders so she could help bear him up. Will refused to lean any of his weight on her, but he did let her wrap her arm around his waist while he moved in short steps toward the copper hip bath in the alcove off the earl's uncluttered chamber.

"How's Nab?" he asked as he climbed into the warm water. His knees had to bend in order to fit, but the warmth was a balm to his sore muscles.

"He'll do. Dorcas told me ye called out at the last for Nab to be cut down and it shamed the men into mercy. They were easy on him," she said. "Only his feelings were hurt."

"For someone like Nab, that sort of wound takes longer to heal than one that bleeds."

"That's as may be, but ye're still bleeding a bit in places and ye'll be black and blue in others well past Twelfth Night." She eyed him critically. "We'll have to bind your ribs once ye get out of your bath."

He didn't argue. Judging from the pain each time he drew breath, a couple of them were likely cracked. William closed his eyes, leaned on the copper backrest, and tried to let the aches drain from his body. At least one good thing had come from his fight with Ranulf. In a moment, Katherine would begin touching him, soaping up a cloth and cleaning every bit of him. Despite his hurts, his skin prickled with awareness, with anticipation.

Nothing happened.

When he opened his eyes again, Katherine was just looking down at him, a taut, drawn expression on her lovely face.

"Well, wife, are ye or are ye not going to bathe an injured man?"

"Ye wish for a scrubbing, do ye? Then that's what ye'll get, husband."

Katherine had removed her arisaid so she was wearing only her thin leine. The hip bath was so full now that William's body was in it, the water was likely to surge over the sides. No point in getting all her clothing wet. She swished a washcloth in the water beside William's knee and rubbed a dollop of the lavender-scented soap Margaret had made of beef tallow and ash in the wet cloth. She slathered it vigorously over William's bruised shoulders.

"Ow! Easy, lass."

"My apologies, milord. I didna ken ye were so tender. Lord knows ye havena shown your hurts to me.

And in case ye're wondering, I'm not talking about these scrapes and bruises."

Will's lips drew into a hard, thin line. "I dinna know what ye want from me. I've told ye how I feel about ye, Katherine."

"I know ye want me in your bed. I know ye wish things were different, that I could . . . but I dinna know how ye feel about . . . about Stephan and the others."

He closed his eyes. "There's no profit in going down that path. How I feel willna bring them back."

But it might ease her burden of grief if he lifted half of it. Clearly he either didn't feel the loss as keenly as she or else didn't care enough about her to share it.

"Sit forward and I'll wash your back," she ordered.

He obeyed. When she caught her first glimpse of his ribs, her breath hissed over her teeth. "Oh, Will."

"As bad as that, is it?"

A dark purplish stain spread from his waist to his third rib on the right side.

"Bad enough." She ran the cloth over his back as gently as she could, but the muscles under his skin still twitched. "Ye ought to think before ye challenge a man, William. And count his allies instead of charging ahead." She shuddered. "If my father hadna come into the hall when Ranulf MacNaught and his friends were beating you to a bloody pulp—"

"I dinna need another whipping. Perhaps ye'll let my bruises speak for themselves instead of laying on with your sharp tongue," he interrupted. "How did ye say Nab is? He took no lasting hurt, did he?"

"He'll be all right. At least he's in better shape than ye. Ye've asked me about him once already. I suppose it's to be expected since ye took a verra hard clout to the head." She took a dipper and slowly poured water over his crown, smoothing his wet hair with her other hand, feeling for lumps. One was swelling behind his right ear. "It was a fine thing ye did for Nab. Foolish, but fine."

Then she began to lather his hair with the soft, sweet-smelling soap, taking care to be gentle.

His shoulders relaxed a bit and he sighed.

There was a time when she'd lived for that sigh. When she and William made love, her goal was always to spend him so thoroughly, pleasure him so deeply, a sigh was all he had left.

And he did the same for her.

Then after the death of Stephan, each time they came together, she was driven to wring the last drop from Will because she reasoned she'd be more likely to conceive. Their joinings became frantic. Desperate. She wanted to give him a son more than her next breath.

She forgot about giving him joy.

And she didn't let William give any to her either.

When they were first married, he lavished her with alternating tenderness and abandon until her world spiraled down to just him, just his mouth, just his hands, just his glorious maleness pounding inside her. He sent her spirit to another place entirely, a place where nothing mattered but their eternal "oneness," their raging need, their shared delight.

It was a lovely forgetfulness. A way to make the world disappear for a time.

When she was trying to conceive, she was too worked up about whether or not they'd made a child to allow him to make her forgetful.

"Keep your eyes closed," she said after she'd finished massaging his scalp.

"Don't think I can open the one."

"Tomorrow, Margie said." She used the dipper again to rinse out the soap. Then she began sudsing up his chest.

Since he still had his eyes closed, she could study him without his being aware of it as she ran her cloth over his hard muscles. When she soaped them, his brown nipples puckered.

She almost leaned down and flicked one with her tongue. She used to whorl her tongue around the tight nub and then give him a little nip. He liked that. She remembered how his breath had hitched the first time she did it and how his eyes had gone dark and splendidly wicked. Just thinking about it made a heaviness, almost a rhythmic ache, gather between her legs. It had been a while since she'd allowed herself to feel that feral drumbeat.

She gave herself an inward shake. No good could come from it.

Then she washed his arms, first the nearest one and then leaning across him to reach the far side. She was close enough that he nuzzled her breasts, taking one tip into his mouth and suckling her through the thin fabric of her leine.

"Will!" Katherine straightened immediately. She covered the wet spot with her hand, pressing a flat palm against her breast to try to still her throbbing nipple.

He grinned at her. With one eye swollen shut, he looked like a right ruffian, but a wickedly appealing one at that. "Ye canna blame me, lass. Ye practically waved them in my face. No mortal man could resist such a ripe pair."

Then he took her hand with the wet cloth and guided it down his body, past his chest and over his flat abdomen. As he gently pulled, she leaned down. The scooped neckline of her gown drooped, baring her breasts to his gaze from this angle. His smile faded and something far more potent than naughty teasing simmered between them.

"I miss having ye touch me, Kat."

The earnest longing in his voice made a lump form in her throat. She couldn't speak.

"And I've missed touching ye, love." His voice was husky with wanting. He reached inside her scooped neckline to cup one of her breasts. Her nipple went suddenly pebble hard and so sensitive her knees nearly buckled.

"Kiss me, wife."

She loved it when he told her what he wanted.

"*Lie still,*" he'd whisper, "*and let me fill ye with my love.*"

"*Climb on and ride me, my Kat,*" he'd dare her. "*And we'll see who tires first, but I promise ye, lass, I can go all night.*"

"*Bend over, love, and splay your fingers on the floor. I'll take ye hard and fast,*" he'd warn. "*That's it. Your sweet pink slit is all ready for me. God, what beautiful hips ye have.*"

The memories made her ache. The early days of their loving were ones of endless discovery and carnal adventures so heart pounding they had to be a sin. But William and she were husband and wife. And even when they were naked, they were not ashamed.

Now, however, she was soul naked before William and that was much more exposed than just baring her body. Since losing her precious bairns—yes, she counted all the little lost ones as her babies—she wasn't sure it was in her to ever be that open again.

"Katherine." His voice called her back from the

dark place to which her mind had wandered. "Can ye not give me a simple kiss?"

His fingers toyed with her nipple, tugging and circling. His need fed her own. She still loved him so much, it hurt to breathe.

"Aye, Will," she said, choking back a sob. She hadn't given him much of anything for the last few months, not since she'd withdrawn from him, hoping to keep her latest pregnancy from failing. "I can give ye a kiss. And a wee bit more."

As she leaned down to kiss him, she also reached under the soapy water and found his cock. When she slid her palm down the hard length of him, he groaned into her mouth.

He cupped the back of her head, deepening their kiss. She stroked his cock in rhythm with the thrusts of his tongue in her mouth, first slow and languid, then hot and frenetic. The way he tormented her nipple with his other hand sent jolts of desire streaking from her breast to her womb.

Body and bones, she ached. She was as empty as a hollowed-out gourd. Need long denied roared to life and she nearly lifted her gown and climbed into the tub to mount him.

But this was about William. Not her. About what she could give him. Lord knew she couldn't give him much else, couldn't fill his quiver with the sons every man needed, but she could grant him this blessed oblivion.

She shoved back his foreskin with each stroke and tormented the spot at the base of the head that she knew was most sensitive. He groaned again and broke off their kiss long enough to say, "Harder. For God's sake, harder."

She took his mouth again while she whipped him into a helpless frenzy. Then she slid her gown off one shoulder, baring a breast and pressing it to his lips. He sucked so hard, her eyes rolled back in her head and she was passion blind for a moment. Her world narrowed to disjointed elements.

Pleasure a knife's edge from pain. Joyful aching. Hurts that heal.

Water surged over the sides of the tub, soaking the front of her gown, but she didn't care. The heat of him in her hand warmed her more than a fire. His mouth at her breast made her womb clench.

Once. Twice. She was almost there. Any moment now and her insides would dance with lust even without him touching her secret place or seating his thick self between her legs.

Then he erupted in her hand. When his release came, William gave a low growl, a feral sound that made Katherine tremble with need. He bit down on her nipple till she thought she'd unravel simply at that, but somehow her own completion, which had seemed so very near, now slipped away. Bliss left her behind while William's body arched.

It had been that way for a long time. She couldn't seem to find release while she was trying so desperately to conceive.

He was still pulsing in her hand beneath the surface of the water, all that life-giving substance wasted.

Though no more so than if he'd emptied himself into her.

When it was over, he wrapped his arms around her and pulled her into the tub with him, settling her on his lap. She needed to be near him too much to protest, to feel his wet skin against her, even if the fabric of her leine still separated them. The warm bathwater rushed over the sides of the tub in wavelets. William's breathing was ragged, and when he gentled her head to rest upon his chest, his heart pounded in her ear.

"Oh, Kat." He stroked her hair and pressed a kiss on her crown. "I've needed you, lass."

Her insides still raged. She was still empty. Still wanting. It had been so long, tears of frustration gathered at the corners of her eyes. She couldn't remember ever aching this much, but she couldn't ask him to—

He reached under her hem and slid a hand up her thigh. She brought her knees together. Despite her longing for him, she still needed to find a way to dissolve their marriage. With such unwifely thoughts, she didn't deserve his touch. It would only make their parting harder.

"Let me, my dear one," he whispered. "I love ye so. I canna bear not holding ye."

Her thigh muscles relaxed and his big hand cupped her sex with such gentleness, it made her weep.

What a mercy to be held so. To be cherished in her most unproductive part. William took her disappointment, her failure, her broken promise in his hand and loved it in spite of her.

She ached so, teetering on the edge of that blessed cliff that would send her spiraling to joy.

He slipped a fingertip between her folds and her insides tightened. Then he grazed her secret place and she came completely undone. Her body bucked with the force of her release and she cried out his name. Not once, but many times.

William. Her determined protector. She chanted it. She practically sang it. When the last convulsion died, she was still whimpering her husband's name.

Katherine collapsed bonelessly back onto his chest

and let him hold her as their breathing fell into rhythm with each other. Her spirit seemed to float above them, oblivious to time or place or the fact that she was thoroughly soaked.

There was no need to speak. No need to think. If only they could stay this way forever. . . .

"My lady!" The sharp voice echoed up the spiral staircase that wound between the family chambers. "Oh, Lady Katherine, ye're needed right quick."

It was Dorcas.

Katherine scrambled out of the tub and bent to wring as much water from her hem as she could. She still dripped onto the stone floor in a regular patter, but by the time Dorcas appeared in the chamber, she'd donned her arisaid over the top of the wet leine.

"Oh! Beggin' yer pardon, I'm sure, Lord Badenoch." Dorcas bobbed a curtsey at the open doorway and averted her gaze.

"Dinna mind me, lass," he said wryly. "In the grand scheme of things, what's a naked man more or less?"

It was a measure of the seriousness of her visit that Dorcas's round face didn't pinken in the slightest.

"'Tis Lady Margaret. There's trouble. Two of the men are bearing her up the stairs in a sling. Oh, come quick, my lady. She's bleedin'."

"Ye mean her waters have broken."

"Nay, she says not, and she'd know, her having birthed five bairns and all. If that doesna make her the knowledgeable one, I swear I dinna know what would." Dorcas finally ran out of steam and breath at the same time. Her face crumpled and she twisted her fingers together. "Please, my lady, I dinna know what to do."

Katherine's heart sank to her toes. Bleeding, with no onset of labor. She knew all too well what that might mean. "Fetch fresh linens and a pan of hot water. Send for the midwife in the village and I'll be with Lady Margaret directly."

Dorcas disappeared back down the steps with a rustle of her skirts. Her little yelping apologies as she squeezed past the men bearing Margaret up the narrow staircase echoed back to Katherine.

She turned to face William. "Can ye—"

"Aye, Kat, I can shift for myself. Go to Margie." But when she made to go, he caught her wrist. "But we are not finished, ye and I. Not even close."

He pressed a lover's kiss on her open palm and let her go.

Heart pounding and sick with dread for her sister-in-law's situation, Katherine hurried to the stairwell in time to precede the men bearing Margaret up to her bed.

Oh, sisters too, how may we do,
For to preserve this day,
This poor youngling, for whom we do sing,
Bye, bye, lully, lullay.

—From "Coventry Carol"

"A song can make a body weep. Can what we do make
a song weep?"

—An observation from Nab,
fool to the Earl of Glengarry

Chapter Eight

"I dinna know what all the fuss is about," Margaret
was saying as she rose from the sling chair and waved
away the men who'd carried her up the stairs. They
fairly bolted out of the room, but she waited till they
were out of earshot before she continued since men
were notoriously squeamish about the details surrounding childbirth. "I spotted a bit of blood with Tam
too. 'Tis not so bad."

"Not so bad?" Kat said. "Ye're white as a ghost."

Her good-sister's skin had a translucent quality, and
the blue vein that ran down the side of her neck was
more stark than usual. Katherine walked around her

under the pretext of helping her out of her clothing. Blood had seeped through Margie's gown to leave a ruddy stain as large as her palm.

"Arms up, dear," Kat said, trying to hide her growing alarm. "We'll get ye changed into something more comfortable."

Margie obeyed, but after Katherine pulled her gown over her head, she gasped at the rivulets of red snaking down her inner thighs. Margie's knees seemed to give way and she had to sit suddenly on the edge of the bed, which Katherine had already covered with a thick pad of cloth. "Och! 'Tis a good bit more blood than I had with Tam."

"Have ye any pains?"

"No, none at all."

Katherine wanted to ask when was the last time Margie had felt the bairn quicken, but the words cleaved to her tongue.

Stephan had stopped moving the morning she began bleeding.

Dorcas returned, muttering under her breath. She helped clean Margaret and dress her in an old linen nightgown. There was no point in wearing one's best to childbed, where it might be stained beyond reclaiming. She disappeared down the spiral stairs with Margaret's soiled clothing, grumbling about how best to clean them without fading the dye in the fabric.

Katherine spread an extra couple of absorbent sheets over the bed. "Lie flat," she said as she eased Margie between them. She gave her sister-in-law a wadded handful of linen to pack between her legs and plumped the pillows to elevate Margie's feet.

The midwife had tried this when Katherine showed blood with Stephan. In the end it hadn't helped her little mite, but it was something to do and anything was better than standing about wringing her hands. In Margaret's case, it did seem to improve the color in her cheeks.

Beathag Hardie, the midwife, bustled into the chamber then and, after a quick look around, nodded approval at Katherine's ministrations. Old Beathag was trusted by all the women of the surrounding glens and had been bringing bairns into the world since before Katherine's mother was born. The woman's face was as shriveled as a piece of weathered leather and her eyes were nearly opaque with cataracts, but she had a kind, albeit toothless, smile.

"Let us have a look-see, my lady, and then we'll ken what's what, aye?" She examined Margie intimately, pressing on her belly with gnarled fingers and feeling for the position of the bairn, nodding and clucking her tongue as she worked.

"The head is down. He's ready to make his journey into the world," the old woman said. "No pains yet?"

Margaret shook her head.

Beathag's mouth pulled tight across her face, making her look very like an old potato with a spade cut across it. "Weel, that could change any moment. Believe it'd be best for me to stay in the castle instead of down in the village so I'll be to hand when ye've need of me."

She pulled a vial filled with green, nasty-smelling liquid from her small satchel and put it to Margaret's lips. Margie made a face, but she drank it down, as dutifully as an obedient child.

"Rest ye for now, my lady. That's the main thing. The time will come soon enough when ye'll have no rest at all."

When Margaret sighed and closed her eyes, Katherine

pulled Beathag across the room and mouthed, "How is the child?"

Fortunately, though the old woman's eyes were going, her hearing was still keen. "He pushed back when I examined my lady. He's still moving." Then her wiry grey brows knit together over her sharp nose. "But I'll not say 'tis not serious. There's a poultice I can apply that will help stop the bleeding but it'll take a bit to prepare. I don't expect Cook will appreciate me in the kitchen. Is there a stillroom?"

"Aye, off the solar. Lady Margaret keeps it well stocked with medicinal herbs and such."

"Good. I'll nip down and see about it then. She'll sleep now. Wish I could." Beathag yawned hugely, every one of her years etched plainly in her tired face. "I'll take meself to Jamison before I return to see can he find me lodging here. Ye'll stay with her, aye?"

Katherine nodded.

"Call for me if the bleeding worsens." She lowered her voice. "Or if she no longer feels movement." The old woman toddled off to find the stillroom.

Katherine went over and perched on the side of Margaret's bed, then took her sister-in-law's icy hand in hers. She'd have Dorcas stoke up the fire if the gabby goose ever returned. The girl didn't seem the sort who'd be especially helpful in a sickroom without a lot of direction, but at least she had a willing spirit.

Margie's eyes opened slowly and she squeezed Kat's fingers. She ran the fingertips of her other hand in slow circles over her distended belly. "I feel much better now."

The pupils of Margie's eyes were so dilated, her expression so flat and unconcerned, Kat was certain that green stuff Beathag Hardie had given her was some sort of poppy juice.

"I think we should send for Donald," Katherine said.

Margaret's eyes flared wide at that. "No. I dinna want him to see me like this."

Katherine bristled. "If my brother saw what you go through to give him children, maybe he'd be more attentive the rest of the time."

"No, I dinna want him to think I've been complaining."

Katherine knew she shouldn't speak ill of her brother, but she was so afraid for Margie, if Donald were in Glengarry now, she'd be tempted to box his ears. "By the Rood, ye've reason to complain. As ye said yourself, the man canna be bothered with his own family for longer than it takes to get ye with—"

"Hush, my dear Kat." Margie reached up and stroked her hair as if Katherine were one of her brood of children. "Dinna fret yourself. 'Twill be all right. Ye'll see. I've wide hips, ye ken. Like a brood mare, Donald says. I've yet to have trouble birthing a bairn."

Then between one breath and the next, Margaret's eyes drifted closed and she fell asleep. Katherine ventured a hand on her belly.

The child made his mother's abdomen undulate under Kat's palm.

"God be praised," she murmured. The miracle of another life gave her palm a little kick.

"How is she?"

Katherine startled at the soft masculine voice behind her and turned toward the sound. It was William. She hadn't heard him enter the chamber. For a big man, he could be as quiet as a cat when it suited him.

"Sleeping. The bairn is still . . ." Somehow saying the child was alive now made the possibility that later he might not be more real. "I felt movement a moment ago."

"Good." He nodded curtly and went to stir up the fire without being told, bless him. "Is she sending for Donald?"

"No, but I think she should."

His eye was still bruised, but thanks to Margie's leeches, it was less swollen. William came over, stood beside her, and peered down at his sleeping sister-in-law. Margaret's lips still had an unhealthy blue tinge.

"Donald should be here," Kat said. The court would always be there. Margaret might not be.

"If ye want, I'll see to it."

"No, Will, don't go to Edinburgh. I mean . . ." She bit her lip. The words had tumbled out before she could catch them. She should want him to leave Glengarry. If there were no more incidents like the shattering one in William's bath, no more times when she succumbed to her need to touch him and let him touch her, it would be far easier to send that annulment request to Rome after Christmastide was over.

But the thought of cutting her remaining time with him short made her chest constrict. If these were the last days she might have with William, shouldn't she wring every drop of joy she could from them?

He smiled at her. "Wild horses couldn't drag me away, sweeting. No, I only meant I'd send someone to fetch Donald home. Of course, I'm staying."

He bent down and pressed a kiss to her crown. A fresh whiff of clean male skin emanated from him. Katherine tipped her chin up and he brushed her lips with his.

But before the kiss could ripen into something more than a peck, Dorcas bustled through the open doorway, linens crammed under her armpits and her hands bearing a pot of water that sloshed over with each step.

The girl cleared her throat loudly and, to Katherine's mind, accusingly.

"Beggin' yer pardon, my lady," she said with a sniff. "I brought ye what ye asked for. Now what should we do for Lady Margaret?"

Katherine tossed him an apologetic glance. "Will, if ye please—"

"I know, I know. There's no place for a man at a time like this." He raised his hands in mock surrender. "I'll see ye after, wife."

Ranulf MacNaught refilled the drinking horns of his compatriots—Filib Gordon, Hugh Murray, Ainsley MacTavish, and Lamont Sinclair—and swept an appraising gaze over them. Since they each owed him a debt they couldn't repay, they were likely enough allies. All of them were minor gentry—landholders who had tenants and kinsmen beholden to them, but not enough to qualify for even a "Sir" before their names.

Not that they weren't ambitious enough to be working toward it.

His little band didn't include the heroes he'd hoped to draw to his standard, but they'd do.

The rest of the castle was quiet, all the drinking and revelry of the holiday season burned out for the night, like a guttered candle. Ranulf reckoned there was a fuss going on in Lady Margaret's bedchamber after the way she'd been carted from the great hall, but that was only the province of women.

Ranulf was more concerned about his men.

They all nursed new wounds and bruises, courtesy of the quick fists of William Douglas. Ranulf tongued the empty place in his gum where an eyetooth used to be and cursed Lord Badenoch afresh.

"Aye, MacNaught, we're with ye on that point," Filib Gordon said as he rubbed his purpling jaw. Even outnumbered, Douglas had gotten in several good licks before Gordon had bashed him over the head with that chair. "We all agree the Laird of Badenoch is a misbegotten bastard, but talk willna change a thing. It certainly doesna do your cause any good."

In England, succession to a title and estate was only a function of bloodlines, as if people were damned livestock, but the folk of Scotland were more practical. All things being equal, the best leader should rule.

And Ranulf was satisfied he was that leader.

Since Lord Glengarry had had that apoplectic fit last winter, Ranulf had been doing all he could to improve his chances of filling the old man's shoes.

"Dinna fret. Bide your time. Your uncle Glengarry is failing," Sinclair said, peering at Ranulf through only one eye, since the other was swollen completely shut.

They'd taken a drubbing and no mistake. Still, there had once been a time when Lord Glengarry could have disrupted the beating of his son-in-law with just his own hard fists. This time, the old man had to call on some of the onlookers to come to his aid while he broke up the gang attack on William Douglas.

"Ye'll get your chance soon, Ranulf," Ainsley MacTavish piped up. He was a bit of a brownnoser, but it pleased Ranulf to surround himself with MacTavish's brand of uncritical devotion. "Another fit like the one he had last year will carry his lairdship off to his reward, like as not."

"Not fast enough to suit me," Ranulf said sullenly. "Glengarry deserves a young hand on the reins."

As the old laird's nephew, Ranulf was not a natural choice for purists who liked to ape English sensibilities and held to niceties like bloodlines. His mother, God rot her miserable, neglectful soul, was only Laird Glengarry's sister, after all. Ranulf was brutal when he needed to be. Benevolent when it suited him. Both traits he shared with his mother, now that he thought on it.

But more importantly, he knew how to rally men to his side—the all-important quality for a leader.

"But what about the laird's heir?" Always the pessimist, Hugh Murray had to bring up the obvious flaw in Ranulf's plans.

"Donald?" Ranulf waved away his rival with a flick of his hand. "He's mincing about at court with the rest of the fops. He knows how to bow and scrape and how to pick a French wine. I know the men of Glengarry."

"So when the time comes, what do ye intend, Ranulf?" MacTavish asked.

He rose and paced the length of the solar. "When the time comes, when the times comes," he repeated. "Ye know, I'm sick of waiting." Besides, a tough old boot like Lord Glengarry could linger for years yet, even if he had another bad spell or two. And in that time, Donald might come to his senses and come home for good. "I'm thinking we ought to make our move before there's need to be concerned about the succession."

"What have ye in mind?" Gordon asked. "I know ye've gathered a good bit of support among the laird's men who are unhappy over Donald's absence, but we canna start a melee within these walls. The laird still holds the advantage, and many a man who's shared a horn with ye and spoken of being dissatisfied will turn back to aid his laird in a pinch. They did take an oath, ye ken."

Ranulf shrugged his massive shoulders. "So did we all. But a man canna be tied to an oath to a doddering old tyrant. Besides, who said anything about starting a ruckus here? It's Christmastide, ye heathen." He smacked Gordon on the back of the head and continued pacing the room.

"Hold a moment," Sinclair said. Of the four of them, Ranulf judged Sinclair to be packing the heaviest load of brains, so he stopped prowling long enough to listen. "Since no one would expect ye to move against the earl before Twelfth Night, would that not be the canny thing to do?"

Ranulf settled into one of the heavy chairs and stroked his beard. "Even so, I'd not stoop to taking what's mine from the inside like a thief. I'll take it like a man. I can put a hundred and twenty fighting men in the field at a call. How many will each of you pledge?"

After much hemming and hawing, between them all, they figured they could rally nearly three hundred men.

"Which doesna do us much good," Murray said. "Glengarry has stout walls and a source of water inside the bailey that'll never run dry. It's never been taken from without and canna be."

"That's only because the right people havena tried it yet. Besides, I have a surprise or two I'm saving for when the time is ripe."

Last winter, he'd stumbled across the remains of something he didn't recognize at first when he followed a wolf into her lair. After he killed the bitch and her litter of pups, he rummaged through the collection of lumber and rusted bolts. The cave was dry enough to have preserved the contraption, but the leather parts had rotted or been gnawed upon by the wolves.

Whatever it was, he sensed it was something important.

When he'd found the huge metal-reinforced bucket, he was certain of it. But it wouldn't do to let just anyone see it, so he'd left it in the cave. Then he traveled to Edinburgh and stood the oldest warriors he could find to interminable pints of ale, pumping their memories for information about engines of war. Finally, he found one whose grandfather's grandfather had seen something that sounded like what Ranulf had found.

"They called it 'trebuchet,' and a fearsome thing it was too," the rough old fighting man had told him. "It could hurl a weight of some three hundred and fifty pounds, enough to knock down the stoutest wall after enough direct hits. And all the while remaining beyond the reach of the best archers."

But the man couldn't tell Ranulf how the thing worked. Just that it took a mathematician to do the figuring. But when it operated properly, the trebuchet was devastating, especially if it delivered flaming projectiles.

"Imagine that, laddie," the fellow had told Ranulf while holding his empty mug up in the hope of a refill. "With the right system of pulleys and wires, a pasty-faced scholar can do more damage than a whole clan of warriors."

After that, Ranulf went to the nearest monastery and asked if there was a priest or monk who had a predilection for numbers. The prior told him about Brother Antonio, an Italian friar from Rome, who was a visiting scholar and mathematician. For what Ranulf thought was an exorbitant donation toward the running of the monastery, he convinced the prior to send Brother Antonio with him to the Highlands. There he'd ostensibly be tasked with teaching the most likely boys their sums and letters in the hope of finding a few who would later serve the Church.

Instead, Ranulf took the friar to the cave and demanded he put the trebuchet back into working condition. At first the little Italian protested, but after Ranulf threatened to dismantle him one digit at a time, Brother Antonio agreed that it would be a fine and glorious thing indeed to resurrect the old instrument of destruction. Ranulf had set his most trusted retainers to guard the friar and his work. And to make sure the little man of the cloth didn't slip away into the Highland mists some night.

But according to the last report, the friar still hadn't figured out how to make the counterbalance function properly.

"I'm all for ye becoming the next Laird of Glengarry, but ye're reckoning without Lord Badenoch, and he isna one we can dismiss lightly." Sinclair's dour words dragged Ranulf back to his present dilemma. "Even if Lord Glengarry should fall, and the men didna rally to Donald, some might support Douglas. He is married to the daughter of the house, after all."

"Being Lady Katherine's husband is a weak claim on the place at best," MacTavish said. "Besides, from what I hear, he may not be wed to her much longer."

Ranulf cocked a brow at him. "Aye?"

MacTavish grinned back. "I've bedded down a serving girl or two in this place and they all say things aren't exactly cozy between Lord and Lady Badenoch. Did she not come here without him at first? And he left his wife's bed that first night to drink with her father. What man would leave such a tempting armful unless he'd been ordered away?"

Badenoch was a problem. With him at Lord Glengarry's side, the remaining defenders in the castle would fight to the last man. But if Ranulf could deepen the chasm between Lord Badenoch and his wife, the man might leave Glengarry altogether. After all, as MacTavish pointed out, they didn't arrive as one.

"We need to provide a bit of distraction for Lord Badenoch," Ranulf said. He couldn't touch Lady Katherine. That would bring down the wrath of the old earl quicker than stewed prunes induced the trots. But beyond his lady wife, what did William Douglas value? A sly smile lifted his lips. "I know just the thing."

My heart of gold as true as steel
As I me leaned upon a bough;
In faith but if ye love me well
Lord so Robin lough.

—Sixteenth-century carol

"A heart of gold would be heavy to bear. No wonder he
needs to lean upon a bough."

—An observation from Nab,
fool to the Earl of Glengarry

Chapter Nine

"Come, Kat and let's to bed."

William's words curled around her ear and sank into her inmost parts.

Oh, aye, she'd go with him. She lived to feel Will's body all warm and hard against hers, all tangled up with him in a soft feather tick. Skin on skin. Heart on heart. To flare with heat at his touch. To drown in his scent and not care a whit. To join with him so deeply there could be no severing, nothing that showed that this much was him and that much was her because they were all in all. To—

"Katherine, love. Open your eyes."

She came more awake then and tried to remember why she wasn't in her own bed. Her neck hurt something wicked. She put a hand to the crick and rubbed it hard. "Och, I'm so tired."

"Small wonder. Ye've been up all night. Ye might have caught a wink or two in this chair from time to time, but nowhere near the rest ye need," William said, taking her by the elbow to encourage her to stand. "Come away and get some real sleep or ye'll be no use to anyone."

It all came rushing back—the urgent need to keep up a brave face, the desperate waiting to see if the blood would stop, the quiet watches in the wee hours, hoping to see her good-sister's belly roll with the child's movement. "What about Margaret?"

"I'm fine, dear, and I dinna appreciate being spoken of as if I'm not in the room," came the calm reply. Margie was sitting up, propped by pillows on all sides while she tucked into a breakfast tray of steaming parritch and fresh bannocks. "The bleeding's stopped— och! I'm sorry, William. You're a gallant man for braving a birthing chamber and all, but ye'll have to stop your ears if ye dinna want to hear more." Without a pause, she went on. To Will's credit, he didn't bolt, but he did take a step or two back. "Beathag says it was a false alarm. The bairn is fine and not ready to come just yet. I'm to eat anything I want." She sighed. "What I'd really love is something fresh and tart, but it'll be months before gooseberries hang on the bushes again. Fortunately, I laid in a goodly supply of jam for the winter."

She popped a suitably slathered bite of bannock into her mouth and grinned at Katherine. "Mind your husband. To bed with ye. Beathag will stay with me now.

She only wandered down to fetch her own breakfast and will be—och, there she is."

The old woman appeared at the open doorway with a tray in hand and bustled into the room with amazing spryness for one so stricken in years. She set down her load on a trunk and busied about her patient, smoothing the coverlet around Margaret's hips before turning to Katherine.

"Ye've done yer turn, my lady. I'll stand the watch now, though I'm thinking it might be days yet before this babe deigns to join us."

"Truly?" Katherine walked toward the bed, carefully putting one foot before the other lest she lose her balance from sheer fatigue. She'd been up and down with Margie countless times in the night, changing linens and sponging sweat from her feverish forehead as Beathag's poultice and vile green medicine did their work. Finally, as the first rays of dawn crept in the window, Katherine had sunk into a fitful, light sleep in her chair.

Beathag eyed Margie critically. "Are ye havin' any pains, m'lady?"

"Only hunger pains, and they're easily remedied," Margaret said between spoonfuls of parritch. "Do ye think there's any more songbird pie in the larder?"

"Satisfied?" William steered Katherine out of the room without waiting for an answer. She plodded up the circular staircase that led to her chamber. Their chamber, hers and Will's, part of her heart reminded her. He followed her with a hand to the small of her back.

It was a comfort, that soft touch, even if it was a bit possessive.

The bedclothes had been drawn back up, but it was untidily done. She recognized William's hand in it and gave him credit for trying. The bed was still so inviting it was all she could do not to stumble into the mass of linen and goose down. Then one of the pillows moved and Angus crawled out from under it, his little furry body wriggling at the sight of her.

"Och, where've ye been, ye naughty boy?" She knelt down to greet him as he leapt off the bed and came to press doggie kisses on her knees.

"He was cowering on the staircase outside Margaret's chamber until Dorcas threatened to add him to the stewpot. Guess she tripped over him more than once," William said with a grin. "Then he gave up and joined me last night. Any port in a storm, eh, Angus?"

Guilt lanced her chest. In the panic of Margaret's emergency, she'd forgotten all about him. "My poor wee laddie."

Now that Angus was receiving a bit of sympathy, he whined to be picked up. Katherine scooped him into her arms and hugged him so tightly he squeaked and squirmed to be put down again. Then he trotted to the doorway and stretched himself as long as he could across the opening, taking up guard duty as if to make sure Katherine wouldn't slip away without him again.

"Will ye eat before ye sleep?" William asked. "I brought ye some breakfast."

She yawned hugely. "Maybe a bite or two."

"Let's get ye out of those clothes first." He put his hand on her waist, sliding into the space between her arisaid and leine. "'Tis still damp."

"I didna have time to change."

"We'll remedy that now." Without waiting for her consent, he undid the belt holding her arisaid at her waist. It was just as well. She was too tired to argue with him. Then he did the same with the damp gown.

As layer after layer of her clothing was peeled off, so did the worry and fear she'd wrestled with all night.

Margie was out of danger, as was the babe she carried. But after fetching and fretting and caring for her sister-in-law during the dark watches of the night, it was beyond fine to have someone doing the same for her now.

Especially someone like William.

His big hands brushed her skin. The calluses at the base of his fingers nicked her skin lightly, but his touch was so gentle, it left a frisson of awareness and anticipation in its wake. He was careful of every brooch and pin that held her clothing just so. Finally, she stood before him as bare as Eve, but unlike that ancient lady, Katherine felt suddenly shy.

Maybe it was because of the way she'd withdrawn from his bed for months. Or maybe it was because the gasping, eyes-rolled-back-in-her-head moments in William's bath were still so fresh in her mind. Perhaps it was the way Will's dark gaze smoldered over every inch of her. But whatever the cause, her body lit up like a candle. She blushed all over. Her nipples were as bright as cherries and she was sure her bum was rosy.

Even so, she resisted covering herself with her hands and stood perfectly still. He was her husband. It was his right to look at her. And truth to tell, she loved the way he was doing it. The hunger in his face made her insides clench and a little thrill of feminine power shot through her.

But all he was doing was looking, and she couldn't fathom why.

Suffering Lord, why does she say nothing? Do nothing? Doesn't she know what seeing her like this does to me?

William gritted his teeth. He would not beg. He also wouldn't swive a statue. She needed to give him some sign that she wasn't going to push him away again.

A word. A touch. God's Toes, even a half smile would be enough.

But she just stood there, her breasts rising and falling with each breath, her eyes wide and searching. Was that a hint of fear flickering behind them?

Fiend seize it, does she think I'd take her unwilling?

He turned away, partly to rummage in her clothing trunk for a clean chemise and partly because his body cheered the idea of ravishing his own wife, willing or not, with far too much enthusiasm. For half a heartbeat, he imagined falling on her in a heated rut. She'd be the one begging for a change. Then if he did it right, she'd be begging him not to stop.

He shoved the unworthy thought away and willed his body to settle. He'd never force her. Of course not. But it was hard to shake the notion that if only he could possess her completely, swive her beyond the ability to think, maybe then she'd finally understand that she was everything to him and nothing else mattered.

If he tried putting his feelings in words they'd just get into another argument. Silence seemed the safest course.

He held up the linen garment and she lifted her arms so he could slip it over her head. One corner of her mouth twitched.

Was that disappointment?

Will had no way to know what was rattling around in that pretty head of hers. After the nonsense about seeking an annulment, nothing would surprise him. But surely after what had happened in the bath, she'd set all thought of that aside.

Then why did he feel the need to tread with as much care as if she were a wary doe he was stalking?

He wanted her to want him. To need him as he

needed her. And if God never saw fit to grant them a child, for him to be enough for her without one.

But he couldn't say the words. They were stuck in his throat.

The hem of the chemise skimmed down her body and came to rest, floating at her ankles. She started to tie the drawstring at her bodice.

"Let me." It was probably a mistake to break the silence, but he took up the ties and made short work of knotting them loosely.

"You're so good to me, Will."

"And you're good *for* me."

"No, I'm not." She sighed and he realized the vicious verbal circle they'd been treading was about to start again. So he did the only thing he could think of to head it off.

He kissed her.

Hard.

He walked her backward till her spine was pressed against the stone wall and held her head in place, unwilling to let her slip away, lest she start arguing with him. Her lips were unmoving under his. No matter. By God, she was his, and he was going to kiss her till she responded to him.

Katherine's arms were wedged between them, her fists against his chest. Her body was as stiff as dry leather, and the sounds she made into his mouth couldn't be mistaken for the small noises she made when he pleasured her.

She wanted to be free.

Then, just when he was about to admit defeat and release her, a minor miracle occurred.

Her clenched fingers uncurled and she grasped the front of his shirt to tug him closer. Her lips, which had been as ungiving as an icebound loch, seemed to melt and part.

In that moment, he forgot his own name.

She wasn't cold on the inside. Her mouth was warm, almost feverish, and she suckled his tongue when he swept it in. He bit her lip lightly and she nipped his back.

"Will," she murmured, and he remembered who he was because he was hers.

He released her head. She wasn't going anywhere. But he still needed to hold her, to connect with her beyond the joining of their mouths and the pressure of his body against hers, so he gripped her hands. Her fingers were icy, slender and fragile things. Bone and tendon, skin and nails, all small parts of his bonnie Kat, but cold parts. He'd warm them.

He'd warm her, protect her, tuck her into his plaid and keep her, all of her, as close as his next breath. He'd love away her pain, if only she'd let him.

With unmistakable need, she groaned into his mouth.

He was lost, diving headfirst into the dark loch of Katherine, not sure whether the waves would bear him up or drag him down. He didn't much care either way. He had to have her, and if he drowned in her, it was the death he'd wish for himself.

There was a pounding in his ears, louder than the steady march of his own blood. It took him a moment to realize someone was banging on the door to Kat's chamber.

"My lady! My Lord Badenoch!"

He heard the voice but didn't answer. Kat's mouth was his whole world, her fresh response to him a new and undiscovered country, and he wasn't ready to leave it for the mundane one of Glengarry Castle.

Finally, it was Katherine who broke off their kiss with a gasp. She tore herself out of his embrace and picked up the shawl draped over her clothing trunk to wrap around her shoulders. "Come, Dorcas."

The door burst open and the serving girl spilled into the room. Her dirty-blond hair had escaped her mobcap and stuck out like the long prickly spines of a startled porcupine.

"Och, my lord, ye must come quick before he does himself harm. Please, oh, please." Her voice strayed upward in pitch as she became more alarmed.

"Who?"

"'Tis Nab, ye ken. First he was just walkin' the parapet, leaping from one crenellation to another, but then he climbed atop the southwest bastion." Dorcas clutched her apron, grinding the fabric between her fists. "I'm afeared he means to jump."

William strode to one of the arrow loops that functioned as narrow windows in the room. Sure enough, the fool was perched atop the cylindrical tower that marked a corner of the curtain wall. He sat with his shoulders hunched, his legs dangling over a sheer drop to the loch below.

"What's got into him?"

"I dinna ken," Dorcas said miserably. "He willna speak to me. He willna speak to anybody."

A crowd had gathered in the bailey, pointing and laughing.

"This is MacNaught's doing."

"I shouldna wonder, milord." It was a measure of how desperate Dorcas was that she latched on to William's arm and gave it a tug. "Please, will ye come? While there's still time."

He looked back over at Katherine. Her lips were kiss swollen, her eyes still languid. Their bodies had almost said what his heart feared to voice. If only they'd had a bit more time, they'd have found each other again. He was sure of it.

"Go, Will," she said softly, pulling the shawl tighter around her. "Else ye'll have regrets hereafter."

"No fear of that," he muttered as he stalked toward the door. "I already do."

On the first day of Christmas,
My true love gave to me
A partridge in a pear tree.

—From "The Twelve Days of Christmas"

"Weel, that's a silly gift. Any eejit kens that a partridge
will do ye more good on a spit than in a pear tree."

—An observation from Nab,
fool to the Earl of Glengarry

Chapter Ten

Cupping his hands around his mouth, Will called out from the parapet, "Nab, what're ye doing up there?"

"Ye have eyes. I'm sitting, o' course." Nab peered over the edge of the spirelike roof. He shook his head and the tiny bells at the ends of his cap tinkled. "Odds bodkins. And I'm the one they call a fool," he muttered.

"*Why* are ye sitting there?"

"Have ye seen an owl in the daytime, William?"

"Come to think on it, I havena. Only after twilight."

"That's because in the day, they sit still as a statue in the crotch of a tree, and after a bit, no one kens they're even there. They disappear in plain sight." Nab's shoulders rose and fell in a deep sigh. "That's what I'm doing, William. I'm being an owl."

"Jump!" someone from down in the bailey yelled.

William sent them a thunderous glare, and the rowdy crowd that had gathered below went silent, shuffling their feet in the snow. He wondered where the old earl was. There was a time when Lord Glengarry would have been in the thick of things, scattering the malingerers in the courtyard and demanding his fool come down from that benighted perch before he did something monumentally stupid like falling and leaving a bloody stain on the stone for others with more sense to have to clean up.

Unfortunately, Lord Glengarry was nowhere to be seen. And Nab was the sort who might be easily spooked.

"Would ye like company?" William asked Nab.

"If I liked company, I'd be in the great hall, would I not?" Then his belligerent tone fizzled away and he cast Will a hopeful glance. "But I wouldna mind it so very much should ye wish to come up, William. Ye're not like the others." Then his ever-wandering gaze darted away. "The view of the loch is verra fine from here."

"If ye've seen one loch, ye've seen 'em all," William grumbled as he clambered up the uneven stone and hoisted himself onto the conical spire of the thatched roof. Then he walked, careful to step from one supporting beam to the next and avoid the icy patches, till he joined Nab on the edge of the sloping roof.

A biting wind swirled a breath of snow around them.

"Seems an odd place to sit," Will said. "There are any number of more comfortable places down in the keep to practice being an owl."

"Aye, but none I deserve," Nab said morosely. His

face seemed to fold in on itself like a crumpled piece of parchment. "I lost it, William."

"Lost what?"

"Yer scepter." He hung his head.

Will's chest constricted and he didn't trust himself to speak.

"Are ye angry with me? Canna say I blame ye. I would be, were I ye."

William's hands had bunched into white-knuckled fists without his conscious volition. That silver rod meant everything to his family. It was a promise and a challenge to each new generation of Douglas males as they took the reins of Badenoch. KNOW BY THIS, it said, THAT ALL THE HOPES AND DREAMS OF THOSE WHO CAME BEFORE YOU ARE PINNED ON YOU. HUSBAND THAT WHICH YOU'VE BEEN GIVEN. INCREASE IT FOR THE SAKE OF THOSE WHO'LL COME AFTER YOU. 'TWILL BE HARD, BUT YOU ARE WORTHY OF THE TASK BECAUSE YOU COME FROM US. LIVE IN OUR STRENGTH. RULE WISELY AND WELL.

And now he not only had no son to hand it down to, he'd lost the scepter itself.

"William?"

"No, Nab, I'm not angry." He was, but not with the fool. William knew Nab. He'd as soon lose his right hand as lose that scepter. The fool was obsessive about things left in his charge. There was no one he'd have trusted with the family treasure more.

"I dinna know what happened. I never let it out of my sight. Honest. But my eyes canna stay open forever, can they? Nay, they canna." Nab picked at his motley as if he might find the scepter somewhere in the folds of his disreputable garment.

"When was the last time you had it?" William asked, his mind churning furiously. None of the other servants

would have dared touch it. As far as he knew, none of
the laird's guests had left the keep, so the treasure was
still within Glengarry's walls.

"It was with me when I went to sleep last night, but
when I woke, there was only this in its place." He lifted
a worm-eaten staff roughly the same length and diam-
eter as the Badenoch scepter. "Ye dinna suppose a fey
prince came in the dark and took it back because I
didna deserve to touch it?"

"I'm certain someone came in the night, but I'll lay
odds it wasna the Fair Folk. Where were ye sleeping?"

Only the laird and his family had dedicated bedchambers. Lord Glengarry's retainers bedded down in
the great hall. If there was a guest in the castle of any
high-ranking stature, he'd be allowed to use the solar
for privacy, but even then, the makeshift bed would be
a hand-me-down collection of straw ticks and linens
that were no longer used by his lordship. Servants had
to make do with pallets in the kitchen, above the stable
in the haymow, or down in the souterrain, curling up
near wherever they worked and as near a source of
heat as they could manage.

It made for a close-knit clan of people in the castle.
Everyone knew everything about each other. And if a
couple in the next set of blankets or cloaks happened
to be doing a bit of a rhythmic canter some night, the
polite thing to do was to roll so one faced away and
pretend not to hear a thing.

"I sleep on a pallet across the doorway to the earl's
chamber. It's where I am"—Nab ducked his head and
finished softly—"most nights."

That made sense. William's father-in-law would want
his fool close by if he woke in the night and needed a
bit of company or entertainment. But it meant whoever

had snatched the scepter was a bold thief, committing his crime so near the earl's chamber.

"How does his lairdship fare of late?"

"He sleeps a lot," Nab said. "Sometimes when he doesna mean to, but never deeply or well. I worry about him, William, indeed I do. But ye canna judge by me." He shrugged. "I worry about everything."

"I dinna want ye to worry. Here's what I want ye to do." As Laird of Badenoch, it was Will's job to solve problems and he'd hit upon a plan to fix this. "Ye're still Laird of Misrule. Tell your loyal subjects ye've arranged for a bit of fun. Ye've hidden the scepter someplace within the castle wa—"

"That's a lie, William. Ye dinna wish me to lie surely. Not with it being Christmas and all."

"Dinna think of it as a lie. Think of it as . . ." The fool was right. It was a lie. Why did the simpleminded make everything so . . . well, simple? Black was black and white was white, and Nab wasn't the sort who'd let a grey untruth tramp across his tongue if he could help it. "Think of it as a play. A bit of make-believe. Ye're pretending to be laird, aye?"

Nab nodded.

"Then all ye must do is pretend ye arranged a game of hide-and-seek for everyone. Only you hid the scepter, not a person."

"But I didna hide the scepter."

"Fine, ye can say something like, 'The scepter has been hidden.' That way ye're not claiming to have done it, and 'tis the truth. The scepter is hidden. If folk think ye did it, 'tis not your fault."

"I didna hide it," he repeated doggedly.

"No one but we two knows that."

"And him who took it," Nab pointed out.

"Aye, him too. In fact," Will said, "I'm counting on him being the one who finds it."

Nab flicked his gaze toward Will. "If he did, then would the thief not ken that we ken that he's the one who took it?"

"Aye, but ye must offer an inducement strong enough for him to risk it."

"What could that be?"

It was a thorny question. Will felt to the marrow of his bones that MacNaught was behind this, but he couldn't accuse the man without proof. What did Ranulf want more than tweaking Will's nose by taking his family's treasure?

"I have it. Proclaim that whoever finds the scepter may take his seat in the laird's chair for the rest of the week." Lord Glengarry had vacated it since that first night. He wasn't likely to complain.

"I dinna know, William. The throne Ranulf and his friends made for me isna verra comfortable. Antlers are verra pointy, ye ken."

"Nay, not that one. Lord Glengarry's own seat." It'd appeal to Ranulf's vanity as nothing else would. But unless Will caught Ranulf "discovering" the location of the scepter, how would he prove that Ranulf knew where to look because he'd put it there? "I need someone to shadow MacNaught till he shows his hand. Is there a likely lad among the pages here?"

Nab scrunched his forehead in thought. "Fergie might do. He's the smallest of the lads in the castle. Makes him try a mite harder."

"Good. After ye tell your waiting subjects about this new game,"—William waved at the crowd below and several of them waved back—"find this Fergie and tell him he's to keep an eye on Ranulf MacNaught on the quiet like. It won't do if the man thinks he's being watched. And tell him to find me at once if Ranulf comes up with the scepter."

William stood and held a hand out to Nab to help him up.

"Where will ye be?" Nab asked.

"Talking to Jamison first. I need to find a rider to deliver a message to Edinburgh, and the seneschal should know who can do the job. 'Tis past time Lady Margaret's husband came home." For the sake of Donald's pregnant wife and his father's uncertain health both.

Nab grinned. "And if yer hide-and-seek game works, yer scepter will come home too."

On the second day of Christmas,
my true love gave to me two turtle doves.

—From "The Twelve Days of Christmas"

"What kind of nonsense is this? A creature that's both
turtle and dove 'tis neither fish nor fowl. And a verra
unchancy sort of gift, indeed, even if it came from a
body's true love."

—An observation from Nab,
fool to the Earl of Glengarry

Chapter Eleven

Not all the castle's servants worked above ground. The buttery, the carpentry, the bottlery, and the abattoir, where game was hung and dressed, were located under the great hall, with doors leading out through a set of stone steps directly into the lower ward. Even after Jamison directed William to the subterranean reaches of the castle, it took him the better part of an hour to find a servant with the intelligence necessary to memorize a message to take to Lord Glengarry's son, and another half hour to locate one who knew the way to Edinburgh.

In the end, he decided to send both of them.

Taking the unmarked paths through the Highlands in winter might be the shorter route, but it was also likely to take longer. The messengers could become lost between one glen and the next as landmarks changed over the seasons. Or they might run afoul of some local chieftain or other as they passed through the territory of other clans. Then there was always the threat from men who lived rough, outside the bounds of a clan, for whom any traveler was fair game.

William gave the messengers enough coin to purchase passage on the ferry that plied the loch as far as Inverness. Then they'd take ship and sail down to Leith at the mouth of the Firth of Forth. From there, they'd travel the short distance to Edinburgh Castle, where King James's court resided. Will gave his messengers one chance in ten of reaching Donald and having him return before Margaret gave birth, but at least he could tell Katherine he'd sent for her brother.

"I wish ye'd let yer runners wait a day or so, my lord," the carpenter of Glengarry Castle said after the men William had chosen for the journey left to raid the kitchen for food to take with them. "Then they could deliver his lairdship's gift to court at the self-same time. 'Tis a bit unwieldy, ye ken, and will take two to make the trip."

Even though Donald was dancing attendance on the young King James, it was politic for the old earl to send him a gift for the New Year as well. But usually a royal present meant a piece of jewelry or a bolt of precious silk, something that would fit neatly into a saddlebag.

"What's Lord Glengarry sending to the king?"

The man grinned from ear to ear. "Och, let me show ye."

It was an ornately wrought trunk of monstrous size. The carpenter's apprentice was putting the final touches on the lid, sanding a bas relief carving of a thistle so lifelike, despite its extreme size, Will expected to be pricked by its thorns. Still, he wasn't sure what the gift was supposed to be.

"It looks like an oversized coffin," William said. Not the most politically astute gift to send to a young king.

The carpenter's face fell. "Nay, my lord, 'tis a chest special made to fit the Honours of Scotland. See for yerself." He lifted the hinged lid to reveal a padded purple velvet lining.

"A royal gift indeed," William admitted.

The man's expression bloomed with pride once more as he waved his apprentice away. "Aye, 'tis verra fine, an' I say it myself. As ye see, there's room for the royal crown, the sword of state, and the scepter. And a monstrous long thing that scepter is too. Came all the way from Rome, it did, back in my grandsire's day. Come to think on it, the sword came from Rome too, only later and from a different pope."

"I'm sure His Majesty will be pleased."

"I hope he will. Och, there's a secret to the chest, as well. I'd not show this to just anybody, but as ye're part of the earl's family, I'll let ye in on it."

The man felt along the edge of the velvet for a silk tab. Once he pulled it, he was able to lift the padded bottom to reveal a hidden cavity in the chest.

"'Tis a hidey-hole for other precious things. Reckon a king has plenty of gewgaws that he wants to keep to himself," the carpenter said. "'Twas my idea, the secret place."

"And it's a good one, but ye ought not show it to anyone else."

"Och, that I havena. In fact, I may even let His

Majesty discover it for his own self. That way, it'll stay a secret."

Even though the workmanship of the chest made it a princely gift, William doubted the young king would spare it a second glance once his state treasures were locked away in it. That secret compartment the castle carpenter was so proud of might very well stay secret forever.

Once William climbed the stairs from the lower ward to the central portion of the bailey, he discovered most of the denizens of Glengarry Castle were roaming over the place in search of Nab's "hidden" scepter. From the corner of his eye, he even caught the dark blur of Angus zipping across the bailey from behind the chapel to the stable. However, he doubted the terrier was after anything except rats. Everywhere Will went, folk were looking under benches, opening cupboards, and peering behind every closed door. When he reached the great hall, he wasn't surprised to find it nearly empty.

There was a small boy playing with a deerhound pup in one corner. Will figured it was probably the lad Fergie whom Nab had told him about because he was perfectly positioned to surreptitiously keep an eye on the only others in the large space.

Ranulf MacNaught and his toadies were tossing knucklebones near the fireplace.

William swore under his breath. MacNaught hadn't risen to the bait yet. But since Ranulf probably knew where the scepter was, there was no hurry.

"Not interested in trying out the laird's seat?" he asked Ranulf as he walked by, fully intending not to stop.

"That seat should only be occupied by the man who deserves it."

"In that, we are in complete accord. Lord Glengarry is entirely worthy of his station." Will decided to give Ranulf a nudge. "But I suppose it doesna hurt for others to see someone else there. After all, no man holds power forever."

Something dark and dangerous flicked across MacNaught's features. It reminded Will of a wolf slinking from shadow to shadow, nearly invisible except for the feral glint that made its eyes glow copper in the dark.

"No man holds power forever," Ranulf repeated. "Words to live by, Badenoch."

"Or die by," Will said.

"Assuredly," Ranulf said. "All men die."

"Aye, that they do. Some sooner than others."

"Were I not a guest in my uncle's home, I'd think that a threat." MacNaught barked out a rough laugh. "But 'tis Christmas and I'm willing to believe losing the treasure of Badenoch has addled your brains, so I'll not hold it against ye. Will ye dice with us then? Losing a few throws will keep ye from taxin' your brain overmuch. Or since your precious scepter has gone missing, has the house of Badenoch lost enough this day?"

"No one said the rod was missing." *Except ye.* That slip of the tongue cinched matters. Ranulf had stolen it. "According to the Laird of Misrule, it's been hidden away for someone to find. And I'm guessing it'll not be found by someone who's content to while the day away with a pair of dice."

Hands clenched by his sides, Will headed for the spiral stairs that led to the family's chambers. Katherine was probably sleeping. He hoped she was after her sleepless night, but he had a fierce need to see her. He wouldn't wake her. He'd just watch her for a bit. Simply being in the same room with Ranulf MacNaught made him want to bash someone's head in. Preferably Ranulf's.

Kat's face in repose always rested him. She smoothed out the wrinkles in his soul and gave him space to breathe. He needed her.

Somehow, he had to convince her of that. If possible without groveling.

He hadn't made more than two turns on the staircase before he was nearly knocked into next week by Dorcas, wielding a broom as if it were a mace. She brought the handle down on his crown a second time with a resounding thwack. Then her eyes flew wide as she recognized him.

"Oh, oh! Lord William, I'm that sorry. Truly I am. I didna know 'twas ye." She whipped the offending broom behind her and bobbed half a dozen curtseys in rapid succession. "Thank ye for seein' to Nab. I'm so verra grateful, indeed I am."

"Ye've a funny way of showing it."

She turned her lips inward for a moment, then chattered on as if she hadn't just clubbed the earl's son-in-law. "How is Nab now that he isna fixin' to leap from the bastion any longer?"

"He was never going to leap anywhere," Will said crossly, rubbing his head. "And I expect he's fine since he's not the one having his head bashed in with a wee broom."

"'Tis dim in the stairwell. I didna expect ye back up to yer chamber till this evening," she said with a sniff.

"Even so, why are ye lying in wait on the stairs as if the castle were under siege?"

"Och, I had to resort to violence to keep the rest of 'em out," Dorcas explained. "There's no shortage of those who hope to find the hidden scepter, ye see, and win the chance to sit on his lairdship's throne. Several of the wretches thought to search the family's chambers. With Lady Margaret under orders to rest and his lordship feeling a mite poorly as well, we canna be having that now, can we?"

"No, we canna have that," Will said, sure a lump was forming on his crown big enough to toss a ring over. "Wait. What's wrong with his lordship?"

"He woke with a fierce headache and told Jamison his left arm felt heavy. I didna hear him myself, mind, but word is Lord Glengarry sounded as if he'd been in his cups, and I know he wasna because Jamison says all the ale and whisky have been strictly accounted for. Something about mod . . ." She flicked her gaze to the right, searching for the word as if it might be hovering in the air beside her. "Mod-er-a-ta-tion. 'Moderatation in all things,' he says, lest we run short."

That explained why Lord Glengarry hadn't cleared the bailey of onlookers when Nab was perched on the bastion. "How is his lordship now?"

"Resting comfortable-like," she said. "Old Beathag knows more than midwifery, ye ken. She fixed him a special tea—willow bark and ginger and meadowsweet and a few things she wouldna tell me. Ye dinna suppose it was anything nasty, do ye? In any case, it seemed to set him to rights, but Beathag insists he should keep to his bed today. So we've two members of the family confined to their sheets."

William chuckled. "Three, if ye count Lady Katherine."

"Oh, she's not abed. Lucas and wee Tam were giving their nursemaid fits fussing to see their mother, and wouldna be comforted. But Lady Katherine told me to wake her if there was anything she could do. So she's in the nursery with her nephews."

He should have known. Kat would run herself ragged before she'd let anything cause Margaret the slightest discomfort before her pains began.

His gut clenched. What else should he have done when Kat was brought to childbed with Stephan? Was there something, anything, that might have made a difference? With effort, he shoved the thought away. It would do no one any good now.

William turned around and headed back down the stairs.

The nursery was located above the kitchen, which was off the great hall. This way, the room occupied by the earl's grandchildren was always warm in winter. It was close enough to the source of food that the lads never knew hunger. Will had overheard Margaret complain more than once that her older boys were in danger of being thoroughly spoiled by Cook and the rest of the kitchen staff.

And now the youngest two were being spoiled by his wife.

Will paused at the open doorway to the nursery. Kat was tripping lightly across the room with wee Tam in her arms and three-year-old Lucas hopping along beside her. She hummed a dance tune as she turned and dipped, graceful as a falling leaf. The boys' laughter made a spritely counterpoint.

William stepped back a pace so he could watch her from the shadows. She formed a small circle of three with her nephews. She balanced Tam on her hip and palmed Lucas's hand for each roundelay as they revolved around each other in the skipping dance.

Will's fingers curled into fists. Why couldn't God see that his Katherine was born to be a mother? She was calm and loving and had so much to give to a child.

Then she collapsed into a chair and began a game of peekaboo with Tam, who was now lying on her lap, his pudgy feet waggling in the air. Lucas found a comfortable spot where he could lounge on the hem of her skirts and lean his head on her knee. The toddler made a small wooden horse gallop across his ankles for a bit and raised the toy to his mouth to gnaw upon its pricked ears. Then Lucas caught sight of William, dropped his toy, and scrambled to his feet.

"Unca Will," he cried and hurried toward William in a bowlegged trot, arms uplifted.

Will scooped him up and tossed him skyward, catching him on the way down. Lucas giggled as if he were being tickled by feathers.

"Have a care," Katherine cautioned.

"He's a lad, not Frankish glass. He'll not break so easy." William gave Lucas another toss and was rewarded with another round of shrieking laughter. "Besides, I willna drop him."

Kat seemed satisfied because she went back to the little hand game she'd been playing with Tam. William tired of the tossing game long before Lucas showed any sign of flagging, and sent Katherine a pointed "help me" look.

"Lucas, why do ye not show your uncle your new pony?" she suggested.

The boy scrambled down from William's arms and scuttled over to retrieve his wooden horse.

"I could kiss ye, lass," Will said with a wink.

"Promises, promises."

Well, that was an improvement. Almost an invitation. If he didn't know better, he'd say he and Kat were flirting with each other.

But the presence of two little boys limited what they might accomplish in that direction, so Will sank to the floor and crossed his legs. Lucas plopped down between them and leaned back on his uncle's chest without invitation, making little neighing sounds and trotting his toy up and down Will's shins. Then as the pony's movements began to slow, Lucas explained in his babyish voice that the horse was tired and needed to "wie down to sweep in da paddock."

The paddock turned out to be William's left boot. Once his pony was safely stabled away, Lucas tucked his thumb in his mouth. His head began to nod and he fell asleep sprawled happily across Will's kilted lap.

"I sent a messenger to fetch your brother home," he said softly so as not to wake his nephew. "I canna promise it will be in time."

"At least ye tried. Thank ye," she whispered back.

Lucas shifted in his sleep and made a wee fussing noise. Will smoothed the boy's downy hair till he settled once more. It was as soft as a spring lamb. And his fat cheeks were still touchably new, after the manner of all young things. The lad's milky breath, his bonelessly relaxed body, they contrived to coax a memory to the forefront of Will's brain. He tried without success to tamp it down.

"How old is Lucas?" he finally asked.

"Almost three and Tam was two only last month. Margaret had them verra close together."

"Hmm. I was just thinking. . . ."

"What?" Katherine shifted Tam to her shoulder and patted his bottom rhythmically, in an effort to send him to join his older brother in a nap.

Will hesitated. "I dinna want to . . . I mean, will it make ye sad if . . ." He sighed. "They would have been of an age, wouldn't they?"

The muscles in Katherine's neck bobbed as she swallowed hard. "Who do ye mean?"

"Lucas and . . . our Stephan."

On the third day of Christmas,
My true love gave to me three French hens.

—From "The Twelve Days of Christmas"

"Weel, I must say, that sounds like a practical gift. But
why do the birds have to be foreign? There's not a thing
wrong with a Scots Grey hen."

—An observation from Nab,
fool to the Earl of Glengarry

Chapter Twelve

Stephan. Will had finally said his name. A cold
corner in Katherine's heart began to thaw a bit.

"Aye, I was confined with Stephan about the same
time as Margaret had Lucas." Was it only three years
ago? Sometimes it seemed another lifetime.

"I didna mean to make ye sad all over again. If 'tis
hard to speak of—"

"It doesna make me sad to hear ye speak his name,"
Katherine said. "'Tis a mercy. It means ye think on him
too."

"Of course, I think on him. He was our child, Kat."
He laid a hand on Lucas's head, but the lad slept on.
Will's voice dropped to a whisper. "He was my son."

"He still is. So long as we remember him." She had plenty of memories of Stephan. It was only the final blood-soaked ones that were painful. She cast about for a happy memory. "I mind the first time I felt him move. I'd suspected I was bearing for some time, but then one morning, I felt this wee flutter inside me. Like a moth in a jar." She closed her eyes and put a hand to her abdomen as if, by willing hard enough, she might somehow feel that slight vibration again. "It was so faint the first time, I couldna be sure I hadn't imagined it."

William chuckled. "I didna have to imagine the time he kicked me in the head."

Katherine laughed with him. "Aye. He was trying to tell ye not to use his mother's belly for a pillow, thank ye verra much."

"Opinionated, even in the womb," Will said. His smile faded. "He'd have been a handful."

One that Katherine would have joyfully accepted. Stephan had seemed so lively, especially in the final months of her pregnancy. Her belly rolled in constant turmoil with his little body pressing against the confines of the small space. Then one day, without warning, he stopped moving.

"When I started bleeding, I hadna felt him move for half a day," she said softly.

"Katherine, ye dinna have to talk about it again."

"But that's just it. There's no 'again.' We never talked about it in the first place."

"Maybe that's for the best." He didn't meet her gaze.

"No, 'tis not. Did ye never think that I need to know how it was, how it is, for ye?" Emptiness yawned between them and she rushed to fill it. "Silence is like death. There's no light, no warmth, no hope in silence. It feels like a noose around my neck that tightens more

with each smothered word, with each time we could
have spoken our hearts and didna."

Will stared at the toy horse on his boot until she
began to wonder if he'd even heard her. Finally, he
raised his gaze to meet hers.

"That's what happened to Stephan. Did ye know
that?" he said woodenly. "The cord was wrapped
around his neck, they said."

His words cut like a knife, but if it could cut the pu-
trefying silence from her marriage, she'd bear it. She
still had no idea how he felt, but at least Will was
naming their son and speaking about him instead of
pretending he hadn't existed. It was a start.

"I didna ever know how Stephan died," she said.
"They wouldna let me see him at first. If I hadna demanded, I think the midwife would have just taken
him away. I was weak from losing all that blood, ye see,
and so tired, but I had to see him. When I started to
drag myself from the bed whether the midwife allowed
me or not, she finally promised to clean him and put
him in my arms."

After two days of labor, sweating through countless
sets of sheets, she had thought there was no moisture
left in her. But if the child hadn't been cleaned up by
the midwife, Katherine could have washed his small
body with her tears.

"I was in the chapel when they brought him to me,"
William said so softly she almost didn't hear him.

"In the chapel? Will, were ye praying for us?"

"Aye," he admitted. "Ye know I've never been a praying man, but I was that desperate. Ye'd labored for so
long, and for much of the while I'd stood outside the
door, digging my nails into the wood each time ye
screamed. I wanted to go to ye, but the midwife said
ye'd not thank me for invading the birth chamber."

His eyes became very bright, and for a moment she wondered if he was going to well up. She felt tears pressing against the backs of her own eyes and her nostrils quivered.

Aye, love. Let them fall, and no slight to your manhood if ye do. Let us weep together until there are no more tears left in us. Show me that our son's life and death meant something to ye.

But then William looked away sharply. Katherine swallowed back the lump in her throat and blinked hard. He wouldn't want to see her tears. It might make him stop speaking and she needed him to keep going.

"The midwife was wrong," she said. In the dark watches of those desperate hours, when her strength was fading and the shadows in the corners of the room seemed to close in upon her between one contraction and the next, she'd have given anything to see William. "I wanted to have ye near."

The lines between his dark brows deepened. "I didna know that. I should have forced my way in to be with ye, but I didna want to add to your troubles in case the midwife was right. I was no good to anyone hovering outside your door like a ghoul, so I went to the chapel. I spent the night prostrate on the stone floor, begging God for your life." When he met her gaze again, the ferocity in his eyes made her flinch. "Ten sons couldna make up for losing ye."

Her chest burned with love for him, but she wished he'd prayed for his son as well. They were quiet together for a moment, the only sound the soft, wet snoring of their sleeping nephews.

"I never thought God would take our son," he finally said.

"But ye did see him."

He nodded. "They brought him to me, all wrapped in a bit of plaid. He was perfect, ten wee fingers and ten wee toes. Tiny little nails glinting like the inside of an oyster. His eyelashes were fine, and pretty enough for a lass. Our Stephan had everything, except breath."

"I wish ye'd come to me right away," she said. The midwife had claimed Katherine needed her rest, but she'd have rested easier if her husband had been by her bedside.

"I couldna. I had some unfinished business."

William had taken care of burying Stephan while Katherine recuperated. It was the dead of winter and the ground must have been like iron when her husband dug that small grave in a patch of unconsecrated ground. William still hadn't told her where the child rested, only that he'd done all he could for him.

"There was still a matter between me and God. He'd spared ye, as I asked, but after all ye suffered, He still took our son. So after I buried Stephan, I went back to the chapel and railed at God for putting ye through hell."

"Oh, Will, ye didna."

"I did. And I'd do it again. I swore. I raged. I dared Him to smite me for it. I screamed until I was hoarse, but there was nothing but silence." William's lip curled. "Either He doesna care or He doesna exist."

Katherine couldn't stop the tears from coming this time. "I dinna want to be the cause of ye losing faith, Will."

"'Tis not your fault. Never think it. God had His chance to show a little mercy and He didna."

"But He did. I'm still here. Ye're still here, and after such blasphemy, I wonder that Father Simon hasna excommunicated ye."

One corner of William's mouth lifted. "No need. I excommunicated myself. Besides, when I first started my tirade before the altar, the priest ran for cover. He expected flaming bolts from on high. In any case, he wasn't in the chapel for the worst of it."

Katherine read pain in William's eyes despite his bold words. He'd needed to lash out and God was a convenient target for his anger and grief. She feared for him. It was no light matter to fling insults heavenward, but she was also strangely comforted that William had taken Stephan's death so hard. It was as if his admission was the first step to bridging the gap that yawned between them. Her soul strained toward him, stretching to graze his spirit's outstretched fingertips. Only a little farther and they'd find each other again. . . .

Then William looked away and shifted the sleeping child on his lap so that his head and neck were better supported. "Let's talk on something else."

Katherine breathed a sigh. They weren't done with Stephan's death, not by a long stretch. The wounds were still deep, but at least now, they'd been reopened so the poison of deadly silence could leach out.

"I heard about the hunt for the scepter," Kat said. "I'm surprised ye're not looking for it."

"'Tis not exactly a hunt as Nab said. This is no game. The scepter has been stolen, but it'll turn up. I'm not worried." A muscle in his cheek ticked.

Katherine knew that tick. He was worried. No matter what he might claim, that scepter and what it stood for meant the world to William.

Wee Tam fidgeted in his sleep and whimpered. Katherine shifted him to her other shoulder and patted him back to sleep.

"Ye know, I've been thinking. There's nothing to keep us from filling Badenoch with wards and foundlings," Will said. "Every child needs a mother, and it doesna follow that it must be the one who carried him for months and brought him into this world."

She smiled sadly at him. "I'd love nothing better. To hear the laughter of children in our halls would be a blessing indeed."

"Then we'll do it."

"But it doesna solve our problem, Will. Ye are not a man who can do what he wishes without thought of your holding. Ye need an heir."

"I, for one, havena given up hope of getting ye with child." He shot her a wicked grin. "And I'm looking forward to the effort verra much."

A warm glow washed over her, but she didn't bask in it long. "I can conceive. There's no doubt of that," she said. "I just canna carry a child."

"The past is no proof of the future," he said.

"But 'tis all we have to go by."

"Now that's a wee bit surprising seeing as between the two of us, ye're the one with all the faith," he said.

Faith had nothing to do with it. There was something wrong inside her, something that kept her from bearing. She felt it to her bones. She was broken. She wouldn't break William too.

"Even if we are never given a son, I'll train up one of my brother's lads to take over the barony when I'm gone," he said as if it were as easy as handing down a used plaid.

Katherine knew it was not. Will's younger brother had been made a father twice already and his sons seemed sturdy and strong enough. But a man's nephew couldn't replace a son of his loins, especially in the Douglas family.

"Ye canna hand down the Scepter of Badenoch to a nephew," she insisted. "It has never been done. Time out of mind, for generations, it has been passed from father to son in a line unbroken."

Will laughed, but it seemed forced to her. "Ye're putting too much stock in bards' tales about that pretty trinket. Perhaps ye'll allow that I can take care of my family's traditions without your fretting."

My family, he said. His family. Not our family. The distinction wasn't lost on her. She might be Lady Badenoch, but she and William weren't a family. That would take a child in the center of their circle.

But before she could say more, Nab appeared at the nursery door. "Fergie says to tell ye MacNaught's on the move."

"I have to go," Will said.

"Why?"

"Because I'm fair certain MacNaught's behind the scepter's disappearance and I mean to catch him at recovering it." He rose to his feet, cradling Lucas in his arm and carrying him over to the bed in the corner, where the lad could finish his nap.

"Seems ye're fretting over the 'pretty trinket' as much as I," Katherine said. "Probably more."

Of course, he was. The symbol of Badenoch handed down through the ages wasn't one he could set aside lightly. The scepter itself might be on the smallish side, but it was weighty and dear—both for the rich metal from which it was fashioned and for the ponderous history it bore.

Will strode across the room and placed a quick kiss on her forehead. "Get some rest, wife," he whispered. "With what I have planned for us this night, ye'll need it."

On the fourth day of Christmas
My true love gave to me four calling birds.

—From "The Twelve Days of Christmas"

"Counting this day's gift, the singer has been given a total of ten blasted birds. Ten. At some point, wouldna someone's true love realize that a body only needs so many gifts with feathers?"

—An observation from Nab,
fool to the Earl of Glengarry

Chapter Thirteen

The sky lowered to meet the earth, washing the world in shades of grey and giving no hope that the snow in the bailey would melt anytime soon. It crunched underfoot as Will strode out of the keep with Nab at his heels. Will's breath streamed out in dragonish puffs, but he didn't mind the chill.

In fact, he had the feeling that he'd escaped the nursery just in time. It was beyond uncomfortable talking to Katherine about their dead son. It was like opening his chest and letting her see his beating heart.

A man ought not to betray that sort of weakness. Not to anyone.

But that wasn't the worst of it. Once the subject had turned to the missing scepter, there was a bite in her tone. He felt a definite undertow in the conversation. It was likely to drag him and Kat into another round of argument, a sucking whirlpool that could only lead to colder depths.

"Where's MacNaught now?" he asked Nab.

"I canna be sure since his boots are not nailed down somewhere, ye ken." Nab had to take two strides for each of William's long-legged ones. Though the effort left him red-faced and huffing, he scrambled to keep pace. "Fergie said MacNaught and his men had left the keep and seemed to be meandering toward the chapel."

"That's where the scepter must be hidden." MacNaught and his cronies were no more likely to be going there to pray than William was.

The chapel was located midway between the keep and the stables, squarely in the middle ward of the bailey. It had been built into a natural hillside so that earth was bermed on the north and west sides of the stone structure, angling up to the thick timbers of the eaves. In fact, the ground was close enough to the chapel's roof on the northwest corner that every so often a goat had to be shooed off the slanting thatch. But the protective earth on two sides of the building made for a sacred space that was warmer in winter and cooler in summer than the rest of Glengarry Castle.

William always suspected it was a silent inducement for folk to spend time there, whether they had a chat with the Almighty in mind or not.

"D'ye think Ranulf might have hidden the scepter under the altar?" Nab asked.

"'Tis bold enough, few would think to look there."

"Odds bodkins." Nab wrung his hands, worrying

under his breath over the audacity of stashing stolen treasure in such a place. When he spoke again, his voice seemed preternaturally loud. "Seems an unchancy thing to do, squirreling away ill-gotten goods under the Almighty's very nose, as it were."

"I dinna think Ranulf is overmuch concerned about the Almighty or His nose."

Pressing a finger to his lips to silence the fool, Will opened the oak chapel door and peered inside. Shafts of faint light streamed in through the green glass of the high windows on the eastern wall of the space. The pervasive moldy damp of smoke-darkened stone filled William's nose first, followed by the pungent fragrance of incense that didn't quite cover the first smell. The altar was alight with tallow candles. Aside from the priest, who was kneeling before the flickering votives, there was no one else in the chapel.

Will closed the door with a soft snick of the latch.

"Are we not going to check under the altar?" Nab asked.

"No. If it was there, it's gone by now, since Ranulf isna in the chapel. I'm doubting he hid it there." Not that MacNaught wouldn't stoop to that level of blasphemy. But the men who ran with him struck Will as the sort to be swayed by the threat of divine retribution. "He'd not use the inside of the chapel at least."

Someone gave a short whistle as if calling a dog. Will turned toward the sound. Not far away, the boy Fergie was perched on the parapet of the curtain wall, his knobby-kneed legs dangling, the deerhound pup still squirming on his lap. Once Fergie saw he had William's attention, he pointed the pup's paw toward the rear of the chapel.

Will nodded as his ears pricked to a whispered sibilance echoing off the stone wall behind the chapel. Someone was there. Several someones.

He started creeping around the chapel. Nab dogged him, the bells at the ends of the fool's cap jingling with each step. Will rounded on him and stared at the offending cap.

Nab's mouth opened in a silent "ah!" He removed his head covering and stuffed it up his sleeve. They started moving again. Will could still hear the bells, but their tinkling was muffled now.

"Look again," a voice whispered furiously around the corner from them. "It has to be there."

"I'm telling ye 'tis not. See for yourself."

Several others joined the hissing conversation, their words tumbling upon one another's without pause.

"Someone else has found it."

"Then why has no one come forward to present the cursed thing and claim the prize?"

"Probably because no one dares sit on Lord Glengarry's throne."

"Fiend seize ye all, I dare!" There was enough voice in the last whisper that William was able to recognize Ranulf. "No one but we five kenned it was hidden here. So which of ye bootlickers has moved it?"

A vehement round of denials followed.

"If I find which of ye has crossed me, I'll have your guts for garters," MacNaught said, forgetting to keep his voice down.

The conversation was proof that Ranulf and his gang had stolen the scepter. But it was also proof that they no longer had possession of it.

Will's gut roiled. Where was it now?

But as urgent as finding the scepter was, he couldn't let this chance to confront MacNaught pass by.

Will put an arm around Nab's shoulders and started around the corner toward MacNaught and his men, talking loudly as he went. "And so then the buxom barmaid said—Ho, now!" He stopped suddenly as if surprised to see the five men. "What are ye doing here, MacNaught?"

"What buxom barmaid, William?" Nab tugged at Will's shirtsleeve in all innocence. "I think I must have missed something. . . ."

"Never ye mind, Nab. Weel, MacNaught, this is an odd place to find ye and your men. No horn nor trencher nor chance to toss a pair of dice in sight." Will's gaze flicked to the lowest corner of the chapel where the thatch of the roof had obviously been disturbed. In troubled times when the keeping of weapons was forbidden, common folk would hide swords and dirks under the thatch of the eaves of their houses. The kirk's roof would have easily hidden the scepter as well. "Looking for a blade, are ye?"

"No need since I've one to hand." MacNaught's fingers curled around the hilt of the dirk at his waist.

"But no Scepter of Badenoch, aye?" William bared his teeth at Ranulf in an expression no one would mistake for a smile. It wouldn't hurt to let MacNaught see that Will knew him for a thief. It also wouldn't hurt to let him think Will knew exactly where the scepter was. When it came to controlling a man like MacNaught, keeping him off balance was almost as good as bashing his face in.

It just wasn't nearly as satisfying.

MacNaught fisted his hands at his waist. "What makes ye think we were after the fool's trinket?"

"A fool's trinket with magic in it, ye mean." Will noticed the quick glance that passed between Hugh Murray and Filib Gordon. He'd been right to think them susceptible to fantastic notions like a fey curse. "That's right. The Fair Folk cast a glamour on the Scepter of Badenoch. Anyone who lays hands on it unworthily will find himself with a red palm."

Gordon and Lamont Sinclair surreptitiously checked their hands. Between grubbing in the thatch searching for the scepter and the cold weather, Will was counting on all their palms being ruddy. He wasn't disappointed.

"Look, William." With an idiot's grin, Nab held up his hand. "My palm's not red."

"That's because I gave ye the scepter to hold for me. It knew ye were allowed to have it. But woe betide the man who takes the scepter with nefarious intent. After a time, the red may fade on a thief's palm, but that's when the *yeuks* start."

"The *yeuks*?" Hugh Murray said, squinting at his own hand.

"Aye, and not just on the hand that touched the scepter, mind, but anyplace on the thief's skin that hand touches thereafter."

Will feared he might be going too far, but even MacNaught wasn't immune to suggestion. He surreptitiously rubbed a hand on his plaid as if he might rub off the effects of the curse.

"I'm told 'tis unbearable. And dinna get me started on the part of the spell about what happens to a thief's manhood after he lays hold of the scepter," Will said, shaking his head. "It doesna make pretty hearing."

Ranulf blanched at this. Ainsley MacTavish gave a deep sigh. "Good thing ye wouldna let me touch it, Ranulf."

MacNaught cuffed Ainsley and told him to shut his face. Then he turned back to William. "I can see your talents are wasted on Badenoch. The way ye can spin a tale, ye ought to have been a bard instead of a laird."

"Yet I was born to Badenoch and ye were born to . . . what exactly?"

They both knew the answer. Nothing.

Ranulf's mother was Lord Glengarry's sister, and might have expected a fairly grand match had she not run off with Archibald MacNaught, holder of a minor steading and possessed of no real title, though he'd styled himself a baronet. Some might say it was actually to Ranulf's credit that since Sir Archibald's death he'd built up his father's holding and amassed more land, more cattle, and more crofters beholden to him. But he'd done it through brutality, coercion, and reiving the fruits of the hard work of others.

He spread over neighboring estates like a cancerous growth. Lord Glengarry had confessed to William that he was concerned about his nephew's intentions. It was one of the reasons he'd invited Ranulf and his cronies to spend Christmastide in the castle.

"Keep your friends close and your enemies closer," the old man had said to William that first night. But the laird's teetering health had left him unable to do much about his renegade nephew.

William figured he was right to worry about MacNaught.

"I have what I have from my own actions." Ranulf cast him an oily smile. "Fortune favors the bold, they say."

"Bold is one thing. Grabby is another. Those who overreach should take care lest they draw back naught but a bloody stub."

Ranulf's face turned a deep shade of purple and he looked as if he was about to fly at Will, but Lamont Sinclair laid a hand on his shoulder. He jerked his head toward the guards filing by on the parapet overhead.

After the beating in the main hall, William was untouchable. Standing orders had been given. If

MacNaught attacked the laird's son-in-law now, he'd be set upon at once by the earl's men.

"We'll leave ye now, Badenoch. But let us know if ye find your wee bauble, aye? 'Twould be a pity should such a treasure be lost forever. What would the House of Douglas do without it?" Ranulf and his men turned and stalked away toward the stables.

William watched them go. His gut curdled. If the scepter were truly lost, what would he do indeed?

Priests were always talking about how the living were surrounded by "a great cloud of witnesses," the souls of the departed. He wondered briefly if his forbears were hurling imprecations at him from heaven for losing the symbol of their family's strength and stature. Then he remembered that he didn't believe anything the priests said.

But it didn't ease his gut one whit.

"Weel, that's that," Will said. "They dinna have it, but I'll warrant they'll start searching for it."

"What do we do now, William?" Nab asked.

"We up the reward. If the scepter isna found by this evening, we'll sweeten the pot." He twisted the gold ring on his pinky that had belonged to his grandsire. "Tell everyone that in addition to being able to sit on the laird's throne, I'll give the finder this ring."

"That's a fine ring, William," Nab said. "But I was just wondering about something else."

"What's that, Nab?"

"What ever happened to that buxom barmaid?"

On the fifth day of Christmas,
my true love gave to me five golden rings.

—From "The Twelve Days of Christmas"

"Weel, that's a relief! I dinna think I could abide more
birds."

—An observation from Nab,
fool to the Earl of Glengarry

Chapter Fourteen

Nab parted company with William in the great hall.
Lord Badenoch headed for the kitchen, so Nab fig-
ured he was on his way back to the nursery to see if
Lady Katherine was still there. Though he'd like to
help his friend William settle matters with his wife,
Nab had another mission in mind. He'd done all that
Lord Badenoch expected of him for now and Lord
Glengarry hadn't much use for him of late.

He crept into the solar, hoping that it was vacant.
Sometimes men who wished for a quiet place in which
to play a game of chess made use of the laird's retreat,
but Nab was in luck. There was no one there.

He pulled the copy of *Le Morte d'Arthur* from under
his motley, ready to put it back up on the shelf in the

correct spot. Nab tried never to keep a book too long, lest it be missed. It was past time to return Camelot to its resting place. Besides, Dorcas hadn't enjoyed the stories of the Knights of the Round Table as much as he'd hoped.

She seemed fixated upon the fact that Queen Guinevere was consigned to the stake for her unlawful affair with Sir Lancelot while the knight in question was allowed to continue to roam free and have all sorts of adventures. The fact that Lancelot roared in to the rescue at the last moment and saved his ladylove from the flames didn't mollify Dorcas in the least.

"I dinna see why she was the only one to be burned in the first place since no one can have an affair by themselves. Why should Guinevere bear the punishment for two? No one tried to burn Lancelot," Dorcas had insisted stubbornly.

"Weel, that makes no sense. If they had, then he wouldna have been able to save her, aye?"

Dorcas was unconvinced. "'Tis still not fair."

That set Nab to scratching his head, since the whole point of the Round Table was fairness, as far as he could see. They pledged to help the weak, to defend the downtrodden, to show mercy to their enemies, and he told Dorcas so in no uncertain terms.

"They may be grand fellows when dealing with other men, but there's not a smidge of mercy in them if it's a woman who's broken the rules," Dorcas had said tartly.

So Nab tucked the book back on its shelf with a pang of regret. He still thought he'd be more at home in Camelot than ever he would in Glengarry Castle.

Nab ran his fingertips over the other books' spines. There was a treatise on animal husbandry. He didn't think Dorcas would be terribly impressed with the intricacies of cattle breeding. The one time he'd read it the book had cured him of wandering near the cattle byre for weeks.

One of the books was titled *The Confessions of St. Augustine.* Nab figured that since a saint wouldn't have much sinning to report, it couldn't be all that interesting.

There was another book he'd never tried—a volume of love poetry. Nab knew a number of ribald limericks, and an epic poem or two he could recite on command, but he hadn't committed any sonnets to memory. Ever since he'd admonished William that he'd need some poems if he was going to woo his wife, this little book of poetry had been in the back of Nab's mind.

It was even in Gaelic. According to the frontispiece, the poems were translations of verses written by monks in the eleventh century. Nab wondered what men who lived lives completely shut away from the world might have to say on the subject of love, but when he opened the book and read the first poem, he was shocked to his curled toes.

He was so lost in a tangle of rhyme and pentameter, not to mention arms and legs, that he didn't hear when someone entered the solar behind him. It was only when that someone cleared their throat loudly that he snapped the book shut and whirled to face the interloper. His face was hot, and the hands that held the book of love behind him were clammy.

But the person who'd invaded the solar was Dorcas, so he breathed a sigh of relief.

"Och, Dorcas, 'tis only ye."

"'Only ye'? What's that supposed to mean?"

"Just that I was afeared ye might be someone else."

"Someone important, I suppose?" she said archly.

"Aye, I mean, nay. That is . . . I mean—"

"I ken well enough what ye mean, Nab."

Dorcas pulled a cloth from her sleeve and began dusting the already clean chess set. The board was in a state of play and doubtless her efforts would not be appreciated, since she was careless of where she replaced each piece. But Nab was loath to say anything about it because of the vehement way she scrubbed the ivory pawn.

"Are ye angry, Dorcas?"

She glared at him. "Aren't ye the knowledgeable one?"

He swallowed hard. He'd always hated it when his parents were angry. It made him feel that there was an upturned hive in his belly. "Who are ye angry with?"

"Who d'ye think?"

Nab cast about in his mind for someone who might have upset her. "Is it Cook? I know ye get yerself in a turmoil when she thinks ye work for her and starts giving ye orders and—"

"Nay, 'tis not Cook." Dorcas shook her head so hard, Nab feared it might roll right off her shoulders. "Ye stupid, stupid man."

Nab was used to being thought a fool, but he certainly didn't expect Dorcas to think he was stupid. She knew things about him the others didn't. She'd heard him read. She'd been to his secret room. He'd have sworn she was his friend. His chest ached strangely.

"Why are ye angry with me?"

She turned to face him then, and her face crumpled. "Ye scared me half to death."

"How?"

"By sitting on the bastion roof. I was out of my mind with fear that ye'd . . . well, that ye'd . . ."

"Ye thought I'd jump? What a silly notion. I told William so too. I just wanted someplace quiet to think for a while. 'Tis not safe to go to the secret chamber in daylight, ye ken. Someone might see and then it wouldna be secret any longer, aye?"

"Sitting on the bastion isna safe either." She slammed the white king down with such force it was a wonder his crown didn't topple off. "That roof is covered with ice. One slip and . . ."

A new idea popped into his head and out of his mouth. "Ye were worried for me."

"Of course I was. Who d'ye think sent Lord Badenoch up there after ye?"

Dorcas had convinced a laird to climb up onto the bastion after him. She was very persuasive. Without realizing she did so, she persuaded him to puff out his chest a bit.

"Weel, now ye know ye need not have worried."

"Aye, I know that." She picked up the black queen and rubbed its carved face with the cloth with such vehemence it was a wonder the piece still had a nose when she was done. "And from now on, I'll do my best not to care a flying fig what happens to ye, Master Nab."

His chest sagged. That didn't sound good. He sort of liked it that she'd been worried.

"Why dinna ye care anymore?"

"I do. That's just the trouble." She replaced the black queen far from its original position so it menaced the white king.

Checkmate, Nab almost said, but then he decided Dorcas wouldn't appreciate a change of topic.

"Ye're the one who doesna care," she said. "Ye dinna care one whit. Ye climb down from the bastion as if nothing's happened and do ye come straight to me to ease my mind? Me, who's the only one who cares a flibbet about ye? No, ye dinna." She swabbed one side of the chess board, knocking a whole phalanx of pawns on their faces. "Instead ye flit about the castle on every other business under the sun."

That sounded vaguely insulting. "I dinna flit."

"Ye know what I mean."

"I wasna flitting. I was doing things for William. Important things."

"More important than letting me know ye are all right?" She gave him her back and returned to scouring the chess pieces.

For the first time in his life, a small fire kindled in his belly. This must be what angry felt like, he decided, but it wasn't his fault. Dorcas was being unreasonable. "If ye kenned I was down from the bastion, ye kenned well enough that I was all right."

A hapless bishop slipped from her hand and rolled across the floor, but she didn't go after it. Instead, Dorcas just stood there. Her shoulders shook and her head hung down.

"Dorcas?" He tiptoed over to her and almost put a hand on her shoulder, but stopped himself at the last moment. He didn't like being touched. Maybe Dorcas didn't either. "Are *ye* all right?"

"No, I'm not." She erupted in full-blown sobs. Then she turned and threw her arms around Nab's neck. He'd have been less surprised if she'd pummeled him.

"Dinna cry, Dorcas. Please, dinna."

At first, when she clung to him, he got that hot and jittery feeling that always accompanied being touched, but as her body relaxed against his, the feeling changed. He decided he didn't mind so badly when Dorcas touched him. Hesitantly, he patted her back with his free hand since he still clutched the book of love poems in the other.

"The man I care about doesna care about me one bit," she said with a sniff.

"Then he's a very stupid man."

She pulled back and looked him straight in the eye. To his surprise, he was able to meet her gaze. "Aye," she said with a crooked smile, "he is that."

Dorcas tried to peer around him. "What is it ye've got there?"

Nab didn't know whether to be relieved or bereft that she was no longer so close. He'd never felt like this before. Her smile, even a crooked one, made him feel as if he'd swallowed a moonbeam. No, a whole jar of honey without becoming ill. No, it was . . . it was . . . well, he wasn't sure just what it was, and he wasn't sure he liked it.

If a body got too happy, it was like a prayer to the devil. Excessive happiness was a sure sign things were about to turn in the other direction. But for now, Dorcas was smiling at him, so he decided to wallow in the moonbeam.

Who knew when he'd ever feel like this again?

He held the book out for her to see. "I was picking out something new to read to you since you didna much care for King Arthur."

"I didna say that. It's just that he didna practice being such a fair king with his own queen."

"Ye must admit she did him a grievous hurt."

"So did Lancelot, but I didna notice him being led to the stake in naught but his nightshift."

Nab sighed. Not this again. He gave himself a shake. Where had the moonbeam gone? "In any case, I thought ye might fancy this book instead."

She eyed the new volume. "What is it?"

"Weel, I havena read it yet myself, ye ken, but 'tis supposed to be love poems."

He'd thought her smile the finest thing he'd ever seen. He was wrong. He'd only seen the smallest part of her smile. It bloomed now like a living thing, like the sun in its radiance. Even if it struck him blind, Nab couldn't look away.

"Read me one," she said, crowding close again.

She smelled of sweet soap and bread and linen that had been dried in the sun. Even if he could tear his gaze away from her long enough to read anything, Nab wondered if his mouth would work.

"Quick," she said, "before someone comes!"

He opened the book and started to read the first poem he came to:

From Fate's cruel wounds I cry 'Alack!'
For Love has turned to me attack.
Her bountiful gifts she keeps from me
And makes me beg on bended knee.
And all because, tho' 'tis not fair,
My well-thatched head has lost its hair.

Dorcas snorted. "If that's what this ninnyhammer of a poet thinks passes for a love poem, I can well believe his lady makes him beg."

"Ye dinna think 'tis on account of his bald head?" Nab didn't think he'd like it much if a lady lost her hair. It stood to reason that shoe would fit the other foot as well.

"Nay, of course not. Bald or old or brick-headed, Love doesna think on those sorts of things."

"Love canna think on anything," he pointed out. "Love isna a person so it doesna have a brain, ye ken."

Dorcas scowled at him. "Sometimes I think ye dinna have one either. 'My well-thatched head has lost its hair,' indeed. Bring the book to the secret room and find me a better poem by nightfall."

She flounced out of the solar with a flip of her skirts.

First she smiled, then she scowled. First she scoffed at his poem, then she demanded another. Nab rubbed the back of his neck. He didn't know which way she'd turn him next.

Still, there was a bit of that moonbeam dancing inside him. So he slid down into a corner of the room with the book and flipped through the pages, looking for a poem Dorcas might like.

Love doesna think on those sorts of things, she'd said.

He was still pretty sure Love couldn't think at all, but if it could, Nab wondered what Love would think on. Would it think on red hair or a slight frame or someone who was thought a fool by the rest of the world?

What sort of things made a body love another anyway?

Or not.

On the sixth day of Christmas,
My true love gave to me six geese a-laying.

—From "The Twelve Days of Christmas"

"And we're back to the winged demons again. What?
Ye dinna think a goose smacks of the Fiery Pit? Ye ne'er
have run afoul of one then, I warrant. There's not a
meaner creature on God's earth. Were I to receive such
a gift, and six of them no less, I'd suspect my true love
didna bear me any love at all."

—An observation from Nab,
fool to the Earl of Glengarry

Chapter Fifteen

Katherine finally relinquished her nephews to the care of their nurse, and since old Beathag assured her that Margaret was resting comfortably, she stripped out of her clothes and lay down on her bed in her shift to catch up on some much needed sleep. She only expected to snatch an hour at most, but the feather tick wrapped her in a thick embrace and she slept like the dead. It was long past time to dress for supper and join the revelers in the great hall below when something finally roused her.

She was used to the noisiness of a castle. In Glengarry, as in Badenoch, there was always someone rattling about during the daytime, even without the press of extra guests and the excitement of the holidays. She could ignore at will the determined hum of a working keep. Or even one bent on frivolity and merriment. But it wasn't the sound of pipes and song wafting up the spiral stairs that pried her from her dreams.

It was the smell of warm bread.

The yeasty summons caused her eyelids to flutter open and her mouth to water. When she came fully awake, she found William standing by her bedside, bearing a tray. Tall, broad, and impeccably dressed in a fresh shirt and plaid, the man himself looked good enough to eat, never mind what was on the tray.

"Time to wake and have some supper, love." His rumbling baritone shivered over her. "The day is spent, and Dorcas tells me ye've not taken a bite."

After first taking care of Margaret, and then the youngest members of her brood, Kat decided it was nice to have someone take care of her for a change. She sat up and plumped the pillows behind her back.

"Ye should know better than to listen to Dorcas," she advised. "She talks too much."

"So I noticed. She also has a wicked hand with a broom," Will said as he settled the tray across her lap. In addition to the fresh bread, the trencher was laden with Forfar Bridies, haggis, neeps and tatties, as well as thick slices of goose with brambleberry relish. For good measure, there was even a bowl of Clootie Dumpling swimming in rich cream.

"I canna eat all this," Katherine said.

"I was counting on that." William helped himself to one of her bridies and took a bite of the pastry. Hitching his hip on the side of the bed, he settled in beside

Katherine. Then he held the bridie out for her. "Try this. I dinna know what Cook used for the crust, but they're light enough to float away. We need to convince her to share the secret with our Mrs. MacGuff. Her pastries are like lead weights. I could use one to hold down the stack of ledgers on my desk."

Katherine laughed. Their cook at Badenoch was a crotchety old lady who hadn't tried a new recipe in decades. "Dinna tell Mrs. MacGuff that or she'll put a spider in your tea."

"Try it and tell me 'tis not worth the risk." He tore off a corner of the bridie and lifted the bite to Katherine's lips.

It fairly melted on her tongue. In addition to the crusty pastry, a unique mix of spices seasoned the savory meat inside, a burst of sensations for her mouth. "Och, you're right. This is worth braving a spider. I'll get Cook to show me how she makes these, and then Mrs. MacGuff will either learn from me or she'll have to suffer my presence in her kitchen from time to time. And we know how she loves that!"

"So," he said smugly, his dark eyes alight with triumph, "ye do intend to come home with me after Christmas, then."

Katherine bit her tongue. Blame it on lack of sleep or inadequate food or simply the fact that William Douglas sitting on her bed was the finest thing a woman could ever hope to see in all her living life, but somehow her plan to petition Rome for an annulment had flown completely out of her head. Now, however, the notion was back with a vengeance.

She helped herself to the flagon of small beer and buried her nose in it. She needed to fortify her resolve.

"I'll take your silence for a 'yes,'" Will said amiably

and speared a slice of goose with his knife. "But I want ye to know I was prepared to court ye, Kat."

"Court me? Whyever for?"

"Because I didna do it properly the first time."

Katherine hadn't expected him to court her before they wed. Their marriage contract had been settled before she was out of leading strings. They knew each other as children. Their families often met for fairs and festivals midway between their two estates.

"Ye're right about that. Ye certainly didna court me properly," she said between bites of her meal. "One of my earliest memories of ye is that summer at the fair when I was minding my own business looking at the chandler's wares. Once my back was turned, ye dipped a full foot length of my braid in a vat of yellow wax."

William laughed at the memory. "Ye canna fault me there. Ye were not paying the least attention to me, which is the worst thing ye can do to a ten-year-old boy. I had to do something."

"Ye commanded my attention all right, but not in the way ye might have wished. Have ye any notion how hard it is to get wax out of hair?" In the end, her mother had simply snipped off the ruined braid. Katherine had vowed eternal enmity toward all lads in general and William Douglas in particular that summer. "I hated ye fine then."

"Weel, if we're bearing our souls, I'll admit I wasna too taken with the notion of such a skinny little flat-chested slip of a girl for my future bride either." His gaze wandered below her chin and down to her breasts. "Of course, it was my great good fortune that ye didna stay flat-chested."

Katherine's nipples tightened under his scrutiny, but she didn't want to encourage him, so she snorted.

"Good thing ye didna stay so irritating." After that

rocky start, their relationship improved over the years, and by the time she was of age, Katherine didn't dread becoming Lady Badenoch quite so much. Her only surprise when she joined Will at the altar for their wedding was how tall and broad shouldered he'd become between one summer and the next.

"Just out of curiosity," Katherine said, "how did ye plan to court me?"

"Weel, ye may not have noticed, but I started already. Firstly, I arranged to spirit ye out of the castle on my trusty steed."

"So ye didna really need extra weight on Greyfellow for him to get his exercise?"

William shook his head and helped himself to a swig of her small beer. "That was just a convenient excuse to have ye to myself. Then, there was the gift I brought ye."

"Oh." Katherine gnawed her lower lip. "I'm sorry to have to tell ye that I lost the muff, Will."

"I know. I found it when I trudged back to the castle in the snow. 'Tis in your clothing chest, though I fear there may yet be a few thorns from the gorse bush stuck in it."

Katherine covered her mouth with her hand. If she could keep from making any sound, perhaps he'd think she was embarrassed instead of trying to keep from laughing. He was trying so hard, but so far, Will's attempts at courtship were the stuff of minstrel plays. Whatever could go wrong invariably had.

She lowered her gaze. When she was able to contain herself, she murmured her thanks. It really was sweet of him to have braved the thorns to retrieve her muff.

She used a piece of bread to scoop up some of the neeps and tatties and nibbled daintily. "Thank ye for supper too. I didna realize how hungry I was. But surely ye dinna think bringing me food is a way to woo me."

"No, wife. Seeing ye fed is my husbandly duty. However, teasing ye with a bit of sweets might fall under the category of courting." He used his finger to scoop up a bit of the dumpling and held his other hand beneath it lest some of the cream drip off while he brought it to her lips.

She accepted his offering, relishing the thick, fruity dumpling, rich with nutmeg and cinnamon spiciness. Then she sucked every bit of cream from his finger. He made a low groan.

"Who's wooing who now?" she asked with a grin.

"I reckon we've taken turns wooing each other over the years." He touched the corner of his mouth to indicate that she had something on hers. She flicked out her tongue, but he shook his head. "'Tis still there. Let me."

He leaned forward and licked at that juncture of warm flesh and moist intimacy, then covered her mouth with his in a sweet, cinnamon-laden kiss. When he would have slanted his lips over hers and deepened the kiss, she pressed a palm to his chest.

"I thought it was your husbandly duty to see me fed."

"Aye, but a man has appetites too, ye know."

"As does a woman. Ye taught me that." She'd been surprised when he'd confessed on their wedding night that he was as untried as she in matters of the flesh. Yet, curiosity and natural attraction had led them to the proper use of their young bodies. "Ye taught me many things."

"And verra pleasurable lessons they've been too, in both the giving and receiving," he said.

They'd explored. They'd savored. By the flickering light of the fire, Katherine's first glimpse of William in the altogether on their wedding night fair took her breath away. Smooth skin pulled taut over tightly corded muscle. A dusting of dark hair whorled around his brown nipples. A thin strip ran from his navel and spread over his groin. Then there was *himself*, that glorious rod of maleness risen like a tower toward her. It was almost an entity unto itself. Of all William's mysteries, the secrets hidden in that part of him were the ones she most wanted to unriddle.

But he'd been intent on uncovering all of her secrets as well. He left no square inch of her unexplored. Every place he touched, her skin sparked with pleasure. She ached in places she'd never thought possible and strained at the hollowness she felt. When he'd finally filled her with himself, she thought she'd never feel empty again.

Neither of them had been disappointed that first night, though it had taken several weeks of trial and error before William discovered the true magic he could coax her body to perform. The first time he drove her to completion, she thought she might die.

Then she did, a little. She died to any life other than one devoted to this man. And then, though she loved William more than her next breath, she had known emptiness again.

The emptiness of a barren womb.

Which was why she had to be strong now and make the decision that was best for him, whether he wanted her to or not.

But if she kept thinking about their wedding night and he kept looking at her with those dark eyes of his, she'd not be able to think straight. Katherine needed to be rational for both of them.

She set the supper tray aside and climbed out of bed. If she stayed where she was, he'd be joining her in a few moments. The way her body ached in certain places, she knew she wouldn't have the heart to say him nay. Hoping to keep him talking, she asked, "What else did ye have in mind for courting me?"

The tenor of the music wafting up from below changed just then. The bagpipes were stilled and the gentle sounds of the harp and lute replaced them.

William rose from his seat on the bed and lifted a hand to her. "I thought we might dance."

"I didna know ye could."

"Donald isna the only one who's spent time at court, ye ken. The winter before we wed, I was in Edinburgh trying to see which of the dukes who'd been reigning in our young king's stead might still be in favor once he reached his majority." Will gave her a surprisingly courtly bow. "In the process, I inadvertently picked up a dance step or two. That song is perfect for the volta. Do ye ken it?"

Unlike the vigorous reels usually danced in long lines within Glengarry's keep, the volta was an intimate dance for just two. Kat's father had thought it a silly extravagance, but before her mother died, she'd engaged a dancing master for Katherine and seen that her daughter could manage the steps of courtly dance.

"Just in case, my Katikins, ye've need to comport yourself well at court sometime," her mother had told her with a wink. She'd sat and watched with approval while Katherine learned to heel and toe. Kat's mother had never enjoyed vigorous health, and in the last summer of her decline, Lady Glengarry was the one who encouraged Donald to start spending more time in Edinburgh.

"Wars are not always won on the field of battle, my son," she'd told him. "More often victory comes after a well-played chess match with the right adversary or an elegantly danced pavan before the right set of eyes."

Katherine's mother would have laughed if she could have seen her now, dipping in a low curtsey as if she were dressed in her best finery instead of just her shift. It had been a long time since she'd danced, but her muscles remembered the steps. Once she executed hers, William answered them with unexpectedly good form.

They moved toward each other and then away, in oblique lines, arms arranged in stylized movements, feet making crisp turns.

"Dance is the essence of courtship, the duality and duplicity of wooing," her mother's voice echoed in her mind. *"I love you. I hate you. Come here. Go away."*

With each pass, they drew nearer to each other. When William made a tight circle around her, his fingertips brushed her hips through the thin linen shift. The way her bum tingled, she was sure his touch had made her skin rosy.

I love you, her heart whispered.

He took her hand and lifted her arm over her head, leading Kat in a slow turn that brought her to rest against his chest, facing away from him. She reached up to stroke his cheek as the dance demanded. The stubble on his chin was both soft and bristly beneath her fingertips. His mouth lifted in a smile.

I hate you. She had to. She owed it to William to free him.

Then she twirled away as the dance required, only to be captured by Will and turned in his arms again. They moved together, floating in time with the delicate music. Then at the melody's climax, Will lifted her high with hands on her waist and turned her in a slow circle as if she weighed nothing.

Come here.

She couldn't help herself. It was like flying. Katherine tipped her head back and closed her eyes. Then he lowered her, close to his body, so that hers slid along his, every muscle, every bulge, every bit of her straining to fit with every bit of him. When her toes finally touched the ground, he didn't release her.

Their breathing hitched from exertion. Katherine could feel Will's heart pounding and knew he felt hers as well. Without a word, without asking, because they both knew he had every right, Will bent to press his lips to her exposed neck.

She couldn't bring herself to even think *Go away.*

On the seventh day of Christmas
My true love gave to me seven swans a-swimming.

—From "The Twelve Days of Christmas"

*"A practical gift since Cook makes a fine roasted swan.
Besides, the loch's nearly frozen over and too many
swimming birds in a small spot of open water might
tempt the waterhorse to show himself. And trust me, we
want that nary at all."*

—An observation from Nab,
fool to the Earl of Glengarry

Chapter Sixteen

Katherine's skin tasted lightly of salt and warm
woman. She melted against him, soft and pliant. That
prickly, temperamental standoffishness was completely
gone. She was no longer a rigid, saintlike touch-me-not.

He had his Kat back again.

She arched into him.

Willing. Shyly enthusiastic, even. God help him, he
hoped she was already as wet and eager as she seemed
to be because he didn't know how long he could wait.

When he kissed her, she kissed him back. Not the
desperate, "give-me-a-child-or-I-die" kisses that had

characterized their lovemaking since losing Stephan. These kisses were gentle, almost questioning. As if she were trying to rediscover who he was by exploring his mouth. He let her, though it cost him dear to hold back.

Still, he couldn't keep his hands from being wanderers, sliding over her, feeling every curve, every dip. He was tinglingly aware of her in a way he hadn't been for a long time. He knew this woman's body, but now he reveled in every remembered crease and angle.

But he noted a few differences from his mental version of Kat too. Her hips were a little wider, her breasts a little smaller. No matter. She was his. He felt very proprietary about every bit of her. Protectiveness swelled in his chest. He could see the dark shadows of her nipples, hard and straining against the thin linen of her shift.

He bent to take one into his mouth, sucking in her taut nub and the shift and the sweet lavender, the herb with which she freshened all her clothing, in a glorious mouthful. Over time, lavender had come to be ingrained on her skin. The fragrance was her. Now he knew what it tasted like, all green and minty with a hint of apple sweetness.

When he finally drew back, he continued to tease the tip of her breast through the shift, letting the linen scrape her charged flesh. Even if she'd been naked, the bedchamber was too dim for him to make out the color of her nipples. It didn't matter. He knew they were a dark berry shade.

They'd been light pink when he married her, but after Stephan, even though she never gave the child suck, the areola around each tip had darkened. It wasn't only physical things about Katherine that had changed.

She'd stopped dallying in their love play, always

anxious to rush ahead to the final event that might result in a child.

But now she surprised him when she stooped to slide her hands under his kilt, up his thighs and then came back to stand on tiptoe for another kiss with her fingers fluttering over his groin.

Teasing. Playful.

His leg muscles went rock hard. His cock was already there. She fondled him, cupping his bag. Lord, he'd missed that, the way she'd take hold of him and stroke him, intent on pleasuring him instead of demanding he serve her and make a child because the moon was right and some old midwife had told her it was the most propitious time in her cycle for conceiving and it had to be now or never.

Of course, she'd kept him at bay for the last four months trying to keep from losing her most recent pregnancy, so he'd begun to look back at those days when she demanded he perform like a stallion with longing. He'd almost forgotten what it was like to make love to his wife simply because he wanted to.

It had been long enough for him to forget other things as well. William raised one of her arms and kissed along the crease of her elbow. He'd forgotten the small mole that hid there in the crook of her arm. He gave it a soft kiss.

"I love ye," he whispered. *Every bit of ye,* he finished silently because his mouth was busy elsewhere. He kissed her temples, her cheeks, along her jaw to her ear.

She made a helpless little noise of need when he took her earlobe between his lips and gave it a nip. It almost made up for the fact that she didn't say she loved him back.

He couldn't remember the last time she'd said it.

Then she distracted him by tugging at the buckle of his belt. Katherine groaned into his mouth with frustration when she couldn't seem to undo the catch.

"Let me before ye break it, woman," he said with a chuckle as he undid the belt that held his plaid at his waist. After that, it was a simple matter to let the great kilt fall to the floor. He pulled his shirt over his head to stand before her bare as an egg save for his stockings and boots.

He took her in his arms again, rucking up her shift in handfuls so he could pull it over her head between one kiss and the next. Her mouth was so sweet he almost couldn't bear to release it for the brief slice of time it took to slip off her shift. Once he got it off her, he tossed the shift into the corner.

Skin met skin. Oh, the feel of her, all soft and smooth. He'd never let her go.

Love me, Kat. The words repeated in his brain like a song he was unable to find the end of. *I've loved ye since I dipped your braid in that wax. Dinna fret about making a child. Let me be enough for ye. Ye're enough for me.*

His heart sang the words, but his tongue couldn't bend around them. Once spoken, words were chancy things. If he said them aloud, they'd hang in the air between him and Kat forever, never to be called back. Even though he meant them consolingly, they might send her down the path of melancholy over her childlessness again.

Or worse, she might decide he wasn't enough.

He deepened their kiss and palmed her bum, lifting her against him. To his joy, she hooked her legs around his waist. Suddenly he didn't need her to say anything.

If that's not love, what is?

He began backing her toward the bed.

She tore her mouth from his. "Not yet."

God's Teeth, if not now, when? He swallowed back his oath and spat out a single word. It was all he could trust his voice with.

"Soon?"

Even that came out like a growl, rough with desire.

"As soon as ye take off your boots, William Douglas. We canna have ye soilin' the linen now, can we?"

"Now?" Katherine gasped. Every muscle in her body strained with the effort of holding back. In the early days of their marriage, William had learned to play her body with a skill to rival the most celebrated harpist. His touch was light when he wanted to tease, determined and insistent when she needed it to be, and gentle when he was drawing out the final ebbing pulses of her release.

Even so, once their lovemaking had become more about making a bairn than shared joy, Katherine had been too tense for pleasure. More than once, she'd pretended. She wasn't sure William could tell the difference. If he'd known she had only played at her release, he didn't confront her or ask what was amiss.

Once again, they hid from each other, cloaked by silence.

It had seemed like a small lie that first time. What could it hurt that she feigned a release that didn't seem likely to come? Then the small lie blossomed into a large one. In a very short time, she found she couldn't tell him what she needed from him, even when he asked. After a while, he stopped asking. It became one more wedge to divide them, one more brick in the wall they'd erected between them.

This time, however, he'd told her to try *not* to come.

And perversely, she'd never been wound so tight. She danced along the edge of release, advancing, then retreating, just like in the volta. *Come here. Go away.*

She ached—blood, bones, and womb—she ached so intensely, she feared she'd shatter like a brittle bit of crockery if he didn't let her come soon.

"Now?" she whimpered.

"Soon, love, soon."

She drew in a deep breath but his warm musky scent shoved her closer to the edge. *Go away.* William had said to wait and she was determined to be honest this time. She was going to try.

Then Will climbed atop her. Balancing his weight on his elbows, he entered her. He drove his full length home in a single, slow thrust. She closed her eyes as his thick shaft slid into her.

Katherine expanded to receive him, stretched taut. It had been so long since she'd held him like this, she'd almost forgotten what it was like to be filled with him. She teetered on the edge of release, fighting the downward spiral in her belly.

Go away, she ordered her impending climax. Will had a plan for them. She was determined to make it work as he wanted this time.

William held himself motionless, willing her to regain control, but in her heightened state of awareness she felt the blood pounding through him like a second heart between her legs.

He was as primed as she.

Why had he not released them both?

He cradled her cheeks with his palms and searched her face, his eyes feral in the dimness. Slowly, he lowered his mouth to hers and began a rhythm with his tongue to echo the thrust of his hips. She rose to meet him, desperation making her sob into his mouth.

Come here.

The wanting was so keen, a sliver's edge from pain.

Did he know she'd lied before? Was that why he wouldn't let her body go now?

Doubt made her release sidle farther away.

Come here.

Whether he said so or not, she was ready to welcome her bliss, but pleasure retreated again. She turned her head to pull her mouth from his. "I can't—"

"Dinna fret about if ye can or can't. Dinna try so hard. Just be, lass."

He knew. He knew she'd pretended. And he'd pretended all along that he didn't know. A lie for a lie. That's what they'd come to.

"Now, lass. I know ye want to," he finally said. "Come to me when ye will."

Of course, she wanted to. With every fiber of her being, she longed to feel those deep contractions pounding around him. She wanted to squeeze him tight without consciously working those little muscles, for her body to claim his and not let go. She ached for pleasure to crackle like heat lightning along her limbs, for the force of her release to make her body buck under his.

But instead, her pinnacle slipped farther away with each thrust. She tried. Her body tensed with concentration as she tried to call back the moment, back to the place where she'd been about to tumble into the waiting abyss and didn't care because William was there to catch her. Bliss would buoy her up.

But she couldn't find it.

Will was saying something in rhythm with his thrusts, but his voice faded in sibilant echoes and she couldn't hear him. She knew he was right there, pumping in and out of her body, but she felt as if he were a long way off.

She was alone. And she couldn't find her way back to him.

Her moisture began to dry up. What had begun as pleasure was turning quickly into burning pain.

A small sob escaped her throat. She didn't mean for it to. She meant to lie very still and bear up until he was finished because she loved him. She didn't want to hurt him by admitting her body wouldn't rouse to him.

William evidently could hear the difference between a sob of lust and a sob of pain. He stopped, pulled out, and rolled off her. Losing him so suddenly made her feel as empty as when Stephan had been taken from her arms that last time.

Will lay beside her, staring up into the thatch of the ceiling, not touching her. His chest heaved. The air was musky with sex, pregnant with unfulfilled promises.

"Lord, Katherine, ye're tearing my guts out." He flung a well-muscled arm up and across his eyes. "Can ye not bear me at all?"

It wasn't that. "Of course, I can bear ye," she murmured.

"Ye just dinna love me any longer."

She loved him fine. She loved him too much. It was all her fault, she wanted to say. He did everything just as she liked. Even making her wait had added so much wicked anticipation to their lovemaking. Until she had too much time to think instead of just feel.

Once she realized he'd caught her in the lie, nothing would go right. Her body didn't work properly. Not to make love to her husband. Not to carry his child.

She owed him that annulment. It was the best thing she could do for him. She couldn't tell him how she loved him or he'd never agree to it.

After this, surely he'd agree to send a request to Rome. That deadly silence was back. It hung between them, rotten as a cancerous growth. She reached over to lay a tentative hand on his shoulder, to soften what she was about to say. He startled as if she were an adder poised to strike and scrambled from the bed.

"William, I—"

"Not a word, woman," he growled as he pulled his shirt over his head. "It took ye too long to answer. Whatever ye might say now will no doubt be a lie. God knows our marriage bed has been."

She flinched at the anger in his tone.

He wrapped his plaid around his waist. He didn't take time to pleat it, but simply strapped on the belt to hold it in place. He plopped into the only chair in the chamber and, with a grunt of effort, tugged on his boots. Then he stood. The room was too dim for her to make out his expression, but pain radiated from his stiff stance.

"I'll trouble ye no more, my lady." Then he turned and disappeared down the spiral stairwell.

On the eighth day of Christmas
my true love gave to me eight maids a-milking.

—From "The Twelve Days of Christmas"

"Fine. Someone to help with the chores. But what good
are milkmaids when I havena got any kine?"

—An observation from Nab,
fool to the Earl of Glengarry

Chapter Seventeen

Nab sat in his tower room, fiddling with the book of poetry by the light of a tallow candle. It seemed he'd been there for hours, waiting and hoping that Dorcas would be able to slip away from her duties to join him. Since Lord Glengarry had been feeling poorly, he'd sent Nab away, saying it hurt to laugh.

"Hurts to laugh," Nab muttered. Of all the foolish things. Laughter was supposed to do a body good. Like medicine, the Good Book said. Yet laughter caused Lord Glengarry pain. "And they call me odd."

But it was just as well. After Nab reminded the revelers in the keep that the Rod of Misrule, which was what he'd taken to calling William's scepter, had still not been found, his followers scrambled to continue the search. Nab had plenty of time to himself. He used it to ruminate on all the poems in the book so he could be certain to present Dorcas with the best one this time. He was worried about making a choice, though, because he'd felt the one about the poor bald fellow was rippingly good.

It had a catchy rhyme scheme and Nab thought "well-thatched" was a clever way to describe a full head of hair. Dorcas hadn't been the least bit impressed.

Nab sighed. There was just no telling what a lass might fancy.

He'd finally settled on a poem, but he fretted about it. For one thing, it didn't even rhyme. For that reason, he wasn't sure what it was doing in a book of poetry, but someone must have thought there was something to it or they wouldn't have painstakingly copied it in ornate script.

He ran through the words again, his lips moving as he read silently.

"Has that book bewitched ye?"

He looked up to see Dorcas climbing the last of the steps. *No, ye've bewitched me,* danced on his tongue. That's what a lover might say.

But Nab wasn't a lover. He was a fool.

"I was just practicing a poem."

"Oh, good. So ye found one, did ye?"

"Aye, would ye like to hear it?" He scrambled to his feet. Somehow, he thought the poem might seem more impressive if he was standing.

"In a bit. I need to rest myself. Between seeing to Lady Margaret and helping out in the nursery and following Cook's every uppity order, I'm all done in." She sank onto the wolf pelt, her legs tucked neatly beneath her skirts. Then she patted the spot next to her.

Nab sat, obedient as a child, and opened the book. He cleared his throat noisily.

"What's wrong with ye?" Dorcas demanded. "Ye sound as if ye swallowed a bullfrog."

"No, I was just fixin' to read ye a poem."

"And I asked ye to wait. Honestly, Nab, can't a lass stretch her legs a bit first?" She suited her actions to her words and leaned back on her arms while she lifted first one foot and then the other a few inches off the floor. Pointing her toes, she drew small circles in the air.

She had neat, slender ankles.

Nab swallowed hard. His tongue seemed to cleave to the roof of his mouth and that hot, jittery feeling— the good one, not the bad—began to spread through his whole body. He couldn't read a poem now even if his hope of heaven depended upon it.

Fortunately, he wasn't expected to even speak. Dorcas was capable of carrying on a conversation all by herself. She went on about which scullery maid was sweet on which stable lad and how many of the laird's guests had found themselves twisted up in someone else's cloak besides their lawful spouse's during the course of the Yuletide revelries.

"There'll be hell to pay when they return to their own homes, I assure ye," she said.

Then she berated Cook for her high-handed ways and complained bitterly that the nursemaid left all of Tam's napkin changing for her to do.

"And it'll only get worse once the newest little bairn is born, for then there'll be two wee bums to keep clean." Dorcas sighed, but then a dreamy smile spread over her face. "But I'll not deny 'tis a fine thing indeed to hold a new little one in my arms."

This confused Nab so much, he was finally able to

find his tongue. "But I thought ye said another bairn would make more work for ye."

"Some work I dinna mind so much. And caring for a new babe is that sort of work. Because they've not been long in this world, they've a bit of heaven's fragrance still clinging to them. That's why ye watch them even while they sleep, lest the angels come to take them back. But that's when they're clean, of course."

"And when they're not clean, even Old Scratch willna take them." Nab made a horrible face and pinched his nose.

Dorcas laughed.

Pride swelled Nab's chest. Usually when people laughed at him, he wasn't quite sure what he'd done or said to make them do it. This time, he'd tried to make someone laugh and succeeded. That the someone was Dorcas made it even better.

And while Dorcas made much of how babies smelled, he thought she smelled pretty good herself. He leaned toward her and sniffed.

"Seems to me ye've a bit of heaven clinging to ye too," he said.

"Och, that's only a slice of mince pie. Would ye like some?" She pulled a wrapped parcel from her pocket, and between the two of them, they made short work of the treat. Nab was a trifle disappointed that she was too busy licking her own fingers to lick his this time. "My old mam always told me the way to a man's heart is through his stomach."

"Really? That seems a bit awkward because my heart is here and my stomach is there." He touched first his chest and then his belly. Then he squinted quizzically at Dorcas. "Just where did yer mother think to make her entry?"

This time when she laughed, Nab had no idea why.

Then her merriment faded and she frowned down at her hands in her lap. "I think a bairn is the cause of Lord and Lady Badenoch's troubles. Or rather, the lack of one."

After what Nab had overheard on the curtain wall on Christmas Day, he was sure of it, but as much as he liked Dorcas, he didn't feel he should add to her arsenal of gossip.

That quiver was already full.

"But if they love each other, it will all come right, dinna ye think?" he asked as he dusted his hands together to shake off the last of the mince pie crumbs since no finger licking seemed imminent.

"I hope so. Ye should see her with wee Tam, though, when she thinks no one sees. Her arms are aching for a bairn of her own and nothing else will fill them." Dorcas leaned her chin in her hand. "And before I came here, I saw Lord Badenoch stalking around the great hall this night like a lost soul when he ought to be in his lady's bed." Dorcas made a tsking sound. "Thinking on them makes me sad. I dinna see what they're to do. I'll be needing that poem now to cheer my heart."

"Oh!" The book had left his hands at some point while they were eating mince pie and talking about Lord William and his good lady and become hidden under them. Nab scrabbled through the mass of old horse blankets and the wolf pelt and came up with it. Then he flipped through the pages till he found the right poem. He started to rise.

"No, stay, Nab. I may not know how to read, but I like to look at the page while ye do. I follow the marks and squiggles with my eyes. 'Tis sort of like a maze on the pages. I find it restful." Dorcas leaned into him and settled her head on his shoulder. "Go ahead. I'm ready to hear my poem now."

Nab drew a deep breath and forced himself to read slowly so he wouldn't stumble over any of the words.

Love me truly!
My heart is constant.
Ye possess my soul.
Ye tangle up my thoughts in silken cords,
But I dinna wish to be freed.
Even if ye're afar off,
My spirit is with ye, not in my poor body.
To know such love is to know the torture of the rack.

"Och, Nab!" Dorcas gasped and threw her arms around him. "I had no idea ye loved me so exceeding fine."

Nab's eyebrows shot skyward. He'd had no idea either. He'd thought he was just reading her a poem.

Then she palmed his cheeks and kissed him right on the mouth. It was a bodhran-busting, bell-jangling sort of kiss and it reverberated clear to his toes.

Maybe he did love her exceeding fine. He decided it was worth another kiss to find out.

On the ninth day of Christmas
my true love gave to me nine ladies dancing.

—From "The Twelve Days of Christmas"

"Whist! I canna talk now. I've a passel of dancing
ladies cavorting about my mind, aye?"

—An observation from Nab,
fool to the Earl of Glengarry

Chapter Eighteen

Will woke when one of the men-at-arms near him loosed a snuffling snore. He rubbed his stiff neck and looked around. Most of the castle's inhabitants were still asleep where they'd collapsed at the end of their carousing last night.

He pushed himself upright from the slouching position he'd assumed sometime during the wee hours. The big Tudor chair flanking the fireplace in the great hall wasn't the most comfortable place to sleep, but it beat curling up in his plaid on the floor. The rushes were none too sweet after a few nights of Christmastide revels, though plenty of Lord Glengarry's guests were sprawled on them. William's other choice had been to head for the stable and make himself at home in the haymow, but little Angus had presented him with so many rat carcasses of late, he decided the chair was his best option.

He'd claimed it for the last three nights.

He damned sure wasn't going to return to Katherine's bed. Her welcome would freeze a man's balls more surely than a wintry blast.

But evidently she didn't have that effect on dogs because the terrier came hopping down the spiral staircase, presumably after sleeping with his mistress all night. He made a beeline across the hall and jumped onto William's lap without an invitation.

"Trying to stay on both our good sides, are ye?" He scratched Angus behind the ear, setting his hind leg thumping. "Or are ye just using me to stay out of reach of the deerhounds?"

From their place before the banked fire, the big dogs raised their heads and curled back their lips to show their teeth at Angus. The terrier barked at them, safely ensconced in Will's arms. A number of sleepers scattered about the hall rolled over, cursed, and then sank back into slumber. The deerhounds flopped back down, jaws resting on their forepaws, studiously ignoring Angus. As long as he had William's protection, the little dog wasn't worth the effort.

"Careful, laddie." Nab's voice came from the foot of the spiral stairs. "Pissin' into the wind is like to get ye wet."

"Angus isna smart enough to heed your advice, Nab."

"Weel, if it comes to that, only a fool would take advice from one." Nab crossed over to squat beside Will's chair as he often did beside Lord Glengarry's.

"But I wasna talking to the dog. I was talkin' to ye, William."

"Me? I'm just sitting here minding my own business."

"No, ye're not. Ye're neglecting yer business. Ye said ye were going to woo Lady Katherine, but ye haven't spoken a word to her the last few days. Odds bodkins, if she enters a room, ye leave it. Whatever's ailing the pair of ye, ye're being stubborn to spite yerself about it."

"Ye're right, Nab."

"I am?" A smile split his lean face.

"Only a fool takes a fool's advice." William put Angus down. The dog scrabbled under the trestle tables, then streaked across the hall to the spiral stairs. The biggest deerhound rose and gave chase but pulled up sharply at the foot of the steps while Angus bounded up them. Lord Glengarry didn't allow his hunting dogs into the family's portion of the keep, but the little terrier had no such restrictions. He was free to go and come from his mistress's chamber as often as he wished.

"Life isna fair, is it?" Nab observed as the big dog returned to her place by the fire.

"No, it isn't," Will agreed, disgusted with himself for envying a damned dog. He ought to give up and go home, but he couldn't leave without the Scepter of Badenoch. At least, that's what he told himself. "Have ye found the Rod of Misrule yet?"

"No." Nab's smile sank like a capsized coracle. "We've been looking everywhere. I dinna think we'll ever find it."

William exhaled noisily. There wasn't much point to the symbol of his family's ruling line if the line was dead. "'Tis a small matter now."

But it wasn't. Katherine was right about that.

However much he protested, he did want children. He wanted a whole castle full of them.

He envied his younger brother's pride in his sons. There was something a bit godlike about the moment when a man sees his own features stamped on his son's face. After a man ran his course in this world, his children were the promise that a bit of him would go on. Since Will had all but renounced the Church, having his blood flow through the veins of his offspring was the only sort of immortality he might hope for.

William pulled his plaid tighter around himself against the morning chill. Dorcas came in and began to poke at the fire, sending sparks flying up the chimney and flames licking at the wood she fed it. After she finished tending the fireplace, she rose and gave Nab a saucy wink.

The fool blushed to the tips of his oversized ears.

"Nab, are ye sweet on Dorcas?"

"Dorcas?" He repeated the name stupidly, as if he'd never heard it before.

"Aye, Dorcas," William said with growing amusement.

"Nay, I'm not sweet at all. Ask anyone." His gaze followed the sway of her hips across the hall until she disappeared into the kitchen. "Why d'ye want to know?"

"Because the way ye're lookin' at her, anyone might think she was the last sugared plum in the bowl."

Nab's eyes grew round. "Dinna tell anyone. Please, will ye not?"

"Why? She's a comely enough girl. If Dorcas returns your feelings—and that wink tells me 'tis more than likely—folk will think ye've done well for yourself."

"Aye, but they'll think she has not. I'm a fool, William. The butt of every joke. For some odd reason,

Dorcas doesna see me that way. But she might if everyone starts pointing it out to her." He stood and wrung his hands. "Just imagine what fun Ranulf MacNaught would have with a fool in love."

As much as Will wanted to continue needling him, he had to admit that Nab had a point. "Your secret's safe with me. But if ye want to keep it from others, ye need to guard your face when she's around. Ye practically melted when the lass did no more than smile at ye."

"Ye mean I should ignore her?"

"If ye dinna want others to know your feelings for her," William said with a nod. "They show plain enough when ye look at her."

"Dorcas wouldna like it if I ignore her." Shaking his head, Nab settled back down on the floor next to William's chair. "Besides, meanin' no disrespect I'm sure, but I'd be more apt to take yer advice in matters of the heart were ye sleeping in yer lady wife's bed instead of in this chair."

William shrugged. "Ye have a point."

A pair of men stalked in from the bailey, stomping the snow from their boots and beating their bodies with their arms to banish the cold that followed them in. Will recognized them as the two he'd sent to fetch Donald home from Edinburgh.

There hadn't been enough time for them to make the journey there, let alone back again.

"We have news for Lady Margaret," one of them said.

William hadn't seen his sister-in-law since she'd been confined to her bed. He was pleased to find her sitting up, her smile as bright as ever and her hands busy with a pair of knitting needles producing what looked to be the smallest cap in the world.

He was less pleased to find Katherine in a chair beside her bed similarly occupied. There was no way to avoid her this time. His heart still lurched whenever she was near. He damned himself for a weakling, unable to walk away like a man. If his wife didn't want him—and she'd made that abundantly clear—he ought not to want her.

Except that he did.

Katherine rose when she saw him, but it was as if a stranger peered at him through her beloved eyes. She started to go.

"No, dinna leave. I willna be long," Will said, raising a hand to forestall her. When Katherine perched on the chair once more, he turned his attention to Margaret. "I've news of your husband, good-sister."

Her face, though pale, brightened at this. "What of my Donald?"

"He sends ye his compliments and wants ye to know he's near."

"Oh, I'm so glad. After that bad turn, I had a feeling this time would be different. Did I not tell ye he'd change his mind and come home for my lying-in, Katherine?" Then a shadow passed over her face. "But there hasna been time to send a message all the way to Edinburgh. The runners left but a few days ago or I'm mistook."

William shifted his weight from one foot to the other. "They met Donald in Inverness."

"He was already on his way! Oh, Kat. Feel my heart." She took Katherine's hand and pressed it to her breastbone. "'Tis racing like a young lass waiting for her first beau. When will he arrive?"

William swallowed hard. "He says to tell ye the whole of King James's court has removed from Edinburgh to Inverness till after Twelfth Night. Seems a white stag was sighted in the Highlands thereabouts and His Majesty is keen to bag it. He and his courtiers ride out daily in search of the beast."

Margaret seemed to shrink back into her pillows. "Donald's down at the end of the loch from me only on account of . . . a deer?"

"A rare deer, to be sure. There hasn't been a white stag taken since my father's father's time. Donald says if he's the one who helps the king find it, the future of Glengarry will be secure."

Margaret's lips tightened into a thin line. "Did the messengers tell him I was in some difficulty with this babe?"

William nodded. "Your husband says to tell ye he prays for ye nightly. God, he reasons, can do ye more good here than he can, and he can do ye and all your sons more good at court than the Almighty."

Donald had said nothing of the sort, but William thought Margaret might appreciate the sentiment. According to the messengers, his actual words had been "Lady Margaret isna having trouble. Ye must be mistaken. If there's one thing that woman excels in 'tis pushing out bairns."

William wasn't about to repeat that.

"And it seems his prayers have had effect," Will said. He didn't believe in prayer one whit, but if it helped Margaret deal with her husband's absence, he was willing to play along. "If I may say so, ye are looking radiant, good-sister."

That was a bald-faced lie. Margaret had the scraped-back look of a woman whose body has been taken over by another. She wouldn't be in full possession of herself again until that Other was expelled. Katherine's skeptical glance told him she wasn't the least fooled by William's falsehoods on Donald's behalf.

Margaret, however, smiled tremulously. "Thank ye, Will. 'Twas good of ye to send word."

He wished he had his brother-in-law in front of him that very moment. He'd shake the man till his teeth fell out. "After the runners rest a bit, do ye wish to send another message?"

"No. No need. I'll not trouble Donald again till after the bairn is born. 'Twill be time enough then. 'Tis the news he's waiting for, after all," she said, staring down at the knitting needles that had fallen quiet in her hands. "I'm tired of a sudden. Leave me to rest, if ye please. Ye too, Kat."

Katherine leaned over, gathered up the knitting, and kissed Margaret's cheek. She filed out of the room ahead of William and started down the spiral stairs.

They hadn't gone two steps before Margaret's soft sobs stopped them. Kat turned and would have gone back up, but Will blocked her path.

"She wouldna thank ye, I'm thinkin'," he said softly. "She asked for solitude. That small dignity is the only gift ye can give her."

"You're right. Donald didna say he was praying for her, did he?"

Will shook his head.

"The selfish beast. Oh, how I wish I were a man," Katherine hissed. "Then I could beat my brother senseless."

"I'd be happy to do the honors for ye."

She smiled up at him for the first time in days. "I believe ye would."

"Say the word and Greyfellow and I are off for Inverness."

"Then consider the word given, but I dinna think we'll range that far afield, laddie." A booming voice came from below them on the stairs. It belonged to

Lord Glengarry and he sounded more like his usual self than he had since Christmas Eve. "I'm declaring a hunt and all able-bodied men are to form up in the bailey as soon as may be."

Evidently, Katherine's father had overheard only part of their conversation. They continued down the twisting stairwell to meet him at the doorway to his chamber.

"Seems Jamison has his garters in a twist over the state of our larder, though I've inspected it and have my doubts about the need for fresh meat," the earl said. "Still, it'll give us an excuse to get out of the castle and blow some of the stink off, aye?"

He tromped down the spiral stairwell, bellowing for Nab to roust the men.

"Well, I guess if ye're off with my father, ye've no time to pummel my brother," Katherine said.

"Lady Margaret wouldna want me to, in any case."

"No, she wouldna. She's a far better person than I." Katherine started down the stairs, but he caught her hand.

"That's not true. To see an injustice and want it made right doesna make ye a bad person. It means ye care. If ye like, I will still go fetch your brother and drag him home. Ye know I will." God help him, he sounded so blasted pathetic, but he couldn't seem to stop the words from pouring out of his mouth. "There's nothing I wouldna do for ye."

One of her brows arched. "Really? Let's test that, shall we?"

Hope surged in him. He was ready to scale a castle wall for her. Should the waterhorse appear in the waves off Glengarry, he'd mount the hell-bound beast and ride it to the depths of the loch if Katherine asked him to. Whatever she wanted, he was ready to attempt if only she'd believe he was hers till there was no breath left in him.

"I want ye to do something for me, William."

"Anything." He brought her hand to his lips.

"After ye return from the hunt . . ."

"Aye?"

"I want ye to spend the night . . ."

He'd do it right this time. Whatever it took, their lovemaking would be all about her pleasure. It was the only thing that would please him.

"In the chapel praying," she finished.

He had not seen that coming. "Katherine, ye know I dinna—"

"Ye said ye'd do anything."

Trapped by the words of his own mouth. "And just what am I supposed to be praying for."

"Wisdom." She stood on tiptoe and kissed his cheek. "I want ye to pray that God will show ye the right path ahead for the two of us."

"I already know what that is."

She tilted her head. It wasn't right that she looked so fetching when she was tormenting him. "I want ye to ask God honestly if 'tis right for us to seek an annulment. I've prayed till I'm blue but I canna seem to hear an answer."

Perhaps because no one's listening to your question, he thought. But she looked up at him with such an earnest expression, he couldn't belittle her faith.

"All right. I'll go to the chapel," he said. "But only for half a night. I'll spend the other half with ye, telling ye the answer."

On the tenth day of Christmas
My true love gave to me ten lords a-leaping.

—From "The Twelve Days of Christmas"

"I'm thinkin' the ten lairds probably heard there were ladies dancing hereabouts. That might account for any amount o' leaping, aye?"

—An observation from Nab,
fool to the Earl of Glengarry

Chapter Nineteen

The hunting party headed into the Highlands, leaving Glengarry Castle far behind. The men split into smaller groups, stalking game trails leading in different directions. Lord Glengarry and William, along with Ranulf MacNaught and his cronies, took the steepest path into the deep woods.

William and his father-in-law stopped at an overlook and leaned on their pommels to gaze back at the castle. It seemed to sprawl along the coastline of the loch in the distance, its grey stone sprouting from the earth like the bones of some long-dead creature risen halfway from its grave.

"It's never been taken from without," the earl said.

"Glengarry was besieged for a whole year back in my six-times great-grandfather's time, but it never fell. O' course, according to the old tales, folk did take to eating rats and boiling their own shoes before help came." He glanced at his nephew Ranulf MacNaught, who was ranging a few yards ahead, laughing with his group of toadies. "Perhaps Jamison is right to see that the larder is full to bursting. We can always salt the meat down."

"We have to find some first. Red deer are shy this time of year," William said. The pair of deerhounds loped alongside them when they started moving again. The dogs rarely sniffed after a prey's trail, but once they caught sight of anything with hooves, they could run it to earth in a few heartbeats. "A good many deer have probably wandered to the Lowlands."

"Yet I see signs of them hereabouts." As they rode past a towering pine, Lord Glengarry pointed to a pile of small round droppings near the base. They didn't appear fresh. MacNaught's laughter echoed back to them again.

"Ranulf," the earl called in a half voice, "ye and your men will scare the deer clear to the coast and send 'em swimmin' out to the Orkneys if ye keep up that racket. I thought ye were going to try Murray's peregrine and see if it can roust up a brace of coneys for the stewpot."

Hugh Murray's medium-sized falcon was a vicious bird, as ill tempered as its master. The peregrine had nearly taken the thumb off of one of the lads who tended the castle mews. It screamed now from its perch on Murray's heavily gloved forearm.

"A peregrine doesna usually take to small game like rabbits." Sinclair, as usual, considered himself the fount of information on every topic being discussed even though the bird in question wasn't on his fist. "It prefers to hunt other birds."

"Aye, and I dinna think much of anything, be it man or beast, that preys on its own kind," Lord Glengarry said with a dismissive wave of his hand. "Take the bedeviled thing out of my sight."

"Verra well, uncle." MacNaught turned his horse's head away from the earl. "We'll descend a bit for our hunt then, since ye seem to prefer Lord Badenoch's company over that of your own blood. I'll leave ye two with the hounds. Good hunting."

Ranulf and his men plodded back down the hillside through the rotten snow. A warm wind had started melting the mantle of white. Once the other men were gone, the woods were still enough that William could hear water running beneath the crust of snow, forming into small rivulets and pooling in shallow puddles in low places.

"Ranulf is just like his mother," Lord Glengarry said, shaking his head after his retreating nephew. "My sister was always looking for offense where none was meant. I've tried to help him along, to give him an opportunity to improve himself, for her sake, though she never showed the least appreciation. Besides, it doesna look as if Ranulf will take any chance I give him."

"I'm more concerned that he'll take his own chances," William said. There is a certain glimmer in the eyes of a stallion who intends to rule the whole herd. Will had seen that same glint in MacNaught's eye more than once.

The earl snorted, whether in agreement or dismissal William wasn't sure. "I canna like his companions overmuch."

"From what I've heard, Sinclair, Murray, MacTavish,

and Gordon are the best of the lot." Rumor had it that MacNaught had offered a haven to every masterless man in the Highlands. His crumbling keep was home to any highwaymen, reiver, or draw-latch who'd swear fealty to him. William shifted uneasily in his saddle. If Ranulf could control them, he'd have a formidable fighting force made up of men who had nothing to lose.

"Sir Ellar Dinglewood is sending his wife back to her father after Christmastide," the earl said softly so as not to spook any game that might be nearby. "He says she willna breed so he's claiming nonconsummation and having their marriage put aside."

It was an abrupt change of topic, but William was used to his father-in-law's penchant for dropping things he didn't want to discuss. Evidently, he wasn't ready to consider what MacNaught's plans might be.

"Dinglewood and his lady have been wed for nearly ten years," William said.

"And ye and Katherine have been wed for four." The earl tossed him an inquiring look. "Are ye planning to send my daughter back to me, William?"

"No, sir."

"I ask because Katherine has been after me to find a friar who can deliver a letter to Rome. What do ye know about that?"

"Nothing." He didn't want to accuse Katherine. "I dinna want our marriage annulled. I gave your daughter my vow. I will never put her away."

Lord Glengarry gave a grunt of approval. Then he frowned. "But she may put ye away. She's headstrong, is my Kat. I thought she'd come home to help Margaret, but after watching the pair of ye lately, I've been wondering if she had another reason to leave Badenoch.

Far be it from me to come between a man and his wife, but . . . ye're not harsh with her, are ye?"

"Never."

"Good. I'd have to throttle ye, if ye were."

If the earl were younger, William might have been concerned. The old man had been a veritable mad wolf of a fighter in his prime. Even now, he could probably land a telling blow or two.

"Her mother had trouble bringing bairns into the world too, ye ken." Lord Glengarry dropped his voice to a whisper now, both because the subject was delicate and because they'd just spotted the twin almond-shaped tracks of their quarry. "Not that she couldna quicken. We lost count of how many times she failed to carry a babe longer than a couple of months. Still, she did manage to give me my heir."

"And your daughter," William whispered back. He wondered if Katherine knew her mother had suffered from multiple losses just as she had. And if that knowledge would make a difference. The deerhounds' ears pricked to a sound the men couldn't hear.

"Aye, and a surprise Kat was too," the earl said, oblivious to the way his dogs' ruffs were rising. "We'd thought we were past more children, especially as my Alva had such trouble bearing them. But then here came our Katikins to be a comfort to my old age. It just goes to show, William."

That I have to wait till I'm a greybeard to become a father?

"It shows ye must never give up hope," the earl continued as if he'd been asked.

Hope was something William was fresh out of, but he was spared from having to reply when the two hounds darted forward in long-legged lunges. The thicket ahead of them rattled. There was a chorus of growls mixed with a plaintive cry that was abruptly cut off.

The men chirruped to their mounts and forged through the dense undergrowth, finding the deerhounds seated next to a goodly sized deer carcass. Their blooded tongues lolled in macabre doggie grins. Lord Glengarry had trained the hounds to stop worrying the prey once it ceased struggling. He praised the pair in more lavish terms than William had ever heard him offer someone with two legs.

"Well, that buck's eighteen stone, minus the rack, I'll warrant. Should feed us for a while." The old man dismounted and started field dressing the deer, but William took the knife from him to spare him the chore of gutting the buck. "Jamison ought to be satisfied now."

The scream of a peregrine overhead made William look up. Murray's falcon wheeled above them. Then it gathered itself into a killing wedge and stooped. Hidden by the forest, it dove into a meadow lower down the hillside. The raptor didn't rise again.

"Looks like your nephew's party made a kill as well."

The earl ignored the comment. "Glad we didna bag a doe. That's the trouble of hunting with the dogs. Ye can rarely see what they're after till they've gone and killed it."

William wondered if he would figure out what Ranulf was after before Lord Glengarry's nephew made a move.

"And ye said he wouldna hunt coneys," Hugh Murray said with a sneer at Sinclair while he fed the falcon a small bit of rabbit liver. Then he tucked the rest of the bloody organ into his other turned-back cuff to feed the bird later.

"I said no such thing. I said peregrines *prefer* to hunt other birds. That's all," Sinclair said with an injured sniff worthy of a court dandy. "If ye'd get your head out of your arse and listen once in a while, Murray, ye might learn something."

"Weel, one coney isna going to make for much stew," MacTavish said, with surprising practicality as he tied the rabbit's hind legs together and affixed the carcass to his pony's pommel. The beast rolled its eyes at the scent of blood but stood still when MacTavish grasped its mane and remounted. "Will the bird hunt again?"

"He might if Murray doesna overfeed him," Gordon said as Murray slipped the bird another tidbit. Then he raised a pointed finger at the western road below their hillside location. "There's a rider approaching the castle. He's wearing your plant badge, MacNaught, or I'm mistook."

Some clans decorated their bonnets with a cockade of colored ribbons. A thriftier method was to tuck a certain plant into a hatband to declare a man's allegiance. Ranulf MacNaught's men wore a sprig of holly when they wanted to make themselves known to each other.

"Prickly and poisonous," Ranulf had explained to his followers when he chose it. "One way or another, we'll be a scourge to all who oppose us!"

Now he squinted into the distance. There did seem to be a red-and-green spray attached to the rider's tamstyle hat. "Gordon, ye've sharper eyes than that bird. Keep on with the hunt, all of ye. Where there's one rabbit, there's a dozen."

"Where are ye off to?" Gordon asked.

"To see what this fellow wearing my badge wants at Glengarry."

He left his followers bickering over which direction to take their hunt. Ranulf muscled his gelding into a plunge down the hillside so he could intercept the rider on the western road. To name it a road was to overdignify it. What Gordon had called the western road was little more than a well-worn path. Still, Ranulf meant to catch the rider before he reached the castle.

By the time he reached the road, he recognized the rider as Duncan Burns, one of the men he'd left to guard the Italian friar. Ranulf stopped and waited for Burns to come to him.

"What news?" he said when Burns drew his sturdy Highland pony to a standstill.

"It took a bit of persuading to get the Italian to work on that contraption, but after Ogilvie cut off one of his fingers, he became fair enthusiastic about the whole idea."

Ranulf's mouth twitched, but he wouldn't bestow a smile on Burns just yet. He needed men who could do what was required, whatever that might be. Ranulf made a mental note to see that Ogilvie was suitably rewarded once he came into his own.

"So what has the good friar come up with?"

"He did all sorts of calculating and measuring and wasted any amount of paper drawing up plans based on the parts ye found in the cave. Long and short of it is, we finally have the thing put together."

"'Tis a trebuchet, not a thing," Ranulf said. "Show a bit of respect. Call it what it is."

Because it'll deliver everything I want into my hands.

"The important thing is, does it work?" Ranulf asked.

Burns cocked a brow and nodded. "We tested it. I figured ye'd want us to. Lost Finley on the first try when he didna heed the friar's instructions and his arm got caught in the gears. We couldna staunch the bleeding."

"Finley was a fool."

"And now he's a dead one, roasting in Hell for his folly. It gave the rest of them pause, I can tell ye. No one ignores the Italian now."

"What's the most weight ye can hurl?" Ranulf asked.

"We've tossed boulders that weigh more than twenty-five stone. Should do a good bit of damage, depending on where ye aim them. God knows they damaged a few of the men lifting them."

Ranulf brushed this off as unimportant. He glanced up the hillside where dark granite broke through the turf at intervals. There was plenty of raw material about that would serve as projectiles. In his mind's eye, he could see work crews hewing rock from the earth, while others transported it to the machine's maw to be loaded and finally flung at his enemies.

"What else have ye thrown besides stones?" One of the old warriors in Edinburgh had spoken of hurling flaming bundles over castle walls.

"We havena tried anything but loads of rock."

That didn't mean something else couldn't be used. The fellow he'd treated to drinks had gotten morbidly misty-eyed when he described how siege armies had gathered up the dead who'd made the mistake of leaving the walled citadel. Corpses thrown back at trapped defenders were great demoralizers.

"It unmanned 'em something fierce," the old warrior had affirmed.

"What's the range of my trebuchet?" Ranulf was feeling possessive of the collection of timbers and gears.

"Over eight hundred yards with consistency on level ground. Less accurate at nine hundred."

Ranulf twisted in his saddle and gazed back at Glengarry Castle. The folk who had situated the first keep on the banks of Loch Ness tens of lifetimes ago had committed a grave error. A steep incline rose to the north. If someone situated a trebuchet on those heights, the range of the weapon would be significantly increased. And the machine, and all the men who worked it and supplied it with its deadly projectiles, would be beyond the range of even the best-drawn longbow.

"Tell the friar I want him to devise a method to hurl flames. And I want him and the machine situated there by Twelfth Night, ready to go." Ranulf pointed to an overlook above Glengarry Castle. "Or he'll lose more than a finger."

On the eleventh day of Christmas
my true love gave to me eleven pipers piping.

—From "The Twelve Days of Christmas"

"Eleven Highland pipers would set up a caterwauling noise fit to wake the deid! I begin to think an Englishman, or someone else who doesna know their arse from their elbow, wrote this song."

—An observation from Nab,
fool to the Earl of Glengarry

Chapter Twenty

The hunt was an unqualified success. In addition to Lord Glengarry and William's buck, other parties brought in several smaller red deer. Ranulf and his friends contributed so many coneys to boil in a cauldron of rabbit stew, it was enough to feed the entire assemblage that night.

However, MacNaught's entourage was conspicuous by their absence at the earl's board.

Even so, William almost failed to notice it at first because Katherine was seated next to him at the table on the raised dais, as a good wife should. They spoke softly together about nothing of importance, but the nothings felt normal. Good. So did her soft thigh brushing against his under the table.

"I dinna see my cousin," Katherine said as she offered William a bite of her bannock. She'd slathered it with butter and it dripped honey, just as he liked it. "Is he not back from the hunt?"

William surveyed the great hall but saw no sign of Ranulf MacNaught or his friends. He leaned toward the earl at his other elbow. "Where's your nephew?"

"Gone. Ranulf came to my chamber and made his farewells as twilight fell. Wouldna even stay for supper. Seems he received a message from my sister asking him to return home. Says she's taken ill."

"Oh?" Katherine leaned forward to peer at her father over William's trencher.

"I dinna believe the sickness is serious. Most like 'tis a light case of catarrh. Now that she's a widow, she doesna do well without her son close by, Ranulf says." Lord Glengarry tucked into his stew with more gusto than William had seen in him for days. Fresh air and the exercise of the hunt had been good for him. "My sister always did want to be the center of attention. She may well be shamming. So farewell to Ranulf, and I canna say I'm sorry for it."

"I am," William admitted. "If there's a snake in the middle of the hall, at least I know where it is. While Ranulf was here in the castle, we could keep an eye on him."

It crossed his mind that MacNaught might have found the Scepter of Badenoch and slipped out of Glengarry with it. Then he dismissed that notion, because Ranulf wouldn't have been able to resist claiming the right to sit in the laird's thronelike chair.

"What are ye saying, Badenoch? Think ye I canna trust my own blood?" A vein popped out on Lord

Glengarry's forehead. "He's my own sister's boy. Ranulf may be rough about the edges, but he's family. I'll not hear a word against him."

"Not even if he has designs on your holding?"

"Who dares say such a thing?" The earl's voice rose to a roar and several diners' spoons clattered to the trestle tables.

William started to rise, but Kat stopped him with a hand to his forearm.

"No one says that, Father," Katherine said soothingly while shooting William a warning glance. "Nab, 'tis still Christmastide," she called out gaily in an effort to forestall further argument. "Give us a story fit for the season, will ye?"

The fool rose to his feet and fiddled with the ends of his multitasseled hat. While he knew plenty of stories, Nab didn't have a bard's ease of delivery in the telling of them. He hemmed and hawed and had to be coaxed to get the tale out. This time, however, Nab glanced over at Dorcas, who was refilling drinking horns at a nearby table. The serving girl tossed the fool a shy smile, and he stood straighter, clearing his throat.

"Perhaps ye will have heard the tale of how the robin got his red breast?" he began.

This was met with nods and smiles all around the great hall. Just because the story was familiar didn't mean they wouldn't enjoy hearing it told again, provided it was well told.

"It came about like this, ye see, that on the night of Our Lord's birth, his mother was fair concerned because of the bitter chill." A puzzled look came over Nab's face. "Makes a body wonder, does it not, why Our Lord chose to come to earth in the dead of winter when he might just as easily have been born on a soft spring night?"

"He came to share our hardships," Katherine whispered to William. "Few things are harder than winter."

Will could think of at least one—his wife's stubborn head once she set her feet on a course. Well, he could be just as stubborn. If she thought he was going to spend his time in the chapel later praying himself into agreeing with her ridiculous scheme for an annulment, she was in for a grave disappointment.

"There was a small fire in the stable for warmth on that holy night, but it had nearly burned itself out and Blessed Mary fretted herself that the Holy Child would be cold." Nab punctuated this with an exaggerated shiver. "So she looked about at the animals in the stable to see if they would help."

Nab scratched his head. "This part of the story always makes me wonder where St. Joseph was, for surely he could have stoked up the fire."

It was unusual for a storyteller to depart from the original and interject his own thoughts into the tale. Perhaps that was why, instead of listening in quiet expectation, Beathag, the midwife, felt moved to add her conjecture to Nab's telling.

"No doubt he was seeing the shepherds who'd come visiting back out the door," Beathag piped up. Margaret was doing so well, the midwife had allowed herself the luxury of dining in the hall for a change while one of the nursery maids sat with the lady. "The last thing ye need in a birthing room is a bunch of fellows who reek of sheep!"

The whole company laughed soundly.

"At any rate," Nab continued with a pointed glare at Beathag for the interruption, "the Mother Mary asked the ox would he blow on the fire, but he'd already settled for the night on his bed of straw and was fast asleep."

"I'm not surprised in the least," Lord Glengarry said, waving an admonitory spoon at Nab for suggesting such a thing might be possible. "An ox is not the most biddable of creatures at the best of times. How much less so on a cold winter night?"

"Aye, I take yer point, my lord." Nab tugged down his motley with exaggerated dignity. "However, may I remind ye that I didna make up the story? I'm merely telling the tale as I heard it told."

"Fair enough, Nab." Lord Glengarry raised his soup bowl to his lips and slurped noisily. "Pray, continue."

"So then, Mary turned to the jackass that had borne her safe to Bethlehem. 'Please, Master Donkey,' quoth she, 'will ye snort on the fire and bring it back to life?'"

"It appears to me that the donkey had already done its part," William said, for the pleasure of watching Nab's ears turn bright red. "As I understand it, 'tis a long, weary way from Nazareth to Bethlehem."

"Aye, and bearing a woman near her time is no light matter," came Margaret's voice from the base of the stairs. When she appeared on the last step, a hand resting on her protruding abdomen, the entire hall erupted in cheers and applause, for they hadn't seen the lady in several days.

Katherine leaped to her feet and scurried over to help Margaret to the empty place on the other side of Lord Glengarry. Margaret protested that she was fine and needed no special coddling, but her sweet smile said she was pleased by it nonetheless.

"I couldna bear to be missing out on Christmastide up in my chamber a moment longer. I'll be fine. Truly, I will," Margaret said to keep Katherine from fussing over her. "I'm sorry to have interrupted your tale, Nab."

"Ye're the only one," he muttered. "Everyone else feels it their duty."

Katherine settled next to William again. He slid his hand under the table and took hers. To his surprise, she didn't tug it away.

Perhaps there's something to what folk say about Christmas miracles.

"We'll listen quiet now, Nab," Katherine said. "Finish the tale, if ye please."

"One by one, Mary asked the horse, the sheep, and the goat for help." No one interrupted the fool this time, but some wag in the corner managed to get in a rather convincing "neigh," "baa," and "bleat" at appropriate times. "But none of them would tend the fire."

"Disheartened, Mother Mary wrapped her baby and held him close. Then she heard a flutter of wings. A small brown bird flew up to the rafters and peered down at her. He cocked his head, like this." Nab gave a fair imitation of a robin eyeing something it intended to have for breakfast. "Now back then, the robin didna look as he does today. He was just a plain mud-colored bird, but beneath those drab feathers, there beat a great heart. Without being asked, the bird flew down to the dying fire and began flapping his wings with all his puny might."

Nab demonstrated by waving his arms before himself like a bellows. He made huffing and puffing sounds till he was quite red in the face.

"That's enough, Nab. We can imagine the rest," the earl said. "I dinna want my fool to fall down trying to imitate a bird."

"Weel," Nab said as he caught his breath, "I wasna done just yet. Ye see, according to the story, the robin sang the whole time too, so I thought I'd—"

"In that case, we definitely want ye to stop!" Lord

Glengarry roared with laughter. Nab's singing more nearly resembled a bullfrog's than a songbird's. "Skip over the song for now and end your tale."

"Verra well, but the song adds a great deal to the telling, I've been told," Nab said with a sniff. "So then the robin picked up a beakful of straw—I'll not be doing the imitation of that since 'tis clear yer lordship wishes me to finish!—and the bird tossed the kindling onto the glowing ash. The kindling burst into flames."

Nab threw his arms into the air, setting the bells at the ends of his cap ajingle. Then he clutched his chest awkwardly.

"The fire flared up and burned the robin's breast as red as a cherry. Did that stop him from fanning the flames? No, it did not. There was an Infant King what needed warming and that little bird didna quit tending the fire till the whole stable was toasty warm and filled with light."

The entire assembly went quiet, caught in the mood of the peaceful cattle byre—the sweet breath of the animals, the homely scent of fresh straw, a young mother's soothing lullaby, and a Child born into darkness who would become the Light of the World.

For a few heartbeats, William wished he still believed it.

"The Baby Jesus slept sweet that night and Mary rewarded the robin. 'Because ye have loved much,' quoth she—people were always quothing back then, ye ken. Sounds a good deal more holy than 'said,' aye?"

"On with it, Nab," the earl ordered.

The fool's head bobbed. "Och, where was I? Aye, now I mind it. The Blessed Mother said to the robin, 'Ye shall wear the symbol of yer sacrifice on the breast, that all generations may know ye thereby. May yer great heart be covered with a red shield from this day forth.'"

Nab smiled, turning his head this way and that so that all could see his beatific expression. William doubted such a look had ever been found on a robin's face.

"And so it is even now that the robin's breast is red," Nab said. Then he brought his hand to his chin and gave it a thoughtful stroke. "But I'm thinking there's yet another meaning to this story."

"Never trust a jackass to do a birdwit's work?" someone called out.

Laughter greeted this all around. Since the hunt that afternoon had been so successful, Dorcas had doled out the ale and beer with a free hand.

"No, that's not it," Nab said in all seriousness. "I think the story means we ought not discount the small things, the seemingly unimportant. Those who are weak, those whose gifts are not so obvious may, in a time of great distress, prove to be far stronger than we suppose." He turned his gaze downward to study the curled-up tips of his own shoes. "Or than even they suppose."

Lord Glengarry rose and leaned his heavy knuckles on the table. "Thank ye, Nab. 'Twas a story well told, but now I'm in the mood for some music. Let's have that piper. Push back the tables and clear some space. I am moved to dance!"

The earl left the dais as the piper began his tune. Lord Glengarry bowed before Lady Dinglewood, requesting the honor of a reel. William noted that Sir Ellar's face turned an unhealthy shade of puce.

Served him right for wanting to put her aside.

Katherine squeezed Will's hand under the table and he noticed she was tapping her toes.

"Would ye care to dance, wife?"

"Aye, my lord." She didn't call him husband, but at least she smiled at him. "Though if ye'd waited but another moment, I'd have had to ask ye."

On the twelfth day of Christmas,
My true love gave to me twelve drummer's drumming.

—From "The Twelve Days of Christmas"

"The last time I heard twelve drummers, the English
were coming over the hill and by sundown the corbies
were feasting. I believe I'll pass on this gift, if it's all the
same to ye."

—An observation from Nab,
fool to the Earl of Glengarry

Chapter Twenty-One

Katherine danced till her feet ached. She grew dizzy
when William twirled her, but she didn't cry off or ask
to sit out any of the tunes. She couldn't bear to cut
their time together short. Who knew when or if she'd
ever dance with Will again.

At the end of the last reel, he led her out of the
great hall without a stop and through the door to the
solar. There was no one else in the room, though they
could hear the low rumble of the crowd in the great
hall and the flourish of the pipes as the tune drew to a
close. They made a swinging turn of the dimly lit
chamber, and as they passed by the door the second

time, Will kicked it shut without missing a step. He gave her a final turn and then released her to finish the dance with a bow.

Breathing hard from exertion, she dropped a deep curtsey and came up grinning. "That was fun, Will."

"Fun is something we've been lacking of late." He gathered her back into his arms. The banked fire in the grate threw only enough light to allow her to see half of his face, but that half was beaming down at her. "'Tis something we'll have to rectify once we get home. Every day, no matter what else is commanding our attention, we must have some fun together."

She didn't want to spoil the moment by reminding him that she wouldn't be returning to Badenoch with him, not if they were moving forward with an annulment. His body felt so good flush against hers, she couldn't bring herself to pull away from him either.

She settled for reminding him that not every day was a holiday and they couldn't expect the frivolity of Christmastide all year.

"No, but even the most ordinary of days can be extraordinary if ye're with the one ye love," he countered.

"No matter what happens, ye must believe that I do—" She stopped herself. What good could come of admitting she loved him if she still intended to separate from him?

"'Tis all right. Ye can say ye love me. I willna hold it against ye. However, I'm enjoying holding something else against ye verra much."

Katherine felt his hardness through the layers of clothing separating them and rocked her pelvis once. His grin carved a deep dimple in the cheek turned toward the fireplace. She couldn't help putting her fingertips to the sweet spot.

"Even if ye dinna admit it," he said, "I see love shining in your eyes."

"Love always seeks what's best for the beloved," she reminded him.

"For me, that's you."

"But, Will—"

"No buts, woman. I know what I want."

"But not what ye need."

"That's a 'but.' I'll have none of it." His hands roamed lower, cupping her bum and pulling her close.

"Bu—"

"Ye're forcing me to drastic measures, Kat." He covered her lips with his in a quick claiming. Then he released her mouth and looked down at her, his dark eyes searching, his face strong and determined. And full of love.

Oh, Lord, why wasn't that enough?

Perhaps it was. For now, at least. She tipped up her chin. It was all the invitation he needed. His mouth descended on hers again, firm and hungry this time.

The chamber seemed to go shadowy around them and the boisterousness of the great hall faded. There was no yesterday. No tomorrow. Only the eternal now. Only his mouth, his hands, his hardened groin against her softness.

And so for now, she yielded, parting soft lips and letting his tongue sweep in. She suckled him. He was her Will, her soft summer night, her warm cloak in winter. His love hedged her round about to keep the world at bay.

His kiss went on and on, drawing her deeper into the fantasy that somehow everything would be all right.

Her mother used to kiss her scraped knees and

"make them better." She knew that for childish nonsense now. Cuts left scars. Heartbreak left wounds that never stopped weeping. But if kisses *could* heal, Will's would surely bind up the broken bits of her and make her new.

Another childish wish.

But she couldn't keep from hoping it as William deepened their kiss. For now, she put aside all else— Stephan's death, her plans to free her husband, her desire for a child that was so intense she sometimes couldn't breathe.

She willed herself not to remember. Not to think. She would only feel.

His chest was a hardened breastplate, heavy muscles under the fine lawn of his shirt. She slid her arms around his waist to hug him closer as her tongue chased his back into his mouth.

Oh, the smell of him, all leather and warm wool and that crisp male tang that was uniquely William.

Longing shivered over her, leaving her slightly light-headed. If his arms hadn't been around her, if she weren't clinging to him, she might have gone down in a wobble-kneed swoon.

Somehow, he'd backed her to the tapestry-covered wall. The ancient cloth depicted one of the battles William Wallace had won against the English years ago. With her spine pressed against the venerable fabric, she tried not to imagine the wide eyes of the defenders of Stirling Bridge in 1297 looking on as her husband lifted her skirt.

His hands slid over her thighs. She ached for him to hold her, to take her most secret self in his hot palm, but he only teased his fingers close without claiming that part of her. When she groaned into his mouth, he relented and took her in his hand.

She was wet. Praise be.

She hadn't had to force it or concentrate or anything. When she stopped thinking so hard, her body roused to William as it should.

This time when he stroked her special little spot, she didn't try to keep her climax at bay. She let it come and it rushed toward her with the force of a gale.

Bliss took her, lifted her, shook her.

She chanted incoherent things all tangled up with Will's name as her release went on. And then suddenly William hitched one of her knees up at his hip and between one contraction and the next, he raised his kilt and slid inside her, sheathed to the hilt, as her inner walls continued to pound around him. He stood motionless, soaking up her pleasure, letting it abate slowly.

When it was finally over, only then did he start to move. She met him stroke for stroke. It was like riding in perfect rhythm with her mount's gait.

He lifted her other leg and she hooked her ankles at the small of his back.

"I love ye, Katherine," he all but growled. "Ye're mine, d'ye hear? Mine and I'll not let ye go."

She wasn't in the mood to argue. He plunged in, hard and fast. She welcomed the claiming.

The ache that had been so lately relieved started building again in earnest. By the time Will threw back his head and arched his spine as his seed pumped into her in hot bursts, Katherine was ready to come again.

Her insides fisted around him, draining him dry.

"Aye, love," she whispered. "Just like that."

He made her greedy. She wanted all of him.

When the steady pulses stopped, William lowered his forehead to rest on hers. His breathing was ragged, but he kept his hold on her so their bodies could maintain their connection as long as possible. Kat didn't know how long they hung there, suspended on a rack of pleasure, but she wouldn't have moved for worlds.

Finally, William broke the silence. "Ye called me love."

"Perhaps ye'll allow it was a moment of weakness."

When he slipped out of her, she unhooked her ankles and lowered her feet to the floor. She had to stand on tiptoe because he still had the twin globes of her bum in his palms and was lifting her slightly.

"Admit it." He grinned down at her. "Ye love me."

"I love . . . holding ye."

"That's not the same thing."

"For the now it is."

"And for the morrow?" His smile faded.

"The morrow will care for itself. Please, Will. Dinna make me think beyond this moment. For now, we're together and it feels . . ."

"Right?"

"Aye. It feels right *now*. But if ye make me take thought for next week or next month or the march of years ahead . . . ye willna like what I have to tell ye."

William dropped his hands and stepped back from her. His kilt and her skirt fell back into place. "After what we just . . . I felt your pleasure and ye felt mine. We held each other's hearts." He looked down at her as if he didn't recognize her. "Does nothing we do together mean a thing to ye?"

She didn't trust her voice.

"I wouldna have thought it, but ye're a coldhearted bitch, Katherine Douglas."

No, she wasn't. She burned for him as much as any woman had ever burned for a man. William was a dance of light in her heart. He was sun on the water, her moon in a clouded sky. Her heart beat as hot as a refiner's furnace for this man.

But if she was bound to free him to do what was best for him, she couldn't tell him how she adored him. She couldn't tell him how she ached with love for him. He'd never let her go if he knew.

So she turned her face away. "Dinna ye have some-place to be?"

"Aye, Badenoch is missing its laird." The anger in his voice turned it into a growl. "I've been gone too long."

"No, I mean . . . did ye not promise me ye'd spend the night in the chapel? To pray about the path ahead for us."

"I think ye've made our path abundantly clear. I dinna have to waste time on my knees about it."

"Will, ye promised."

"And so did ye, Katherine." His voice rose to a roar as he paced the small chamber, trying to bridle the rage that roiled within him. "Ye promised to love, honor, and obey me. I could do without honor and I've no hope ye'll obey me, but by God, woman, I expect my wife to love me."

I do! her heart cried, but she bit her lip to keep from voicing the words.

"So ye're determined to take the veil, are ye?" His voice was lower now, but the softer he spoke, the more menacing he sounded.

She nodded miserably.

"I canna see ye making a good nun." He stopped before her, hands fisted at his waist. Even though he was no longer shouting, she'd never seen him so angry. "Not when ye've such a hot mound. But only when it suits ye, aye? Maybe ye'd do better as a light-skirt. That way ye can choose your johns and send them on their way when ye're done with them, lighter in the pockets but with a smile on their idiot faces. Lord knows, ye've played me for a fool."

She lashed out. Almost before she knew she was going to do it, she struck him on the cheek.

Another man might have slapped her back. William simply stared down at her, his brows drawn together. "If ye're done with me, m'lady, I'll be taking my leave."

Without waiting for her to speak, he strode from the room.

"Oh, Will." Katherine's knees gave way and she slid down the wall, sinking to the stone floor. Her thighs were still slick with his seed. She clutched at her chest. It hurt so, she was certain her heart was going to burst forth at any moment. Tears streamed down her cheeks. "I love ye, William Douglas. God help me, I'll love ye till I die."

I come from heaven which to tell
The best nowells that e'er befell
To you the tidings true I bring
And I will of them say and sing.

—From "Balulalow"

"O' course, all the nowells and tidings in the world
dinna matter a flibbet if a body doesna want to hear
them."

—An observation from Nab,
fool to the Earl of Glengarry

Chapter Twenty-Two

William stuffed his few belongings into his leather
bag and strode out of the keep. Since the snow had
been melting, the bailey churned with mud during the
day, which refroze by night. So rather than cutting
across the open space to the stables, Will kept to the
stone path that led from one structure to the next. He
passed the well house that protected the castle's supply
of fresh water, drawn up from the depths. A plume of
smoke rose from its small chimney, proof that one of
the Glengarry lads, Fergie perhaps, was keeping a

small fire going within to ensure that the well didn't freeze.

The path wound over a hillock, by the mews, and past the chapel. Light spilled out the green glass windows in slanting bars onto the snow on the eastern side. William slowed his pace.

He had promised.

He stopped and glared at the small house of worship. A wet wind lashed him, cutting through his jacket and plaid as if he were standing naked before it. If he started riding for Badenoch now, he could expect a bitterly cold night of it. Starting at dawn made better sense, but he couldn't return to Katherine. Or even go back into the keep to wait for the sun. He had no wish for company.

The chapel would be warmer than standing in the bailey.

He turned aside and shoved open the door.

A few candles flickered before the altar, casting their light on the crucifix carved in bas relief on the wall behind. The space seemed deserted. He didn't wish to unburden himself to some fawning priest, who would no doubt press him to do just that. He was only there to pass the time till he could leave.

He walked toward the altar. The scent of stale incense hung in the air, accented by the acrid tallow of the guttering votives and the moldy smell of dank stone.

"The stink of piety," he muttered.

So the chapel at Badenoch had smelled the night he'd pleaded with God for the life of his son.

He stood staring at the crucifix. The soughing of the wind outside became a muted whisper as it slipped through the thatch overhead. William fancied he could hear air moving in the sacred space, slipping around columns and circling above him in ever tightening eddies.

If he were the type to be easily swayed by that sort of thing, he might believe he sensed a Presence in that soft sibilance on the edge of sound.

The injustice of his situation flowed over him along with the swirling current. It wasn't fair. He'd poured his heart out to the God he'd known from childhood and all he got in return was this wispy silence.

"On the off chance that there's anyone there, Ye may as well know the last time we spoke, I thought it was the worst day of my life."

The air current sighed.

"Turns out I was wrong. The day I buried my son was only the beginning of a long downhill slide. *This* is the worst day of my life."

He had to bury his love for Katherine. She'd made it abundantly clear she didn't want it and it hurt too much to drag it around inside him any longer. He wanted to cut her out of his heart, but she'd become so deeply ingrained in him, he didn't know where to begin.

Who was he if he didn't love Kat?

"Is this all it comes to? This silence and nothingness?" He strode forward and brought his fist down squarely in the center of the altar. "A man makes a vow. He swears not to change. And yet somehow, the world changes around him. I take on the mantle of my clan as I was born to do. Dinna think Ye're not to blame for making me firstborn among my brothers. But if I were not Laird of Badenoch, there'd be no need for an heir and Katherine wouldna—" He stopped and shook his fist at the ceiling. "But I take a wife and promise to love her. Ye know I have. And I do. Yet Ye deny us a child and render the Scepter of Badenoch useless even if I knew where the damned thing was. And now Ye'd take my wife as well."

Once Katherine entered a convent, she'd be as dead to him as Stephan.

"Why d'Ye not pluck out my heart and be done with it?" he shouted to heaven. "'Twould be kinder than watching me twist on this spit."

He glared up at the crucifix. The artist's rendering was a bit crude. There was no flowing hair, no artfully placed cloth wrapped around the Christ figure's loins. No one would claim this was a masterwork, but the suffering depicted was undeniable.

"Maybe Ye're not there." Will's voice dropped to a whisper but it still seemed to echo around the chapel. "Maybe Ye're too weak to help me. Or maybe Ye just dinna give a damn." His shoulders slumped as some of the fight drained out of him. "I dinna know which of the three is worst."

"I do," came a small voice from the alcove where the silver candlesticks, the monstrance, and the chalice used for mass were kept in a locked cupboard. Nab scuttled from the shadows.

"What are ye doing there?" Will demanded.

"I'm not there. I'm here. You're there, William." The fool shook his head. "Dinna feel bad. Dorcas has problems with that too."

"No, I mean . . . never mind. Why are ye not with his lordship?"

"He sent me away. Seems I've taken to snoring of late and the earl didna want me sleeping across his threshold. And I canna go to my secret pl—weel, that's neither here nor there, so to speak. I canna go elsewhere because there are so many people about. If I

was to slip off to a certain someplace not generally . . .
Odds bodkins, the chapel was lovely and quiet till ye
came in and started yelling at God, William."

"I'm done yelling." Will sat down on the steps leading up to the altar. "I'll not disturb ye further."

"Ye're not disturbing me. Though I dinna suspect
the same can be said for the Almighty."

"By my lack of faith, ye mean."

"Och, no. Ye have faith. If ye didna, ye wouldna be
talking to God at all. So ye see, whatever ye may say,
somewhere inside, ye believe that He hears. Though
ye'll allow yer means of address is somewhat less cordial
than He's accustomed to."

William snorted. "He hasn't smitten me for it yet."

"Has He not? Did ye not say this is the worst day of
yer life? That sounds like a smiting to me. And a rippingly good one, at that."

Nab came over and sat beside him.

"Are ye not afraid to be close to me in case He decides to smite me again?"

"Och, no." Nab fiddled with the ends of his fool's
cap, setting the small bells jingling. "The Almighty is
a gentleman, ye ken. He never smites anyone who's
already down."

"I am that." In fact, William didn't think there was
much further down a body could go. It hurt to breathe.
It hurt to think. It hurt to love.

"D'ye really think the Lord weak, William?"

"I dinna know. If He isna, if He could help me, why
does He not? So either He's unable to help, which
means He's weak, or He doesna care."

"Doesna give a damn, I believe ye said."

"I thought ye were concerned with my less than
cordial way of expressing myself."

"If the Almighty doesna smite ye for it, why should I? But have ye not considered another option?"

"What's that?"

"We live in an odd world."

"Truer words were never spoke, but I'm curious as to why ye say so."

"This world, 'tis not at all what God intended. Remember the Garden. Everything perfect. Then suddenly, it was no more and not because of anything the Almighty did. We brought our exile on ourselves. Ye might even say we chose it. And that makes the world odd."

Nab wrapped his hands around one knee, pulled it toward his chest, and warmed to his subject. "Take me, for instance. If the world were as God intended, d'ye think I'd have been born a fool?"

At the moment, Will didn't think Nab was a fool at all.

"No, the world is as men have made it and the evil in it is on our hands," Nab continued.

"But God could fix it." William couldn't get past the fact that the Almighty could give Katherine the child she craved if only He would.

Nab looked back at the crucifix. "I think He already did. The roots of the oddness, at any rate. O' course, that doesna mean that evil willna still befall us. 'Tis too much a part of everything not to. This world will still be odd so long as we've breath."

It wasn't the most satisfying answer to his questions, but William couldn't think of a better one.

"I'm sorry about yer son, William," Nab went on. "Sorry as I can be. And I think ye're right to feel pain. But I'm thinkin' the Almighty feels it too, right along with ye. He does care. If He didna, that would be the worst. I dinna know for sure, but I believe when we weep, He weeps."

But Will hadn't wept. Not even as he'd dug that small grave. He'd kept all his tears, all his hurt, all his sorrow tucked away in a dark corner of his heart.

His eyes burned. Then his vision swam and the back of his throat ached. He stood abruptly and walked away lest Nab catch him with weak eyes. "For what it's worth, Nab, I've never heard a fool make more sense."

"Where are ye going, William?"

"To see my wife." He was going to show Katherine that black pit inside him. And then if she still wanted to be free of him, he wouldn't be able to blame her.

Katherine wasn't asleep, but she didn't stir when she heard William's soft tread as he approached the bed. She barely breathed. She'd been so certain he'd left her, left the castle, she almost thought she was having a waking dream.

But when he peeled off his clothes and lifted the blankets to slide in beside her, she decided she wasn't imagining things.

And her heart sang a quiet song of selfish hope. She'd wanted him to come back so badly, she hadn't dared wish for it. Still, he made no move to reach for her under the covers.

So she lay frozen in place, listening to him breathe.

Then she heard something else. A small sob. She rolled toward him and saw his profile by the light of the banked fire. His cheek was wet. His mouth was a tight line.

The man was weeping.

"William—"

"Oh, God. Katherine. Our son . . . all our unborn

bairns . . ." He covered his eyes with a splay-fingered hand.

She wrapped her arms around him and felt him shaking. He drew a ragged breath.

"He was so small." Will's chest shuddered. "And there was nothing I could do."

"Ye did all ye could for Stephan. Ye rested him." She pressed soft kisses to his cheeks, his eyelids, tasting the saltiness of his tears.

"'Tis not right. Sons should bury their fathers. A man shouldna bury his son."

"I know." She palmed his face as her tears joined his. "I know, love. 'Tis not right. 'Twas my fault."

"No. Never say that. It isna your fault." He grasped both her hands and met her gaze, his eyes awash with tears. "Nab says it happened because the world is odd, and I think he's right. Because evil still hunts us. And . . . and God weeps with us, Katherine. Am I making any sense at all?"

"Oh, Will."

They held each other and let their grief flow. Katherine had cried over Stephan countless times, but now, for the first time, William wept with her. Something dark and decayed inside her seemed to burst. In its place something new fluttered—a small sliver of hope.

They'd joined in love in their early days. They'd been yoked in heartbreak at the loss of their son, both dragging the weight of it, but not pulling together. Now, finally, they were joined again, this time in shared grief. In that moment, the load Katherine had borne was lighter because Will lifted half of it.

The intimacy of shattered dreams was a fragile foundation, but as their hands found each other under the blankets, Katherine dared to wish for the first time that they could find each other again as well.

Get ivy and hull, woman, deck up thine house,
And take this same brawn for to seethe and to souse;
Provide us good cheer, for thou knowest the old guise,
Old customs that good be, let no man despise.

—From "Get Ivy and Hull"

"Dinna mistake me. I'm all for decking up a house, or a castle, for Christmastide, but a line must be drawn when a woman decides 'tis time to deck up her man."

—An observation from Nab,
fool to the Earl of Glengarry

Chapter Twenty-Three

The chapel was a good deal quieter after William left, but not a smidge warmer. Nab paced the small space, beating his arms to warm them. He usually didn't mind when Lord Glengarry ordered him away from his threshold, but on this particular night a couple had spread their cloaks dangerously close to the secret entrance to Nab's tower stairs. He didn't dare chance slipping into it in case someone should discover him and his hidden chamber.

Nab wasn't comfortable around crowds of people

when they were upright. When they were sprawled about the castle all around him, snoring, farting, or swiving, he felt as if he'd crawl out of his skin. It was his good fortune that Father Argyll, who tended to the souls of all who dwelled in the castle, was an elderly fellow who rarely kept the canonical hours, and preferred to counsel his parishioners by daylight. Nab could count on the chapel being empty all night.

He just couldn't count on it being comfortable. If he was in his tower room, he'd be all wrapped up in the wolf pelt and old blankets, snug as could be. And if Dorcas happened to be there with him . . .

He cast a glance at the altar and hurried over to light another candle. It wouldn't do to dwell on what might take place if he and Dorcas were tangled up in the same set of blankets. He was in church, after all.

The door to the chapel creaked open behind him. "William, I thought ye—"

"There ye are, Nab." Fergie's voice crackled with a growing boy's squeak and then dropped into a lower register. "Ye're a hard one to find."

"Why are ye looking for me? I thought ye were in the well house, Fergie." It had been Nab's first choice when the earl exiled him, but though the small space had the advantage of a fire, it was still very small. He didn't think he could share it with the boy all night.

"I was, but then Dorcas came and booted me out and sent me to find ye." Fergie shot him a toothy grin. "Ye're to hie yerself there on the double-quick or she'll not save ye any of the sweeties she brought for ye."

If the lad's sticky-looking cheeks were any indication, Fergie had helped himself to a few of Dorcas's sweets before he did her bidding.

"Go on wi' ye," he urged. "A lady doesna like to be kept waiting."

"Dorcas isna a lady. At most, she's a lady's maid."

Fergie shook his head. "Ye'll never make her *yer* lady with that sort of daft thinking. Go on, Nab. She's expecting ye."

Nab wasn't sure he should take advice about women from a boy whose voice couldn't even decide which octave to live in, but he certainly didn't have any wisdom of his own to draw upon. This thing, whatever it was, between him and Dorcas had simply sprung into being of its own accord. It was like a mysterious river he'd been swept into without warning. He had no idea how to keep it flowing or how he might direct its course.

"But where will *ye* go?" Nab had no trouble with the thought of sharing the small well house with Dorcas, which surprised him in no small measure, but not if Fergie insisted on spending the night there too. Just the thought of the three of them in that compact space made it hard for him to draw breath.

"There's always room in the stable for the likes o' me." Fergie shivered. "A bed of straw is warmer than here in the chapel."

And more likely to be shared with rats, mice, and other small creatures, Nab thought but didn't say. He thanked Fergie and pulled his plaid over his fool's cap for extra protection from the elements as he pushed out of the chapel door. He sprinted to the well house and ducked inside. The wind whipped through the bailey behind him with a keening wail.

"Quick. Close the door," Dorcas ordered. "Ye'll let all the heat out."

Nab complied and leaned against the portal. It rattled behind him despite the thrown bolt. "The wind is fierce this night."

"Ye're lookin' a bit fierce yerself." Dorcas tipped her

head, eyeing him speculatively. He wasn't sure he liked it. She looked a bit like a tabby before a mouse hole. "But we'll deal with that later. I've brought ye some tarts and an apple fritter."

The sweet, yeasty scent of the pastries filled the small space. He let the end of his plaid slide off his head and reached for a tart. It dripped with currants and honey. Between the warmth of the well house and the good food, Nab's cold-stiffened limbs thawed quickly.

"I didna know I was hungry till ye brought out the food." As he fell to, he had a slightly holy thought, which he blamed on his time in the chapel with William. "Do ye suppose that's why God gave Eve to Adam—to let him know what he needed before he even knew he needed it?"

Dorcas smiled at him.

Usually her smiles made Nab feel all jittery inside in a good way, but this time, his innards flittered with a bit of foreboding. He hadn't really done anything to warrant a smile. Gifts weren't generally given without an expectation of something in return.

What did Dorcas want for this smile?

"'Tis right glad I am to hear you say so," she said, "because I've summat in mind that ye need and I dinna think ye know it."

"What's that?" he asked as he picked a few crumbs from the fritter off his shirtfront.

"Ye need a haircut, Nab."

"My hair is not bothering me in the least."

"Weel, 'tis bothering me. It wants cutting," she replied. "And a wash," she added for good measure. "Now sit ye still while I get my shears."

He considered bolting, but where could he go? The

laird had banned him from his quiet threshold. The keep was overrun with people and the chapel far too cold for comfort, especially after the warmth of the well house. He supposed he could join Fergie and the other rodents in the stables, but then the lad would know he'd failed to do what was necessary to make Dorcas his lady.

It was one thing to be thought a fool by all the adults in the keep. To have a mere boy think him ridiculous chafed Nab's soul.

He took off his fool's cap and scratched his head. Most of his hair had been braided into seven or eight, or maybe ten, thick strands a few months ago, but there were any number of snarls around and between them where some of his hair had worked free.

Dorcas shook her head at him. "How long has it been since ye had it cut last?"

Since before he came to Glengarry. His father had despaired of bringing order to his chaotic mind and his mother felt the same about his hair. "It's been a while."

"Weel, never ye fear. I'll fix things." Then she began snipping off his many braids, dropping them to the stone floor beneath their feet like so many bright red worms.

"Have ye cut a man's hair before?" he asked as the shears snapped by his ear.

"No, but when I lived with my mam and pap, I sheared plenty of sheep."

"Ye dinna intend to shear me surely?"

"I havena decided yet. It may take that much cutting to rid ye of all the snarls. We'll see."

Nab fingered his cap nervously while she continued

to snip. The pile of hair on the flagstones grew. "What made ye think of doing this?"

"I was just watching ye while ye told the story of the Blessed Mother and the robin and about all the animals and—"

"Did ye like the story?" It was important that she did. He was always waiting for her to discover what everyone else knew, that he was a fool. If she admitted to liking a few things about him before that realization hit, he might stand a bit of a chance of keeping her regard afterward.

"Aye, I liked it verra much," Dorcas said. "Ye tell it exceeding fine, but it seemed to me as ye were doing it ye were looking a bit wild."

"Weel, I was imitating a goodly number of beasts."

"Not *wild* beasts, though. As I recall, ye did a passing fair ox, an ass, a horse, a—"

"So ye're saying I want taming?" Something about this idea made his chest swell. It felt good to be thought a bit wild.

"Aye," she said with a laugh. "That's it."

More hair fell to the floor. "What if I want to stay wild?"

"But ye dinna. There. I think that'll do. At least until 'tis clean and I can see what's what. Now, for the wash."

"I dinna think I need—"

"Oh, aye, ye do. Did ye not just say that God gave the first man a woman to point out to him what he needed?"

"Aye, and that may well be one of the most poorly considered holy thoughts I've ever had." Nab sighed. He should have kept it to himself. He didn't used to say so many things he regretted. At least, not so quickly. Usually he didn't realize he'd made a mistake till he was wrapped up in his plaid ready for sleep while the day's events fumbled around in his brain.

"I've warmed the water," Dorcas said. "Here, lean over this bucket."

With a resigned sigh, he did as she bid and the cup of water she poured over his head nearly scalded him. He yelped and straightened abruptly, sending hot droplets flying.

"Dinna fuss so. Let me add a bit of fresh water to cool it. There, now." With a hand to the back of his neck, she tipped his head down and poured another cup of water over his head. "Is that better?"

It was, but he didn't feel like letting her know it. "That's like asking the overdone bannock if a bit of clotted cream will make it better," he grumbled.

"Ye shouldna complain. I'm only trying to help. Now, hold still." She reached into a small satchel and pulled out an earthenware jar. When she opened it, a delightful fragrance filled the small room.

"What is that?"

"Some of Lady Margaret's special soap."

Nab usually made do with a mixture of mutton fat and wood ash. "Smells good."

"It should. She makes it of olive oil shipped to Inverness from some ungodly land far to the south. Then she adds soda and lavender and a few aromatic herbs I dinna remember the names of, but they're frightfully dear." Dorcas put a liberal dollop on Nab's head and began to massage it into his scalp. "Lady Margaret gave me this a few days early. 'Tis for Hogmanay." New Year's eve.

It felt like a bit of heaven oozing from her fingertips. "But this is yer gift. Ye should save it for yerself, Dorcas."

"There's still some left. Besides, I want ye to have it." She continued to rub his head, drawing her thumbs along the center of his skull. Then she kneaded his scalp in slow circles.

He'd thought her kiss was something special. This was beyond his imaginings. Pleasure dripped down his neck along with the soap. He sighed.

"Like that, do ye?"

He couldn't speak for bliss. He could only close his eyes and make an "mmm-hmmm" sound. Fortunately, he wasn't required to say anything else. Dorcas had launched into another of her one-sided conversations about everything and everyone within the castle walls. He didn't even have to listen all that closely to enjoy the running diatribe. Just the sound of her voice soothed him so that he almost nodded off to sleep.

"Lean over the bucket and we'll rinse now."

He jerked back to full wakefulness and did as she instructed.

"And I'll take care to make sure the water's not too hot this time," she promised.

It was perfect. She was perfect.

But he was not. He didn't know why she hadn't already seen it.

Then she draped a cloth over his head and rubbed vigorously to dry his shorter locks. "There," she finally said. "Now let me just trim up the stragglers. Hold still."

She got out the shears again and began cutting in small sections. His wet hair reached just below his earlobes and tickled along the back of his bared neck.

"Close yer eyes," she ordered.

When he did, to his surprise, she sectioned off a good bit of hair and cut it short across his forehead. He ran a hand over the wispy ends.

"There. Now ye look a right proper gentleman," she declared as she put away her shears.

"I'm not a gentleman, Dorcas."

She turned back to him and dusted a few fritter crumbs he'd missed off the folds of his plaid. "A man can be anything he sets his mind to."

"My mind has already pretty much set itself on being a fool with no help from me at all." He crammed his cap back on his head. With less hair, it didn't feel right. In fact, it threatened to fall down over his forehead and cover his eyes. He had to push it back behind his ears, which he was sure made them stick out all the more. He'd been right when he'd told William that change was almost always bad. He didn't like this haircut business one bit.

"There's where ye're wrong, Nab. I ken yer secrets, remember. Ye've a fine mind. Ye can read. Ye're a learned man, whatever folk may say." She walked her fingertips up his chest and then teased his chin. "Ye could make something of yerself."

"I thought I already was something. If I'm not something, I'm nothing." He decided to dazzle her with a little Latin. It should end the argument. "*Ego sum non nihilo, ergo aliquid.*"

"I dinna ken what the rest of that gibberish means, but ye're not at all liquid. Yer hair's nearly dry already."

Evidently Dorcas wouldn't be cowed in any language. He decided to take another tack. "What made ye want to cut my hair in the first place?"

"Why, to help ye, o' course." She batted her eyes at him, as coquettish as a mare in heat. "When a man starts thinkin' of takin' a wife, 'tis only natural that he look for ways of bettering his situation. A haircut canna hurt."

"I'm not thinking of taking a wife."

She blinked at him several times, all traces of co-quetry gone. "Are ye not?"

"No, who would I marry?"

"Me, o' course."

Panic clawed at his belly. A few stories. A few kisses. A poem or two. How had it come to this? "Did I ever say I wanted to marry?"

"Not in so many words, but ye showed me yer secret room—"

"As I recollect, ye found it on yer own," he corrected. She'd followed him, most like.

Dorcas lifted her chin. "At any rate, ye invited me to come back again."

If Dorcas was right, his memory on that point was a bit fuzzy. It seemed to him that she'd just assumed she'd be returning to the tower room.

"And ye read me stories—"

"Which ye didna like a bit." It was still a sore point with him that she couldn't seem to grasp the wonder of Camelot, where might didn't make someone right. Perhaps she'd never felt small and powerless and in need of a code of chivalry to balance the scales in her favor.

She cast her gaze down so that her pale lashes lay like feathers on the swell of her cheekbones. "I liked the poem."

"Not the first one. The one about the bald fellow," he said. She'd been most emphatic on that point. "Was that poem what put ye in mind to do something about *my* hair?"

She waved the thought away. "No, I havena given that poem a second thought. But I liked the love poem, Nab. I liked it verra, verra much. I can even recite it back to ye."

Her eyes slid to the right as if the words might be found hovering beside her ear.

Love me truly!
My heart is constant.
Ye possess my soul.
Ye tangle up my thoughts in silken cords,
But I dinna wish to be freed.
Even if ye're afar off,
My spirit is with ye, not in my poor body.
To know such love is to know the torture of the rack.

Her gaze flicked back to him. "'Twas the most beautimous thing anyone's ever said to me. Did I remember it aright?"

"I think so. I dinna know for certain without the book in front of me." He cocked a brow at her. "How did ye do that?"

She shrugged. "We have different gifts, ye and I. Because I canna read, I remember what I hear verra well. I have to, ye see. But 'tis easy to remember if the words please me."

Nab was good at remembering the gist of stories, but to recite one word for word was an art he'd not mastered. Certainly not after only one hearing. Dorcas really was smart.

Much smarter than he.

That irritated him more than the haircut.

"Ye needn't have bothered cutting my hair," he said testily. Thinking he was the smart one in their little whatever this was had made him feel in control for the first time in his life. Now he realized he'd been wrong. Dorcas had managed everything from the very beginning. "I willna be needing to improve my situation because I'll not be taking a wife."

"But—"

"Not you. Not anybody. I'll not marry ever."

For the first time in his life, he raised his voice at

someone. He couldn't seem to help it. The idea of being shackled to another person for the whole of his life, even someone like Dorcas, whom he tolerated better than anyone, was unthinkable. It made his insides do a jittery reel. All he craved was solitude, safely away from the laughter and snide comments of others. When he was alone, he was in good company.

"Get it out of yer head, woman!" he shouted. "And the next time ye decide to improve a body, ye might try asking do they wish it before ye start."

Nab expected her to fist her hands at her waist and shout back at him. He was used to people yelling. He could deal with that by ignoring her. She'd give up eventually, figuring he wasn't intelligent enough to realize the stickiness of the situation.

Sometimes, it was good to be thought a fool.

Instead, her little chin quivered. Her eyes became overbright. A tear trembled on her lashes.

This was far worse than being yelled at. And he couldn't ignore it.

"Dorcas, dinna cry. Please. I didna mean—"

"Aye, ye did," she said between sniffles, "else ye'd not have said it."

Nab pulled a handkerchief from his sleeve and offered it to her. He couldn't vouch for its cleanliness, so he wasn't surprised when she didn't take it. Instead she covered her face with a bit of her arisaid and sobbed into it.

"I take it back, Dorcas. Can ye not forget I said anything?"

"No, I canna. Ye know I canna. Words in my hearing dinna fade away. I store them up, do I wish it or no."

It was true. She'd just demonstrated how well she'd

remember his hatefulness. He felt lower than the icy slush on the bottom of his boots.

"Dorcas, please . . ." He reached a tentative hand to her. It was hard for him to do it. Touching and being touched was not something he enjoyed, but he didn't mind it so much with Dorcas. Who knew if he'd ever feel that way with anyone else. And he felt if he didn't touch her now, he never would again.

She jerked away from him as soon as his fingertips brushed her shoulder. "Stay away from me, Nab."

Swiping at her eyes, Dorcas hurriedly gathered up her things and put them into her satchel. He saw now that she'd spread a blanket for them on the other side of the wellhead near the fire. There was even a jug of something—ale or small beer—they hadn't opened yet. His haircut was only the beginning of the night she had planned for them.

Part of him wished he'd held his tongue and just let events wash over him. Dorcas was a good planner. He probably would have enjoyed it, whatever it was.

He tried once more to stop her at the door.

"Step aside, Nab," she said without looking at him.

"Not until ye let me tell ye—"

"Why should I let ye speak when I'm afeared of what ye'll say?" Tears coursed down her cheeks. "But I'll say this. I used to stick up for ye, ye know, when some of the others would speak ill of ye. I willna do so anymore. Ye dinna ken when someone truly cares for ye. And ye havena the sense to care for them back." She met his gaze then. "Ye really are a fool."

Then she threw the bolt and slipped out the door. After she was gone, he banged his forehead on the hard oak a few times, wishing he could call back the moment that he'd opened his mouth to complain.

He should have said he loved his haircut. He loved the idea of improving his lot in life.

He loved her.

Then Nab, who would rather have had his own company than anyone else's, sank slowly to the stone floor. All his life, he hadn't minded being alone.

He minded now. And he feared he would for the rest of his days.

Farewell advent and have good day.
Christmas is come, now go thy way.
Get thee hence, what dost thou here?
Thou hast no love of no beggere.

—From "Get Thee Hence,
What Dost Thou Here?"

"Beggars and fools dinna deserve love in the first place. I'm proof of that."

—An observation from Nab,
fool to the Earl of Glengarry

Chapter Twenty-Four

Katherine's knitting needles clicked in time with Margaret's plodding around her chamber.

"I wish there was something I could do to hurry this one along," Margaret said wistfully. "Sometimes, I think I'll die pregnant."

"Whist! Dinna tempt the devil," Katherine said, surreptitiously making the sign against evil. "Are ye sure ye should be out of bed?"

"That's the one thing I am sure of." Margaret ground her fists into the small of her back as she walked. "If I lie there another moment, I'll go dafter than Nab."

"He does seem a bit more barmy than usual," Katherine said, comparing the stocking she was working on to the one she'd finished to make sure it wasn't already longer than its mate. "He told William he'd dreamed the scepter was hidden away where no one would find it for hundreds of years."

Dorcas, who'd been flitting about the chamber tidying up, began remaking the bed. In silence, for a change.

"I'm surprised Nab would bring the scepter up since he's the one who lost it in the first place," Margaret said. "That must be a sore point with William."

"It is, for all that he's not complained, but that's not the least of it. Nab claimed that in his dream *William* was the one who hid it! Wonder what's gotten into him." Katherine shook her head, then gaped at the way the maid was pounding the pillows. "Be easy, Dorcas. Ye'll have feathers everywhere. What do ye think you're doing?"

The maid stopped flailing away at the bedclothes and folded her hands before her, fig-leaf style. She dropped a reflexive curtsey. "I'm just plumping Lady Margaret's pillows, m'lady."

"More like beating them into submission," Katherine said. "That'll do. If we need to subdue any of the other linens, ye'll be the first to know."

"I'll be in the nursery then." Dorcas curtseyed first to Margaret, then to Katherine and padded down the spiral stairs.

"There's something a bit off with Dorcas of late too." Margaret stopped before the window and looked out on the loch.

Katherine tied off a row of stitches and laid her

knitting aside. "She's not talking our ears off for one thing."

"If I were myself instead of two of me, I'd get to the bottom of it. There was a time when nothing passed in this keep without my notice, but my belly preoccupies me. I suspect I'll not be descending or climbing those stairs again till this bairn comes. Ah, well, I'll deal with what I can." She turned and cast Katherine a shrewd glance. "It was good to see ye and William sharing a trencher last night."

Katherine allowed herself a small smile. "'Tis not all we've been sharing of late."

Margaret waddled over and sat on the stool Katherine had been using for her feet. "Tell me."

Katherine loved her sister-in-law dearly but she couldn't reveal the way William had bared his heart and his grief to her. She wouldn't share that with anyone. It was too private.

Too . . . holy.

In the darkness, amid that deep sorrow, their souls had found each other again.

And then their bodies followed suit.

It was a tender joining because they were both so fragile. Once united, their ascent was slow but steady. Grief mixed with joy. Sorrow with unspeakable gladness. Kisses salted with tears. And at their pinnacle, the rightness of a homecoming, weary and spent but grateful to return to a place where the world made sense again.

Safe in each other's love.

The next morning, she'd wakened with William's arms around her, his leg thrown over hers, all tangled up in that vulnerable net of sleep. Even now, she could call up that drowsy, "all's-right-with-the-world" feeling.

But it still felt so tenuous. As if she danced on a spider's web. Their days were filled with pleasant moments and speaking glances and their nights with more whispered confessions and sometimes laughter that ended with another heart-stopping joining.

Even so, she feared being too happy. Their problem was only half resolved.

She was still barren.

"Och, that's all right. Ye don't have to tell me. I can see on your face how pleased ye are," Margaret said when the silence between them had stretched past the point of comfort. She grimaced and rubbed her swollen belly. "Besides, once this bairn decides to come, the last thing I'll be wantin' to think about is marital bliss. When the pains start, I'll be imagining myself beaning your brother on the head, not welcoming him back to my bed."

"Ye've had no pain?"

She shook her head. "The little darling is taking her time."

"Her? Ye think the child is a girl?"

"No, I only hope." Margie rocked a bit on the stool, a comforting rhythm for her and the child inside her. "I suppose I should set myself to have another boy, but it would be so lovely to have a little girl. Oh, dinna mistake me. I love my boys. But as soon as they're old enough not to irritate Donald, he'll have them with him most of the time, lest I spoil them. A girl-child would be mine to dote upon as I please."

"Till Donald arranges a match for her."

"My, what a long view ye're taking this day, and for a bairn not even born yet."

"I'm trying not to. I dinna want to worry about the future. Sometimes, it just comes upon me." Katherine took up her knitting again. She'd missed a stitch and had to unravel a row. "'Twould be so fine if all we had to fret about was now."

"'Sufficient unto the day,'" Margaret quoted.

"But surely we aren't meant to ignore our obligations." She still felt keenly the need to provide Will with an heir. But before she could say more, Fergie appeared with a polite cough at the open doorway.

"Beggin' yer pardons, m'ladies," he said, tugging respectfully at his forelock. "Lord William says ye're to come quick, Lady Katherine."

"What is it?"

The boy grinned but shook his head. "'Tis a surprise. Please, m'lady, he'll think I've not done my job if ye dinna come."

"Go," Margaret said, raising her ponderous bulk to her feet and ambling back to the window. "The sooner ye go, the sooner ye can return to tell me what's afoot."

Katherine didn't need to see her sister-in-law's face to know Margie hoped the surprise was that Donald had ridden back to Glengarry or sailed down the half-frozen loch and was unexpectedly going to be present for the birth of his sixth child. It was why she kept going to the window.

Kat suspected she was destined for disappointment.

After wrapping a warm brat around her shoulders, Katherine followed Fergie down the twisting stairs and through the great hall. It was Hogmanay, the last day of the year, so the yeasty scent of baking spilled out of the kitchen and into the hall. The little ones who called Glengarry home would make their rounds as soon as the sun set, begging for treats.

An old song from her childhood flitted through her mind.

Hogmanay, troll-a-lay, Hogmanay, troll-a-lay
Give us your white bread and none of your grey.

Katherine used to think she was singing away the trolls and other evils that might threaten those she loved through the coming year. If only evil could be turned aside by a song. If only life were that simple. . . .

Still, she hummed the tune to herself as she and Fergie continued outside and across to the bailey.

"Where are we going?" she asked.

"To the stables."

She wondered if a new litter of pups had been born, but she didn't remember noticing that any of her father's deerhound bitches were in whelp. Still, if there were puppies, William would want to show her. He knew how she doted on small new things of any stripe. And speaking of small things . . .

"Have ye seen Angus about lately?" she asked Fergie. "The wee fellow has been making himself scarce."

Once her terrier had gotten the lay of Glengarry Castle, he'd made it his personal hunting grounds. He still stayed clear of the deerhounds, but beyond that, he might be found anywhere—winding around Cook's ankles, hoping for something delicious to drop to the floor in the kitchen; licking up the drippings in the brewery; looking for a friendly word or an idle pat from the folk who worked in the carpentry and stone-mason's shops.

"Aye, yer wee Angus is part of why we're going to the stable, m'lady. Ye'll see."

William and Nab were waiting for her just inside the big double doors.

"There ye are," Will said with a wide grin. "Wait till ye see."

His excitement was infectious and she grinned back. "What is it?"

He took her arm and led her to the slanting haymow ladder that was almost a staircase. Will gave her a gentle push upward and followed closely behind. A few slats of sunlight shafted in through holes in the thatch, setting the dust motes swirling. The air was heavy with the sharp scent of fodder and warm beasts, along with an undernote of the less wholesome smells of a stable.

There, on the topmost mound of hay was Angus, sitting upright, with his ears perked and his eyes bright. As if he were some kind of doggie potentate, he had the Scepter of Badenoch clenched fast between his teeth.

"He's the one who stole it?" Katherine said.

"Nay, he found it, I should think," Nab said. "We're pretty sure the original thieves hid it in the thatch of the chapel roof. Ye mind the low northwest corner"—he waited for her to nod, indicating that indeed she did know of that spot on the chapel roof where goats were wont to roam on occasion—"weel, that's where the wee beastie found it, I'll be bound."

"How could ye know that?" she asked as William took the scepter from the terrier. To Angus's credit, he didn't put up much of a fuss beyond a brief whine.

"Because we caught them looking for it there—Ranulf MacNaught and his friends," William explained as he stooped to give Angus a pat on the head and a scratch behind one ear. "But they were outfoxed by a wee dog."

"Has the scepter been damaged?" Katherine swallowed back an unworthy knot of disappointment. That scepter and all it represented was why she'd fled Badenoch in the first place. It was a painful reminder that Will had no son to whom the rod could one day pass.

Will ran a finger along its length, pride in the symbol of his family's line radiating from his face. "A few scratches in the silver, but those can be polished out. All in all, 'tis not much the worse for wear. Here, Nab. Take it back to the great hall to show everyone that it's been found."

He scooped up the terrier and held him out to Nab as well. "Ye promised whoever turned up with the scepter would be seated in the laird's chair. Ye never said it couldna be a dog."

Nab accepted Angus but drew back from the silver rod. "Nay, William, I canna take it. Ye've seen how slippery a thing it is in my keeping. Ye'd do better to trust it to the wee beastie."

"In a few days, it'll be Twelfth night." William pressed it into Nab's hand. "Ye can give it back to me then."

Nab relented and took the scepter. Bearing both Angus and the rod, the fool scrambled back down the ladder, missing his footing and nearly tumbling off completely. But when his feet touched the lower level of the stable, he scurried toward the keep. Fergie ran ahead of them, shouting the news that the scepter was found and the "hero" would shortly be seated on the laird's thronelike chair.

William made no move to follow.

"Ye dinna care to see the spectacle of a wee dog in the laird's judgment seat?" she asked.

"No, this is Nab's moment. Let him enjoy it."

After they climbed down the ladder, she hooked a hand in his elbow. "It doesna bother ye to turn loose of the scepter?"

"Aye, o' course it does. The fool is like to lose it again." William shrugged, but she knew he wasn't as indifferent as he tried to appear. "But if I dinna give him a chance to succeed this time, he'll always fail."

That was one of the many things she loved about him. William always gave people another chance, and when he did, they were usually so grateful they'd lop off their right arm rather than disappoint him.

He'd certainly given her plenty of chances.

"I've been chosen to be the first-foot for your father's crofters," he said as they strolled back toward the hall.

"That doesna surprise me a bit. Ye're perfect for the job."

The custom of the first-foot decreed that the first person to cross a threshold after midnight on the first day of the year would determine the luck of the household for the coming twelve months. Since a fair-haired visitor was considered unlucky, a well-favored, dark-haired man was usually chosen to serve as the designated first guest for all the homes in the surrounding area.

"'Twill take a while to ride out to all the crofts, and since there'll be no moon tonight, I'll need someone who knows the way," he said. "Will ye go with me?"

It had been a couple of years since they'd performed this service for their own people. Katherine had started fearing that no matter how fine her tall, dark husband was, *she* was unlucky and her presence might lead to misfortune for their crofters.

But William obviously didn't think so.

"Aye, I'll go." Things had been so good between them, if he wanted her along, she wasn't about to say him nay. "I'll need a bit of time to arrange for the gifts." She'd have to organize the small parcels they were to deliver from the castle's stores—a coin, bread, salt, coal, and a small flask of whisky for each of their stops.

"If we're to be the harbingers of prosperity, food, flavor, warmth, and good cheer, it willna do to neglect any of the symbols," Will said. "Though truth to tell, most of the menfolk would be satisfied with just whisky."

"All the symbols are important," she reminded him.

"So they are."

The Scepter of Badenoch wavered in her mind. It was a potent symbol for the Douglas clan. A few days lost in a stable hadn't diminished it. Being brandished by a fool for the season of Christmastide didn't lessen its pull on her husband. The rod meant continuity, the perpetuation of a strong family for the good of the people who depended upon them.

"We'll ride double on Greyfellow, then," William said as they parted ways at the door to the great hall. Katherine would have to venture into the souterrain to assemble the gift parcels.

"Remember what happened the last time we rode out on that gelding." She stood on tiptoe to plant a quick kiss on his cheek. "Let's hope ye're luckier this time, Will. Ye dinna want to end up walking home again."

At Christmas be merry and thank God of all,
And feast thy poor neighbors, the great and the small.
Yea, all the yearlong have an eye to the poor,
And God shall send luck to keep open thy door.

—From "Get Ivy and Hull"

"It does seem to be a rule that's been woven into the fabric of things that whatever ye give, ye get. Only it's been my experience that the getting oftimes comes long after the giving."

—An observation from Nab,
fool to the Earl of Glengarry

Chapter Twenty-Five

The night was moonless, but it didn't matter. The sky was so thick with clouds, that not even starlight penetrated to the narrow game trails William and Katherine took. Fortunately, she was cat-eyed enough to recognize the correct way even in the gloom, and the cloud cover kept the night from being as stingingly cold as it might have been.

Riding at a leisurely pace, Katherine snuggled up close to William, pressing herself against the warmth of his strong back. She was slightly foxed from too many cups of ale, for every cotter they visited had insisted upon toasting them. A low fire glowed in her belly from the alcohol, and the sharp wool and leather of William's scent made the glow dip lower in her body to simmer between her legs.

Will was her man, to do with as she pleased. And it pleased her to touch him. She slipped her hand around to run her palm under his kilt and along his muscular thigh.

"What are ye doing?" he asked.

"Passing the time between crofts." She brushed his stiffening member, reveling in her power to rouse him. "Do ye not like it?"

He made a noise that sounded suspiciously like a growl, but she knew he was pleased. "That's not in question. The thing is, how can I hope to first-foot for your father's crofters when my cock is like to be the first thing through the door?"

She laughed and gave him a hard stroke from root to tip. He was so warm in her hand, almost feverish.

"Mercy, woman."

"I have none." She raised herself and nibbled behind one of his ears. When she took his lobe between her teeth and gave him a nip, he reined Greyfellow up sharp.

Will was off the gelding's back in a heartbeat and pulling her down with him. His mouth was on hers, demanding and gaining entrance. He tasted of ale and heather honey from the sweet cranachan they'd been served at the last croft.

His hands parted her cloak and found their way in around the folds of her arisaid. He kneaded her breasts. He pinched her sensitive nipples the way she liked, and still she wanted more. She wanted his mouth on them, sucking and biting, but this wasn't the place for prolonged love play.

When he pressed her spine against a broad yew tree and raised her skirts, she hooked a knee around his hip to help him. He wasn't the least gentle, but she didn't want him to be. She was wet and ready, and when he thrust in, she tilted her pelvis to meet him.

She'd never felt so wanton. The thrills swirling over her skin had nothing to do with the cold. She wanted this man to take her, to pound into her body, to drive himself home and claim her indelibly. She wanted to take him into herself and never let him go. If a whole troop of woodsmen chanced past them at that moment, it wouldn't have mattered a bit. She was beyond shame.

They came at the same time, with pants and helpless noises of release, limbs jerking. The connection between them pulsed with life.

When the last contraction was over, she sighed and rested her cheek against his chest. "Oh, Will. Ye do me so fine, ye know."

"If by that ye mean I took ye like an animal in rut, I'll have to plead guilty." He stroked her hair and cupped the back of her head, holding her close.

"Ye're always so in control. Sometimes, it pleases me for ye to lose command of yourself for a bit." She glanced past his shoulder. "Dinna look now, but ye're about to lose control of our mount. Greyfellow is wandering off."

Will pulled out of her and ran after the gelding. The horse had stopped on the other side of the clearing to paw at the snow in hopes of finding some grass beneath.

"Weel, this is what comes of vexing me, woman," Will told her as he helped her up onto the gelding's pillion once again. Katherine was a little sore, but she was totally satisfied with the result of his "vexation." "'Tis what ye may expect when ye tempt a man beyond bearing."

"Do ye promise?" She snuggled against him once he mounted ahead of her. Sated and still slightly tipsy, she was likely to fall asleep before they reached their next stop. Katherine was in no danger of falling off the horse, though, for William had wrapped the end of his plaid around both of them.

It occurred to her that she'd gone all day without thinking of Stephan or conceiving or the empty cradle in their chamber at home. And it was a good thing.

"If this is what happens when I vex ye," she murmured as her eyelids drifted closed, "dinna be surprised when I do it again. Often."

The croft of Sawney MacElmurray was the northernmost and farthest from Glengarry Castle of all the households that counted themselves attached to Katherine's father. But it was certainly not the least. MacElmurray boasted eleven strapping sons and seven pleasant daughters.

And one very overworked good-wife.

Still, Mrs. MacElmurray was a veritable Martha of a hostess and presented Kat and Will with hot cups of spiced cider after William "first-footed" through their door. After all the ale, Katherine accepted the cider with gratitude. Mrs. MacElmurray insisted they take off their wraps and have a bit of broth to warm them as well.

The MacElmurrays were a musical family and, accompanied by a homemade harp and small bone flute, the brothers and sisters sang half a dozen carols for William and Kat before they had finished their cider and broth. When William rose to give them thanks and make their good-byes, Mrs. MacElmurray pulled Katherine aside.

"Afore ye go, my lady, ye must needs hear what my wee Hew has seen." She motioned to one of her offspring. "Hew, fetch yerself here and tell our noble guests what ye stumbled across yesterday."

Wee Hew turned out to be a lanky young man who was so tall he had to duck to avoid the ceiling beams in the low croft. He nodded respectfully to Will.

"I was trapping north of here when I seen 'em." Hew tugged on his bottom lip and his brow wrinkled, clearly concerned. "I'll not get into trouble for hunting off Glengarry land, will I?"

"Not with Lord Glengarry," Will said. "I canna answer for the landholder ye were poaching from."

"Och, I take yer point. No harm in telling ye then." His legal questions assuaged, Hew launched into his tale with broad hand gestures. "Anyways, whilst I was setting some snares, I chanced to see Ainsley MacTavish and nigh onto fifty men tromping through the woods after him."

"My Hew can count all the way to a hundred, my lord, so ye can trust his word," his mother cut in with a beaming smile.

"I take it these men weren't hunting," Will said.

Hew shook his head. "They scared away the game for miles with all their clankin' and jawin'."

"Clanking?"

"Aye, there be some in armor and some in mail. They bore crossbows as well as swords. Ten were mounted."

"Where were they headed?"

"From what I overheard—they was bumping their

gums something fierce as they marched along, ye ken—they was on their way to MacNaught's stronghold."

"Do ye think MacTavish means to attack my cousin?" Katherine asked.

"No," Will said, his face grim. "I think your cousin means to attack your father. He's gathering fighting men and MacTavish is turning away from the earl to support MacNaught's challenge. Doubtless the rest of your cousin's cabal are following suit."

"Surely Ranulf doesna mean to besiege the castle."

"That seems to be his plan unless he has a way over the wall."

A denial died on her lips. It was exactly the kind of thing grasping, defiant Ranulf would do. In the absence of her brother, Donald, her cousin had become restless and ambitious. Her father was growing older, more feeble. Without a visible heir, without Donald to keep the fighting men loyal to Glengarry, allegiances had shifted.

"We need to warn my father." Katherine thanked the MacElmurrays for their hospitality and William counseled them to move to the safety of the castle as soon as possible.

"What about our stock?" Mrs. MacElmurray asked.

Katherine had counted one shaggy milk cow, two goats, and half a dozen hens in the listing stable, but they no doubt represented a goodly portion of the family's wealth.

"Bring them with ye to Glengarry," she told the woman. "Dinna tarry. If an army marches through here, there'll be no safety for any of ye."

"Hew, take three or four of your brothers and visit the other crofters hereabouts. Ye mind where they all are, aye?" William said as he wrapped his plaid around his shoulders. "Tell them to make for the castle with all speed. We've no idea how soon MacNaught intends to move. Come, my lady."

William didn't need to urge her to haste. She ran beside her husband to the stable, where Greyfellow was sheltered with the MacElmurrays' beasts.

The earl was fond of boasting that Glengarry Castle had never been taken from without. But if her father's people weren't safely inside Glengarry's walls, if her father didn't make preparations to defend its battlements, the castle might just fall.

The ride out to all the crofts had been at an unhurried pace, punctuated by a decidedly hurried but supremely satisfying moment of "vexation." The trip back to Glengarry, lit by a sickly dawn, was much different. There was no time for Kat to even contemplate "vexing" her husband. The countryside whipped past in an icy blur as William urged Greyfellow to as much speed as possible. Katherine clung to Will to keep her seat, with the wind biting her cheeks.

Once they clattered into the keep, they sent Nab to wake her father and, while he dressed, waited for him in the solar, rousting Sir Ellar and his lady from their makeshift bed. Apparently, the quarreling couple had reconciled over Christmastide and he was no longer planning to put her away, so they'd claimed use of the solar as ranking guests. They were more than a little put out at being roused so early, but William gave him such a storm cloud glare, Sir Ellar stopped his complaint in midsentence and dragged his wife from the chamber.

As soon as the earl made a grumbling appearance, William told him everything they'd learned from Hew MacElmurray and what had been done about it.

"What d'ye mean by ordering my crofters to gather here?" Lord Glengarry roared. "Jamison is finally satisfied with the state of the larder. The influx of all those additional mouths will send him into a foaming-mouth fit."

Actually, Katherine's father looked more likely to succumb to that malady than his seneschal. A vein bulged on the earl's forehead and his color was too florid to indicate good health. She fought the urge to encourage him to calm down because nothing was more likely to agitate him further. The laird paced the length of his solar like a caged wolf.

"I gave the order because it's what ye'd do yourself once ye think about it. Ye have to protect your people from MacNaught. He's coming. Ye know it in your heart," William said. "Ranulf may be your kin, but there's no love lost between ye. He means to take your place or I'm much mistook."

"Ye're more than mistook, Badenoch." Lord Glengarry shook a fist at his son-in-law. Calling William by his title instead of Will or "laddie" was an indication of how upset he was. The earl quivered with rage. No one but he made decisions about his people, and he wasn't about to let William start. "Your orders betray ye as a coward and ye'd have me be one too. Fleeing behind the walls and shutting the gate. And against my own nephew!"

Katherine's gut churned furiously. She hated seeing the men she loved most in the world at odds with each other. Will was showing remarkable restraint, but the way that muscle in his jaw ticked, she knew his patience wasn't endless. "Father—"

"That's enough, daughter." The earl cut her off with a dismissive gesture. "'Tis bad enough I must listen to your husband. I'll not take counsel from a woman."

With every appearance of meekness, she sank into one of the Tudor chairs. Katherine wished she could convince her father that Will had done the right thing. She longed to describe the look of gratitude on Mrs. MacElmurray's face when William offered the protection of the castle to her family, but her father would likely send her away if she said another word.

"'Tis true I rarely saw eye to eye with Ranulf's mother, not after she married against our father's wishes," the laird said, "but I've done nothing to cause my nephew to turn on me."

"Ye didna need to do anything," Will said, his tone measured and low, a sure sign he was struggling to keep his temper in check. "'Tis not personal with MacNaught. He only wants your position, your place. It doesna matter to him if you're in the laird's chair or Donald or even wee Angus. Mark my words. He means to claim Glengarry for himself."

"That's against all law and precedent. Glengarry is not his to claim. When I pass, the earldom goes to Donald. No court in the world would rule otherwise."

"Aye, but MacNaught's not taking ye to court. He means to take your castle. Remember, possession is eleven points in the law and they say there are but twelve. Once he has the castle, the title will follow," William said, "and Donald isna here to defend his inheritance, is he?"

Katherine bit her lip. Nothing would anger her father more than a slur against his heir.

"Ye've not a shred of proof against my nephew," the earl bellowed. He couldn't defend his son's perpetual absence, so he turned back to blaming William. "I'm thinkin' ye still hold a grudge over the black eye he gave ye in that wee bit of roughhousing a few days ago."

"Roughhousing? In case ye've forgotten, MacNaught

and his men had beaten me senseless before ye stopped them."

Katherine knew it cost Will to bring that up. No man liked to remember such a crushing defeat even though it had been an unfair fight.

"I'm wondering if I stopped them too soon," the laird said. "I suppose ye think Ranulf was behind that scepter's disappearance too."

"He was."

"I'd like to see your proof."

Will folded his arms over his chest and clamped his lips together.

"As I thought. Ye have none. And now ye order all my crofters to converge on the castle on the strength of nothing more than what Hew MacElmurray claims he saw. And while he was unlawfully trapping on someone else's land, to boot." When William didn't respond, the earl stopped pacing and seemed to settle a bit as he considered what he'd just said. Even the bulging vein on his forehead stopped throbbing and shrank. "Ye believe Hew?"

"I do," Will said. "He has no reason to make up this tale, especially since it brands him a poacher."

"There is that. What man admits to wrongdoing to offer a false warning?" The old earl sighed and rubbed the back of his neck. "But still, I wish ye hadna acted so hasty. I blame myself. Ye're a young laird yet, Badenoch. Ye dinna know that projected strength is oftimes a man's best defense. Dinna look as if ye expect an attack and ye'll not encourage one."

William nodded, taking the admonishment along with his father-in-law's capitulation. "I hope I'm wrong."

"Ye are," the earl assured him. "I'd bet my best plaid."

Will's mouth twitched. "The one with the hole in it?"

"Aye, laddie, I was never one for puttin' on airs. And besides, as quick as Margaret mends it for me, I always manage to catch the cursed thing on something and rip it again." Kat's father chuckled and her husband joined him. "May as well let the hole stand. I seem to fare better with breeks."

Sensing reconciliation in the air, Katherine stood. "Time will tell and then we'll know whether ye'll forfeit your plaid, Father." She headed for the door, stopping when she laid a hand on the heavy latch. "In the meanwhile, why don't I fetch breakfast for the pair of ye and ye can plan out the castle defenses together, just in case? Besides, it felt like snow this morning. Ye may as well have something to do that'll keep ye warm and inside."

"I suppose it wouldn't hurt to fill the cauldrons over the murder holes and set a watch," her father said as he took the seat she'd vacated. William settled into the chair opposite him.

"We might organize an archery tournament for this afternoon," William said. "Just to see how many bowmen we have to hand."

The earl nodded. "That's a good thought. A drill or two to gauge how quickly we can man the walls might not come amiss either. It'll give us an idea of how many fighting men we can muster. Now ye mustn't expect much from the crofters. They've willing hearts, but they havena much experience with armaments and the like. What d'ye think about . . ."

Katherine slipped out, satisfied that between the two of them, they'd meet Ranulf's threat. But as she filled their trenchers with steaming parritch and fresh bannocks, something William had said came back to her.

"Donald isna here to defend his inheritance, is he?"

If Will had no heir, was he courting the same sort of challenge from a rival a few years hence? Would Badenoch Castle become a bone of contention for every member of the Douglas clan who thought their particular branch of the house ought to take charge since William's line had ended?

Her chest constricted with that same old ache, only now a fresh twist of guilt was added. Ultimately, would men die because she couldn't give her husband a son?

For within the Rose
Were heaven and earth in a single, little space.
Miraculous thing.

—From "There Is No Rose"

"Too many people dinna realize how fine a thing a single, little space is, or how much like heaven it can be to one who feels lost in a big space."

—An observation from Nab,
fool to the Earl of Glengarry

Chapter Twenty-Six

Nab wished with all his heart that he was in his single little space up in his secret tower. William had been trying to teach him to shoot a longbow all afternoon, but the yew bow was not kind to his clumsy hands. Nab had to strain with all his might to draw the arrow back, and when he released it, the missile often went so wrong, everyone within the keep had given the pair of them a wide berth.

"Has it crossed yer mind that some of us were not meant to be archers?" he asked William after one of the arrows narrowly missed Angus. The terrier went yapping across the bailey, more scared than hurt, but it was a near thing. Nab would never have forgiven himself if he'd hit the wee bugger. He lowered the bow and scowled down the archery butts at the target, which was in no danger from him.

"Ye must try, Nab." William handed him another arrow. "Every man should be able to defend both himself and others who are weaker than he."

Nab suspected there were few in the castle weaker than he. *Maybe the lads in Lady Margaret's nursery.*

He loosed another arrow, which fell short of the mark by some ten yards.

The younger lads, he amended as he rubbed his shoulder. It ached from all the unusual exertion.

William didn't chide. It was one of the things that made his company so much easier for Nab to tolerate than most people's. Instead, Lord Badenoch demonstrated the proper technique once more. He pulled an arrow from his quiver, drew it back to his ear in a smooth, seemingly effortless motion, and loosed it. The shaft flew true and sank halfway into the target.

"A well-placed arrow from a longbow can even pierce armor, ye ken," William said. "I dinna understand why ye never learned to shoot. I heard that some years ago Lord Glengarry had ordered all men between fifteen and sixty to practice with a bow at least once a week."

Nab gave a halfhearted nod. "He did, but I was excepted from the law. When it became apparent to his lordship that I'm only suited to telling stories and making people laugh."

Even though half the time he wasn't sure why they were holding their sides with mirth.

"What about a sword or a dirk?" William asked. "Have ye ever wielded a blade?"

"Other than my meat knife, no, and I've only ever menaced a shank of mutton with that."

"Collect your arrows and give it another go then," William ordered.

"I dinna see the point."

William's face went as hard as the stone of the curtain walls. "The point is, if it comes to it, ye need to be able to acquit yourself like a man, Nab." Evidently, William could chide when he wished. "If I order ye to the wall and call for a volley, ye must follow directions. Ye dinna need to aim then. Just point the tip upward and let fly. Nock. Draw. Loose." He demonstrated each step again, and the result was another shaft embedded in the target. "But until we come to that, ye need to improve your skills. Now go gather your arrows and try again."

Nab wandered after his errant arrows. William was clearly worried. All the whispered gossip he'd heard about Ranulf MacNaught's army coming might be true.

He noticed that Dorcas had sauntered out into the bailey to watch the practice from the hillock near where the chapel stood. Since she was looking on, he stood straighter and picked up his pace down to the raised mounds of earth where several round turf-covered targets had been set up. He refilled his quiver, determined to give her something worth seeing. Lord knew, she hadn't spoken to him since he'd made such a mess of things.

And surely he'd do better with the bow knowing Dorcas was there.

Just as he stooped to pick up the arrow that had come nearest to hitting the mark, a sound like a giant hornet buzzed over his head. There in the center of the turf target near him, a fletched shaft quivered.

He straightened and peered down the butts to see

a tall, thin fellow nocking another arrow on the string. Nab waved his arms over his head. "Och, man, do ye not see me here?"

He quickly scooped up the last of his arrows and skittered to the side as another missile zipped past him.

"O' course, I see ye," the young man called back, cupping his hands around his mouth.

Nab stomped back to him. "Ye might have hit me, ye ken."

"No might about it. I would have hit ye," the fellow said agreeably, "if I'd been aiming for ye."

William clapped a hand on the archer's shoulder. Nab wondered what that sort of approval felt like.

"Hew MacElmurray can shoot out a coney's eye at a hundred yards," Will said. "Ye were in no danger, Nab."

No danger, he says. Maybe not, but when that arrow had flown so close over Nab's head, his trews were in imminent danger of needing a wash.

"Mr. MacElmurray, ye must be hungry after all that practicing," Dorcas called down. Even though she spoke only to the new fellow, all three men looked back up at her. Dorcas's cheeks were kissed with becoming patches of pink, bright roses in a world of grey. She'd never looked so comely. "Cook just took a fresh batch of tarts from the oven. Shall I bring ye one?"

All that practicing, she says. Hew MacElmurray had let fly only a couple of arrows and Dorcas was ready to bring him fresh tarts for his piddling effort. Nab had been hard at it all afternoon and she didn't offer him so much as a moldy crust.

"Are they as sweet as ye?" Hew called back to her.

"That ye'll have to decide after ye've had a bite," Dorcas answered saucily.

Something burned in Nab's chest.

"In that case, I'll come try one," Hew said. Nab hoped he was talking about the tarts. It was hard to be sure. "I dinna need more practice here."

Hew's words would have been quite a boast if they weren't true, Nab thought ruefully.

"Shall I walk ye back to the keep then?" Hew asked.

Dorcas smiled at the tall bowman.

She used to smile at Nab like that. Why, oh why had he made such a muddle of things? The burning sensation spread from his chest up his neck and singed the tips of his ears.

Hew slung his bow and quiver over his shoulder and hurried up the slope to join Dorcas. Leaning toward each other, they ambled off toward the keep. Dorcas's laughter floated back to Nab. He wondered what the beanpole of a crofter had said to her to make her laugh.

"Bet he canna read her a poem," Nab muttered.

He turned back toward the turf targets, nocked an arrow on the string, and drew with all the fury his body possessed. The fletching on the end of the shaft brushed his ear and he loosed.

The arrow flew true and buried its pointed head in the target. It wasn't dead center, but it was close.

"Well done!" Will pounded his back. "A longbow man should be able to loose ten or twelve birds a minute. Do it again to make sure that wasna an accident."

Nab nocked another arrow and drew back the hemp, ignoring the way the muscles in his arm and shoulder protested. He let fly, tracking the course of the arrow through the crisp air till it joined its fellow in the target.

"I dinna know what ye're doing different," Will said,

"but ye're definitely getting the hang of this. Keep up the good work."

William left, probably drawn back to the keep by the promise of fresh tarts, but Nab pulled another arrow from his quiver. He could have told William what he was doing differently.

He was imagining Hew MacElmurray's face dead center on the turf-covered target.

His camp is pitched in a stall,
His bulwark is a broken wall;
The crib His trench, haystalks are His stakes,
Of shepherds, He enlists the troops.
And sure of wounding the foe,
The angels sound the trumpets alarm.

—From "This Little Babe"

"*The way the carolers tell it, ye'd think the Christ Child*
was invading the stable. Alone in a world that didna
want Him overmuch . . . mayhap He was at that."

—An observation from Nab,
fool to the Earl of Glengarry

Chapter Twenty-Seven

Katherine rolled over in her sleep, conscious only that warmth had fled from her bed. Her hand groped for Will and found only an indented pillow. When she opened her eyes, she saw him standing by one of the arrow slits that served as her chamber's windows. His dark form was kissed by starlight and faint flickers from the banked fire. The small hairs on his arms and legs were edged with alternating silver or gold. Beautifully formed, he was as still as a statue as he peered through the slit into the night.

"Will, come back to bed."

He turned at the sound of her voice. "I canna sleep and didna wish to wake ye with my restlessness." But he came to her in any case, sliding under the coverlet, bringing the much needed heat of his bare skin back to the bed.

For days, the castle had hummed with feverish activity. The Earl of Glengarry's crofters poured through the gates with their livestock and household goods. Parts of the bailey resembled a fair with makeshift tents and stalls, but there was little of the gaiety associated with an open market. Instead a quiet drone of murmured rumor made the castle a beehive whose inhabitants hadn't quite made up their mind to swarm.

The men of the castle had drilled each day. The fletchers produced arrows at a breakneck pace. The smith's forge flared all night, turning out swords and axes. The cooper ceased barrel making and instead prepared round targes covered with hardened leather and studded with metal discs. The small shields would turn an enemy blade in close combat or shelter a fighter from a hail of arrows.

But with each passing day, the strain of waiting for something to happen frayed tempers. William had broken up a number of petty fights. If MacNaught didn't come soon, Katherine's father was likely to send everyone home.

"Waiting is the worst thing in the world," Will said with a sigh.

"Tell that to Margaret. She's about to pop." Katherine snuggled next to him, soaking up the warmth of his body. "Ye've done all ye could."

"Tell that to the earl."

"Would ye have done anything differently if this were Badenoch ye were defending?"

"No."

"Then ye've nothing to reproach yourself for." Fortunately, Badenoch was at peace with its neighbors, but if the worst happened in William's absence, his four brothers—Eadan, Kieran, Ross, and Sean—would stand shoulder to shoulder against all comers. Sean, the youngest, was only fifteen, but he could already look William in the eye and was probably going to be the tallest of the brood. The five Douglas brothers were a force to be reckoned with.

Unfortunately, only one of them was in Glengarry.

The smell of baking wafted up the spiral stairs. Below in the kitchen, Cook and her gaggle of helpers were already hard at work even though dawn wouldn't come for some time.

"Winter nights are long," Katherine said with a sigh.

William patted her rump. "God be praised."

"Hmph. Speaking of the Almighty, 'tis Epiphany, ye know," she said. "Will ye go to mass with me?"

"Aye, I'll go. God and I are no longer at war."

"Good. Ye'll enjoy the miracle and mystery play Father Argyll has prepared. He's gone all out since the castle is so full of souls for him to save. Wee Tam is playing Baby Jesus this year, but I'll not say he's warmed to the role."

William's belly quivered with a chuckle. "He's a good lad. Just not the sort to take to 'swaddling clothes' without a fight, I'll be bound."

"No, Tam's the one who's being bound and that's just the trouble. About the time Father Argyll gets him all bundled tight, as the Scriptures say, and settled in the manger, he pitches the most unholy fit."

A cock crowed. This was followed by a slamming

door, the tramp of feet, and a muffled call as a few of the castle's residents began to wake and stir. William threw back the blankets and swung his long legs over the side of the bed.

"If I canna sleep, I may as well walk the walls. The hours before dawn are the worst for a watchman. It'll do the lads good to have some company."

"Maybe ye'd like some company too." Katherine slid out of bed after him and drew on her arisaid, belting it tightly over her leine. "Besides, I willna sleep more without ye."

The terrier, Angus, had no such trouble. Now that his humans had vacated the bed, he left his spot at the foot and wormed his way up to burrow under the pillows till only his stubby tail showed. After chasing vermin, going to ground among the linens seemed to be his second favorite pastime.

"I'm glad to hear it. I dinna want ye to sleep without me," Will said. "Not here. Not back at Badenoch. Not anywhere."

It was William's way of reminding her that she'd threatened to send to Rome for an annulment after Epiphany. Katherine still hadn't told him whether she'd given up on the idea or not.

Mostly because she didn't know herself. She and Will were closer now than they'd ever been in their marriage. They'd finally wept together. They'd loved each other through tears and emerged from the torrent all the stronger. They'd started to behave like a normal man and wife again.

Better than normal. They talked and laughed together, even though the castle was in turmoil. And they swived each other with enthusiasm every chance they got, without considering whether or not they'd created a child.

In Margaret's case, that wasn't so usual.

"Your brother Donald is verra parsimonious with his seed," she had confided to Katherine. "He spends it to make a child and when that task is accomplished, he's off to tend to other interests in other places. Storing it up for the next time I need to be gotten with child, no doubt. Leastwise, I hope he's storing it up."

William certainly wasn't. He gave himself to Kat at every opportunity without reservation.

More than their intimate life was being reborn. In other ways, the connection between them grew stronger each day. They finished each other's sentences. They shared secret glances in the most public of places and understood the thoughts behind them without a word.

But Katherine still wasn't sure an annulment wasn't the best thing for William, so she hadn't ruled it out. Their marriage was all that was warmth and light in her world, but that didn't signify when measured against the coldness of her cradle and Will's need for an heir. The reasons behind her decision to seek an annulment still applied.

But could she love the man enough to set him free? That was the rub.

Wind whistled through the arrow slits, keening like a lost soul.

"I'll be glad for your company," Will said as he draped her cloak over her shoulders and handed her the new muff. "But bundle up. Sounds colder than a banshee's tits out."

"And since when do ye know about any other tits but mine?" she asked tartly.

He pulled her close and fondled her through the layers of her clothing. Her nipples perked at his touch despite the wool and linsey separating them. "I do only imagine, love. Yours are the only tits for me."

He dropped a kiss on the tip of her nose and they headed down the spiral stairs. Katherine sneaked a glance into Margaret's chamber as they passed and saw Beathag dozing in a chair beside the bed. Margie seemed to be resting comfortably.

"Careful," William whispered as they continued down. "Nab's sprawled out here."

How the fool could sleep with his head on the earl's threshold and his body draped over a couple of the stair risers was a wonderment. But Nab's stentorian snore proved he managed it well enough.

Katherine and Will picked their way through the great hall, successfully avoiding the many retainers, crofters, and guests who'd wrapped themselves in their plaids and claimed a bit of floor space. One of the deerhounds near the massive fireplace lifted his head as they passed, thumped its tail, and settled immediately when it recognized them.

Outside the great hall, the bailey was swathed in a low-lying fog that muffled sounds and obscured the pathways. The brewery, the well house, the chapel, and other outbuildings rose from the white haze like islands in a becalmed sea. William grasped Katherine's elbow and steered her to the stairs leading to the top of the curtain wall.

A sentry challenged them and was embarrassed when he saw who they were, though William praised the man for his thoroughness.

"What news?" he asked.

"Nothing, my lord," the fellow said. "Leastwise I hope 'tis nothing. The woods have been rustling something fierce this night, but it may just be the wind."

The new moon was setting, but there was enough light to make out the dark pines and bare-limbed alders that began growing halfway up the slope to the north of the castle. Their trunks were swathed in mist, but their topmost boughs rose above it like pointed spears or bony fingers clawing heavenward. Katherine leaned on the crenellations as the eastern sky lightened to pale grey. A flash of something deep in the woods caught her eye.

"There's something there, William," she said softly, pointing to the place where the meadow left off and the forest began. Another flicker made her breath hiss over her teeth. "Is that—"

"Hush." Will cocked his head to listen. It was a low, plodding crunch, the footsteps of hundreds of men marching through packed snow. As more of the mist lifted, dawn reflected off another bit of armor.

Glengarry was situated on a spit of land that thrust out into the loch. The dark waters of Loch Ness served as its rear guard. It was only accessible and only vulnerable from the north, where the woods stood on a steep slope. As the world turned a sickly greenish grey, Katherine saw that among the trees, there were men-at-arms.

Hundreds of them.

As the light strengthened, she saw more of them. Someone gave a shouted command and they formed up, a long snaky line that cut off both access to the castle and escape from it. When the last of the natural fog faded, the men's breath rose in the air, an unnatural dragonish haze.

Grim-faced, William turned to the sentry. "Wake his lordship."

The man tugged his forelock, his face as white as the fog had been, and scrambled down the stairs.

"There are so many," Katherine said. She was no expert, but it seemed the men outside the walls outnumbered those inside by three or four to one.

"But we are safe behind the walls of Glengarry." Will pulled one of her hands from her muff and pressed it to his lips. "No need to fear."

"Ye'd say that whether it was true or not."

Will's mouth lifted in a half smile. "It was worth a try. But it is true that your cousin will break his forces on the walls of Glengarry if he tries to scale them. We are more than enough to defend this castle. Dinna be afraid."

"I'm not afraid for myself," she said, though something inside her that had nothing to do with the cold was beginning to make her shiver uncontrollably. "Not so long as I'm with you. But what about Margie? And all the children, hers and all the crofters'?"

"They'll need to be kept inside. Out of the open bailey and as low in the keep as ye can arrange."

She nodded breathlessly. They'd been preparing for this, but it still seemed unreal. She turned to go, but he didn't release her hand.

"Kat, we haven't spoken of it in a while, love, but . . . weel, I just wanted to make sure ye've put away any thought of sending to Rome." His dark gaze burned through to her inmost part. Even if she wanted to tell a lie, she couldn't. He'd know it. He knew her heart as well as she did. "Tell me ye've changed your mind."

She was spared from giving an answer by an unexpected helper—her cousin Ranulf. At that moment, he broke through the tree line, mounted on a beautifully caparisoned palfrey. Filib Gordon fell in beside him on a less impressive mount, bearing a white flag of truce. The pair rode down the slope toward the gates of Glengarry and stopped about a hundred yards shy of the wall.

"What now?" Katherine asked.

"Looks like he wants to parley. I'll ride out with your father and see what he has in mind."

Katherine scanned the long row of fighting men. They were too far away for her to be able to read their expressions, but their forms bristled with weaponry. "I think it's fairly obvious what my cousin has in mind."

"Aye, but if Ranulf wants to play the gentleman and offer terms, we'll do him the courtesy of listening."

"My father will never surrender."

"Of course not, but we might learn something that will help us turn the tables on him."

She'd resisted the urge to accuse her cousin of treachery, but now he'd convicted himself of it by amassing this contingent of fighting men around Glengarry's one vulnerable side. "But what if Ranulf doesn't mean to play the gentleman?"

"He knows better than to try anything under-handed beneath a flag of peace, but just in case . . ." William signaled to another of the watchmen and told him to order the archers to the walls. "May as well give MacNaught an incentive to remain honest."

Katherine put her arms around him, heedless of who might be looking on, and pressed a quick kiss on his lips. "Be careful, Will. My heart goes with you."

"And mine remains safe in your keeping." He kissed her back, hard and determined. "What evil can befall us?"

Then he strode away. Katherine looked back down at her cousin, who still waited beneath his white flag. As if he felt her gaze, Ranulf turned his head in her direction and bared his teeth at her in a wolf's smile.

What evil indeed?

Herod, the king, in his raging,
Charged he hath this day
His men of might, in his own sight,
All young children to slay.
That woe is me, poor Child for Thee!
And ever mourn and sigh,
For thy parting neither say nor sing,
Bye, bye, lully, lullay.

—From "The Coventry Carol"

"Kind of makes a body wonder why we make so merry at Christmastide since the first one led to the deaths of so many innocents."

—An observation from Nab,
fool to the Earl of Glengarry

Chapter Twenty-Eight

William chafed at the delay, but Lord Glengarry insisted on wearing his station in rich velvet and satin instead of his customary drab plaid. His mount was saddled with the finest Spanish leather tack, and the hilt of his sword glinted with a carbuncle big enough to choke a horse.

"What do I care if that snot-nosed bastard's arse is sore from sitting his horse so long?" the laird growled. "He's the one who came calling unwelcome. He ought not be surprised that I make him wait."

The earl mounted his horse and kneed him into a brisk trot through the raised portcullis. Will followed and, as he'd ordered, the iron bars lowered behind them after they cleared the gate. He didn't look back, but he knew the curtain wall was lined with bowmen waiting for the shouted orders "Nock! Draw! Loose!" Will's archers would turn MacNaught and his second into pin cushions if they put so much as a toe out of line.

"Well, nephew," the laird began in a low tone, "does your mother ken ye've turned on your own blood?"

"Aye, she does," Ranulf returned in a surprisingly cordial tone. "Mother sent me off with a benediction and, since ye're her favorite brother, she said for me to tell ye she prays that your death will be swift and nearly painless."

The distended vein on the earl's forehead pulsed but he said nothing.

"Look around, MacNaught," William said. "Ye've amassed a sizeable force, I'll grant ye, but they're no match for the walls of Glengarry. Have a care for the lives of your men. If ye launch an assault, the corbies will feast."

"Let me worry about my men. Trust me, Badenoch, ye'll have enough to fret about yourself before long. Besides, ye're not laird here," Ranulf said, then skewered the earl with a penetrating gaze. "Now, to business. Surrender now, Uncle, and I give ye leave to ride out of Glengarry with your family and the clothes on your backs, but no weapons and no wealth. The people, the livestock, the stores, ye'll leave for me and my men."

Lord Glengarry laughed mirthlessly. "And I give ye and your men leave to freeze your balls off outside the walls whilst we lie snug by the fire with plenty of food laid by and an inexhaustible supply of fresh water."

"We saw nothing but abandoned crofts on the way here, which means ye've far more mouths to feed than usual." Ranulf smiled unpleasantly. "Lots of women and children too."

Lord Glengarry leaned on the pommel of his saddle. "No worries on that score. Long before we feel the slightest pinch of a siege, King James will hear of it and come to rout ye. My son, Donald, has His Majesty's ear, ye ken."

"As I understand it, our young king is thoroughly occupied with a chase for a white stag at present. He's not likely to want to give up a portent like that. Not even for your precious Donald." Ranulf narrowed his eyes at William. "Besides, no one will be able to break through our lines to deliver a message to His Majesty in any case. We'll kill any who try. Depend upon it."

"Show some sense, man," the laird said, his face now a livid purple. "Go home, Ranulf, and let your men live out their lives. A siege has never worked at Glengarry. The walls are too stout."

"A siege has never worked because I have never commanded one," MacNaught said. "I give ye one last chance and that only because we share a bond of blood. Will ye yield, Uncle?"

"I'll see ye in hell first."

"I was hoping ye'd say that." Ranulf raised his hand in signal and a commotion started behind his line of men. Two long lines of Highlanders pulled a heavy, wheeled platform out of its concealment among the trees and onto a level spot. Upon it stood a tripod of timbers with a complicated system of ropes and pulleys. William had never seen the like before and didn't know what to make of it.

However, Lord Glengarry obviously did, for his eyes grew wide and his cheeks drained of all color. His mouth moved, but he seemed to be having trouble forming the words. The left side of his lips drooped, but he finally managed to whisper, "Trebuchet."

"Aye, Uncle, I've a trebuchet and the will to use it. Dinna ye wish ye'd taken me up on my offer?" Ranulf said. "I'd make it again, but ye've vexed me sore with your refusal to give me what's due me. So now, I'll just raze the castle walls and take what's mine."

Lord Glengarry babbled a string of nonsense sounds and dropped the reins because his left arm suddenly hung loose. He swayed uncertainly in the saddle. Will grasped him and turned both their mounts back toward the Glengarry portcullis with as much speed as he dared.

Ranulf's laughter followed them the whole way.

From her place on the curtain wall, Katherine couldn't hear what the men were saying beneath the flag of truce, but she knew something was wrong when her father nearly lost his seat while his horse was standing still. She skittered down the stone steps and lifted her skirts to fly across the bailey toward the portcullis.

As soon as Will and her father cleared the gate, Will was off his mount without stopping and was pulling her father down from his. The laird couldn't stand without assistance, and one whole side of his face drooped in sagging pockets of flesh.

"Ge' me t' the wall," he garbled as he leaned on William.

"He needs to be put to bed," Katherine said, positioning herself to support her father on the other side.

William shook his head. "If he can bear it, I need him to see what's happening and explain it to me."

Her husband half dragged, half carried her father up the stone steps to the crenellated top. Katherine followed miserably. When her father had had his bout with apoplexy last year, it had taken them a few days to hear of it and rush to his side. By that time, he was on the mend. His speech had almost returned to normal, though his left arm would never be as strong as it once was. Seeing the indomitable earl in such a weakened state frightened her more than all the fighting men and that strange contraption beyond the gate put together.

"What is it?" William pressed the earl to speak. "And how do we defend the keep against it?"

His lordship's speech was gone again. He made sounds that echoed the rise and fall of normal conversation, and the steely look in his eye told Katherine her father thought he was making sense, but the words were gibberish.

"Beggin' yer pardon, my lord," said Sawney MacElmurray. Katherine was surprised to learn the man could talk because when she and William had visited Sawney's croft on Hogmanay, he couldn't seem to get a word in edgewise with his large brood gabbing all at once. "I believe I ken what it is. Not that I've ever seen one, mind. Only that my grandsire's stories told of it. To tell ye the truth, I thought he was pullin' our legs."

The earl growled out some frustrated incomprehensible nonsense.

"Well, what is it, man?" William said.

"A tre . . . trebbie bucket."

"A trebuchet, ye mean."

"Aye, that's it," Sawny MacElmurray said. "I thought ye didna ken what it was. My mistake." He shuffled back to his place on the wall.

"No, wait." Will stopped MacElmurray with a hand to his shoulder. "All I know is what it's called. What does it do?"

A screech of gears made every gaze turn toward the machine halfway up the hillside. A crew of men swarmed over the scaffoldlike apparatus like ants on a bread crumb. They were preparing it for something.

"As to what it does, I'm afeared we'll know soon enough. I just remember my grandsire saying the laird had to limit the number of men on the walls when that . . . that trebbie-bucket thing was in use."

That went against the rules of war. In a siege, the more men at the curtain wall with bows to hand, the better. If a battering ram was used, the team at the murder holes was ready to pour scalding water on any who breached the portcullis. If somehow Ranulf's men managed to mount ladders and started to scale the walls, Glengarry would need every able-bodied fighter to beat back the attackers. How could they defend the walls if they used fewer men?

The earl babbled again and pointed emphatically. His color was high again and the vein on his forehead throbbed.

There was a loud clanking and shouts and the men who'd been working on the machine scrambled away from it now. Then suddenly its tall arm dropped down and another sprang up, launching a large stone like a giant slingshot. With a zing of ropes and pulleys, the timbers fell back into position while the stone flew toward the castle.

William pulled Katherine behind him as if his body would protect her from the several hundred–pound weight hurtling toward them. Left unattended, the earl collapsed to the parapet, but Katherine couldn't get past Will to reach her father. There was such a crush of so many bodies on the wall no one could move to avoid the oncoming projectile.

The flying stone crashed into the wall a scant fifteen yards from Will and Katherine, above the portcullis, near the men tending the fire under the cauldron for the murder holes. Defenders screamed and shouted as they were showered by shards of granite. One man fell into the flames that heated the cauldron and rose shrieking along the parapet. He lost his balance and fell headlong into the bailey, landing in a smoldering heap at the foot of the stone stairs.

"Merciful Christ," William said under his breath, then ordered the archer nearest him to go beat out the flames and move the man. Kat suspected the fellow on fire was past caring, but the last thing they needed was for the flames to spread.

The earl began convulsing at their feet.

Katherine's chest constricted with panic, but she forced herself to remain calm as she dropped to her knees beside her father. She took his hand and tried to say something soothing but feared she was making no more sense than the earl. This time, he didn't answer. He didn't even babble.

"Sawney MacElmurray, Nab!" William shouted. "His lordship is unwell. Take him to his chamber and put him to bed. Katherine, ye go as well to see that he stays there."

The clanking and shouts from MacNaught's camp began again as they readied the trebuchet for another volley. She met Will's bleak gaze for a sickening heartbeat.

"Hurry," he said and then turned away from her to order all but every tenth man from the wall.

Katherine hurried down the steps ahead of the fighting men. Mr. MacElmurray stooped and slung the earl over his shoulder, leaving Nab to scoop up his weapons and follow after. Once in the bailey, they trotted across what used to be open space but was now filled with the temporary tents and stalls of the crofters. Shrieks and muffled cries rose up from the families huddling in those flimsy shelters. The sickening thud of another stone striking the wall made Katherine turn back, like Lot's wife, to look.

A chunk of the protective crenellations was gone near the east corner of the curtain wall. Men were scrambling to obey Will's command to empty the parapet of all but a little more than a dozen defenders. With room to move, the men could avoid the flying stone and shout out where it would land to the rest of the force milling ten feet or so from the foot of the wall in the bailey. As far as she could tell no one was killed by the second volley, but several were bloodied by flying debris. William was striding along the parapet offering encouragement to the few men who served as both targets and lookouts.

The clanking began again and Katherine realized another shot was being prepared. At this rate, the trebuchet would slowly eat up the curtain wall in relentless bites. Once there was a breach big enough to admit a large force, her cousin would throw his rested fighters at William's beleaguered ones.

"My lady." Nab tugged at her sleeve. "William said for us to put the laird to bed."

"You're right. Let's away." She led Sawney MacEl-murray, who shifted the burden of her father's inert form on his broad shoulders, into the great hall. Nab stumbled along behind, bearing her father's fine sword and heavy targe.

A cold lump of dread congealed in her belly. Her father might be dying. Every soul in Glengarry was in mortal peril.

But all she could think was that she should have told Will she loved him while she had the chance.

From His mother He came to us quietly
As dew in April that falls on the grass.
His mother's labor was painless and quiet,
As dew in April that falls on the grass.
As His mother lay there, He came quietly,
As dew in April that falls on the flower branches.

—From "I Sing of a Maiden"

"A bairn that comes into the world quietly? That would
be a Christmas miracle indeed."

—An observation from Nab,
fool to the Earl of Glengarry

Chapter Twenty-Nine

Katherine met Dorcas coming down the spiral
stairs. Because the space was so narrow, the maid had
to turn around and head back up to where the earl's
chamber veered off in order for Katherine and the
men to continue climbing. The maid followed them
into the laird's room and skittered around MacElmurray and his burden to pull back the counterpane on
Lord Glengarry's bed before they reached it.

Katherine noticed that the maid shot a quick glance
at Nab and then studiously ignored him, unnecessarily

smoothing the linens that were bound to be rumpled again soon.

When Nab tugged off her father's boots, he didn't stir so much as an eyelash. Katherine tucked the coverlet up to his chin and was relieved to see that it rose and fell. He was still breathing.

"May I have yer leave to go? I was just off to fetch Beathag, my lady," Dorcas said breathlessly. "Lady Margaret is in a bad way."

Katherine's heart sank to the tips of her kid-covered toes. "Go. And after ye've found Beathag, get ye to the nursery and collect my nephews. Tell Nurse she's to mind them in the souterrain till Lord Badenoch says different." All the small round faces of the children who had descended on the castle with their humble parents rose in her mind. "We have to get the crofters out of the bailey as well. Tell them to take their little ones to the souterrain too."

"All of them?"

"All. The mothers too. They can help Nurse keep watch over them." The castle would have to be razed to the ground before the trebuchet would reach the children there. "'Tis the safest place."

"Beggin' yer pardon, milady," Sawney MacElmurray said, twisting his bonnet in his work-rough hands. "I dinna think I can do his lordship much good here. My boys are all with Lord Badenoch on the wall. If ye'll give me leave, I'd like to join them."

"Verra well, Mr. MacElmurray," she said woodenly as she hitched a hip on the side of the earl's bed.

Normally her father's cheeks were ruddy, but now his complexion was like fine alabaster, pale and fragile looking. She had no idea what could be done for him. Since he was unconscious, he couldn't be fed strengthening broth or given any healing herbs, even if she knew what those might be. She didn't think leeches would help, and in any case, she couldn't bear the thought of breaking out Margaret's store of the slimy things.

So she did the only thing she could do. She put a hand to Lord Glengarry's chest, closed her eyes, and loosed an arrow of a prayer skyward. Her father was in God's hands and she would have to leave him there.

"Nab, I need ye to stay."

The fool had started to trail Sawney out of the chamber. "My lady? William wants all the men to—"

"Not you. Someone must stay with his lordship. In case he wakes."

"And what should I do if that happens?"

"Keep him in bed. If ye can." Another crashing boom sounded closer this time, and a collective scream rose up from the bailey. Katherine flew to the window. The brewery roof was staved in by a large chunk of granite, the timbers of the rafters snapped as if they were no stouter than a child's dollhouse.

Another wail sounded, this time one much closer than the bailey. It was so full of anguish it made Kat's chest ache.

"Lady Margaret," she said.

"But milady, I dinna think I—"

Katherine left Nab still jabbering his excuses of how inadequate he'd be to tend the earl. She fled from her father's chamber and up the circular stairs to her sister-in-law. Margie was in her bed, but struggling to climb out of it.

"What are ye doing?" Kat asked. "Should ye not be lying back?"

"Not anymore." Margaret rolled to one side, dangled her legs over the edge of the bed, and tried to push herself into a sitting position. "My waters have burst and the bedclothes need to be stripped or it'll seep through and ruin the feather tick."

"Trust ye to be concerned with such a mundane thing as a mattress at a time like this." Katherine hurried to her side to help her rise to her feet.

"Oh!" Margie cradled her belly as another contraction hardened it and more of her birth waters pattered to the floor between her legs. A guttural groan escaped her throat, and she dug her nails into Katherine's forearm hard enough to leave marks.

"I ask your pardon, Kat," she said between gasps. "I didna moan so with the others. D'ye think it means a girl-child?"

"God knows."

Along with the mildly sweet smell of Margie's birth water, memories of her own childbed ordeal flooded Katherine's senses. When she'd labored with Stephan, she'd needed to move. She must have paced miles within the confines of her chamber in a gritty struggle as her body fought to expel him. The respites between contractions were all too brief. Her attendants' whispers sounded like a hissing ball of adders as she sank into delirium.

Katherine cleared her throat, hoping her voice would not break. "Will ye walk a bit?"

"No." Margaret trembled. "This child is coming. I need the chair."

Katherine stayed beside her, supporting her until the pain subsided. Then she moved the birthing chair from its place in a corner of the room to a central location before the fire.

The special chair was made of pine with a U-shaped seat to support Margie's thighs. But the open seat left plenty of room for the child to slip through into the midwife's waiting arms when the time came. It had a reclining back, curved to match Margaret's spine, and had been painstakingly sanded till it was as smooth as glass all over.

The chair brought back more memories. Katherine had thought her labor was nearly finished once she settled into her chair. The pains were close together. Her midwife had assured her all would be well. Instead, she'd labored for hours to bring forth a child who couldn't seem to be born.

When Stephan finally arrived, the sudden silence in the chamber was a physical thing, a weight like a shroud. She wondered if she'd been struck deaf, except that the silence echoed not in her ears, but in her heart.

The child made no cry.

From the tail of her eye, she'd seen the midwife carrying away a small, still bundle. Then someone had put a cool cloth to her brow and lied soothingly about how next time everything would be different.

Katherine blinked back tears. It wouldn't do to show weak eyes to Margie while she was birthing her bairn. Instead, she arranged her sister-in-law's skirts around her so that if anyone should happen into the chamber, she'd be decently covered.

Before Katherine was brought to childbed with Stephan, she had dreaded losing her dignity while giving birth. She was determined to remain in control of herself. After a very short while, the illusion of being able to control anything fled. Her body was not her own. Forces as old as the tide swept her past Death's door. She had no say in whether or not it would send her rushing headlong through it.

Another contraction started and Margie gritted her teeth for as long as she could, but a cry of pain pushed past her lips despite her efforts. Her whole body stiffened.

"This is different." She panted shallowly once the moment had passed. "It feels . . . I can scarcely draw breath. Something's wrong."

Katherine dipped a cloth in the water basin and applied it to Margie's forehead. "'Tis the way of things. All mothers-to-be think something's amiss, my midwife said."

"But something *was* wrong for ye." Margie bit her lip and squeezed her eyes shut. "Ye knew it. D'ye not think a woman knows?"

"Hush now. 'Twill be all right. Just breathe, my dear one, till the next pain comes."

Where on earth was Beathag?

She crossed to the bed and stripped off the soiled linens. Another crash sounded out in the bailey, but Margie cried out again and Kat hurried back to her. Margie's grip ground the bones in Katherine's hand against each other, but she didn't pull away. Margie needed her. No matter if the castle was shattering around them, she couldn't tear herself from her sister-in-law's side.

"Nock! Draw! Loose!"

In the interval between the flying rocks, William had lined the curtain wall with archers. Their shafts flew in a high arc toward the deadly machine on the hillside, but fell far short of the mark. A cheer went up from MacNaught's men, and a long line of them bent over and flipped up their kilts to bare their arses in a show of contempt. Then they began reloading the trebuchet.

"He's got it all planned out, my lord." Hew MacElmurray pointed off to the right. "Ye see the crew workin' over there. That's where they're getting the stones. There's a goodly sized outcropping of granite."

Will ground a fist into his palm. All of MacNaught's men were out of range of even the best bowmen. The Glengarry defenders were outnumbered too severely for Will to consider abandoning his defensive position. But the trebuchet was negating the advantage of the thick curtain walls with each volley. He'd ridden Greyfellow over the hillside that rose to the north of Glengarry countless times, but now he surveyed it with a strategic eye.

"There's a bit of a dip in the land halfway between us and that damned machine. It would shelter a group of archers. D'ye see where I mean?" William asked Hew.

"Aye, that'd do. And it would put us close enough to do some damage," Hew said with a nod. "Shall I gather some men and make for it?"

"Not now."

MacNaught had at least twenty mounted men flanking the trebuchet. A cavalry charge would decimate men with nothing but bows in their hands. MacNaught had also stationed a group of his own bowmen at the ready about twenty yards in front of the trebuchet. Ranulf was a better general than William had expected.

"Pick the best archers we have and assemble a team, but we'll wait for dark. They won't be expecting us to sally forth then."

Hew gave his forelock a tug in respect and loped away to do Will's bidding.

"Trebuchet!" someone shouted. "Headed for the western ramparts!"

A three hundred–pound weight of stone hurtled through the air and crashed with a sickening thud against Glengarry's wall. One of the defenders hadn't scrambled away in time and was thrown from the parapet like a rag doll.

William cast an eye at the sun, wishing there was a way to speed it along its pathway. Shouting orders to redeploy the men along the curtain wall, he thanked God that winter days were short. Darkness was their friend, and the desperate sortie he had in mind was like to be their best hope.

Margaret wasn't moaning any longer. She was screaming. She'd even stopped apologizing for it during the short rest periods between contractions. Katherine had reached the end of what she knew to do for her. She could only let Margie squeeze the life out of her hands and pray that Beathag would come soon.

Finally, the midwife dragged herself up the spiral stairs. A strip of muslin had been tied over her head and under her jaw, covering what looked like a jagged cut along one of her cheeks.

"Beathag, what happened to you?"

"I was in the brewery when the roof collapsed, my lady. Dorcas helped pull me out." Beathag waved a bony-knuckled hand. "Dinna fash yerself on my account. I've a bump on my head and a cut on my cheek, but I'm well enough for all normal purposes. Lord knows there's them what are worse off than me."

One of those unfortunates was ensconced in the birthing chair. The midwife bustled over to Margaret and settled herself on the short stool in front of the lady's elevated knees to take stock of the situation. Her brows lowered in a frown and she made a tsking sound with her teeth and tongue.

"That's bad, it is," she muttered. "The babe's turned 'round."

Margaret's chin had sunk to her chest as if she'd swooned, but now she lifted her head. "What do you mean? I thought you said the child was ready to come."

"He was. But sometimes they take an odd notion at the last moment. This one's coming feet first." Beathag forced a smile to her thin lips now that she realized Margie was still sensible enough to hear and understand her. "Dinna fret, my lady. 'Tis not the first breech bairn I've brought into the world and, God willing, 'twill not be my last."

Another boom sounded in the bailey and another chorus of screams rose to greet it. The pull toward the window was strong, but Katherine couldn't answer its summons. Margie was in the throes of another contraction and Kat wouldn't take her hand away.

Besides, if Will was in the path of one of the flying boulders, she didn't want to know.

Be thou poor or be thou rich
I direct up thine eye
And so in this we be all like
For one and all shall we die.

—From "Death Began Because of Sin"

"If we all have to share in something and I'd had my druthers, I'd have wished that we all had red hair. Aye, 'tis a bit of a curse at times, as I've good reason to know, but it beats dyin' by a long chalk."

—An observation from Nab,
fool to the Earl of Glengarry

Chapter Thirty

With the darkness came a blessed stillness as well. MacNaught seemed satisfied with the damage he'd done to Glengarry's curtain wall that day. As twilight deepened, the machine stopped clanking and tossing death and destruction toward the castle. Fires burned at intervals along the hillside, and occasional laughter rose from the camp of the men giving siege to the castle as they enjoyed their evening meal.

Why shouldn't they laugh? Will thought. *There's no one to bury in MacNaught's camp.*

William made the rounds, searching out the family members of the men who'd fallen defending the wall. One of the crofters' children, a small boy named Jamie, had died when the brewery was struck.

"He wasna a bad boy," his mother said tearfully. "But he'd a fear of underground places. Wouldna set foot in our root cellar. When I called for him to join me and the other children headed for the souterrain, he ran away."

His small, broken body was found where he'd hidden away amid the hogsheads of beer and barrels of hops. For now the dead were laid out in the chapel side by side in their makeshift shrouds. William feared the small church would soon not be big enough.

"Now, my wee laddie will lie underground till the Last Trump sounds," young Jamie's mother said, her shoulders shaking with grief.

"Not so," Will said. "If the great and mighty can be interred in the walls of cathedrals, we can carve out a niche here in the chapel for your boy."

The power of speech deserting her, the woman grasped William's gloved hand and pressed a kiss to it.

"Dinna fret, mother. I swear I'll see it done." Will moved on to the next grieving family to offer comfort. He steeled himself not to feel. If he let himself, he'd be too bogged down by the sorrow around him to be any good to anyone.

As many people as could fit were crowded into the great hall. There, cheek by jowl, they were served a thin stew and bread. A few grumbled, but if the siege lasted long, they'd be glad Cook was thrifty from the start. Will found the MacElmurray family huddled together as near the fire as they could manage.

"Are ye and your company of archers ready, Hew?" Will asked.

The young man nodded. "Aye, they're to be waiting at the portcullis for yer orders, milord."

"By yer leave, I'll be joining ye too, Lord Badenoch," Sawney MacElmurray said. "I canna let my youngest son follow ye if I fear to go myself."

Both men kissed Mrs. MacElmurray on the cheek, shouldered their quivers and bows, and followed Will into the night. He found a dozen men milling by the gate.

"Once we clear the castle, there's to be no talking," William told the assembled group. "Dinna nock an arrow till I give the signal. We'll have a chance for perhaps a dozen volleys before we meet resistance. Then we hightail it. Our task this night is to sting them."

"Not to defeat them?" Hew asked.

"That'll come, Hew," Will said. "For now we need to inflict some pain and show them we aren't cowed by their damned machine."

By all accounts, Ranulf's men were not overly fond of discipline or much familiar with the concept of loyalty. With any luck, MacNaught's loosely bound group of warriors would think twice about their leadership after this nasty surprise caught them unawares. William was counting on some of MacNaught's fighters slipping away from the siege as an unprofitable venture that was likely to get a man killed when he wasn't looking.

"When I call retreat, ye're to make for the castle without looking behind ye. I'm taking fourteen men out. I mean to bring ye all safe to your families once this night's work is done," Will said with a grim smile.

To a man, they grinned gamely back at him. Too often, lairds spent the lives of their pledge-men cheaply, using them as archery fodder in set battles. Besides having genuine concern for these volunteers' lives, William didn't have a single man to spare.

He wished he could go mounted, but feared the sound of a horseman would be louder than men on foot. He ducked through the postern gate, the smaller opening that didn't require the portcullis to be lifted.

"Be at the ready to let us back in," he ordered the porter as the last bowman passed through.

The new moon was shrouded behind heavy clouds, for which Will gave thanks. It meant his small party climbing the snow-covered hill might seem to be nothing more than undulating shadows to any watchman. No alarm had been raised by the time they reached the depression William had pointed out earlier.

He tugged off his gloves and clicked his fingers, the signal they'd all agreed would replace the verbal commands to nock, draw, and loose. The hiss of arrows as they winged toward the campfire nearest the trebuchet could easily be taken for the stinging breath of the winter.

Shouts and screams told them some of the arrows had struck true. William gave the signal for another volley in the same place. The third group of arrows was directed at another prechosen fire. More cries of surprise and pain rose from the camp.

The old Vikings told tales of the Valkyries, disembodied choosers of the slain. Will's arrows were like those mythical death-bringers. They sang a song of doom as they whizzed through the air and found their marks. Over the cries of the wounded, William heard MacNaught shouting but couldn't hear the words well enough to tell what he was ordering.

If their positions were reversed, Will would be calling for the cavalry to mount up, so his ears pricked for any sound of horses. He gave orders for more volleys in rapid succession.

"Back to the castle," he ordered when he heard

hooves pounding their way. His men took to their heels, having been warned that this was how a sortie was conducted—a bold strike after leaving a defensive position and then a swift retreat.

How much damage they'd done, Will couldn't say. Unless they'd managed to hit the fellow in a friar's frock who seemed to be ordering the operation of the trebuchet, this foray was more to undermine morale than to deal a decisive blow.

Hopefully, it would wipe the smugness from Ranulf's face when he realized his men weren't as untouchable as he thought.

Will charged after his men, half running, half sliding down the snow-covered slope. As they neared the gate, he did a quick count and found himself one man short. He turned back to see Hew MacElmurray still in place, emptying his quiver, his movements fluid and full of deadly grace. There was barely a stop between one shot and the next.

"Hew!" Will shouted. "Retreat!"

"Only a few more," came the answer. Half a dozen of MacNaught's horsemen were almost upon him.

"No!" William drew his sword and ran back up the slope. Hew ducked at the last moment, barely escaping a horseman's blade that would have sheared off his head like a rabbit's.

Hew's father shouted at his son to retreat but the lad loosed one more arrow at an oncoming rider before taking to his heels. The horseman took the arrow full in the chest and toppled from his mount, but five more barreled after him. Hew rushed past William, who braced his feet and wielded his claymore with both hands before the pounding charge.

As a rider bore down on his position, William dropped to one knee and gutted his mount as they flew past. The horse screamed in agony and tumbled headlong down the slope, taking the warrior on his back with him in a devastating fall. William hated the wanton destruction of dumb beasts in battle, but it was easier for a man on foot to take out the horse than the rider.

The archers he'd stationed on the wall began to shoot at the men on horseback as they came within range. The shafts zinged into the hillside around Will and his attackers. Since Hew was safe, he turned to flee while the riders milled in confusion. The archers kept the riders at a respectful distance. When they managed to bring one down in a frenzy of screaming horse and man, the rest abandoned the fight and made for MacNaught's camp.

Battle rage still roaring in his veins, William pounded down the slope and through the postern gate. Once he was inside, the heavy bolt was thrown.

"Why?" Will grasped Hew by the collar and slammed him against the stone wall. "Why did ye not obey orders?"

Hew stammered an incoherent excuse, but Sawney MacElmurray hung his head. "I blame myself, milord. The fault is mine. Hew was ever headstrong but he was such a bonnie hunter and a fine hand with a bow, I didna teach him to mind as I should have."

"If he canna follow orders, he's of no use to anyone," Will snarled. "There are enough ways for a man to die, Hew. I dinna want to have to tell your mother ye got yourself killed because ye were stupid. Now get out of my sight before I have ye whipped."

Red-faced, Hew bolted away. Will swallowed back his fury. Young MacElmurray was the best bowman in the castle and he'd nearly lost him.

"Thank ye for risking yerself for my boy, milord."

Sawney's eyes were moist. "Hew's his mother's favorite, ye ken."

William dismissed his men to find their families. An uneasy quiet settled on the night as each side licked its wounds, but Will couldn't afford to rest.

He passed quickly through the bailey, into the great hall, and climbed the spiral stairs. Nab met him at the opening to the earl's chamber.

"How does Lord Glengarry fare?" he asked wearily.

"The same. He hasna twitched so much as a nose hair," Nab said. "Jamison has come to sit by him for the rest of the night. What can I do to help ye, William?"

Will sighed deeply. Nab was no fighter. He'd improved a bit with his bow, but a few lucky shots did not a warrior make. If it came to hand-to-hand combat, Nab wouldn't last more than a few heartbeats.

"I don't know how ye can help," Will said honestly.

"I'll just bear ye company then," the fool said. "Sometimes that's enough."

"I thought ye didna much care for the company of others."

"I dinna." Nab pulled off his fool's cap and twisted it in his hands. "But yer company I dinna mind so much."

Will shrugged. "Come then and we'll see how it goes with Lady Margaret."

Nab went owl-eyed at the prospect of visiting a lying-in, but fell gamely into step behind William as he mounted the stairs.

The rest of the castle might be enjoying a tentative peace, but Lady Margaret's war went on. Will peeked into the chamber to find her seated in the birthing chair, her face glistening with sweat, her hands gripping the arms.

Katherine was at her side, smoothing her hair back and murmuring urgent encouragements. Kat's face was as taut with anxiety as Margie's was with pain. Then the contraction subsided. His sister-in-law's head lolled forward and her arms relaxed.

Katherine straightened and happened to glance his way. Her face lit with joy. She abandoned Margie and flew to him, throwing her arms around his neck.

"Oh, Will, thank God." She buried her face in his neck. "I heard ye'd led a sortie beyond the walls. I was so afraid for ye."

Will hugged her fiercely. The welfare of every soul within Glengarry was on his shoulders, but she was all he was fighting for. This woman, this moment, all warm and silvery, there was nothing else for him in the world.

But he couldn't lay aside his responsibilities and lose himself in her as he wished. Without releasing her from his embrace, he whispered in her ear, "I need to know if there's a secret way out of the castle."

She pulled back to look up at him. "A secret way out? If there is one, I dinna know of it. Do ye mean to abandon Glengarry then? Are things that bad?"

"No, we aren't evacuating, though it may come to that. I need to send a messenger to Donald in Inverness, and going out the main gate isna an option."

After the sortie, Ranulf had no doubt reinforced his net of watchmen around the landward sides of the castle.

"Donald?" Margie's voice was as frail as a piece of parchment stretched thin enough to tear. "Is Donald here?"

Katherine sent him a quick look of apology and hurried back to Margaret's side. "Not yet, dearest. But soon." She blotted her sister-in-law's face and neck with a wet cloth. "Donald will be here soon, won't he, Will?"

He will if I have anything to say about it, and the bastard had better bring a hundred horsemen with him. Will swallowed back that thought and took a step or two into the room. "We need to send word to him that his child is coming, good-sister. Is there a way to leave Glengarry besides through the portcullis?"

Badenoch Castle had a complex warren of tunnels branching off from a locked cell in the dungeon. They led to a natural cave system that wandered below ground. A man, or a hundred of them, could leave Badenoch unseen and reappear miles away. It was a closely guarded secret, known only to him and his brothers. He hadn't even told Katherine about it. He made a mental note to do so at the first opportunity.

"No, there isna a secret way out of the castle," Margie said between gasping breaths. "I asked Donald once why there wasn't a way to launch a boat from the castle since the loch is so near, but he said it would undermine the walls to have another opening besides the portcullis. The walls of Glengarry are our protection." She grimaced as another contraction seized her. "And our prison."

Will felt a tug on his sleeve. It was Nab.

"Ask me, William. I know a secret way."

*O great mystery
and wondrous sacrament,
that animals should see the newborn Lord
lying in their manger.*

—From "O Magnum Mysterium"

*"Great mystery, ye say. I'll tell ye a great mystery. 'Tis
the wonder of a fool what canna keep his big mouth
shut when no one has even asked him a question."*

—An observation from Nab,
fool to the Earl of Glengarry

Chapter Thirty-One

"But I dinna know the way to Inverness, William."
Nab slogged up the crumbling stairs of his secret tower
with Lord Badenoch at his heels.

"There's naught to know. Stick to the loch shore
and head northeast. When ye run out of loch, follow
the river's course and it'll lead ye straight to Inverness.
Anyone can tell ye where the king's court is after that."

When they reached the tower chamber, it seemed
smaller than ever with William in it too. But small or
not, it had been Nab's. Now that Lord Badenoch knew
about it, it would never be his again.

Why, oh why had he said anything?

"Stop at the village of Abriachan to see if the ferry is there, though it may be across the loch at Dores." William pressed a purse that jingled into his hand. "If ye can catch the ferry, it'll speed your journey."

Nab didn't want a journey, speedy or otherwise. He'd never been farther than the boundary of Glengarry lands in his whole life. His belly squirmed like a bucketful of eels.

William leaned his head out the small window and gauged the distance to the frozen loch below. "Aye, this'll do. We've rope enough to lower ye down and the ice at the loch's edge should bear your weight. If ye hug the shoreline, the land is steep enough as it rushes down to the loch that ye're not likely to attract the attention of MacNaught's watchmen."

"Not likely? Can ye not do better than that, William? Not likely means there's a chance I will be seen."

"The fortunes of war, my friend." Will grinned at him, clearly trying to buck up his confidence. "There are no guarantees, but I like your chances."

"I'd like my chances better if they were somebody else's chances," he said as William tied one end of his rope around Nab's waist.

Will's falsely cheerful smile faded. "I'm countin' on ye, Nab. We all are. And in truth . . ."

"In truth, ye canna spare anyone else," Nab finished for him. "I understand. I canna fight, but I can bolt like a hare if need be."

"God gives us all different gifts, Nab." Will started to lay a steadying hand on his forearm, but seemed to remember how Nab felt about being touched and stopped himself. "It may well be that your gifts will be the saving of us all. D'ye remember the message?"

Nab rattled it off word perfect.

"Good." William looped the other end of the rope around his own waist so he could help Nab control the rate of his descent. "Now off ye go before dawn catches ye in the open."

"Guess I'd best return this first." Nab took the scepter from his belt. William took it from him solemnly.

"Ye were the best Laird of Misrule I ever saw."

"Thank ye, William."

"No, 'tis I who should thank ye. Ye're done with play and are acting like a laird in earnest. I'm counting on ye, Nab."

He'd never known what it felt like to be trusted with anything of importance.

He still wished he didn't, but he climbed into the small window in any case. Then he rolled over and lay with his belly on the sill so his arse and legs dangled over the loch below. If he looked down, he'd never have the courage to do it. He had to back into this descent. He grasped the rope with both hands, took a deep breath, and closed his eyes.

"Wait, Nab! I'm coming!"

It was Dorcas.

The rope slipped a bit and Nab had to scrabble his boot tips against the castle stone to remain in the window. Dorcas popped up at the head of the stairs, eyes wide when she saw where he was. Heedless of Lord Badenoch, she flew to Nab.

Without any preamble she palmed both his cheeks and kissed him right on the mouth in front of William and God and everything!

"Lady Katherine told me what ye're doing. Nab, I'm so proud of ye I could burst."

Nab's belly stopped squirming and glowed with something he suspected was pride.

"But I'm that angry with ye too," she said.

He'd never know it by the way she kept peppering his face with kisses, bussing his cheeks, his forehead, his closed eyelids.

"Why would ye leave without giving me a chance to tell ye good-bye, ye wicked, wicked man?"

He couldn't have answered if he'd wanted to because just then she thrust her tongue into his mouth. When Dorcas finally let him come up for air, he said, "I thought ye were taking up with that Hew MacElmurray."

"I only wanted ye to think so. To make ye jealous."

"It worked."

William cleared his throat. "The sooner ye go, Nab, the sooner ye'll be back."

"Aye." Suddenly he knew what he needed to do to keep from being afraid. "Dorcas, will ye marry me?"

"Now?" Her brows shot skyward. "Ye ask me that now when ye're about to go get yerself killed?"

"That's the point, ye see. Even a fool has to keep his word. If I promise to marry ye, I canna let myself be killed, can I?"

Her warm-as-a-summer-day smile washed over him, though it didn't quite reach to his nether regions. His arse hanging over the loch was colder than a well-digger's knee.

"Aye, Nab, I'll marry ye." She kissed him one last time. "And now ye must keep yer word, but 'tis not the word of a fool. 'Tis the vow of the man I love. I'll have words with anyone, even you, who takes ye for a fool."

With those fine words ringing in his heart, he pushed off and let William lower him down the lochward wall. Dorcas leaned out the window, her little heart-shaped face filled with both yearning and fear.

If he saw his own face in a mirror just now, he suspected he'd see the same unchancy mix.

* * *

"Push, my lady," Beathag urged from her place on the floor before Margaret's spread legs. "'Tis almost done, lamb. I see a wee footikin peeping. The child may be coming backward but he's finally coming."

Margie growled in response and bore down. Then when the contraction ceased, she trembled and panted, her head lolling on Katherine's arm. Kat had been supporting her through the pains, and that arm felt as if hundreds of pins were pricking it, but she wouldn't move it out from under Margie for worlds. The firelight should have bathed her sister-in-law in shades of gold, but her complexion was as pale and translucent as wet muslin.

"Kat," she whispered.

"I'm here, dearest."

"I feel myself going, so I do."

Katherine cast a worried glance at Beathag, but the midwife only returned a tight-lipped grimace and lifted her shoulders in a small shrug that said, "'Tis in God's hands."

"If I should die, I want ye and William to foster this bairn."

"Dinna speak so. D'ye wish to tempt the devil?" Katherine clutched Margie's hand tightly, but her sister-in-law's grip went limp. "Besides, Donald might have something to say about that."

Anger flared in Margie's eyes, and for a moment she looked more like herself. "Dinna fret on that score. Donald would have to be here first before he'd have anything to say, would he not?"

That spark of contentiousness died as the next contraction swept her up.

"Lady Katherine, do ye press down on her belly," Beathag ordered.

Kat added her force to Margaret's waning strength.

"Aye, that's it. She's coming."

"She?" Margie stopped groaning long enough to ask.

"Aye, the head's not out yet, but both legs are free. There's enough bairn here for me to see that ye've almost got a new daughter, my lady."

"God be praised." Then Margie grunted like an old sow and the child came forth. "A wee lassie! Oh, I so wanted a girl-child." The bairn sucked in her first breath and wailed her little head off. Margie chuckled weakly. "Maybe just not such a noisy one."

"'Tis a beautiful noise." Katherine hugged Margie and kissed her cheek. Beathag didn't say anything. She was too busy tying off the birth cord.

"Here, Lady Katherine. Kindly take the bairn and give her a proper cleaning before ye present her to her lady mother." The midwife pressed the squirming bundle into Katherine's arms. "Lady Margaret, yer labor isna quite done, but I promise 'twill be much easier now."

While Margie passed the afterbirth, Katherine took the child to the washbasin and sponged off the blood and mucus. The baby's skin was softer than a mole's belly. As Kat washed her, the little one stopped crying and blinked slowly, her dark eyes enormous. A crest of fine hair of indeterminate color topped her perfectly shaped head and she had all her fingers and toes. Katherine didn't think she'd ever seen anything quite so lovely in all her life.

A Christmastide miracle with feet.

Kat swaddled the babe tightly and then hugged her close, inhaling her newness, a last whiff of heaven.

Judging from the midwife's chatter, things were going well with Margie now.

Kat breathed a silent prayer of thanks. Margie deserved something easy. She carried the child back to Margie, whose color had improved out of all knowing, and placed her in her mother's arms.

As she watched Margie and her new daughter become acquainted, a fist formed in her heart. She shoved the feeling away. She didn't want it claiming space in her heart. It was unworthy.

Jealousy was a bruise that never went away. It hurt to touch it, so she made a conscious effort not to.

But it was always there.

"I'm going to name you Katherine, after your beautiful auntie," Margie told the bairn. Then she looked up at Kat. "But we'll call her Kitty so there'll be no confusion." She clasped Kat's hand. "Thank ye for being here for me. I couldna have . . . I wouldna—"

"Come, my lady," Beathag interrupted. "Ye've had a long and trying day . . . and night, come to that! Past time we got ye into bed. Lady Katherine, if ye'll send for the wet nurse—"

"No," Margie interrupted back. "I'll suckle this one myself."

"Weel, that might be for the best, my lady," Beathag said. "It'll make ye less likely to bear again so soon."

"Why have ye never said so? If 'tis true, that's the sort of thing that ought to be more generally known. If someone had told me before this, I'd have nursed all my bairns," Margie said, some of the usual vinegar creeping back into her voice. Then she cast an appraising eye at Katherine. "Ye should find your bed too, Kat. Ye look all in."

"Trust ye to think of others even at a time like this."

Kat pressed a kiss to the crown of Margie's head and stroked her niece's cheek. "I'll see ye both in the morning."

Wearily, she slogged up the stairs to her chamber, wondering if she'd be able to fight sleep long enough to peel off her clothing. When she reached her room, she was met by a sight that assured she'd stay awake.

William was waiting for her there, naked as Adam. He was seated in the earl's copper tub. Flickers of firelight kissed his bare chest and steam curled from the surface of the water.

"Will ye care to join me, wife?"

The time of grace has come—
what we have wished for,
songs of joy.

—From "Gaudete"

"I suspect every soul on earth could use a little grace—
a little receiving of that which we dinna deserve but
need as surely as our next heartbeat."

—An observation from Nab,
fool to the Earl of Glengarry

Chapter Thirty-Two

Katherine shrugged out of her clothes as she crossed the room, letting the pieces fall to the floor unheeded. By the time she reached the steaming tub, all that remained was her leine, and she made short work of that, pulling it over her head in one smooth motion.

Will's gaze sizzled over her. He lifted a hand to help her into the bath. "Ye do know how to make a man's heart glad, Kat."

With a contented sigh, she settled between his legs and lay back against his chest, letting the rising water lap at her breasts. "The castle is under siege. Everything is upended. How on earth did ye manage this?"

"Your father has no need of his tub just now. And before ye ask, Jamison says the earl's resting quietly and even roused enough to take a little broth, though he still isna speaking sensibly," William said. "In any case, after I sent Nab on his way to your brother, Donald, I had Hew MacElmurray move the tub up here and fill it."

Heating and hauling water for the bath was the province of Dorcas and the other maids. "That must have grated on him."

"He wasna inclined to complain. Hew has a debt to pay."

William reached around to hold her breasts. He didn't tease along the underside of them. Didn't torment her nipples into tight peaks. Instead, he just held her as if they were the most precious things in the world. She'd had so many demands on her all day, the fact that he made none now allowed all the tension to drain from her body.

"Lady Margaret is well?"

"Aye, she is and was this night made the mother of a fine wee daughter." That fist clenched in her chest again.

"Good for her."

"Aye, good for Margaret. She wanted a girl this time." Katherine hated herself for the smoldering ball of envy in her heart but she couldn't seem to stop it from flaring. Her arms, like her womb, would always be empty. It wasn't fair.

Why not ever good for me?

A tear streaked her cheek and she swiped it away, hoping Will wouldn't realize she wept.

"I know 'twas hard for ye to be there with her, but ye

made me proud by it." His chest rumbled against her spine as he spoke.

So much for her secret tears.

"'Tis hard for me too," he said. "Do I wish things were different? Aye, I do. Sometimes in my mind's eye I see the sons and daughters we should have had and I wish—"

"Then ye shouldna fight me about sending to Rome." Assuming they made it out of MacNaught's siege, of course.

He put a hand to the crown of her head and smoothed her hair. "Ye didna let me finish. I may sometimes think on what we dinna have, but I never lose sight of what we do. We have each other. Do ye ken how rare a thing that is? We are a family, Katherine, you and me. We may be only a circle of two but 'tis enough." He hugged her tighter to his chest. He was all broad bands of muscle and sleek skin in the warm water. "If I had ten sons and didna have ye, I'd be a pauper. Ye are all I have and all I need. Ye are my home."

Her soft palate ached from trying to hold back tears. "Oh, Will."

"D'ye know why I never fear to go into battle?"

She shook her head, unable to speak.

"Because if I should fall, 'twould not be the worst that could happen to me. The worst would be losing ye."

She'd never felt more unworthy. Or more grateful. Her insides might be in turmoil, but Will's love was a calm sea on which to launch her soul. He'd always bear her up.

She turned in the tub so she could wrap her arms around him and lay her cheek against his wet chest. "I do love ye so, Will."

He drew a ragged breath. "Feels like forever ago since I heard ye say that."

"I love ye so much it hurts," she went on. "And yet I wouldna stop the aching for worlds."

"I dinna know what will come tomorrow," Will said. "But that's the condition of every man. All we have is now. This night. This moment."

She rose up and kissed him, his mouth both familiar and strangely new. "Then we'd best not waste it."

William didn't know if kisses could heal. No matter how many times he and Kat loved each other, there were some hurts nothing would mend. They'd been so innocent when they first pledged to love each other till one of them laid the other in the arms of God. So naïve. Life had not yet smacked them down. Their hearts hadn't bled.

But not all wounds were mortal. Their hearts went on, calloused and bruised, but still beating.

He rose dripping from the tub with Katherine in his arms and carried her to the bed. They tumbled into it in a tangle of limbs and a flurry of kisses. The feel of her skin against his was heaven enough to drive rational thought from his mind as blood pooled in his groin.

Everywhere she touched flared with heat. Everywhere she kissed burned with forgiveness and hope. They knew the best and the worst of each other. And they had not turned away.

It was a minor miracle.

Her skin was his favorite flavor. He wanted to taste every bit of her. Each sigh was the music he most wanted to hear. Her fingertips made love to the old scar on his ribs. He played a lover's game on her secrets. Something inside him nearly burst when she came under his touch.

Then she wrapped herself around him and he sank into her. Complete.

One.

She was lightning to his answering thunder. Chaos roared in his veins. She rose to meet him with such abandon, he didn't know if he was taking or being taken. When he came, he cried out something unintelligible, something in the language of demons or angels, he wasn't sure which.

Spent and gasping, they both sank into the feather tick, still entangled with each other, still connected.

If he could magically go back to their first days of loving, he wouldn't. Things might have been simpler before they buried their stillborn son.

Now they were more real.

It was the screams that woke him. William leaped from the bed and crossed the chamber to the narrow slit that overlooked the bailey in a few bounding strides. Plumes of black rose from the stables and tongues of orange licked the edges of the gaping hole in the thatched roof.

"Merciful Christ," he swore as he pulled his shirt over his head. "Ranulf is lobbing fire at us now."

As if wall-busting boulders weren't enough.

A bucket brigade formed up and hostlers braved the smoke and falling ash, ducking into the burning building to lead terrified horses to safety. There was no saving the stables. Once the hay caught, the best they could hope was that the fire wouldn't spread to other buildings.

There wasn't time to drape and belt a plaid, so William tugged on his trews. Katherine scrambled from bed to find his jacket while he donned thick stockings and boots.

"Stand still a moment," she said as she helped him shrug into the jacket.

It would probably be the last time he'd see her all day—he wouldn't allow himself to think it might be forever—so he hugged her fiercely and pressed a kiss to her forehead. If he kissed her lips, it would be all the harder to leave her. Then he glanced up at the underside of the thatch above their heads. "Get yourself out of this tower. Margaret and her bairn and your father too."

The keep and its tower were located close to the lochside wall. "Surely Ranulf's machine canna reach so far."

Maybe not from where it was now. But if all the men in Glengarry were pulled from the walls to fight fires, there'd be nothing to stop MacNaught from moving the diabolical thing closer. A sharp breeze caught a whiff of smoke from the stables and sent it through the arrow loops.

"Just do it," William said as he made for the stairwell. "And quickly."

"Oh, my lady, I'm that glad to see ye." Dorcas skittered to Katherine's side when she appeared in the souterrain. Margie's boys raised a cheer and surrounded their mother, hopping up and down and demanding to see their new sister. Jamison supported the earl, who was favoring his left side and not speaking beyond monosyllables, but at least he seemed aware of his surroundings. The seneschal found a barrel the right height to serve as a seat for the laird and propped it in a corner so Lord Glengarry could be supported by the stone walls at both his shoulders.

"How is everyone faring here?" Katherine asked Dorcas after greeting as many of the women and children as she could in the crammed space.

"As well as might be expected. 'Tis cold and cramped and damp. We made do with winter apples for supper and expect more of the same for breakfast. Can we not send to the kitchen for aught else?"

"Cook is busy feeding the men who are defending the castle," Katherine said, remembering the way Cook's orders had rung in shrill tones as she'd passed by the kitchen. No general ever demanded—or received—such instant obedience. "I dinna think she has time for much more, but I'll see what may be done."

William had assured her the souterrain was the safest place in Glengarry, but to Kat's nose, beneath the acrid smell of the torches and the press of too many unwashed bodies, it had the moldering stink of a crypt. She'd take any excuse to climb the uneven stone steps back to daylight.

"Wait, my lady." Dorcas reached out a hand to stop her, then seemed to remember herself and drew it back. "I dinna suppose ye've heard from Nab."

Katherine shook her head. "'Tis fifteen miles to Inverness. With luck, he's made it there, but we canna expect him back this soon even if he turned around and walked all night."

Not to mention that it was the dead of winter and Nab had never been to Inverness before. Katherine hadn't voiced her concerns to William about his decision to send Nab, but the fact that all hope of rescue rested on the shoulders of a man who couldn't even keep the Scepter of Badenoch safe did not give her comfort.

"I should have gone with him. Four eyes are better than two." Dorcas worried her lower lip. "Even if he makes it past MacNaught's watch, what will Nab do once he reaches Inverness?"

"He must only find the king and his court," Katherine said with more confidence than she felt. "Then my brother will know what to do."

If he believes the word of a fool.

Nab couldn't feel his feet. His nose hairs were so frozen, they'd never unthaw and he'd have those little shards of ice in his nostrils forever. Nevertheless, after a terrifying night of dodging MacNaught's men and startling at every owl's hoot, dawn found Nab on the Abriachan ferry, drawing closer to his destination.

The chimneys of Inverness were belching out a dark cloud of smoke on the horizon. As he disembarked and drew nearer, he forgot about being cold and began to fret about getting lost. He'd never seen such a big town.

"If I were king, where would I lay my head?" he mumbled.

There was a castle situated on a high bluff overlooking the River Ness. Or at least part of one. It looked as if it too had been bombarded by MacNaught's machine at one time. Nab decided to head for that structure since it was still the largest and arguably the most defensible one in town.

Once he was admitted at the town gate along with a farmer and his draught wagon laden with hens bound for market, he made for the street that looked as if it might lead him to the castle. He hadn't gone very far when a gang of three men singled him out.

"And what might yer business be in Inverness, yokel?" one demanded as he placed himself directly in Nab's path. As much as Nab generally disliked association with others, he'd have given his left pinkie to see a familiar face from Glengarry just then.

"We dinna want any more beggars in town," another said, grasping Nab's arm and dragging him into a narrow side street.

"I'm not a beggar," Nab stammered. "I'm a fool."

"Like as not, that's true," said the first with a laugh that was anything but mirthful. "Ye do look a fool."

"It is, and I am—fool to the Earl of Glengarry, that is. What I mean to say is that I bear a message for a member of the king's court, Lord—"

"Lord love him, listen to that. He expects to be let in to see the king! We've no need for such a ninny-hammer here in Inverness. The parish coffers are stretched enough with our own bird-wits," the biggest man said. "Ye'd best turn around and be gone, gaber-lunzie."

The men had mistaken him for a licensed beggar. Nab realized he must look a fright after his wild scramble through the woods dodging MacNaught's sentries and traipsing along the loch's rugged shore, but he'd never begged in his life. Not for money, at any rate. He'd begged to be left alone plenty.

"I'm not a gaberlunzie," he said.

"Show us yer purse then."

Unfortunately, he'd spent all the coin William had given him on the ferry. "I have nothing ye'd want."

"Maybe I just want to give someone a beating this fine morn and methinks ye'll do." The man's fist shot out in a blink and connected with Nab's jaw. The blow twirled him around. Then he toppled like a felled sapling. The frozen ground rushed up to meet his chin.

As his vision tunneled to blackness, he realized he'd be lucky to end up hanging by his heels this time.

Holly stands in the hall, fair to behold:
Ivy stands without the door, she is full sore a cold.

—From "The Contest of the Holly and the Ivy"

"This doesna seem at all a fair contest to me. My coin,
if I had any, is on the one with the most prickles."

—An observation from Nab,
fool to the Earl of Glengarry

Chapter Thirty-Three

The bombardment kept up all day. The only saving grace was that it seemed MacNaught's men had trouble launching fire, so only three more flaming bundles were lobbed toward Glengarry. One fell mercifully short and fizzled in the snow a few feet from the base of the wall. The other two struck the stable again, now only a burnt-out shell, its charred skeleton still smoking.

Most of the horses had been saved, but not all. Their dying screams still rang in Will's ears and the scent of seared flesh filled the air. As he'd helped toss buckets of water on the blaze, William had seen little Angus tearing out of the burning building, but the terrier was moving too quickly for him to catch. He hoped the dog would find Katherine in the depths of the keep. It would be a comfort to them both.

"Trebuchet!" one of the watchmen on the walls shouted, and William's gaze followed the trajectory of the boulder as it hurtled toward the eastern bastion. With a shuddering crash, it took out the steeply sloped roof above the corner watchtower along with one of the sentries who hadn't scrambled away quickly enough.

"They're getting better at it." Hew MacElmurray leaned over the crenellated wall to peer down its length. Since his disgrace over disobeying Will during the sortie, the young man had been hovering at his elbow, looking for ways to redeem himself. "Their aim is improving."

Will nodded, wishing there was another way to see things. "Without reinforcements, it'll be a matter of only a few days before the walls are breached."

"Judging from the number of meal fires burning on the hillside, it seems MacNaught's forces are holding despite the stinging we gave 'em in that sortie."

"Ranulf's the type to give orders to kill his own deserters," William said, wondering how many of his men would slip away if they could. He wasn't going to wait around to find out. The need to do something burned in his veins.

Another boulder came soaring toward them. It cleared the wall and clipped a corner of the chapel.

"Saddle up Greyfellow and a mount for yourself."

"Aye, my lord, where are we going?"

"To stop that damned trebuchet."

Within a quarter hour, he and Hew were riding out the main gate under a flag of truce. The bombardment ceased, but it took Ranulf another quarter hour to deign to present himself along with one of his lieutenants. Ranulf brought Sinclair as his second this time.

Slick bastards, the pair of them, Will thought, but held his peace as they took their time picking their way down the hillside.

Twilight encroached on the short winter day, casting long grey shadows. Will's men lined the curtain wall, brandishing torches to light the proceedings. Ranulf's troops stood shoulder to shoulder in a surprisingly well-ordered line before their hulking machine. None of the fighting men could hear the parley, but every ear strained in the direction of it in any case.

"Had enough, Badenoch?" MacNaught asked.

"The question should be whether *ye* have," Will returned smoothly. "Ye hope to be master of Glengarry when this is over. Do ye really mean to rule over naught but a pile of rubble?"

"If need be. I'll raze the place to the ground if I must." Then Ranulf's hard expression softened a bit. "The offer of safe conduct still holds for Lord Glengarry and his family, should he wish to surrender."

"How touching, but the laird will not abandon his people to ye."

Ranulf scanned the curtain wall. "I dinna see the dear earl, and he didna seem so healthy when we parted last. How fares my uncle?"

"Well enough to send ye to hell."

MacNaught's laughter bounced from the walls of the castle and echoed on the hillside. "Maybe in his prime the old wolf might have bested me, but he'll never do so now."

It was the opening William was waiting for. "If 'tis single combat ye wish, I shall oblige ye."

"I didna say that."

"Did ye not? It sounded that way to me." William turned to the man who bore Ranulf's standard. "What think ye, Sinclair? If a leader has a care for the lives of his men, what better way to show it than to agree to single combat to settle the matter?"

Sinclair's mouth opened and then shut abruptly. The glare Ranulf sent him would have melted steel.

"If I win, your men will be allowed to return to their homes provided they leave the trebuchet," William offered to Ranulf. "I vow there will be no retribution on them."

Ranulf bared his teeth. "And if I win, your men will be allowed to stand aside protecting their own arses while we rape the women and plunder the castle."

It wasn't a fair exchange, but he didn't expect one from MacNaught. "When shall we meet?"

"I'd say why wait, but 'tis getting too dark. Besides, I want my dear cousin on the wall watching while I turn the snow red with your blood."

"Dawn then," William offered. "And there's to be no more bombardment in the meantime."

"Verra well." Ranulf's lip curled but he nodded curtly. "I want ye rested when I skewer your liver, Badenoch. Give my regards to your lady wife, my cousin. She was ever a fetching piece. Tell her I'll see her soon."

Gossip always travels fast within a castle. It takes wing when the castle is under siege.

Young Fergie, who'd sneaked out of the souterrain and had been peering over the wall with the rest of the defenders while William parleyed with MacNaught, came flying back to Katherine's side with news of the impending single combat, that he had overheard Will telling his men about when he'd returned to the castle.

Katherine's chest constricted and her vision wavered uncertainly, but she schooled her face into an impassive mask. "I see. And where is Lord Badenoch now?"

"He's taking his turn on the watch," the boy

beamed. "Just as though he were any other man. Only he's not. Not at all. I figure he's about the finest laird there is."

"That he is." Katherine allowed herself a small smile and handed Angus to the boy. Since the stable had burned, the terrier had been under foot and claiming her lap every time she sat down. If the lad didn't hold him, Angus would probably trail after her and she didn't have time for the wee dog at the moment. "Now I want ye to do something for me, Fergie."

"Oh, aye?"

"I need to see my husband, and Lady Margaret needs someone to watch over her and her little ones while I'm gone. Will ye be her extra pair of hands and eyes?"

His lips, pouty as a girl's, tightened into a thin line. Fergie was nimble-minded enough to realize this was also Katherine's way of making sure he stayed in the relative safety of the souterrain. But his frank idolatry of William was strong enough that he couldn't say no to her.

Katherine went first to her chamber to retrieve a warm cloak for Will. He'd left the scepter on the clothes trunk. Something about seeing it there, discarded with the other things they'd abandoned when the tower was evacuated, made her realize William really had given up on his dream of continuing the Douglas line.

Sadness, hope, despair, fear—there was such a boiling soup of emotions simmering inside her; she wasn't sure what she was feeling. But she knew she didn't want to leave the scepter where it was. She wrapped it in the cloak and then stopped by the kitchen for some food for William.

The bulk of the men had been dismissed for the

night. They streamed toward the keep to find their families. A few watchmen were still posted on the landward curtain wall. Katherine recognized Will's profile near the ruined eastern bastion.

"I can hear your belly rumbling from here," she said with false brightness as she approached him. "Trust ye not to take a moment for yourself."

"I was taking a moment. A grand moment actually," he said as he fell to eating the bannocks and sliced cold mutton she'd brought. "I was just standing here wondering at how unnecessarily beautiful this world is, what with the loch and the mountains and the trees all around. And why I'd never really noticed till now."

His tone was casual. There was a smile in his voice, but it was a brittle smile. His words were those of a man who expected to be leaving the world soon.

She didn't know what to say. She'd half hoped to be able to talk him out of meeting Ranulf in combat tomorrow, but she realized he'd never go back on his word. He'd made his bargain with her cousin. William would keep it.

So she chattered about Margie's new baby while he ate, nattering on about how lustily she cried, how well she nursed, and how intently she met everyone's gaze. She reminded herself of Dorcas, but she couldn't seem to stop her tongue from wagging.

"She's sober as a judge, but bonnie as well as wise. A most precocious lass is our new niece," Katherine said as she ran out of things to share. "I expect Donald will have to beat the lads off with a stick once young Kitty comes of age."

William laughed. "I'd enjoy seeing that."

Then his laughter faded. Katherine put a horn of warm cider in his hand. He held it between both palms for a bit before draining it to the dregs.

Finally, she couldn't stand the silence that began to grow between them. "Is there no other way?"

He didn't pretend to misunderstand her. "No. If I don't engage MacNaught in single combat, Glengarry will be overrun. The mason tells me another solid blow to this eastern corner will see it crumble to the ground. There will be a breach large enough we willna be able to defend it." He glanced toward the east and Inverness.

"But what about Nab?" she asked. "He might be bringing reinforcements even now."

Will handed her back his empty horn. "Do ye really want to trust the safety of all the souls in Glengarry to the fool?"

"No." She unrolled the cloak she'd brought and draped it around his broad shoulders. "I'd rather trust the Laird of Badenoch." Then she handed him the scepter. "Take it with ye on the morrow. For luck."

He tucked it through his belt as if it were a long dirk. "If I should fall—"

"Whist!" She pressed two fingers to his lips. "Ye dinna want to tempt—"

"The devil. Aye, I know." He kissed her fingertips, then curled them inward and pressed her fist to his chest. "Listen to me, Katherine. If I should fall, your cousin has promised no mercy. Dinna let yourself be taken, ye or Margie or her bairns."

She swallowed hard as she realized what he was telling her. What he was asking of her.

"D'ye have a blade?"

"Aye." There was a slim dagger concealed in the busk of her bodice. In a pinch, it would do. If the time came, could she steel herself to the gruesome task? If William was killed, she'd already be dead inside.

They say the dead feel no pain.

She shook off the morbid fancy, surreptitiously making the sign against evil with one hand. "Will ye come and rest a while?"

"I should be praying in the chapel, but I thought I'd stand the watch so others could rest. Besides, I'll rest when this is done." He looked up as the sliver of a new moon disappeared behind scudding clouds. "And I can pray just as well from here."

"I'll stand watch with ye, then." *And pray,* she added silently as she leaned on the crenellations and watched the fires in MacNaught's camp burn on the hillside.

William came behind her and enfolded her into his cloak with him. With his solid chest at her back, his heart beating against her spine, she was suddenly warm and comforted.

If she'd learned anything this Christmastide, it was that while she'd always tried to plan for years into the future, life was really only a string of moments. And each single one was all anyone ever had.

This one moment, standing on the battlements with the man she loved, was a shining one. Damn whatever might come with the dawn. William was right.

The world was unnecessarily beautiful.

"So if Badenoch wins, we're supposed to lay down our arms and simply go home?" Filib Gordon asked Sinclair, careful to keep his voice low. MacNaught had already turned in for the night, but who knew which of the men milling about might be ready to report a disloyal word. Ranulf had already hanged two of MacTavish's retainers who'd tried to slip away after the hail of arrows had rained down on the camp. It was brutal, but Gordon couldn't argue with the results. The hangings rendered the rest of the men sullenly obedient and there had been no more attempts at defection.

"That's about the size of it," Sinclair said as he tossed a snow-covered pinecone into their fire and watched it sizzle open. "Badenoch wins, we go home. But if MacNaught wins, we get to do whatever we want, take whatever we want from the castle and everyone in it."

"That's more like it," MacTavish said. "My men willna take kindly to freezing their balls off for nothing."

"Seeing home again with their balls intact isna nothing, I'm thinkin'," Sinclair said.

"Then ye're a coward," Murray said. "Ye hold your manhood too cheap. We've set ourselves to bring down Glengarry and we damned well ought to do it. Whether Lord Badenoch falls or not."

"We canna go back on the agreement made in parley," Gordon said.

"Then we make sure MacNaught wins." Murray glowered down at the castle. "D'ye see the pile of rubble at the eastern corner, where the roof of the bastion came down?"

MacTavish twisted around to look. "Aye."

"I'm thinking that under cover of darkness, a single man could work his way around to the loch and then come up along the eastern corner without being seen by their watch," Murray said.

"To what end?" MacTavish asked.

"To the end of being close enough to put a bolt through Badenoch's heart if it looks like he's about to best MacNaught," Murray grumbled. "God's Teeth, I'd have to draw this one a picture to teach him to take a piss."

"At least I'm willing to do something instead of just talk about it, which is more than I can say for ye, old man," MacTavish said, rising in a huff and slinging his crossbow over his shoulder. "When this business is done, Murray, ye and I are going to have more than words."

He stomped off into the night.

"MacTavish is younger and faster than ye, Murray," Sinclair said. "Yet ye dinna look worried."

"Naw, after he puts a bolt through Badenoch, he'll have betrayed his position and someone from Glengarry will see him right there under their noses," Murray said. "Whatever happens, MacTavish won't have a fart's chance in a skillet of making it back to our line."

It came, a floweret bright,
amid the cold of winter,
when half spent was the night.

—From "Lo! How a Rose E'er Blooming"

"I canna think of aught good that comes in the middle
of the night. Or in the wee hour of dawn either, for that
matter."

—An observation from Nab,
fool to the Earl of Glengarry

Chapter Thirty-Four

Katherine woke curled up on the parapet with Will's heavy cloak tucked beneath and around her. She'd meant to stay up with him, but anxiety and more than a few sleepless nights had a way of wearing on a body, and she must have drifted off surrounded by the warmth of his cloak.

Now the parapet around her was filling with the Glengarry defenders, all jostling for position in order to best see the drama unfolding below.

He didna even say good-bye.

Her heart was a prickly ball of thorns. Katherine scrambled to her feet and peered over the wall. On the

trampled snow about one hundred yards from the
castle, Will and Ranulf dismounted and handed the
reins of their horses to their seconds. Hew MacElmurray and Lamont Sinclair led the horses a safe distance
away from the combatants.

William and Ranulf seemed to be speaking to each
other, but strain as she might, she couldn't make out
any of their words. Her cousin turned and, as if he felt
her eyes on him, stared straight at her for a blink.
Then he gave her a mock salute, raising his claymore
above his head.

William didn't glance her way.

It was a good thing because Ranulf used the gesture
to initiate his attack. Will barely had time to draw his
sword from its shoulder baldric and meet MacNaught's
blade.

Katherine had often listened to her father and
William discussing fighting styles over their meals. She
wished she'd paid closer attention now. She might
have been able to make more sense of what she was
seeing. There was no finesse. No strategy. Her husband and her cousin seemed to be taking turns trying
to split each other in two.

She felt every bone-jarring parry. Her breath fled
away with each thrust. She dug her nails into the
granite wall so hard that they bled.

Her vision tunneled till all she could see was Will.
Circling with deadly grace. Leaping back to avoid
Ranulf's blade. Returning a vicious stroke with a blis-
tering one of his own.

The cacophony of steel on steel strafed her ears so
loudly, she didn't hear her father's approach until
Lord Glengarry, supported by his seneschal, Jamison,
was beside her on the wall.

"Good lad," her father said through one side of his

mouth. The left side of his face still sagged as if it had melted. He laid a heavy right hand on her shoulder.

He meant well, but it was little comfort. Not when her heart was out there, dodging each blow along with William.

The combatants seemed to be tiring, for their movements slowed. The snow they trampled underfoot was turning slushy and slick. Kat's breath hissed over her teeth when William lost his footing and went down on one knee.

With a roar, Ranulf pressed his advantage. He came flying, his blade poised to be buried in the juncture of Will's neck and shoulder. At the last moment, William caught Ranulf's claymore with his own and, with a quick circular stroke, tore the sword from MacNaught's hands.

Will rose to his feet, his sword tip pointed at MacNaught's chest. "On your knees, if ye value your life."

Ranulf panted from exertion but remained upright.

"Yield, damn ye." Despite the cold, a bead of sweat trickled down Will's spine. "I dinna wish to murder my wife's cousin if I can help it."

"Do what ye must," MacNaught said and ripped open the front of his shirt. He took a step toward William. "I willna beg."

Before Will could deliver the final blow, utter surprise widened Ranulf's eyes. He toppled like a felled pine with a crossbow bolt protruding from his back.

"Damned fool," Gordon said. "MacTavish missed and killed Ranulf instead."

"Even better," Murray muttered, and then raised his voice in a shout that he hoped could be heard by the cowering masses behind Glengarry's wall. "Treachery! Some coward from the castle has murdered MacNaught by stealth. Kill them all!"

Murray drew his sword and led the charge down the hill. The men at his back were eager for a fight, pouring after him like a raging stream. After days of doing nothing but lobbing rocks and dodging arrows, they relished the chance to blood their swords.

He didn't need to kill everyone in the castle. If they only managed to kill Lord Badenoch, that would do. It would take the heart out of the defenders, and Glengarry Castle would fall into his hand like a ripe plum.

His hand, not Ranulf MacNaught's. Murray was the next strongest and the only one with the cunning to make the most of this unexpected development.

If MacTavish survived this morning's work, he'd have to find a way to thank him.

Katherine's relief at Will's victory was short-lived.

William shouted up to the archers on the wall, probably ordering a volley, but his words were whipped away by wind and the banshee howling of the advancing force. A few arrows flew, but it didn't result in the kind of devastation a sustained release would have produced.

Her father tried to speak but couldn't form the words. He only managed to point at William.

"To arms," Katherine shouted. "Every man to his blade and Lord Badenoch."

She wasn't sure it was the right order when she gave it, but her father nodded. Men flooded through the gate to stand before the onslaught. For good or ill, the word had been given for the last stand of Glengarry. The battle was joined.

A melee was something men might speak of with each other, but none discussed hand-to-hand warfare before their women. Katherine was unprepared for the carnage that erupted before her.

There was no order. No semblance of a battle plan on either side. Only the need to keep moving or die. She lost track of William's dark head and despaired, only to find him again in the center of another circle of desperately battling warriors.

Her cousin had amassed so many men. The Glengarry defenders were hopelessly outnumbered, but Kat couldn't look away. As long as William was still upright, still fighting, she'd bear it with him.

Her father went down, his one good leg no longer able to support him. She could hear Jamison fussing over the earl beside her, but Katherine remained at the wall. She had to keep watching William.

Part of her knew she couldn't change anything happening before her eyes, but a more primitive part of her mind argued that as long as she could see him, as long as her spirit yearned toward him and prayed for him in a place too deep for words, he would somehow be safe.

Glengarry's numbers dwindled by the moment. Katherine covered her mouth to keep the scream building inside her from escaping.

Then she heard the hunting horns.

A phalanx of riders burst out of the trees on the eastern road. Her brother, Donald, was in the lead and the Douglas men, William's brothers, were hot on his heels. Behind them came another hundred seasoned warriors on horseback, swords drawn and ready for the fight. Someone on a Shetland pony was bringing up the rear, bouncing along as if the saddle was fitted with springs.

"Nab!" she shouted with joy.

But when she looked back down at the melee again, she couldn't find William anywhere.

The unexpected arrival of cavalry changed the direction of the battle in a heartbeat. Murray's men had neglected to make use of the horses they had and probably rued their impulsive decision to follow him blithely into the fight. They took to their heels to avoid the slashing hooves and the blades of the men on the horses' backs. Most were cut down, but a lucky few made it to the safety of the thick forest and disappeared into the Highlands.

Katherine abandoned her father on the wall and hurried through the open gate. The wounded were starting to return to the castle, some leaning on their fellows, others tottering on their own in a daze. She'd have to oversee a makeshift hospital to deal with them, but first, she had to find Will.

The corbies had already discovered the bloody hillside, being drawn by the clash of swords and shouts of battle. Now they feasted. Katherine tried to shoo them away, but the carrion birds were a belligerent bunch and resettled on the corpses as soon as she passed.

She swallowed back the rising bile. "Please God, let me find him."

Donald and the men with him returned to help with the wounded, but none of them had seen William.

"I'd help ye look," her brother said, "but I need to find Margaret just as urgently."

"Ye've been gone this long," she said testily. "Why such a hurry now?"

"Because when the fool told us the castle was under siege, all I could think was that I might lose her. I never realized till now just how much I . . . I've been gone too long chasing a fool's errand. I suspect I have much to atone for."

His suspicion was correct.

"Margie and the boys are in the souterrain, safe and sound," she said as she marched away to continue her search. "As is my new niece."

She'd call the bairn Donald's daughter once he started acting like her father.

Katherine wandered from one group of the fallen to another, both sickened and hopeful. After a time, not finding Will became the goal. If he wasn't in the growing ranks of the dead, she could still hope.

In the next tangle of bodies, movement caught her eye. A man pushed another body off him and staggered to his feet.

It was Will. Her fierce hug nearly knocked him down again.

"Easy, woman. Let a man find his feet."

"Where are ye hurt?" She pawed over him, feeling his arms and legs, running her hands over his chest and belly.

"Nay, 'tis someone else's blood ye see. I dinna think I'm wounded," he said with a hand to the growing knot on his temple, "except for the wee knock on the head I took there at the last." He bent down, retrieved the Scepter of Badenoch from the lifeless hand of Murray, and tucked it back through his belt. "The man thought he'd liberate this from me, and decided to use it as a mace. Looks like my sword split his gizzard just as he gave me a love tap with the crystal."

She hugged him again. Only her William would call a blow that rendered him unconscious a "love tap." She fingered the swollen spot and then palmed his cheek.

"I thought I'd lost ye."

"Couldna happen," he said as he drew her into an embrace. "Ye and I are one heart. No matter what happens, I carry a bit of ye in here." He pressed her hand to his chest and then laid his palm on hers. "And ye are stuck with me wherever ye go. Love is stronger than anything, outlasts anything. Even death."

She nodded. "And once we're both gone, if our love is all that remains, 'tis enough."

Yea, all the yearlong have an eye to the poor,
And God shall send luck to keep open thy door.

—From "Get Ivy and Hull"

"I thought I'd used up all the luck God will ever send a fool on that trip to Inverness, but then He gave me Dorcas."

—An observation from Nab,
fool to the Earl of Glengarry

Epilogue

Masons estimated it would take years to repair the damage to the castle. Margaret claimed it might take longer than that to repair the rift in her marriage unless Donald lived up to his promise to spend more time in Glengarry. So far, he was showing every intention of doing so.

"I'm not here just because the earl is still incapacitated," Donald professed in a hissed whisper while they were all seated on the raised dais where the family ate in the great hall. Lord Glengarry's speech was improving, but he'd never be the same man he'd been before his most recent apoplexy. Donald had stepped into the daily running of the earldom on his father's behalf and the earl seemed pleased to let him. "I'm weary to my soul of court life and have been longing for ye and our bairns."

"Ye had a strange way of showing it," Margaret said, refusing to be mollified too easily.

"Will ye not forgive my neglect? I was only gone so much because I was seeing to your welfare," he said. "What must I do to convince ye?"

"I'm not sure yet," Margaret said with the faintest of smiles, "but I give ye leave to try."

Good for ye, Margie. Katherine tipped up her horn of ale and leaned toward William so as not to overhear any more of her good-sister and brother's conversation. "I understand Nab and Dorcas are to be wed as soon as the chapel is repaired."

"Aye, that'll give time for the swelling to go down," Will said as he sopped up the last of his mutton broth with a bannock. Nab had taken a horrible beating in Inverness at the hands of those town ruffians he'd encountered, but fortunately Lord Donald's squire happened by and recognized him before his face was too bloodied. He'd been whisked into the royal presence and been able to convince Katherine's brother of the dire circumstances at home that required his immediate attention. "And as a reward for his service to Glengarry, Donald has declared that Nab is to be given sole use of that derelict tower room. The walled-up door will be refurbished and the staircase leading to it is to be repaired, as well as the small fireplace."

Katherine glanced over to where Dorcas was leaning in to refill Nab's drinking horn. "I don't expect he'll be the sole occupant for long."

"And speaking of long, we've been a long time from Badenoch." Will stood and offered her his arm. "We'll start home in the morning, but there's something I need to do this night, and I'd have you with me for it."

She expected him to lead her up to their bedchamber, but instead, he squired her from the great hall and down into the depths of the keep to the carpenter's shop. They stopped before a large, ornate trunk.

"What's this?"

"Glengarry's parting gift to His Majesty now that Donald is home for good. The earl is sending this trunk for King James to use to store the Honours of Scotland. It's been specially sized to house the Great Scepter, the Sword of State, and the Crown." Will opened the trunk to reveal the velvety inside. "And it's perfectly sized for something else as well."

He gave a tug on one corner and the bottom of the trunk lifted to reveal a secret cavity below. Then he took the Scepter of Badenoch from his belt and laid it in the small space.

"Will, what are ye doing?"

"It served its purpose and Badenoch needs it no longer," he said. "Only tradition and this scepter guaranteed that the title passed from father to eldest son. After I'm gone, the fittest man will rule in my stead. It'll be one of our nephews, most like, but only time will tell who has the mettle to be the next laird."

"So ye willna need a direct heir of your body," she said slowly, realizing the enormity of the gift he was giving her.

"No. The barony will be better served by the best man, not just one with the right blood." He closed the lid on the scepter, and the trunk hid its presence completely. "And now that worry is over. We can concentrate on filling Badenoch's keep with fosterlings if that's your pleasure."

"There are children aplenty who need love," she said, slipping her arms around his waist.

He snugged her close, the hard planes of him against her softness. "So long as ye dinna forget barons need love too."

"And ye have mine. Always and completely, Will."

"So no more running away for Christmas?"

"No more running away ever. Ye told me once that I am your home. Ye are mine as well. We are a family, we two, a complete circle of love. Whether we choose to shelter any fosterlings within that circle doesn't add to or diminish it. Our love is enough. It can be divided without becoming smaller. It grows with each breath. There will never be an end to it, either in this world or the next."

"I dinna wish to fret about the next world just now." William's smile turned wicked. "Not when there's a bed in your chamber waiting for us in this one."

Author's Note

I decided to tackle the theme of childlessness after my sister served as a gestational surrogate for a couple who could not conceive. Infertility is a difficult enough issue in the twenty-first century, when we have access to in vitro fertilization technology and a host of other options. It was devastating in the sixteenth century, when there was no help for childless couples at all. But no matter the time period, the emotional pain is the same and my heart goes out to all who grapple with infertility.

I'm sure some readers will wonder why William and Katherine didn't simply adopt a child. Unfortunately, there was no such thing then. Fostering was common, and noble houses would accept wards, but there was no law governing legal adoption in the United Kingdom (including Scotland) until 1926. Bloodlines were paramount to the laws of inheritance, so even if adoption were legal, adopted children still wouldn't be able to inherit. The Badenoch patent stipulates the barony passes to "heirs whatsoever." It will allow someone not in William's direct line, but still related to him by blood, to inherit. (Will expects it will be one of his nephews, but with the "whatsoever" designation, it could well be a niece!)

Finally, a word on the Scepter of Badenoch. Recently, my husband and I visited Scotland and viewed the Crown Jewels in Edinburgh Castle. There we learned that the Honours of Scotland had been stored away in a large trunk in 1707 when the Treaty of Union dissolved the Scottish Parliament. Over the years, their whereabouts were forgotten. In 1818, Sir Walter Scott was given permission to conduct a search for them, and after turning Edinburgh Castle inside out, he finally recovered the Crown from Robert the Bruce's time, the jewel-encrusted Great Scepter, and the Sword of State, all still in the large trunk.

Along with the Honours, a much smaller scepter of unknown provenance was found. It is this scepter I used as the inspiration for my Scepter of Badenoch, the symbol of the continuing Douglas bloodline. By giving up the scepter and hiding it away, William was telling Katherine, and the rest of us, that continuing love trumps all.

Wishing you continuing love,
Mia

P.S. After a challenging surrogate pregnancy that ended in a difficult delivery, my sister gave birth to healthy twins, a boy and a girl. And then she gave these precious gifts to a grateful couple.

Is she heroine material or what?

Want to read more holiday Highland romance from
Mia Marlowe?

Check out this sneak peek of
PLAID TIDINGS,
available now!

If only one of the MacOwen girls could make a profitable match, a rich bride price might be just the thing to tide the family over until the money from her father's newest invention came in.

Lucinda reached into her pocket and pulled out the book she'd picked up in a shop off Leicester Square. It was a silly extravagance. Books were so very dear, but she couldn't resist using the last of her pin money for this one. She ran her fingertips over the title: *The Knowledgeable Ladies' Guide to Eligible Gentlemen.*

It was filled with a fairly current roster of the notable gallants to be found in London as well as many chapters of advice for those who wished to be "knowledgeable" ladies on a number of romantic topics.

Not that Lucinda was likely to capture a beau. It was hard for any fellow to get past the tricks Brodie MacIver played on her would-be suitors.

Yet she wished again for Brodie's protective presence and not just because she'd stumbled into Lord Alexander Mallory. If Brodie were here with her, she wouldn't feel so alone in this royal spider web of a court. But she understood why Brodie MacIver couldn't come to

London with her. Traveling was uncomfortable enough for the living.

It was downright dangerous for a ghost.

Out in the wide world away from his usual haunts, if Brodie weren't tethered to her somehow, he might float away and never find her again. As far as either of them knew, Lucinda was the only soul on earth who could see and hear him.

Lucinda sighed and opened her guidebook. She decided she might as well study some of the entries. There might be a gentleman who would suit for one of her sisters.

At least, that was the reason she gave herself for leafing through the book. Instead, she gravitated immediately to the *M*s and located the information about the man she'd all but tripped over in the hall.

"**Lord Alexander Mallory**, b. 1794. Second son of the Marquis of Maldren," she read silently.

He'll have more than two coins to rub together, I'll be bound.

Lucinda shook her head. No good could come from imagining more about the fellow. What would a marquis's son have to do with the daughter of a Scottish inventor?

There was no point to reading on, but she couldn't help herself.

Near the top of every marriage-minded mama's short list of eligibles, Lord Alexander's name occupies a well-deserved spot. He is courtly, quick of wit, and has an excellent seat on a horse. The excellent seat of his trousers is not to be lightly dismissed either.

Lucinda's cheeks heated. She'd had no idea this guidebook would take such an earthy bent. But the creeping blush didn't make her stop reading.

When Lord Alexander sets himself to charm, any woman in his path will be hard pressed not to be swept along by his dangerous allure.

Lucinda could testify to that. She'd forced herself to be cool and disdainful to him when in fact the man had quite taken her breath away. Thank heaven his unremarkable friend was there, too. Sir Bertram Clarindon was a comfortable sort.

Still, her gaze was drawn back to the guide for more information about the decidedly *uncomfortable* Lord Alexander.

However, the young Mallory has never, to this observer's certain knowledge, debauched a virgin or ruined an otherwise reputable widow. That in itself is hearty commendation for someone so closely attached to the dissolute court of King George IV.

Not having debauched a virgin or ruined a widow is setting the bar for good behavior rather low. Seems like they're damning him with faint praise.

But it didn't stop her from reading on.

Well-informed readers will recall that unpleasantness about his mother years ago, but in truth, the least said about that, the better. Neither of the marquis's sons has shown any propensity for madness. Lord Alexander may be safely regarded as a thorough catch by one and all.

Madness in the family is no impediment, eh? I wonder what it would take for the Ladies' Guide to Eligible Gentlemen *to disqualify someone.*

Then Lucinda's gaze fell on the last line of the entry.

However, he shows no signs of allowing himself to be caught.

She closed the book with a snap. *It seems Lord Alexander has disqualified himself.*